SLAVE
HARVEST

D1646162

BY ANDREW BUTCHER

The Time of the Reaper
Slave Harvest

Look out for . . .
The Tomorrow Seed

SLAVE
HARVEST

ANDREW BUTCHER

Atom
An imprint of
Little, Brown Book Group
100 Victoria Embankment
London EC4Y 0DY

An Hachette UK Company

www.atombooks.co.uk

ATOM

First published in Great Britain in 2007 by Atom

Copyright © Andrew Butcher 2007

The moral right of the author has been asserted.

*All characters and events in this publication, other than
those clearly in the public domain, are fictitious
and any resemblance to real persons,
living or dead, is purely coincidental.*

All rights reserved.
No part of this publication may be reproduced,
stored in a retrieval system, or transmitted, in any
form or by any means, without the prior
permission in writing of the publisher, nor be
otherwise circulated in any form of binding or
cover other than that in which it is published and
without a similar condition including this
condition being imposed on the subsequent purchaser.

A CIP catalogue record for this book
is available from the British Library.

ISBN 978-1-904233-95-4

Papers used by Atom are natural, recyclable products made from
wood grown in sustainable forests and certified in accordance with
the rules of the Forest Stewardship Council.

Typeset in Baskerville by M Rules
Printed and bound in Great Britain by
Mackays of Chatham plc
Paper supplied by Hellefoss AS, Norway

SWINDON BOROUGH COUNCIL	
6472216000	
JF	£5.99
04-Jan-08	

Little, Brown Book Group

Andrew Butcher Love UK Ltd

Atom.co.uk

For everyone at Paradox Comics.
No pictures, I'm afraid, but plenty of words!

ONE

She shouldn't be here.

Jessica Lane felt that strongly. She felt it as soon as she heard the boy screaming, saw him, one of the Harrington boys supposed to be on watch, racing into the Great Hall with the terrified cry of 'Outside! *Outside!*' on his lips. She felt it as the party was instantly forgotten, everyone abandoning their dancing or their drinking and surging out into the quad, faces marked with apprehension and anxiety and fear, herself borne helplessly along with them. She felt it as she emerged squinting and dazzled into a night that had lost the quality of darkness.

She felt it most acutely of all when she realised why.

Spaceships studded the sky. Alien spaceships. Jessica didn't need a crash course in extraterrestrial technology to recognise them for what they were. Human beings had never constructed such craft. Vast of size, colossal in dimension, they sliced through the night like blades of silver fire. Their design reminded Jessica, as far as her numbed brain was capable of coherent memory at this particular moment, of the sickles or the scythes farmers had once used to harvest their crops in fields of gold. The ships were fashioned like the crescent moon, and on almost the same scale, it seemed, their twin tapered points hundreds of metres apart. They were like the

1

sheerest of mountains, like silver icebergs on the sea of the sky, plying their course with imperious disdain for the tiny knot of youngsters huddled far below. So many craft, innumerable, identical. And the heavens throbbed with the rumble of their engines and the earth shook in awe at their presence.

Jessica suddenly realised that Mel's hand was in her own and squeezing, squeezing so hard her friend's nails were all but breaking the skin. Mel's black hair streamed as she gazed wide-eyed into the sky; the eldritch light from the spacecraft exaggerated her genetically pale complexion into ghostly whiteness. Around her, Jessica's other friends and companions. Linden clinging to Travis as if she imagined the aliens had come to take him away from her, Travis's mouth gaping as he stared up at the fleet, but his eyes still piercing, still strong, like chips of blue steel. Antony, blond like herself but with his tight curls resembling one of those marble statues she'd seen in Greece, his arm raised to shield him from the engines' furnace glare. Richie Coker blinking stupidly, opening and closing his mouth like a troubled fish. Simon Satchwell, the lenses of his glasses bright silver mirrors as the spaceships soared above him.

And some of the community were silent, and some were not. Shocked shouts, cries of dread and dismay from among the older kids, the little ones squealing, shrieking. They'd seen films. They'd watched alien invaders atomise the world's land-marks. They knew what to expect.

Jessica thought she did, too. Which was why she shouldn't be here. And maybe she didn't need to be here. Maybe she could simply close her eyes, shut out the threatening, treach-erous present, transport herself to another place, somewhere silent and secret and safe. She'd done it before.

*

2

The Sickness had been the reason then. The mysterious disease that had swept across the globe, infecting everyone in its pandemic path. Every adult, at least. Teenagers, toddlers, anybody under the age of about eighteen appeared inexplicably immune. And the government had said it could cure the Sickness but it couldn't, and whether it had given up trying before its members died, Jessica didn't know. The Prime Minister, the Chancellor of the Exchequer, the Home and Foreign Secretaries, breathing air thick with the poison of plague. All the Right Honourable Gentlemen, so used to power, so complacent in their seats of authority, gasping out their final, tortured breaths while the Sickness carved its trademark scarlet circles in their flesh as with a knife.

But horrible though those days had been, the deaths of people known only through television, the deaths of people in far-off countries and in unvisited cities, of neighbours never spoken to, deaths of that nature could still be kept at a distance, Jessica had believed. She could cope. As long as her own family could be protected. As long as her own parents survived.

They hadn't.

Her discovery of their bodies had proved too much to bear. Jessica *wouldn't* bear it. Something had happened to her then, and whether she'd been its victim or its willing accomplice she wasn't sure. She only knew – now, after her recovery, and because Travis and Mel had told her – that she'd retreated inside herself, withdrawn from reality, shut down all conscious thought and fallen into what Travis had called a catatonic trance. She vaguely recollected darkness and closeness, like hiding in a closet during childhood games. Physically she'd still functioned, because she'd surrendered

3

her senses in her own home, and by the time she'd regained them, woken back into the real world, she'd left her house and her parents and Wayvale where she'd lived far behind. She'd found herself here, in a boys' public school built like a castle in the countryside. Harrington. Her friends had brought her here. Travis, Mel – it had been their decision, she knew – they could have left her behind but they hadn't and Jessica supposed she ought to be grateful for that. Part of her was. It meant they loved her. But still, as the alien armada continued to fill the sky to all horizons, like a net thrown over the world, most of her felt she shouldn't *be* here.

Jessica closed her eyes like she must have done before, willed herself into that secret, small, unconscious place again.

And nothing happened.

She could shut her eyes, but the bright fire of the space-ships burned through her eyelids and forced her to see. The aliens' reality could not be denied or ignored. No retreat for Jessica Lane. Nowhere to hide.

She shouldn't be here but she was. And it would have been unfair to expect her friends to tend to her again. Jessica could afford to be a child no longer. Somehow, she was going to have to make her way herself.

At last it ended. The final spacecraft passed overhead, and as they vanished like their predecessors beyond the range of sight, the light they'd brought dimmed like the fading of a vision. Night returned to its rightful place, a cool and velvet darkness. The air was silent once again. The ground had ceased to tremble.

'Trav.' Linden's lips were brushing his cheek, she was that

close as she whispered. He felt her shuddering in the thin white party dress she'd chosen for tonight from the community's shared stock of clothing, the gooseflesh rising on her bare arms. 'What were they? What *are* they?'

'Spaceships. It looks like we've got visitors.'

'Aliens?' It wasn't that Linden actually required an explanation, more that she could scarcely merit the truth of her own deductions. 'There's no such − aliens don't exist, Trav.'

'Perhaps somebody omitted to mention that fact to the extraterrestrials themselves, Linden.' Antony, his green eyes narrowed grimly. To Travis: 'Did you see that one come in to land?'

Travis nodded tensely. To begin with he'd thought the entire fleet might be landing, but they'd obviously only been adjusting their height for whatever reason. The sole spacecraft he'd observed physically descending to earth had seemed to put down beyond the range of hills to the south of the Harrington School. A fair distance away for now, but perhaps not, Travis feared, far enough.

'Vernham Hill's ten miles exactly,' Antony provided. 'We used to stage cross-country runs from here to there before the Sickness. The ship might have landed a few miles further still.'

'What are you saying?' prompted Travis.

'It wouldn't take us long to get there.'

Or for the aliens to get here, Travis thought. He exchanged a nervous glance with Antony. 'First things first. The Head Boy needs to take charge.'

The community was clustering around Antony Clive, whether they'd been students at Harrington or not. More

5

than sixty frightened faces turned to him for direction, reassurance, decision. The younger children were crying – not, Antony felt, an unreasonable response to the current situation – while some of the girls were trying to comfort and quieten them. The responsibility of leadership weighed on him as never before, like a solid force. He had to find the strength to bear it, in himself and in what he believed. People were relying on him.

'Clive, what are we going to do?' Leo Milton, his deputy – along with Travis now, Antony reminded himself – stepped forward, his freckled face flushed with agitation. 'We ought to—'

'Inside, Leo,' Antony said. 'Everyone. Back into the Great Hall. And please, don't worry.'

'Who's worried?' Mel muttered to Jessica. 'But if I was someone who chewed their nails when they were stressed, my fingers would be stumps by now.'

In the Great Hall, the party was definitely over. The rush to the quad minutes before had scattered and smashed glasses, spilled cans, upturned benches. The instruments the musicians had been playing lay lonely on the floor, like corpses; the dance space was empty. Already, Travis thought, the evening before the intrusion of the spaceships seemed to belong to another time altogether, a different era, like his life prior to the Sickness. They'd have to adapt again – if they could.

'Listen. Everyone, listen.' Antony stood on the platform where Harrington's masters had once used to dine. Travis and Leo Milton flanked him, and maybe it was coincidence and maybe it was not, but as everyone else crowded close, the boys who'd been students at Harrington tended to favour Leo's side of the platform, while those who'd arrived at the school since the Sickness inclined towards Travis. Apart from the desolate sobs of the little ones, the assembly was silent. 'We all know what we saw out there. We all saw the same. Spacecraft, impossible as it may seem, spacecraft belonging to an alien race, piloted, crewed – we have to assume – by extraterrestrials, beings from another world. Now that much seems self-evident, but its implications are not. We obviously have no idea why they've come or what their intentions are, but what we must not do is panic. We must remain calm. For all we know, these aliens might be able to help us. They might be just what we need to get our society started again. That's for tomorrow. For tonight, I'm ordering lights out now. Go to bed. Go to sleep. I'll double the watch. You'll be safe, I promise. Harrington hasn't let anybody down so far, has it? Myself, Leo and Travis, we'll discuss and decide our best course of action. For tomorrow. But now, as I say, I think it would be wise if we tried to get some rest.'

'You don't think people *are* actually going to be able to sleep, do you, Clive?' said Leo Milton when he and his fellow deputy had joined Antony in the Headmaster's study. 'We ought to have told them our plans before we sent them to the dorms, given them confidence that we're in control of the situation.'

'Yeah.' Travis uttered a hollow laugh. 'In control of the situation. Right.' And with an alien spaceship half an hour's drive away and with countless others fanning out across the world, for all he knew, he was ashamed that it *still* felt satisfying to earn a glare from Leo Milton. Fellow deputy? *Rival* was nearer the mark.

Antony shook his head, ran his hands through his tight blond curls. 'No, you're probably right, Leo,' he sighed. 'If we knew what our plans are.'

'If we knew who these *aliens* are,' Travis said, 'and what they want. What we do is bound to depend on what *they* do, what they're here for. If they're like ET, fine. But if they're hostile . . .'

'Why would they be hostile?' Antony frowned, his tone strangely defensive. 'A people intelligent enough, advanced enough to have mastered interplanetary travel . . .'

'How can we be sure they're even aliens, Naughton?' challenged Leo. 'Those ships might be American or Russian or Chinese, the products of technology secretly developed in case of just such a global catastrophe as the Sickness. Our saviours might be aboard those ships, and they might be human.'

Rival? *Enemy* was nearer the mark still. 'You don't really believe that, Leo, do you?' Travis said with a mixture of pity and scorn. Surely the ginger-haired boy was simply being contrary. 'You had your eyes open out in the quad, didn't you? Aliens. No question.'

'But what if Leo's . . .?' Antony groped for hope. 'If they are human, that would explain why they're appearing now, to aid the survivors of the Sickness. Perhaps somebody's found a cure and—'

'Antony,' interrupted Travis. 'Don't. Don't even . . . You're deluding yourself.'

'The trouble is, Travis,' Antony winced, 'if the ships are alien, and, all right, I know they are, what can *their* possible reason be for arriving on Earth at the very moment when human civilisation is so utterly shattered? I can't believe it's a coincidence.'

'No,' agreed Travis. And he knew where the blond boy was going with this. It had been at the back of his mind too from the moment he'd entered the quad and looked up, only he'd not dared to acknowledge it, like a patient refusing to accept the tumour growing inside him, slowly killing him. Leo no doubt secretly felt the same. Probably everyone did.

'But if not coincidence,' Antony continued remorselessly, 'then we have to assume intent. The aliens have arrived among us now because they meant to, because they've been watching us, watching the Earth. All those ships. Think of the logistics required to gather together a fleet of that size. This is happening by design. It's planned. And if it's been planned . . .' Antony's voice trailed away with his courage.

'If it's been planned' – Travis took over – 'then whoever those aliens are must have known about the Sickness. But how could they have known? Unless they caused it.' He felt his words to be true even as he spoke them, even as they sickened and terrified him. 'We were looking in the wrong place for blame. Terrorists. Biotech experiments gone wrong. We were looking down when we should have been looking up. The Sickness didn't come from Earth. It came from space.'

Antony turned away, as if he could face neither Travis nor his conclusions. His eyes sought refuge in the portrait of Dr Stuart that hung on the wall. Dr Stuart, Harrington's late and last Headmaster and the man who'd appointed Antony Clive Head Boy. The artist had captured perfectly the Headmaster's quiet, confident certitude, perhaps as a reminder for those who would come after him. Dr Stuart had believed in decency, fair play and giving others the benefit of the doubt. So did his protégé.

Antony returned his gaze to his deputies. 'You could be right, Travis,' he conceded, 'but you could also still be wrong. Perhaps the aliens have been observing Earth and wanting to make peaceful contact with us for a long time. Perhaps they've been deterred from doing so through fear of our reaction, because they've witnessed from space little else but wars, acts of terrorism, hatred, violence, the kind of things we know the human race has become rather expert in over the years. Perhaps now they've seen the decimation the Sickness has caused, they've finally judged it's safe to show themselves. That's possible, isn't it? They could still be here to help us.'

'It's possible, Antony,' Travis said without conviction, 'but possible doesn't mean certain.'

The blond boy nodded. 'And we need to know for sure. In which case, our course of action is clear. We have to establish contact with the aliens ourselves. As soon as possible. As soon as it's light.'

'I don't agree, Clive,' Leo Milton objected. 'It would make more sense to leave the aliens to themselves and to address first the question of our own safety. We should stay here at Harrington. We can defend ourselves here. We've done so before.'

'Against Rev and his bikers,' Travis reminded him caustically. 'Oh yeah, and a few guys in cars. Yeah, and a commandeered bus. If these aliens are hostile, Leo, I think they'll have more to throw at us than a handful of Molotov cocktails.'

'If they're hostile, Naughton,' retorted Leo, 'why offer ourselves up so readily for the slaughter?'

'All right, all right,' Antony said. 'Differences of opinion are healthy so long as they're voiced with respect. Unfortunately, we don't have time for debate. As Head Boy, I recommend we send a party to the ship at Vernham Hill with the aim of establishing friendly relations with its occupants. What do my deputies say? Leo?'

'I say no.' Unsurprisingly. 'I say we reinforce our position within these walls, strengthen our defences . . .'

'Stick our heads in the sand,' Travis added by the way.

'Travis,' reproached Antony, 'there's no need for that. Leo's entitled to his point of view, as are you. And it seems yours will be the deciding vote.'

Travis glanced between the two Harrington boys. Leo Milton was already gnawing at his lower lip in barely disguised fury. He knew which side of the fence the newcomer was on. Travis didn't disappoint him. 'We go to the ship.'

Travis wasn't unduly surprised to find his group waiting for him in the dormitory he shared with Richie and Simon, even though it was now past midnight and, according to the rules, girls were not permitted in the boys' accommodation at any time. Still, under the circumstances, he felt an exception could be justified. Funny, too, in a way, that he should still think of them as 'his' group, when technically they were all now part of the wider Harrington community. Mel, Jessica, Simon, Richie, they were perched awkwardly on his bed as he entered, like their limbs were frozen. One person missing.

'Trav!' Mel relaxed, brightened when she saw him.

'Where's Linden?'

'She's with the little ones. Juniper, Willow and the others.' Linden's fellow Children of Nature, the extended family of eco-warriors they'd all belonged to before the Sickness. 'They were too frightened to even try to sleep without her.'

'What if I told you I was too frightened to sleep without *you*, Morticia?' advanced Richie Coker.

'I'd tell *you* to get used to bags under your eyes, Coker,' snorted Mel.

'Can't you both shut up with the smart remarks for once?' Simon complained peevishly. He was rubbing his thumbs and his forefingers together constantly, without realising he was doing it. 'This isn't the time for trying to be funny. We've got to be serious. Who knows what . . .?' He shrugged, defeated by his own question.

'It's all right, Simon.' Jessica placed her hand on his. 'Did you decide anything, Travis?'

He told them the plan. 'So at first light half a dozen of us are going to make our way to where the aliens landed – I doubt we'll have any problems finding the ship – and, I guess, introduce ourselves. Or something. We'll have to see what happens when we get there.'

'Are you sure it's a good idea, Travis?' Mel ventured, concerned. 'I mean, it sounds dangerous to me. It could be – are you sure?'

'I don't think good or bad idea comes into it, Mel,' Travis admitted. 'I don't think we have any choice. We just have to go out there and pray *our* aliens haven't seen *War of the Worlds* or *Independence Day*.'

'How do you pray?' grunted Richie Coker. 'But these half-dozen guys, Naughton. Six? Do they know who they are?' He looked vaguely fearful.

'Don't worry, Richie.' Travis smiled thinly. 'You're not one of them.'

'Just as well,' Mel said. 'God only knows what the aliens'd think if the first human being they saw was Richie Coker, complete with baseball cap.' She dropped her voice an octave lower. 'I thought the monitors reported *intelligent* life on Earth, Captain.'

'Thin ice, Morticia,' grumbled Richie, pulling at the peak of the baseball cap in question.

'Who *is* going, Travis?' Jessica wanted to know. She seemed to colour a little, not that anybody noticed. 'Is Antony . . .?'

'Yeah, Antony. Me. Hinkley-Jones. That little Giles kid. And two others who went to Harrington I don't really know, Tolliver and Shearsby.'

'Hinkley-Jones,' noted Mel. 'Supposedly the best shot we've got.' She frowned. She'd hoped the small arsenal the Harringtonians had amassed from neighbouring farms and the like wouldn't need to be pressed into service again.

'And Giles is fastest on his feet,' Simon put in. 'That's why he was chosen to be the runner when Rev attacked. I was partnered with him.' And had mistakenly thought Giles to be the boy's first name. It had turned out to be his surname: the school's formalities of address died hard.

Richie chuckled. 'Had the runs yourself now and again, Simes, huh?' Simon wanted to retaliate but didn't dare. 'So that ginger plonker Milton's not going with you?'

'Leo's in charge here till we get back.'

'Oh my God.' Not a popular promotion with Melanie Patrick. 'Sure there isn't room for a goth chick on this otherwise sexistly male jaunt of yours, Travis? Get back *soon*, you hear me?'

13

'And safely, Travis,' Jessica added, her green eyes earnest. 'You and Antony. And the others. Be careful.' Boys who could shoot. Boys who could run. It seemed like the group was preparing for trouble. 'Promise you'll be careful.'

Travis reached out and stroked Jessica's long blonde hair. 'I promise,' he said.

Stroking a girl's hair seemed to be becoming a habit of his. Linden's was much shorter than Jessica's, of course – she'd had it cropped close to the head, she'd told him, when she and her mother had first joined the woodland encampment of the Children of Nature. It was different in colour, too, a russet tint, putting Travis in mind of tumbling autumn leaves, though Linden was very much alive. Her eyes might be closed but her lips were slightly parted in her breathing, her chest rising and falling peacefully as she slept. Maybe sleep was the only state where peace could be found in the unrelenting nightmare the world had become.

Maybe he shouldn't disturb her after all.

But he'd had to see her before he left for the alien ship. Outside, dawn was already breaking; by the time the sun set again they'd know *something* about their likely fates. For better or for worse. It struck Travis how, before the Sickness, whole months of his life could pass by with blithe mundaneness, without any deviation from their ordinary routines, without disruption, months that he could hardly remember now because nothing of note seemed to have happened in them. Maybe he should have tried harder to make his life special, to make it count for something in the world that had gone. Now he had no choice. Now, post-Sickness, a lifetime could be concentrated into a single day, and nothing ever stayed the same, and every precious moment of living mattered.

He wondered, was this the last he'd see of Linden?

If so, it would be a good memory to carry with him. In her dorm, Linden had pushed two beds together so there was room for the younger children to sleep with her. Juniper, Willow, Rose, River, Fox, all of them crowded under the covers. Travis's mouth twitched a mischievous smile. *There were six in the bed and the little one said* . . . No. Best not to say anything. No need. He'd be back. He'd already made a promise, and his dad had taught him always to keep his promises.

He leaned down, kissed Linden lightly, tenderly on her lips. She sighed in her sleep but didn't wake. By the time she did, Travis would be long gone.

They didn't take any of the cars. Antony thought approaching by road would be too conspicuous, that it would be more sensible to conceal themselves from alien eyes, if stealth was even going to be possible – 'and however many eyes the aliens might have,' little Giles had added – at least until they'd given themselves a chance to survey the ship from closer quarters; they could determine how to proceed from there. So they travelled by foot and across country. They did, however, take with them a shotgun each – except for Giles, who being a first year and twelve years old was deemed too young to bear firearms even in the present crisis – and plenty of spare ammunition in pouches slung over their shoulders. They didn't bother with the bows that had helped to repel Rev and his gang; the odd arrow probably wouldn't make much of an impression on a spaceship twenty storeys high. Truth to tell, the shotguns would hardly reduce the aliens to quaking in their boots, either – 'if they wear boots,' Giles had pointed out, 'and if they've got legs' – but the weapons made the boys feel better, like comfort blankets made of metal and wood. If Hinkley-Jones was indeed Harrington's best shot, Travis was assured that Tolliver and Shearsby ran him a close second and third.

Antony set a brisk pace from the start. For once, he'd dressed in something other than the Harrington uniform and his Head Boy's tie, a more practical sweatshirt and jeans like the rest of them, dark colours to provide a semblance of camouflage. After three miles, Travis was struggling to keep up with the Harringtonians.

'Hey, Antony,' he called, 'I know you said you used to do cross-country runs over this route, but we're not doing one now.'

'Ah, state-school pupil,' Antony grinned. 'Unfit. Lack of competitive sporting opportunities. It's because the government sold off all your playing fields for development, you know.'

'Thanks for that. 'Preciate it.'

'Sorry. Soapbox. I suppose politics don't matter much any more.'

'That's where you're wrong.' Travis increased his effort, found the energy from somewhere to catch up with Antony and match the public schoolboy stride for stride. 'They matter as much as ever, today most of all. When we come face to face with these aliens—'

'If they even have faces,' contributed Giles, kind of bobbing up alongside the older boys.

'When we *meet* them,' Travis revised, 'it won't be just as

16

individuals. We'll be representatives of the entire human race.'

'Like ambassadors,' Antony approved. 'My father would have enjoyed that.' He smiled wistfully. 'I told you he was a diplomat, didn't I?'

'But what I want to know . . .' Giles interrupted again. His teachers must have loved him, Travis thought. 'What I want to know is what the aliens will actually look like. Will they be like us, sort of human, give or take a head, or will they be monsters with tentacles, or will they be like robots, not flesh and blood at all?'

'I think we can probably ignore all those cheap sci-fi-show clichés, Giles,' Travis said. *If only we could ignore you, too.*

Antony was nodding. 'The real issue isn't appearance. It's communication. How are we going to communicate with an entirely different species? The language barrier. My father told me once, if one can understand another's language, one can understand his mind. Share words and one begins to share ideas, identify common ground, build trust, mutual co-operation.'

'Let's hope they speak English, then,' said Travis.

'If they don't, we'll find another way.' Antony gazed serenely into the bright early-morning sky. 'I know we've taken precautions, but the more I think about it, the more certain I am they'll prove unnecessary. Whatever language the aliens speak, they're a civilised race. They must be. Only great civilisations produce great technology – their ships. And I believe that civilised societies by their very nature embrace the same core values: freedom, equality, the dignity of life. We share those common values, don't we? That'll be enough to begin establishing a relationship.'

'It *sounds* good, Antony,' Travis conceded, though heavily implying a *but*. 'It sounds *easy* . . .'

'It'll be fine, I'm sure of it. My father always placed his faith in discussion and negotiation. Everyone can be reached by reason. Respect others and they'll respect you.'

Unless, of course, thought Travis darkly, they didn't. But he kept his doubts to himself. He thought of his own father. Keith Naughton had been a police officer but he hadn't lived long enough to perish in the Sickness with everyone else's parents. Dad had been stabbed to death in the street by a thug high on drugs. No doubt he'd tried to reason with the junkie first, had reached out to him. It hadn't worked. Discussion and negotiation were all very well, everything Antony had said, mutual this, common that, his underlying assumption that everyone was like him really, all very well – in an ideal world. Travis had not believed in an ideal world since he'd been fetched from class at ten years old and escorted to the Head's office to be informed that his father was dead. The Sickness had only confirmed what he believed. That the world was flawed. That life was a struggle. That while you hoped – while you *strove* – for the best, you had to be prepared for disappointment. You had to be ready for those who did *not* respect you or anything you held dear, who despised you, who would not listen when you talked, who had no interest in your words. And when confronted by such an irreconcilable enemy, Travis believed, you had to make a stand. You had to fight.

Tightening his grip on his shotgun, Travis moved inexorably closer to Vernham Hill.

*

'He should have woken me,' Linden said. She sought explanation from Jessica and Mel. 'Why didn't he wake me?'

'He probably didn't want to upset you, Lin,' suggested Jessica.

'Well *that* didn't work, did it?' Linden's eyes were red, as if she'd been crying.

'Travis always does what he thinks is right,' Mel sighed. 'It can be a downer sometimes, but that's Trav. He won't change.'

'I don't want him to change,' said Linden. 'I want him here.'

And Antony Clive with him, Jessica found herself thinking.

The girls were standing outside in the school grounds, staring off in the direction they knew Travis and his companions had taken. The boys had been gone two hours. Mel remembered a Great War poster she'd once seen of a woman in white with long black hair (like hers, though she never wore white) striking a dramatic pose on a shoreline, evidently forlornly awaiting the return of her soldier lover/boyfriend/husband from the Front. Mel had mocked the poor woman mercilessly. 'Wasting all her time waiting for a man to come back,' she remembered scoffing. 'Stupid tart should get a life.' She supposed that was irony.

Mel wasn't out here just for Travis, however. Where Jessica went, she went.

'How long before they get there?' Jessica was wondering now.

'I don't know whether I hope it's soon,' said Linden, 'or never.'

'So this is where you're hiding.' A familiar voice from behind them. Simon trotting through the archway that led to the quad.

19

'Hiding, Simon.' Mel looked pointedly at the open spaces around her. 'Right.'

'You're not inside.' Simon frowned. 'We all need to be inside.'

'Why?' Linden's heart raced. 'Has something happened?'

Simon glanced nervously up at the sky as if he entertained a powerful suspicion that something *might*, and that the event could well consist of an alien ship appearing overhead to blast the Harrington School to dust. The reality was that Leo Milton had called a meeting in the Great Hall, attendance compulsory for every member of the community.

'Didn't take Ginge long to start throwing his weight around,' Mel said acidly. She followed the others in heading to the Great Hall nonetheless.

Jessica placed a sympathetic hand on the bespectacled boy's shoulder. 'How are you holding up, Simon?'

'Fine,' he said tersely. Because he could do without being patronised by Jessica Lane. She didn't care about him. If she did, she'd have voted against Richie Coker joining up with them. But oh no, she couldn't do, could she? Jessica Lane hadn't been in any condition to cast a vote one way or another the night they'd fled from Wayvale, because she'd been totally out of it, a zombie, dragged along by Mel, unable even to feed herself. If it hadn't been for them, Jessica wouldn't even be here. She'd be lost and alone somewhere (if blonde girls with fit bodies ever stayed alone for long), in despair. And yet now she had the gall to ask him how *he* was 'holding up', pretending concern, all this touchy-feely sort of crap. She had probably only invited him to her parties back in the old world because her parents knew – had known – his grandparents and had taken pity on him. Like he was a stray dog or something.

It was a stupid question, anyway. It deserved a lie for an answer. He wasn't fine. How could he be fine? How could anyone be fine with an army of aliens poised to overrun the planet? That was what the occupants of the spaceships were here for, whatever anyone else said, to make them all victims. Simon possessed expertise in such matters. He'd been a victim his whole life.

Here was his tormentor-in-chief now. Richie Coker, slouching against the wall at the back of the Great Hall. 'Keeping out of the way in case Leo's looking for volunteers, Richie?' Mel goaded as they passed. Richie Coker, heavy, sullen features – *Crimewatch* features, ugly, brutish, that stupid bloody baseball cap. Richie Coker, who'd bullied and tormented him pretty much every day of his school career, who last night had made it clear to Simon, with the aid of violence, that he could expect pretty much the same treatment to continue even though school was out for ever and the teachers were all dead. If the aliens' arrival could change that somehow, then there might be something to be said for them.

He was suddenly aware that Jessica was still looking at him, her brow creased in puzzlement. 'Simon, are you *sure* you're okay?'

'I'm sure,' he said.

'Look at this, though,' Mel said disapprovingly. 'Look at this. While the cat's away . . .'

Leo Milton was pacing the platform from which Antony had spoken as if staking out new territory. Mel, Jessica, Linden and Simon approached no closer than the fringe of the assembled community; maybe Richie was right to keep his distance after all. 'Everybody here?' Leo's eyes darted from side to side. 'Good. We've got plenty of work ahead of us, so I'll keep this brief and to the point. I believe Clive was wrong to actively seek contact with these aliens.' Murmurs from the floor. 'I want you to know I objected to the proposal last night and I still disagree with it now. Our first priority should be self-preservation. What we must do is fortify our position here, within Harrington's walls, build barricades, not bridges, wait for the aliens to come to us if they choose to do so, but we must be in a condition to defend ourselves if necessary. To that end, I am making the following changes to the work rosters . . .'

'No!' The vehemence of Jessica's outburst surprised even herself. Mel was staring at her agog. But the *assumption* Leo Milton was making, she couldn't let him get away with it. 'You can't do that. You can't change anything . . .'

Leo Milton peered coldly across a sea of heads, all of them turning towards Jessica. 'Do you have something to say, Lane?'

She suddenly felt abashed, her cheeks flared red, but she couldn't lapse back into silence now. She didn't want to. 'Yes, I . . . You're not Head Boy, Leo. You're not our leader. Antony is. You don't have the authority to change anything without Antony's consent, and he's not here to give it.'

'Precisely.' A malign smile played at Leo's lips. 'Neither, I believe, will he be coming back.'

'What do you mean?' Jessica's protest was joined by Linden and Mel, and some of the others. But not all. Not even many. Scarcely any, Mel realised, among the original Harringtonians.

'They'll be back, all of them,' Jessica cried. 'Of course they will. Of course.'

'Wishful thinking.' Leo Milton shook his head in artificial sadness. 'They were lost the moment they left the protection of Harrington behind them. At least, we who remain must proceed on the basis that they are.'

'Why?' Mel yelled. 'Why must we? This is all about *you*, Leo, you . . .'

'We cannot afford to wait for Clive's unlikely return. Or Naughton's. We cannot delay doing what needs to be done.'

'You bloody—'

'In the absence of Clive and in the absence of my fellow deputy,' Leo Milton declared, 'the leadership of Harrington by right devolves to me. I am the new Head Boy.'

'You little *shit*.' But Mel could hear cheering from some quarters.

'And there are going to be some changes to how we operate and organise here, let me tell you,' Leo continued triumphantly. 'To begin with, this nonsense Clive was about to introduce last night, renaming this institution the Harrington *Community*, that will not happen. Its true title, its only title, is the Harrington School, and that is what we shall continue to call it.'

'Did you hear what I called *you*, Leo?' Mel shouted.

And Simon was trying to shush her, his eyes round with fear behind his glasses. *The little weed.* 'Mel, I don't think you should – I don't think we should make a fuss.'

'Maybe now isn't the time, Mel,' added Linden. Like Simon, she'd noticed stony glares directed towards them from several of the Harrington boys.

'And *because* this is the Harrington School,' Leo Milton announced, 'those of us who belonged here before the Sickness, those of us who attended as students, it is only fair

23

and just that we be granted certain privileges in recognition of that fact. It's only right that the rules are made and enforced by us, for example. We, after all, are the true Harringtonians.'

Fresh cheers from the Harrington boys, louder, more confident, almost swaggering, in fact. Mel was astounded, more so that the few voices that had been raised in opposition to Leo were now stilled – including her own.

'Those of you who have sought shelter here since the Sickness . . .' *What?* Mel anticipated. *Will be expected to grovel in servile gratitude?* She didn't do grovelling. '. . . You will not be denied it. You are refugees, and the Harrington way has always been to extend the hand of charity to those in need. But you must know your place. You are here not because you have a right to be but because *we* allow you to stay. You will therefore treat true Harringtonians with the respect we deserve. You will obey the new order of things.' Leo Milton's eyes fixed on Mel, Jessica, Linden and Simon. 'Or you will suffer the consequences.'

About halfway to Vernham Hill, and as if by one accord, the Harrington party fell silent. Perhaps it had occurred to them that they would soon be closer to the aliens than to the school. Perhaps they were beginning to wonder whether the extra-terrestrials might have emerged from their ship by now, might be closing in on the expedition this very minute, or lurking just ahead, within that thicket, beyond those trees.

It seemed natural that Hinkley-Jones should take point, and he prowled forward warily, vigilantly, his shotgun poised to fire. Tolliver and Shearsby followed a few paces behind him to right and left, the three of them forming a protective arc around Antony, Travis and little Giles. Travis could see in the younger boy's eyes that he was afraid. His ridiculous prattle about aliens with multiple heads or oil for blood had been a defence mechanism, an attempt through exaggeration to mask the genuine dread he was plainly feeling at the prospect of encountering beings from another world. Travis wished he hadn't grown irritated with the boy earlier; Giles deserved only his understanding.

But no aliens appeared in any case. No traps were sprung. And now the ground was rising as they began to climb the thickly wooded incline of Vernham Hill itself. Perhaps, on the other side, the spaceship might be spread out below them, the alien creatures milling around breathing the air of a planet not their own. Travis felt his heart beat faster, and not simply because of his physical exertions. Weariness, in fact, seemed to have deserted him. He was advancing now more quickly, more purposefully than ever. So were the others. So near to their goal, they were almost breaking into a run. The need to *see* outweighed their fear and impelled them forward.

Hinkley-Jones crested the hill first. He cried out in awe, staggered to a halt, swayed as if he'd fall. 'It's here. My God, we've found it.'

Travis did run now, gasped the final metres to the summit, to the brink of Vernham Hill's second slope, a declivity that swept down to a broad valley, a further range of hills ascending on the far side. The topographical niceties of the scene did not, however, impinge on Travis's consciousness.

Between this hill and the others, the giant blade of its scything curve spanning the valley, its silver exterior glistening in the spring sunshine, the alien ship stood at rest.

Travis was unsettlingly reminded of an executioner's axe. Antony fancied the craft was reaching out its arms to embrace the Earth. That didn't stop him from seeking cover behind a tree, however, as his companions had done instinctively. Giles began to whimper.

The ground immediately surrounding the ship had been scorched and scarred by the landing, the undercarriage of the craft itself having compensated somehow for the unevenness of the terrain so that it had settled in the valley perfectly horizontally. In flight, every surface had been sheathed in the favoured silvery metal, but now the inner curve of the crescent had in part dispensed with what it seemed had been shields; its lower section, perhaps a dozen levels, burned with lights, red and blue and green, like jewels among a conqueror's spoils. A background hum of energy emanated from the ship, but no doors or hatches or portals were open, no ramps extended, no personnel or machinery dispatched outside that the boys could see.

Travis wasn't sure whether the aliens' apparent reluctance to venture out into the Earth environment relieved or perturbed him. 'Looks like they don't want to be disturbed,' he said in a whisper.

'They might be carrying out tests,' Antony returned in similarly hushed tones, as if alien ears might possess the ability to detect sound at considerably greater distances than their human counterparts, 'establishing whether they can live in our atmosphere without suits or something . . .'

'Clive,' hissed Giles, 'what if these ships aren't manned at all? What if they're fully automated, run by computers?'

Antony breathed in deeply. 'That's one of the things we need to find out.' He turned to the others. 'Who's coming with me?'

'Down . . . *there?*' faltered Shearsby, as if such an intention was as foolish as throwing oneself from a clifftop.

'It's what we came for,' Antony reminded him. 'We need to make contact with them. We need to communicate.'

Antony was right, of course. Travis knew that. But, as so often before, doing the right thing was not easy. However, 'I'm with you, Antony,' he said.

'For Harrington,' said Hinkley-Jones. Tolliver and Shearsby nodded nervously.

'I'm coming too.' For little Giles, being left on his own was a far more daunting prospect than meeting an alien, whatever it might look like.

'All right then,' Antony said. 'Let's go.'

Grouping together more closely than they'd done so far, taking advantage of the screening foliage, the boys began to descend. On this side of Vernham Hill, unhappily, there was more natural cover near the top than lower down. Almost as if, Travis imagined disconcertedly, the trees themselves were in retreat from the aliens. The undergrowth would not obscure the party from the ship's sight for more than a few metres further. If they were still unable to see the aliens after that, the aliens would sure as hell be able to see them. And that was if their presence hadn't already been detected by the spaceship's instruments, if their progress was not already being monitored every step of the way.

'Carry your guns at your sides,' Antony was instructing. 'Don't make any aggressive motions with them. We don't want the aliens to think we're hostile.'

'Clive,' Shearsby said, marvelling at the ship, 'I don't think it's going to matter what they think we are.'

As the trees, like traitors, gave the boys up.

As a slight hiss, almost of derision, escaped the spacecraft.

As, above the multitude of lights, a wide aperture opened in its hull, gleaming doors sliding back, a black and grinning mouth.

'Is this good or bad or what?' worried Shearsby.

A second ship suddenly shot from within. The boys cried out involuntarily. A second ship, identical to its parent in every respect save size, and even so it was still larger and boasted a wider wingspan than any aircraft Travis had ever seen. He kind of hoped its appearance was unrelated to their own. He kind of hoped it had business elsewhere.

It wasn't and it didn't.

Engines glowing at each tapered point of the scythe, the ship wheeled in the sky towards them, hung in the air directly above them, a hovering bird of prey.

Little Giles had seen enough. He screamed, his hands balled into terrified fists.

Shearsby was howling: 'Let's get out of here! We've got to get out of here!'

But Antony was adamant. 'We can't do that. Shearsby, there is no going back.'

Ludicrously, Hinkley-Jones was raising his shotgun as he might during a shoot on his late father's estate.

'No!' Antony seized the barrel and pulled it down again. 'What do you think you're doing? What did I tell you?'

'But Clive . . .'

'This may not be an attack. They may have come to greet us. We have to give them . . .' *The benefit of the doubt*, Antony was going to add.

Until silver panels slid open in this second ship too, in its undercarriage, disgorging even smaller flying craft, tiny, these, relatively, hardly larger than the size of a man, oval in shape, like eggs or pods, the lower half metal and the upper half a transparent substance like glass. Six of them.

Six of *us*, Travis thought, fear clawing at his insides. He was stepping backwards almost without realising it. They all were, even Antony.

'No.' But the Head Boy forced himself, willed himself to stop.

The pods circled overhead between the boys and the ship. They were occupied. Through the glass Travis could make out a compartment, a cockpit of a kind, with a pilot seated in each, a figure humanoid in form though highly unlikely to be a man.

'We have to reach out.' Antony flung down his weapon, threw his arms wide as if preparing for crucifixion. 'We have to show them we're no threat.' He moved apart from his companions.

Travis had to concede, Antony Clive had courage. Especially as the aliens seemed wholly and uncompromisingly encased in some kind of armour. Their garb might have been an innocent type of spacesuit or flying suit, he supposed, but he was put more in mind of medieval knights, warrior knights, and the armour was glittering and dark, like black ice, except in one case where it dazzled as its wearer looped above the boys' heads, the brilliance of gold.

'Can you hear me? Can you understand me?' Antony was appealing to the aliens at the top of his voice. 'Please, talk to us. We only want to talk.'

But the helmets the aliens had donned concealing their features flitted past Travis's straining sight like the heads of strange and savage beasts, each different but all either tusked or fanged or horned, cast in the violent image of creatures that had never trod the Earth. Their aspect did not appear conducive to mutual co-operation or the establishment of common areas of interest.

'We want . . . we want to be your friends.' But even Antony seemed less certain than before.

And below the glass cockpit of each pod, a circular hole was suddenly opening, white light crackling within. A gun port.

'Forget it,' Travis yelled. 'Antony!'

Hinkley-Jones was swinging his shotgun up to his shoulder, his finger quick to the trigger.

But the aliens were quicker.

Six bolts of energy flashed simultaneously from the pods. Each one struck Hinkley-Jones, enveloping him in blinding brightness. The rays blazed like white fire but the boy froze like ice. He didn't even cry out. Couldn't. Hinkley-Jones, the best shot in the Harrington School, pitched forward and thudded to the ground and did not move again.

Travis gaped in horror, though it occurred to him bitterly that their mission had at least been successful. The boys had wanted the aliens to communicate with them, and the aliens had. In no uncertain terms.

They hadn't come to help. They'd come to kill.

TWO

'Run!' Tolliver and Shearsby were already on their way, the opportunity to demonstrate their marksmanship forgotten as they dropped the shotguns that would only slow them down. 'Antony, run!' Travis grabbing his friend's shoulder.

'No. No.' The blond boy groaning in painful despair.

'*Yes.*'

But not so much despair that he didn't want to live. Turning on his heel, Antony fled too. Abandoning their useless weapons as Tolliver and Shearsby had done, he and Travis raced for the trees. The cover offered by the wood was their only chance.

'Giles!' Antony yelled ahead – the younger boy was already outstripping them all. 'Go like the wind. Warn them at Harrington. Warn Leo.'

The pods swooped lower. Travis could see the shadow of one of them zeroing in on him over the grass. He didn't dare glance up towards the pods themselves. *Look up, you might trip. Trip, you might fall. Fall, you'd die, no might about it.* So he only heard the ominous crackle of the death-ray recharging. His back wasn't especially broad, but he bet it still made a good target.

He darted to the left, suddenly and with all the speed he could muster. An energy bolt sizzled to his right. Would have hit where he'd been; missed where he was.

And the ground was rising more steeply, but that meant the concealing trees were nearer. Travis powered on, burning lungs and muscles preferable to immersion in the aliens' flame. The pod that had failed to shoot him down was having to circle round for another attempt. Antony, glimpsed from the corner of his right eye, was zigzagging too, keeping distance between them. Giles, ahead, was plunging into the wood. They might make it. They might all yet—

Twin bolts of energy ended Tolliver's interest in the post-Sickness world. Shearsby paused in his own retreat to cry, 'Robert!' It was the first time Travis had heard the Harringtonian call his friend by his Christian name, and the last. A static target was easier to hit than one on the move. The aliens took advantage, briefly diverted. Shearsby was screaming before the rays hit him, silent thereafter.

But he'd given Travis and Antony crucial extra time. They hurtled headlong into the thicker undergrowth among the trees, and though their pace was slowed, the shadows of the pursuing craft were lost among those cast by the canopy above their heads. Travis prayed that meant the aliens had lost sight of them as well.

He glanced across to Antony, maybe thirty metres away. The blond boy was altering direction now, running towards Travis. They'd hide from the aliens and when it was safe find their way back to Harrington together. Travis felt a surge of hope.

The trees that separated the two of them exploded.

Shards of timber flew and the force of the detonation knocked both boys to the ground. On his back, no choice for Travis but to look up now. He could see the pods wheeling above the wood. A new strategy for the hunters. Flush their prey out into the open by destroying the habitat that sheltered it.

The aliens' weapons blazed again. More trees erupted in pillars of fire. And now the rays that spouted from the pods were yellow in colour, not white like those that had murdered Shearsby, Tolliver and Hinkley-Jones. That was probably important, though not as vital as immediate survival.

Travis scrambled to his feet, looked for Antony. Dense, drifting smoke obscured his line of vision and there appeared to be no sign of the other boy. 'Antony!' No answer. He couldn't be dead, could he? Travis's mind refused to consider that possibility.

But *he'd* be dead if he didn't shift. The trees around him were igniting like firecrackers. He couldn't stay here, and Antony wouldn't want him to. Travis propelled himself forward, higher, into the green again, trusting that somewhere nearby his friend was doing the same.

He hadn't to think of the agony racking his body. He had to distance himself from pain, physical, mental, close his mind to it. Operate by instinct rather than thought. If he was being hunted like an animal, he had to respond like one. Or would that simply confirm what seemed to be the aliens' assumption, that human beings were nothing more than beasts? No. Only those who attacked and killed without reason were truly bestial, even when they flew in spaceships.

Travis stumbled into a clearing. A mistake. He'd allowed himself to become distracted. Automatically he gazed upwards. Another mistake. And he'd been doing so well in that regard.

An alien pod hovered above him.

It jabbed at him like a boxer's fist, almost plummeting to

earth before rearing back to its original height. Travis cried out, staggered back. Tripped. Fell. He knew what that meant. The alien who would kill him wore golden armour. The blast that would kill him was forming, flaring within the gun port. There was no escape. He sucked in his breath, his final breath.

The energy bolt flamed to the ground six inches to the left of his head.

He was still alive. *Still alive.* And he intended to stay that way, rolling over now with renewed vigour, jumping to his feet. So the alien's one-of-a-kind outfit hadn't been awarded for services to shooting. Travis sprang back under the cover of the trees. Best not to grant him a second chance, though. And maybe it was just wishful thinking, but the pod didn't seem to be giving chase, no yellow lightning combusting his surrounds.

Unless it had accelerated on ahead. Unless that was it, the craft Travis could spy through a break in the foliage skimming the very summit of Vernham Hill.

The craft that was tracking Giles.

Travis moaned in dismay. He could glimpse the boy running, desperately, hopelessly, in and out of the trees. It looked like he was crying. The alien was toying with him, could have put Giles out of his misery time and again even as Travis watched. Playing games with human lives. *Bastard*, Travis cursed.

'*Bas—*'

A kind of rugby tackle brought him to his knees. 'Down and quiet or do you want them to see you?' A voice he was only too pleased to hear again.

'Antony, how did you . . .?'

'Same as you. Ran like hell. I've found somewhere we can hide.'

'Okay, but' – Travis's attention drawn once more to the frantic figure of the younger boy in the distance – 'Giles . . .'

Antony looked on too, ashen-faced. 'Run,' he urged, softly but fervently. 'Run, Giles, like you've never . . .'

But the alien must have grown bored. The white ray flashed. The game was brought to its inevitable end.

'Here. Travis, here.' Antony pulled at his arm. 'It'll be after us next. I've found . . .' A hollow in the ground. A depression large enough for several bodies to cram into it, to cover themselves with leaves and twigs. Antony and Travis did all that. 'We can't outrun them. But we have to make them think we have, hide here and hope they think they've lost us.'

Lying on his front, Travis peeped through a screen of forest debris towards the place where Giles had fallen. The pod had remained sentinel above it. 'What's it waiting for? To check he's dead?'

'*That.*' Antony stabbed his finger skywards.

The ship that had launched the pods loomed over Vernham Hill. A beam of white light issued from its undercarriage, circular and of a diameter far broader than the pods' energy bolts. There was something more peaceful about this new manifestation of alien technology, almost serene. The beam extended from the ship to the soil. It encompassed the spot where little Giles lay. And it lifted him up.

'What the hell . . .?' Travis was both appalled and fascinated as the boy's limp form floated into the air within the light's embrace.

'It's a tractor beam. They're taking him away.'

'But why would they want his body? Dissection?' A word Travis immediately regretted uttering. The thought of it made him want to retch.

'Maybe – maybe Giles isn't dead. Maybe none of them are.' Harringtonian optimism. A trace of colour was finding its way back into Antony's complexion.

'You can make a case for that?' Travis challenged hopefully.

'Maybe their white energy bolts just stun. Hinkley-Jones and the others, I didn't see any blood, and the aliens used . . .'

'. . . yellow blasts when they were doing their bit for deforestation. Sounds plausible, I guess.'

'Unfortunately, every answer begs a question.'

'Meaning?'

As the body of Giles disappeared into the belly of the ship and the tractor beam was extinguished, Antony focused his gaze penetratingly on his companion. 'If they want us alive, Travis, what do they want us alive *for*?'

'Okay, so only the grey blazer types get a say in how everything's run, only they get to carry weapons, and the rest of us have just got to know our place, stay in it, and not rock the Harrington boat.' Mel snorted in disgust. 'Leo's staged what in the old days would have been called a coup. And you know what?' Mel glanced from Linden to Jessica to Simon and back again, pretty much ignoring Richie. 'I'm not standing for it.'

'What are you going to do?' Simon's own gaze kept straying to the dormitory door. It was firmly closed and made of solid English oak, but he still feared the possibility of eavesdroppers pressing their ears to the other side. Conspiracy made him uncomfortable.

'I'm leaving, that's what I'm going to do,' said Mel. 'I'm going to go after Travis and Antony and let them know what nasty little liberties Leo's taken in their absence.'

'His supporters are guarding all the doors,' Jessica pointed out.

'Nobody's allowed outside,' Linden added.

'For their own protection.' Mel mimicked Leo's voice unflatteringly. 'For the duration of this present emergency. God, he even *sounds* like a politician. If it wasn't for the Sickness, I reckon in thirty years or so Leo Milton would have been running this country. But don't fret, Jessie. I doubt the blazers can keep an eye on *all* the doors. And the worst thing is, this *is* an emergency. Aliens in spaceships. We should be coming together, presenting a united front, not breaking up into factions. I thought after the Sickness there'd only be one class of humans left – survivors. Seems I was wrong.'

'You only need two people,' Simon commented bitterly, 'for one to be a victim.'

'Mel, even if we do follow Travis and Antony,' Linden said, 'they'll be at the alien ship by now.'

'If the ship's still where we only *think* it is,' Mel countered. 'They could just as easily be on their way back here having found nothing, and somehow, if they *are*, I don't reckon Leo'll be putting out the welcome mat. Not now he's got his grubby little paws on some power.' She crossed to the window. 'So like I said, I'm out of here. Anyone want to join me?'

Linden nodded. 'I'd have gone with Travis in the first place if I could.'

'I don't think we've got any choice,' said Jessica. 'Antony will put things right.'

'Simon?' Mel pressed.

Simon's heart had been sinking throughout this hastily, clandestinely convened meeting of their original group. He preferred to hide in the margins of life, unnoticed and therefore hopefully unpersecuted. He wasn't used to standing up for himself or anyone else, he wasn't used to taking sides, but neither did he relish the possibility of finding himself isolated at Harrington without the others' solidarity. 'I'll come,' he said.

'Richie?' As if she wasn't really bothered either way.

'Never wanted anything to do with this poncy bloody school anyway,' Riche Coker grunted, which was interpreted as a yes.

'Okay.' Mel moved decisively towards the dormitory door. 'Well there's no time like the present.'

'Wait.' Linden. 'I can't leave Juniper and the other little ones. Not again.' The memory of how she'd run out on the junior Children of Nature at their camp in the forest still shamed her.

'We don't want to be lumbered with a bunch of bawling kids,' Richie objected. 'I'm not a bloody babysitter.'

'I'm sure the babies of the world are glad about that,' said Mel. 'We'll pick Juni up on the way, Lin. Now let's . . .'

Mel threw open the dormitory door. Leo Milton stood in the corridor beyond, accompanied by several Harringtonians complete with school uniform. And shotguns.

'And where do you think you're going?' said Leo.

*

The ship with the tractor beam departed almost as soon as it had abducted Giles's body. Travis and Antony, burrowed as deeply into their makeshift foxhole as practicable, had feared that the pods would at least continue to search for them, or worse, indulge in further wanton destruction of the woodland. One fear thankfully unrealised. The yellow rays were not fired again. Doors slid open a second time in the larger craft's undercarriage and the pods returned inside. Then the crescent ship itself accelerated out of sight. It seemed the aliens had more important matters to attend to elsewhere. Travis hoped Mars.

Even so, the two teenagers waited until dark before crawling out from their refuge. The long hours of immobility had taken their toll; the boys' limbs were stiff and their muscles felt invalid weak. They were also increasingly aware they'd had nothing to eat or drink since before they'd left Harrington, and now they were faced with a further ten-mile trek back to the school.

'The sooner we start . . .' said Antony.

'Yeah.' Travis regarded him bleakly. 'The sooner we tell the others we're finished.'

Because that was the only conclusion he could draw from what had been beyond doubt the most catastrophic day since the Sickness, with its ramifications likely to prove just as devastating and far-reaching. Maybe more so, Travis thought. The virus after all had only infected adults, with anybody under eighteen or so inexplicably immune to its ravages, but that invulnerability patently did not extend to alien weaponry. With their ability to defend themselves reliant on a few puny shotguns and rifles, the unpalatable truth was that the Harrington community, and probably every other surviving community in the world, was completely at the aliens' mercy. And mercy was a quality which, for the present at any rate, seemed to be in short supply among the extraterrestrials. None of this meant that Travis was about to give up any time soon, march to the aliens' mother ship with his hands in the air or throw himself under a pod or something – surrender wasn't true to the spirit of his father, or to his own sense of what was right – but he harboured no illusions about the outcome of any resistance they might wage against the invaders. He was as prepared to make a stand as ever, only chances were it'd be a *last* stand.

Antony was probably thinking much the same thing. He was certainly unusually withdrawn as they made their way homewards. The two of them trudged in silence.

It must have been past midnight when they finally came within view of the Harrington School. Travis's heart quickened, not just at the sight of the familiar crenellated structure, looking more like a castle than ever silhouetted darkly in the moonlight, but at the knowledge of who was inside. He couldn't wait to see the girls again, to see Linden again. He started forward more eagerly.

'Something's wrong.' The sharpness in Antony's tone halted him in his tracks.

'What . . .?'

'No lights.' Indeed. Harrington was nothing but an inky, hulking mass. 'We always leave some lights on for the watch. And where *is* the watch?'

Travis felt his pulse race faster again, and not for positive reasons. Antony was right, of course. They were virtually on the school's doorstep and they'd not been challenged at any point. Where was the watch? Surely Leo wouldn't have neglected to post guards tonight of all . . .

'My God, Travis, what if the aliens have been here?'

But Travis had already broken into a run. The pods earlier. Why waste time scouring a hillside for two errant humans when there had to be easier pickings nearby? He pounded out of the trees into the shadow of the main building, which was black with foreboding. He heard Antony chasing behind him. 'Travis, be careful. We don't know what we'll find. We ought to think before . . .'

Only one thought worth thinking: where were his friends?

Travis sprinted through the arch into the first of Harrington's two quadrangles. The doors on all sides, the doors that provided access to the building itself, every one of them open, gaping as if in shock. He yelled as he charged inside. 'Hello? Can anyone hear me? Answer me! It's Travis!'

'Leo? Anyone?' Antony weighed in. 'Is anyone here?'

It appeared not. The boys' shouts echoed emptily from walls of stone. Desertion lurked in the corridors' darkness, abandonment, despair.

'Travis, we should check the Great Hall.'

'You can. I'm going to the dorms.' If his friends were anywhere, that was where. He bounded up the staircase.

'Okay. Wait for me, Travis. We ought not to get separated.'

'No time to wait.' Glancing back over his shoulder once and once only. 'Keep *up*.' Darting along the corridor towards the girls' dormitory. Its door was closed, like the room held a secret. But all Travis would have to do was fling it wide and he'd be greeted by the sight of Linden and Jessie and Mel asleep in their beds because all that was really, actually wrong was that the generator had broken down and Leo Milton had neither fixed it nor, in his incompetence, remembered to post the watch. That was all. Mechanical failure and human error. Nothing to do with aliens. It couldn't be. He wouldn't let it be.

The girls were gone. The dormitory beds had not been slept in tonight. 'Nonono.' Travis flipped the light switch: nothing. But that was good, wasn't it? Maybe the generator *had* packed up. And if he was right about that, there was still hope that . . . 'Antony, we need to check the other . . .'

Antony wasn't at his back to hear. But he couldn't have left him that far behind. Travis froze. 'Antony?' He edged out into the corridor again, squinting back the way he'd come, into almost total darkness.

Someone was standing there, metres away, the night congealing into more solid form.

It wasn't Antony.

Because the aliens *had* visited Harrington. At least one of them was still here.

A figure in armour like jet, like oil, a figure with the head of a beast, ferocious and feral, striding implacably towards him. A figure with a gun in his right hand, the weapon as black as its owner's armour, like a pistol with a hexagonal barrel. It was pointing at Travis.

'What have you done with the people who were here?' Anger overcame fear. 'Can you understand me? What have you done with them?'

In what might have constituted an answer as well as an action, the alien fired his weapon. Travis just had time to register the colour of the energy bolt before it hit him. White. And it was cold, not hot, icy, and Travis couldn't feel his body at all or even the flagstones of the floor as he fell. He couldn't feel anything, sinking into a darkness deeper than the night.

Fight it, he urged himself. *Don't give in to it. Don't close your eyes.*

The alien towered above him. The sideways slant of his head suggested curiosity at Travis's continued consciousness.

'Who . . . you . . . looking at?'

The alien touched a stud on his neck. At once the fluid, organic lines of his helmet stiffened, flattened, retracted from his throat upwards like a blind being raised, slithered over his skull to hang down at the back like a hood or a cowl.

Travis was grateful his numbness stopped him shrinking from the sight of the alien revealed.

The head was utterly hairless and disturbingly white, like a skull peeled of living flesh; there was skin, but of phantom pallor, as though drained of blood, and it was stretched tautly across the bone as if, on the alien's home planet, skin was in short supply and needed to be applied sparingly. A hard buttress of bone protruded all along the forehead, jutting out aggressively and overshadowing deep-set eyes. The eyes, in fact, might have been where the creature's blood had flowed to: they were deep red, like scarlet blisters, without pupils or irises or, ironically, given the alien's prevailing pigmentation, whites. Their colour reminded Travis of circular crimson scars on human bodies, the sign of the Sickness. The remaining features were similarly unprepossessing. The ears were little more than lumps of cartilage on the side of the head with a crescent flap sliced into them, the nose could have belonged to any heavyweight whose boxing career had gone on for one fight too many, and the lipless mouth resembled a wound that had failed to heal.

'I can . . . see you . . .' Travis breathed.

The alien opened his mouth in what might have been a smile. There was red inside. 'Not for long,' he said in perfect English.

Which might have prompted a reaction from Travis even given his paralysis. If he'd been able to stay conscious long enough.

The lack of pain was something. As his senses returned to him, Travis had expected an accompaniment of agony, but he felt no after-effects of the alien's attack at all.

Apart from the fact that he wasn't now where he'd been before.

'Travis, are you okay?' Antony was kneeling beside him, studying him with concern.

'They got us both, then.'

'I'm afraid so.'

'At least you were right about the white ray. As for am I okay . . .' Travis sat up on the floor where he'd been sprawled. 'Okay is a relative concept.'

He deduced their location at a glance. A featureless rectangular room, the dimensions of a large lounge, cast in the silvery metal of which the aliens seemed so fond. The low hum in the air and the slight throb of motion beneath his fingers as they pressed against the floor. They were aboard an alien craft, probably the ship with the tractor beam, and they were in flight. The context of their journey the bareness of their accommodation also made plain. The room could more accurately be described as a cell. They were prisoners.

Which almost certainly meant the others were, too. Which meant they were alive, Linden, Jessica, Mel, all of them, even

Hinkley-Jones and little Giles. Travis stood. He felt surprisingly strong. Right now, alive would have to do.

'Any idea how long we've been out?'

'A few hours, I suppose. Look over here.' Antony drew Travis's attention to a strip in one of the cell walls. From a distance the panel seemed formed of the same metal as the rest of the room, but closer inspection showed it to be transparent. It was daylight outside, and they were indeed passing over the hills and woodland surrounding the Harrington School. 'I haven't been conscious long myself. When I came to, we were still on the ground.'

'No prizes for guessing where we're going,' Travis said grimly.

'If they're taking us to their mother ship, that could be to our advantage.' There was a pale eagerness in Antony's face.

'You mean if the others are there too? They must be.' Travis recognised Vernham Hill ahead. 'All of us together, we might be able to break out or something, find a weapon we can use against these creatures. I saw one of them, Antony, the one that shot me. Without his helmet. We're talking natives of Planet Ugly.'

'I didn't mean that. I *mean*, if we're taken aboard their mother ship, we might get a chance to talk to their leader, their captain, commander, make him see sense, explain . . .'

Travis regarded his friend with stark disbelief. 'Explain what, Antony?'

'That this is all a misunderstanding . . .'

'Hunting us down in those pods, incinerating half of Vernham Hill, probably kidnapping the entire population of Harrington – a misunderstanding?' Travis shook his head incredulously. 'I think they know what they're doing, Antony, and why, and it's not good.'

'And it's not necessary,' Antony burst out. 'We can live alongside these people . . .'

'They're not people, Antony, not like us.'

'We pose no danger to them.'

'Ain't that the truth.'

'There's no reason for us to be in conflict. It doesn't make sense. And if we can only just talk to their leader, discuss the situation like reasonable beings, I'm sure we can come to some kind of mutually acceptable—'

'Antony. Antony.' Travis couldn't bear to hear any more. He clamped his hands on his friend's shoulders, shook him. 'Listen to me. Shut up and listen. That's not going to happen. That's not going to work. You've got to face facts. Whatever these aliens want, it's not friendship, it's not co-operation and it's not tolerance. We can't negotiate with them. We can only fight them.'

'But my father always used to say . . .'

'Your father's dead, Antony. All our dads are dead. And the world they lived in, that's dead, too. But we're alive, and if you want to stay that way you've got to face up to the fact that the rules have changed, for ever. You've got to accept that and change with them or you won't be any use to us, Antony, or to yourself. Do you understand?'

'But Travis, everything I believed in . . .' There were desolate tears in Antony's eyes, tears almost of bereavement. 'If it's all useless, all worthless, what good am I?'

And Travis felt pity for his friend. Maybe he'd been too harsh. He could remedy that. 'You want to know what good you are? You have to ask? You're Antony Clive, Head Boy of the Harrington School. You're still a leader, Antony. We need you.' *And now,* he thought, as the ship swooped down over the far side of Vernham Hill towards its parent below, the doors they'd seen before opening in anticipation.

Antony was also aware of the mother ship's proximity. 'All right. All right.' He nodded, took deep breaths, visibly pulling himself together. 'Then you've got me. And Travis – thanks.'

'No problem,' Travis said warmly. 'But listen, there's something else, something I haven't told you. When I saw the alien without his helmet, I heard him as well. God knows how, but they speak English.'

'Do they?' Antony forcibly injected the confidence into his voice again. He'd betrayed weakness in front of Travis. That deserved a demerit. Head Boys of the Harrington School were not appointed to display weakness to anyone. 'Then we can make them understand us.'

Both teenagers remained close to the viewing panel as their vessel glided between the open doors of its larger counterpart, as if it was a morsel of food swallowed by a mouth. It immediately came to rest on what was clearly the mother ship's flight deck. Travis could make out another of the tractor-beam models that had abducted Giles standing by, aliens moving about in reddish armour this time and without helmets. His renewed acquaintance with the naked white skulls and the bulging ridged foreheads no more endeared him to the aliens' physiognomy than had his previous encounter; it didn't surprise him that Antony's first reaction to their captors' appearance was one of distaste. 'My father used to tell me one must never judge by appearances,' he said coldly. The scarlet slash of the mouth. The livid crimson eyes. 'Perhaps that was another matter in which he was mistaken.'

They weren't given long to gawp at the aliens, however. Suddenly the viewing panel seemed to be sliding up the wall, slipping between it and the ceiling and out of sight.

Travis stepped back, startled. 'What the . . .?'

'It's not the wall moving up,' Antony realised. 'It's the floor and the ceiling moving down. Through the decks.'

Which was true. Travis felt their descent now in his stomach and through the soles of his trainers. 'Cell and lift all in one. So where's it taking us? Ground floor, freedom?'

'Wherever it is, we're there,' muttered Antony.

Their elevator cell ceased motion. A door slid open in what the boys had imagined thus far to be a sheer wall.

Through the doorway they glimpsed what seemed to be an identical cell, though deeper, larger, figures shuffling about, some squatting or slumping on the floor with the apathy of the incarcerated. Some in grey blazers and trousers. Some female.

One with an elfin face and short russet hair.

'The Earther prisoners will enter the adjacent cell at once.'

Travis and Antony didn't need a disembodied alien voice to tell them. In a second they were through that door, and they were shouting out with relief and elation. The door closed and melted away behind them but they scarcely noticed. In another second, Linden was in Travis's arms, her body soft and her lips moist against his, and for that second at least, nothing else mattered.

Richie Coker was kind of glad to see Naughton again. Not as glad as Hippie Chick, of course, who was all over him like a rash soon as he stepped through the door that hadn't been there a minute ago. Not as glad as the other members of Travis's harem, either, Morticia and Jessica Lane getting in on the lip action as well (how did Naughton *do* it?). Nah, Richie Coker didn't go in for visible displays of emotion, not even the wimpish sort of handshake Simes was sharing with Naughton now. Best thing was, safest thing was to keep your feelings to yourself – that way nobody else was likely to trample all over them. So a brief, approving sort of nod was all he offered when Naughton glanced towards him.

'You all right, Richie?' Sounding like he was genuinely concerned.

'Guess so.' Trying to sound like he didn't care. But yeah, he was kind of glad to see Naughton back.

Jealous, too, in a way, a little bit, though there was no reason why he should be. He was bigger than Travis Naughton, taller, stronger, had kicked more heads in. Nobody messed with Richie Coker – or hadn't, in the time before the Sickness. But there *was* a reason for the envy if he was being honest, which was not a condition that came naturally to Richie. Other kids *liked* Naughton; they respected him, looked up to him (even when they *were* taller). It was obvious from how they responded to Naughton's reappearance, thankful, joyful, clamouring around him and the rich kid even though most of them had only known Travis a couple of weeks. Why? What did Naughton have in him to make that happen? Richie didn't understand. If he'd been the one suddenly turning up again after a period of being missing, the reaction would be cool disinterest at best, open disappointment at worst. Nobody cared right now whether he was there in the cell with the rest of them or not. With the probable exception of one person, of course. Travis Naughton.

Richie turned away. Back in Wayvale he'd hung around with plenty of mates. He'd been a leader himself back then, had demanded and been shown respect. People had done what he'd told them to do. But only because they'd been shit-scared he'd have kicked their heads in if they hadn't. He knew that was how it had been, if he was honest. But kids would follow Naughton – *were* following, obeying him, letting him lead them – not due to fear or threats, but voluntarily, freely, because he *inspired* them somehow, with his do-gooding self-belief and his blue eyes that saw right through you. There was a magic in Travis Naughton, an authority, something he remembered Dr Shiels at school calling integrity, and it cast its spell over anyone who came into contact with it. Which frightened the crap out of Richie Coker. Because he was falling under its influence, too. In a way. A little bit. If he was being honest.

He was glad to see Naughton alive. Not kind of. Just glad. Because part of him wanted to *be* Travis Naughton.

'*Weren't* we, Richie?' Morticia's voice, summoning him back into the group.

He gravitated towards them, feigning offhandedness. 'What? Weren't we what?'

'I'm telling Trav what happened at the school. We were shut up in the dorm, weren't we? Leo and his blazers placed us under what he pompously called house arrest, like we were criminals or something.' Mel's blue eyes flashed as she directed her contempt towards the defeated figure of Leo Milton, slumped and disconsolate on the floor. 'We were a disruptive influence, that's what he said, wasn't it? We might have a demoralising effect on the rest of the community. Load of crap. Should have left a girl in charge, Antony. How does it feel now *you're* in the cells, Leo? Pretty demoralising now, huh?'

'All right, Mel,' said Travis. 'We get the picture.'

'Told you,' Richie put in, 'we can't trust nobody in that poncy bloody uniform.'

'That's not true.' Jessica certainly seemed to feel that one of the Harringtonians was worthy of her faith. After Travis, she'd flung welcoming arms around Antony, too. While they weren't clasped about his neck any more, they were still lingering close to him, brushing against him. As was the rest of her. 'What Leo did Leo can be blamed for. No one else.'

Travis agreed. 'Given what's happened since, I suppose it's not important now anyway.'

'We couldn't have done anything to stop the aliens even if we'd been free to try,' Linden said. 'They swarmed over Harrington with those ray guns of theirs in a matter of minutes. I don't think we inflicted a single casualty.'

'Not even the army would have been able to stop them,' moaned Simon.

'The army isn't here, Simon,' Travis said. 'We are. And we have to find a way.'

'Naughton!' Richie couldn't restrain a burst of hollow, disbelieving laughter. 'You're talking out of your arse. You actually think we can stand up to these guys?'

Travis gazed at the boy in the baseball cap. 'If we don't stand, Richie, we fall.'

And Richie Coker was silenced. Not for the first time, the conviction and the resolution in that blue stare robbed him of words, even those containing four letters.

Antony, meanwhile, had remained broodingly deep in thought throughout the previous exchange. Now he seemed to have made his mind up about something. 'It *is* important,' he said coldly, forcefully.

'Antony?' The expression in his face Jessica had not seen before, angry, bitter.

'It is important what happened at Harrington, what Leo did. It's important because it was a betrayal. You're a stinking Judas, Leo, you know that?' He bore down on his deputy, fists clenched and violence in his eyes.

Leo, probably sensibly, leapt to his feet. 'Don't you come near me, Clive.'

'Or what? What are you going to do? Cowards like you don't fight face to face, do you? You wait until someone's back is turned before you stab them in it.'

'Antony.' Jessica sheathed one of his fists in her hands. Appealing: 'Travis?'

Travis stepped between the Head Boy and his would-be successor. 'Not the time. Not the place.'

'Why did you do it, Leo?' Antony demanded regardless. 'It's not just turning against me personally, you betrayed everything Harrington stands for. Duty. Fairness. *Trust.*'

'I'm not the traitor here, Clive,' Leo retorted. '*You* are. You betrayed the values of Harrington by letting these others in.' He sneered disdainfully at Travis's group and their fellow new arrivals. 'Plebs. Yobs. Girls. Snivelling infants. Harrington was never intended for the likes of them. Real Harringtonians are *better* than them, and if you were no longer willing to preserve what was truly fine about our school, then I was.'

'You?' Antony lashed out, grabbed and twisted the lapel of the ginger-haired boy's blazer. 'Leo, you're a disgrace to this uniform.'

'Don't touch me, Clive,' the deputy warned.

'All right, all right, that's enough,' Travis intervened exasperatedly, yanking Antony's hand from Leo's blazer. 'I thought the public-school system was supposed to foster maturity. I'd ask for your money back if I were you. Take a look around, remind yourselves where we are. In a cell. On an alien spaceship. And you're arguing over who belongs and who doesn't belong in a building we might never see again. Get real. Open your eyes.' He broadened his message to include the whole cell. 'That means the rest of you who supported Leo's little coup, as well. It's not about class. It's not about sides. We're all in this together, and if we forget that we can forget everything.'

Antony looked around him. He could see dismay etched on his community's faces, Harringtonian and newcomer alike, and misery, and fear. And he was ashamed that his argument with Leo Milton had probably contributed to their distress. The younger children were sobbing, Juniper, Rose and their little friends holding desperately on to Linden. Some Head Boy he'd turned out to be. 'You're right,' he said. 'I'm sorry.' He heard Leo mumble something similar.

'Good.' Travis was also surveying the cell, his expression one of sudden puzzlement. The number of prisoners incarcerated here and his understandable delight at the reunion with his closest friends had conspired to prevent the matter from registering until now, but: 'Where are Giles and Hinkley-Jones? Tolliver? Shearsby?' None of their already captured companions were present.

'We haven't seen them,' said Jessica. 'You mean they're not still free?'

'The aliens caught them before they caught us,' said Antony. 'Before they caught you.'

'Maybe they've put them in another cell, Trav,' suggested Linden.

'Maybe,' Travis conceded, 'but I'd like to know why.'

But the answer – if there was one – would have to wait. The walls, the floor, the ceiling, suddenly were screens. The pale and hostile face of an alien stared pitilessly at the prisoners from six directions. The younger children squealed, Juniper clasping Linden's hand more tightly than ever. Some of the older teenagers cringed from the image.

Travis stood where he was. *The face of the enemy.* He returned the alien's gaze as fearlessly as he could manage, more fearlessly than he felt, he hoped. A defiant gesture, he hoped.

The crimson eyes didn't even notice him.

'Earther prisoners.' There was blood somehow in the alien's voice, and the winter of a sunless world. 'I am Shurion, born of the bloodline of Tyrion of the Scytharene race. I am the commander of this ship.'

Antony opened his mouth as if to speak. He thought better of it.

'You will obey implicitly and immediately the orders given to you by myself or any member of my crew or you will be punished. Aboard this vessel there is only one punishment for disobedience and that is death.'

'Ohgodohgodohgod.' Travis heard Simon moaning under his breath. He sympathised.

'Children of Earth, be clear. Your old lives are over. Your planet and your parents have been taken from you. Your names, your identities, your very sense of selfhood will follow. For you have no value now but the value we place upon your heads, and you have no significance now but to serve us.

Reconcile yourselves to this reality at once or your sufferings will be long and hard. Know, children of Earth, that for you, freedom is a word without meaning. From this moment on you belong to the Scytharene. You are our property. Know also that we are slavers, and from this day forward every last survivor of the Sickness, every single child on Earth, is our slave.'

THREE

Slaves. Travis struggled to come to terms with the import of Commander Shurion's words. They were slaves. Not chained below decks, crammed into the fetid, rotting hold of a slave ship to be transported across a trackless ocean to a distant foreign land, but sealed in silver cells, abducted from their homeworld, prisoners condemned to a voyage of no return into the fathomless depths of space. The details changed; the barbarity did not.

And in the cell, a general groan rose up, a sound that had echoed down through the centuries of man's own inhumanities, all the occasions of one race or nation subjugating and exploiting another, a collective utterance of despair that transcended time and language. Spartacus would have recognised it smarting under the Roman whip, and the Africans toiling in plantations of cotton or in the jungles of Haiti. It was an expression of hopelessness more bitter than death.

'Trav.' Linden, eyes wild with desperation, the eyes of a trapped animal. 'Travis, what are we going to do?'

'I don't know.' What *could* they do? 'Something. Don't give up, Lin. Never give up.'

'You will be processed,' Commander Shurion announced. 'We must determine whether you are strong enough, physically, emotionally, psychologically, to survive what awaits you.

The processing will commence immediately. Again, obey instructions without hesitation or your lives end today.'

Shurion's image vanished. The screens were simply the surfaces of the cell once more.

The younger kids couldn't stop crying now. Linden had to let go of Travis to cuddle Juniper and her other charges. Mel embraced him instead. Clamours of anguish and anger battered at the walls like fists, but to no effect. Leo Milton had crumpled to the floor again; he was sitting cross-legged and his head was in his hands. Simon's horror was beyond expression of any kind. For Richie Coker, after years of playing the bully, it was finally his turn to be the victim. Antony, Jessica by his side, was shouting something, evidently trying to impose some kind of calm, some kind of order. Trying and failing.

Only when a Scytharene voice cut through the air like a knife did the majority fall silent. Linden hushed Juniper, Rose and Willow, stroked their hair with trembling hands.

'Processing begins,' the voice said without inflection. 'Two doors will open. Males will enter through the door on the left. Females will enter through the door on the right.'

'Travis.' Mel squeezed him. 'Oh, *God*.'

'You're strong, Mel,' he impressed upon her. 'Be strong for Jessie and Lin.'

'I will.' Not that she felt strong, tears spilling from her eyes.

'They can't separate us! They mustn't!' Linden turning in terror to Travis. 'We have to stay together.'

'We can't do that, Lin. The only chance we've got is to do as they say. It won't be for long. We'll be back together again before you know it. I'm sure of it.'

She was in his arms, seizing him fiercely, possessively. 'I'm not going to let you go. Not this time. I'm not.'

Mel glanced towards Antony and Jessica. Well, Jessica, really. Antony in any case was busy with a cluster of panicking Harringtonians. She reached out her hand and Jessie took it. 'We'll be all right,' she assured the blonde girl. 'I won't let anything happen to you, Jess.'

'Processing begins. Two doors will open. Males will enter through the door on the left. Females will enter through the door on the right.'

In the wall opposite that which had provided access to the cell for Travis and Antony, two doors did indeed begin to form, materialising in the metal as if from nowhere. They slid open. Beyond lay further cells, it seemed.

'Guess we're lumbered with each other a bit longer yet,' Richie said to Simon, he wasn't sure why. Simon's only response was to hang his head in desolation.

People were not moving towards either door. They were shrinking back from both.

Antony recalled the work they'd done in History on the Holocaust. Men to the left, women to the right. Every fibre of his being cried out against obedience to the Scytharene's orders, but at the same time he had no doubt that Commander Shurion's threats were real. There was no refusal possible. 'Listen! *Listen!* Everyone. We have to go through those doors. We have to stay alive. Now quickly . . .'

'Antony.' Jessica slipped her hand out of Mel's, placed it in Antony's instead. Mel stared at her open palm, her empty palm. 'Be careful. Be safe. Please.'

'You too,' Antony said. 'Jessica.' The sorrow in her eyes tore at his heart. He hadn't realised before how beautiful she was.

'I'll look after her,' said Mel.

And Travis was running his fingers through Linden's hair, stroking her cheek and neck and shoulder. 'See? We won't be far away. The thickness of a wall. Nothing bad is going to happen to either of us, but you have to go with Jessie and Mel.'

'I know. I know.' But shaking her head, yearning otherwise.

'You've got to look after Juniper and Willow and Rose as well.'

'I know. Come here, sweeties.' The little girls didn't need telling twice. They clung on to Linden like she was their mother.

'I'll take River and Fox. Boys.' Whimpering, they held Travis's hand. 'Lin. I'll see you soon.'

'You'd better,' said Linden.

'Lin, come on.' Mel seemed to have taken charge of the score or so of girls among the Harrington community. 'We have to . . . See you, Trav.' They edged warily towards the right-hand door.

'Travis, Antony, take care,' called Jessica.

Don't turn away, Travis was thinking. *Don't turn your backs to us*. All the while he could see their faces, the girls were safe. But they did turn away, Linden, Jessica, Mel, and they entered the next cell, and there was nothing Travis could do to bring them back.

'Travis, we ought to go too.' Antony was indicating the left-hand door.

Travis nodded. He'd vowed to Linden he'd see her soon, and he would. Whatever he had to do to make it happen – like stepping from one cell into another. And as the last boy, who chanced to be Leo Milton, followed him through, the door slid closed behind them.

In the girls' cell, which was identical to the one they'd just left, there was plenty of space for the few of them. The boys would find themselves a little more cramped.

'Good girls.' Linden leaned down to hug her three younger charges. 'That wasn't so bad, was it? We don't need to worry, do we?'

Jodie, the guitar player who'd joined Harrington from the village of Midvale, was comforting the several other small children similarly.

'So what now?' Mel said.

'Processing continues.' A disembodied voice spoke.

'You had to ask,' said Jessica with a weak, brave smile.

'Prisoners will remove clothing. Clothing will be placed on the floor. Prisoners will be naked for the next stage of processing.'

'What? They want us to strip?' Linden sounded more offended than afraid.

'They're men,' Mel muttered. 'Of course they do.'

'Somehow,' Jessica countered, 'I don't think this is just so they can leer at us, and I don't think we have any say in the matter.' She pulled her sweater off over her head.

'I suppose you're right,' said Linden, unbuttoning her blouse. 'Kids, are you all right undressing?'

Reluctantly but resignedly, the girls began to take off their clothes.

'Well, at least there's one thing,' Mel observed with a nervous laugh, trying not to glance in Jessica's direction, Jessie whose jeans and trainers and socks had already joined her sweater in a little pile on the floor. 'At least Travis and the others aren't here.'

'I wish they were,' said Linden, shrugging out of her bra.

'That's good, Juni. That's good, Willow. Yes, it's silly we haven't got any clothes on, isn't it?'

'Mel, what are you waiting for?' Jessica, her underwear in her hands, frowned at her friend. 'Why aren't you undressing?'

'I am. I am.' Fumbling with buttons. 'I'm just slow, that's all.'

'You don't need to be embarrassed,' Jessica said.

'*You* don't need to be embarrassed,' Mel retorted under her breath.

'I wonder if the boys are going through the same thing,' Linden said.

They were, and for some, stripping in front of others was indeed a discomforting experience. The Harrington contingent, used to communal showers, for the most part removed their clothes quickly and efficiently. Travis, too, whose mind was less on his state of attire than on what any later stages of processing might consist of, and even more unsettlingly, what the fate might be of any of them deemed by the Scytharene *not* to be physically, emotionally or psychologically strong enough to pass the test.

Richie was recovering a semblance of his old swagger. He was rather proud how his body compared to the others'. That rich kid Clive, he might be a bit of a ponce but he was well muscled, to be fair, well proportioned, must have worked out, but the other posh kids were feeble. The freckled look didn't hold out a lot of promise for Ginger Milton's future prospects with the birds. As for Naughton, he might inspire with his words and his eyes, but Hippy Chick and Morticia might not be quite so impressed by the rest of him. No, Richie didn't have much to worry about

61

physically: he was taller than the others, stronger – all that. As a proof of his returning confidence, he kept his baseball cap on.

But Simon was suffering. He remembered once, to his shame, when he was six or seven years old, some of the other boys at school holding him down in the classroom when the teacher had gone, holding him down and laughing and they were going to pull down his trousers and his pants and find out once and for all whether Simple Simon Satchwell really was a proper boy or, as they suspected, not. If the teacher hadn't come back for something she'd forgotten, they'd have done it, too. The sense of degradation, of humiliation, had stayed with Simon a long time and he'd never forgotten it. He was feeling it again now. Naked, he stood bony, bowed and shivering, though the cell wasn't cold, and he covered his modesty with his hands, and he blinked tearfully and owlishly behind his glasses.

'Simon.' Travis was seeking him out, the two little boys River and Fox trailing along with him. 'Try to keep your head together. Try to stay strong.'

'What for? We're dead.' The misery in his voice was almost palpable.

'No, we're not. And we won't be if we play by their rules.' Travis's eyes burned into Simon's as if he could impart courage by strength of will alone. 'They want slaves, that's what this Commander Shurion said. That's something we can hold on to. Dead slaves have no value. They'll keep us alive if we don't step out of line.'

'Travis, how can you be sure?'

'*Trust* me.'

'Prisoners will be naked for the next stage of processing.'

The Scytharene was repeating himself. 'Headgear will be removed. Spectacles will be removed.'

'They can see us,' Travis realised, instinctively glancing around. The room's bare walls gave nothing away. 'They're watching us.'

'They want me to lose the cap?' Richie protested. 'Bastards.'

But he'd heard Travis trying to boost Simon's spirits. Not stepping out of line was good advice. Grudgingly, he bade farewell to his baseball cap.

'No, I won't,' Simon baulked. 'I can't take off my glasses – I can't do without my glasses. I'll be blind.'

He wasn't the only boy wearing glasses, of course, but the order to dispense with them affected him more than the others, petrified him, in fact. Naked, and rendered practically sightless, Simon would be totally vulnerable, more helpless than ever.

'You've got to do it, Simon. Now,' Travis urged as gently as he could. His patience wasn't as limitless as he'd like. 'They're watching us.'

'But I won't be able to see. I won't know what to do.'

'I'll tell you. Keep by me. I'll guide you.'

Sniffling, Simon lifted one reluctant hand to his glasses. 'All right, Travis, but I don't – it's not – this is wrong.'

'No argument there,' said Travis.

Simon's eyes were puffy and red. He deposited his glasses with his clothes. 'Promise you won't leave me behind, Travis.'

'I never have so far, have I?'

'Travis,' Antony alerted him. A door was appearing and opening in the far wall. 'How much deeper into this damned ship can we go?'

'Processing continues. Prisoners will enter the corridor.'

Because for the first time the doorway did not lead into another cell. The corridor was long, narrow, entirely featureless and seemingly ended in a blank wall. The boys padded into it with trepidation. 'Keep with me, Simon,' instructed Travis. Richie wasn't far away, either.

No sooner had they all entered the corridor than the door behind them followed the example of its peers and faded into smooth, seamless metal. At the same time, dozens of doorways imprinted themselves along the full length of the corridor, at even intervals and on both sides.

'Processing continues. Prisoners will each select a door and stand before it.'

'No,' Simon panicked again. 'They're going to split us up, too. Don't let them do it, Travis. I can't be on my own.'

'Simon, calm down. Take it easy. You're frightening River and Fox.' Who were gazing up at Travis with anxious eyes. 'It's okay, boys. Look, all we need to do is walk along here a little bit. Choose a door.' He led the children further into the corridor. 'Simon. The sooner we get through whatever this processing involves, the sooner they'll put us all back in the cell. The girls, too, I reckon.' He paused. 'You want that one, Fox? Okay, River, you stand next to him. I know it's a funny game. Simon, take the other side of me.'

The boys shuffled about until they all faced a door as directed. Richie had opted for the one adjacent to Simon's and Antony stood alongside him. 'They're used to big numbers,' the latter called to Travis, registering perhaps a dozen doorways superfluous to immediate requirements, and that with over thirty prisoners in the corridor. 'There must be at least one more area like this on board – where the girls are. Assuming processing's the same for everyone.'

64

'We'll ask them,' returned Travis, 'when we see them.' He'd banished *if* from his vocabulary.

'Processing continues. When the doors to the assessment cells open, prisoners will enter immediately and follow the instructions of their Scytharene assessors.'

Travis felt his heart thudding as every door in the corridor slid open simultaneously. He ruffled River's hair. 'Be good, both of you.' His encouraging smile included Fox as well. 'I'll see you soon.'

'Good luck, everybody,' rallied Antony, like a captain in the Great War about to lead his men over the top. 'Travis . . .'

'You too,' Travis acknowledged. 'Richie. Simon.'

'Travis, please . . .'

And Simon's pleading whine was the last thing he heard before he stepped through the door. Into a room much smaller than any he'd seen so far aboard the Scytharene ship. A room conical in shape, tapering towards the ceiling. A room hung with wires like spiders' webs, throbbing with power he could feel through the soles of his feet, lined with computer instruments, scanners and screens, several displaying genderless silhouettes of human beings. A room already occupied by two male Scytharene, clad in the same red armour as the aliens he'd seen on the flight deck.

'Come forward, slave,' snapped one of the aliens irritably.

The alien who'd spoken – one of the *assessors* – was regarding him with undisguised contempt, almost disgust. *You should look in a mirror sometime*, Travis thought. His colleague seemed more amused by Travis's nudity, the details of his body. 'Stand here, slave,' he said. 'Place your feet here.'

Two depressions in the floor and in the exact centre of the room, directly below its highest point. Travis's feet fitted into them easily, though he'd have preferred them not to be quite so far apart.

'Stretch out your arms, slave. Lift them to the height of your shoulders.'

Colouring in humiliation, Travis had no choice but to obey. The assessors went to work. One in front of him, one behind, they looped restraints like cables around his arms so that he could no longer drop them to his sides even if he wanted to. Descending from the ceiling, the restraints resembled a puppeteer's strings, and Travis the puppet. His ankles were clamped more securely where he stood. Next the aliens affixed thin wires to him, glittering metal threads tipped with circular adhesive pads, applying them to his temples, his throat, above his heart, lungs, his other major internal organs, to the palms of his hands, to his muscles, his biceps, his pectorals, calves, thighs. Elsewhere, too. It hurt him to think that Linden, Mel and Jessica might be receiving the same attentions. The aliens handled him as if he was without dignity or personality, like he was nothing. Like he was a slave.

They wove the wires around him, and if the wires were like a web, Travis was the insect caught in its heart.

He was being fitted with sensors of some kind, he guessed. He dared to find out for sure. 'What are you going to do to me?'

'Silence, slave,' ordered the first assessor.

'You will be subjected to certain stimuli,' his associate revealed more amenably. 'Our instruments can easily diagnose your physical state, but before we invest resources in transporting you to our own world for sale, it is necessary also to appraise your mental and emotional condition. We must be certain that both physiologically and psychologically you will be able to withstand the ordeal that lies ahead of you. Slave.'

'My name's Travis,' he declared.

'You have no name,' said the Scytharene.

Didn't sound promising. Travis would have clenched his fists if the sensors in his palms didn't prevent him from doing so. He realised he was breathing more raggedly, the effect of stress. The human silhouettes on the walls were flickering into a kind of life. The computers were gathering readings, measuring the acceleration of his heartbeat, the increased activity of his sweat glands as fear became physicalised and leaked from his pores. He felt like an experiment. But he didn't feel like a slave. He swore he never would.

'Prepare for assessment.' The talkative Scytharene placed a slim visor over Travis's eyes and secured it behind his head. It was black, but the teenager could see everything as clearly and in the same colours as before. He could see that the disdainful assessor had crossed to an instrument panel in the wall and was keying information into it. His colleague joined him.

Above Travis, a hum of increasing power. He looked up, cried out. It was as if a shower had suddenly been turned on and was drenching him in blood. It wasn't blood, of course. It wasn't even liquid, though it tingled against his skin. A kind of spotlight had lowered itself from the ceiling and was bathing Travis in lurid scarlet illumination. But only him. The new source of light created a cone within a cone, and Travis's world turned red.

Briefly.

Then he was in a hospital, the reception area of a hospital. He knew it was that because he could see doctors and nurses and porters as well as members of the public.

They were all dead.

They were slumped on seats or heaped against walls or curled in strange positions on the floor, their flesh marked with the fatal circles of the Sickness. All dead. Travis's heart wrenched with horror and grief. It was like Wayvale General, when he'd gone there while his mother was still alive. It *was* Wayvale General. Somehow, the Scytharene had transported him back home.

And back in time, too? No. He doubted time travel was possible even with alien technology.

And he was gliding through the corridors, through the wards, and the dead crowded and narrowed the corridors, and the beds on the wards were occupied by corpses.

He didn't understand. How could he be here? How could . . .? He glanced down at himself. Naked still, and his feet, though seemingly free again, motionless and the distance apart that they were in the clamps in the assessment cell. His arms, extended and at shoulder height. No sign on his body of the sensors; the visor had vanished. As he hovered above the dead like a wingless angel, Travis tried to move his limbs. Couldn't. Invisible though they were, the restraints were still in place. Because he hadn't gone anywhere. He was still aboard the Scytharene ship. And this wasn't Wayvale General. It was a generic hospital, virtual reality, a holographic environment designed to evaluate his resistance to emotional pain. They were analysing his response to the genocide of his species. They were measuring his reaction to murder. And as Travis continued his enforced inspection of the morgue that had been a hospital, he realised the aliens must be inflicting this suffering on the others, too.

He wondered if it was ever rational, ever excusable, to hate an entire race.

Not far away, Jessica was crying. She couldn't help it and she couldn't stop. It wasn't so much what she was witnessing, the great pits brimming with bodies, the soldiers in protective suits and masks dousing them with petrol like watering a garden, igniting the fuel, and the al fresco crematoria burning, blazing, incinerating. It wasn't that, though that was unbearable enough. She knew the grotesque panorama wasn't real. Might have been, had been weeks ago, but it wasn't happening now. Yet the lifeless men and women emptied from army trucks into the mass graves brought her own immediate bereavement to mind. In the face of every man she saw her father; in the face of every woman she saw her mother. She'd seen her parents dead, side by side and scarred by the foul red rings of the Sickness. And now here she was, splayed and bare and helpless. A slave, those hideous albino aliens said. Here she was, forced to remember, compelled to relive an overwhelming loss. And she wasn't sure that she could cope after all.

The holograms shifted. The holograms changed. Past Antony's vision, the great cities of the world blurred. London, New York, Paris. Ablaze. St. Paul's an inferno, the Empire State, the Louvre. The Statue of Liberty breathing fire from its mouth, spouting flame from its eyes. Above the cities hung the ships, the scythes that had cut down the days of humankind like sheaves of wheat. The vessels of the Scytharene. The harbingers of death. Antony was crying out in impotent rage. It wasn't simply life they'd taken but the context of life, the order, the structure, the certainty and shape of things. Governments. Institutions. Laws. The very glue of society. Eradicated within weeks. And for the survivors, all that remained was anarchy, chaos, savagery, slavery. He wanted his school back. He wanted the rules back. He'd do anything for the security of rules.

Richie had always loathed rules and despised those who abided by them. You did what you could get away with doing, and if you were strong, you could get away with a lot. The Scytharene were strong. He saw them emerging from their mother ships, in flight, pods swarming like locusts, blackening the skies with their numbers, on foot, marching in ruthless armoured battalions, each boot stamping a bruise on the weak and pallid soil of Earth. Ranks of warriors converging on Richie, Richie powerless to evade them. They would trample him into the ground without qualm, crush him without question. All his life he'd deluded himself that *he* was strong, too. He wasn't. He never had been. And Richie was afraid.

Simon, too, who'd left Earth far behind. He'd been propelled into space without ship or suit or breathing apparatus of any kind, but in virtual reality none of that seemed relevant. The infinite dark of the universe enveloped him. At incalculable distances, stars came to birth in eruptions of hydrogen gas light years across, galaxies scattered like dust, like grains of sand. The vastness of the void intimidated, demoralised him. His own insignificance terrified him. He was nothing, a mote, a speck in the eye of the cosmos, less. He'd never mattered, never. Alive, no one had wanted him. Dead, no one would miss him. The endless night of space was the blackness of his own despair, and Simon wept.

Linden gasped. The planets whose surfaces she had

skimmed, incredible. Cities in the sky above oceans of magma. Civilisations hewn from the rockfaces of mountains hundreds of miles high. Landscapes in gold and red and blue. Worlds with three suns and worlds with none. The products of a creation beyond the comprehension of her mother and the Children of Nature. Were these what awaited them, these marvels? And the living beings culled from a thousand different species. Creatures like stone, massive and grey. Creatures like air, barely substantial, dancing in the light like sunbeams. Races winged like bats, carapaced like crabs, beaked like birds, finned like fish, ugly and beautiful and strange. Life, Linden thought. Even in the midst of death. Somewhere, somehow, life would go on. In all its diversity and variety and wonder. And she would go on, too. Linden would live, and she would live her life to the full.

The alien peoples didn't impress Mel. They'd startled her to begin with, as had her holographic grand tour of the galaxy, but she understood what was happening and that helped her distance herself from the scenes unfolding around her. These were the races the Scytharene had already conquered, already enslaved, she reasoned, so there was no need to be fearful of *them*. They were the universe's losers. Processing was about ascertaining whether she'd be able to overcome the sense of dislocation her captors obviously expected her to feel if she was shipped out to slavery among the stars. She would be able to do that. She would. Even if those guys with the tentacles and the portcullis mouths turned out to be her cellmates. She wasn't some crying, cringing little girl. Mel could look after herself. She'd cope. As long as she had Jessica with her. And Travis. As long as she had the two of them.

And outside the holograms but within the cells, the assessors monitored readings, drew conclusions, developed profiles. The female with the long black hair: strong-willed and therefore perfectly capable of survival, but likely also to be insolent; physical chastisement where appropriate must cure her of that. The female with the short red hair: responded positively to new experiences, suggesting adaptability and open-mindedness; could well over time forget her former life on her own planet and accept her new existence without demur. The sobbing male: of minimal physical value, overemotional, prone to depression and unlikely to flourish in his altered circumstances. The male with the shaven head: physically impressive but extremely limited intellectually, suitable for only the meanest manual tasks; the star mines paying well for such specimens of late. The blond male: would struggle initially with the loss of his home and the destruction of his way of life but essentially conformist and unlikely to rebel once familiarised with new expectations and patterns of behaviour; a clerk, a follower of regulations. The blonde female: emotionally suspect but physically robust, by established human standards of beauty the most desirable female in the batch; might create amusement and novelty as a pleasurer. The male with brown hair: significant ability to master and control his fears; notable single-mindedness and self-discipline; likely to reward investment given the right market, but must be closely monitored and his instinct for self-determination eliminated.

'Assessment completed. Processing completed.'

Travis heard the Scytharene again before he saw them. The next instant, however, deep space vanished and he was returned to reality. No more red light, either. The second assessor removed his visor.

'Hell of a ride.' Travis didn't want the aliens imagining he'd been cowed by it, but there was a certain dread in him nonetheless. If the examination was over the results must be in. 'How did I do?'

'In some telepathic cultures,' scowled the first assessor, 'a slave without a tongue is a possession of value. Be careful that your mindless prattle does not have the unintended consequence of equipping you for such a position.'

Which at least, Travis thought, clenching his teeth, suggested the Scytharene were thinking in terms of selling him. Which meant they were keeping him alive. Which meant there was still a chance to escape. If he only knew how.

The door to the assessment cell opened. A third Scytharene entered. Travis wasn't sure who reacted with most surprise to this presumably unexpected intrusion, himself or his two assessors. The latter blanched even paler than the natural pigment of their skin, difficult though it was to credit. Their reason for doing so was a mystery; his own startlement was not.

The newcomer wore gold armour.

'Lord Darion.' The first assessor thumped his right fist against his chest and bowed his head. 'It is an honour to receive you.'

'I'm sure it is,' said the Scytharene in gold.

'Is there any way we can serve you, Lord Darion?'

'By continuing your work, to begin with.'

Which the assessors did hastily, detaching the sensors from Travis's body, releasing him from clamps and restraints. He let his arms fall and there was no objection.

So the hue of the armour was related to rank, and gold was somewhere near the top. Maybe gold symbolised quality

73

and achievement throughout the galaxy. And was this Scytharene the warrior who'd failed to capture him on Vernham Hill? The visitor was no longer wearing the individualised helmet Travis would certainly have recognised, so it was impossible to tell. He doubted he'd be able to distinguish between the aliens by physical appearance alone at any rate. But this Lord Darion *could* be the one. Did the Scytharene remember him?

Was that why he was here?

There was no hint of familiarity as Lord Darion cast his eye over Travis now. Perhaps, though, a ghost of pity. 'Processing is over, is it not? Then the Earther can be clothed.'

'Of course, Lord Darion.' The first assessor, his contempt obviously reserved only for his inferiors, scurried to a panel beneath one of the silhouettes. At the press of a button it split in two to reveal a small compartment. The alien withdrew its contents, a tunic and trousers, both folded, boots, all in grey. He thrust the items at Travis. 'Put these on, slave.'

Gratefully, Travis did so. The garments were not exactly bespoke, but they fitted comfortably enough. The tunic and trousers looked as if they'd never been worn before and there was the smell of new leather about the boots. Maybe the Scytharene ran up uniforms for their slaves while they were undergoing processing.

'You may leave,' Lord Darion was saying to the assessors.

'But Lord Darion, the slave. . .'

'I require a private interview with the Earther. I will return him to the cells myself when I am finished with him.'

'Yes, Lord Darion.' Both assessors made their salute of deference, the punch to the chest, the bow of the head.

Both left the cell.

Dressed again, Travis felt more confident, less vulnerable. Or was he fooling himself? Had the situation just got better or worse?

'You will come with me,' said the Scytharene.

'Will I?' Take a chance. Test him out.

'You will.' The alien produced a weapon from a thigh holster. Travis had seen its like before, though the energy blaster that had shot him at Harrington had been black, not gold. 'Or this time, I will not miss.'

Simon had almost wept with relief when he'd been handed the clothes to wear. What with the processing apparently concluded too, perhaps the worst was over. Oh God, he hoped so. If only they'd give him back his glasses. The aliens assessing him made no mention of them and he didn't dare to ask.

So the corridors of the Scytharene ship were kind of misty as he was conducted through them. Back to the cells, he supposed. Back to Travis and Antony. Back to the girls.

He was right about the cells.

'Inside, slave,' the assessor behind him ordered, and he didn't need the additional prod of the energy blaster to enter the cell. But it was a different cell to those whose hospitality he'd sampled before, even Simon's limited vision could deduce that. It was unfurnished, as bare as ever, but the ceiling was panelled and the room was rather smaller in size.

Perhaps because it was accommodating rather fewer inmates.

Eight others besides himself. No Travis. No Antony. No Mel, Jessica, Linden. None of the little kids Linden was caring for. Not even Coker. His fellow prisoners were sitting or lying dejectedly on the floor, all of them in the same grey clothing. The only member of the group Simon knew by name was a Harringtonian called Digby. Digby who was on the plump side, like a couple of the other boys incarcerated with him. And several of them, they'd also worn glasses. And one was coughing quietly in the corner. And the only two girls present were scrawny and pale and clung to each other as if they suspected the worst.

They weren't alone in that. Simon felt fear crawling up his spine. He'd never entertained any illusions about his physical prowess or potential. None of his immediate companions looked like they'd ever been first pick for the football team, either. '*We must determine whether you are strong enough to survive what awaits you.*' He recalled the commander's ominous words.

Because what if he was in the place where the weak were sent?

'Digby. Digby, where's Travis?'

The Harringtonian shook his head and shrugged.

'What about Antony? Have you seen Antony? Jessica Lane?'

'It's just us, Satchwell,' mourned Digby.

'No.' And Simon knew why.

'Earther prisoners.' That toneless Scytharene voice again. 'You have been judged incapable of enduring the ardours of a slave's existence. You have failed processing. Therefore you are no longer of any value to us.'

'No . . . you can't . . .'

'Therefore, pray to the gods of your people that they will receive your souls.'

'No!' Simon screamed. 'No!'

'You are all to die.'

FOUR

It was difficult to focus the mind while an alien warrior was jabbing one's back with the barrel of an energy blaster, but Travis did his best. Knowledge could well prove to be the key to survival. As Lord Darion conducted him through the corridors of the Scytharene ship, therefore, the teenager kept his eyes open and his wits about him.

A couple of things already. Up close, it became clear that what the aliens wore was not after all armour in the King Arthur sense, not a suit of iron. If the material was any kind of metal, it was an alloy so far unknown on Earth. Light and flexible, it was probably closer to Kevlar, more like the body armour Travis had seen riot police wearing in the news and on TV shows. Almost certainly the Scytharene had clad themselves in metal armour once, during their ancient history, but technological advances had rendered such primitive protection obsolete long ago. The fact that their present garb still paid visible homage to it suggested to Travis a culture both militaristic and obsessed with tradition and heritage, proud of its martial past. It would be unwise to look to the Scytharene for compassion.

He was also beginning to get his bearings. Lord Darion kept him moving in the same direction, and shortly the nature of the corridors changed. The harsh metallic surfaces became tinted with blue as they left the cells behind. Doors did not appear and disappear at a hidden Scytharene's whim, but behaved more conventionally and stayed where they'd been put. Notation in the aliens' language was inscribed on the walls – Travis didn't understand it, obviously, but he recognised it as similar to the markings on the strange cylinder Antony had shown him soon after they'd met at the Harington School, the cylinder that had smashed through a farmhouse's walls during its descent to earth. They'd thought its origins lay with a foreign power; now Travis realised the cylinder was the work of an extraterrestrial one.

Other aliens passed by, almost all of them in red, a small number in black, every one acknowledging Lord Darion with the fist to the chest and the respectfully lowered eyes, not one of them thinking – or daring – to question why the Scytharene was escorting an Earther slave through what was evidently now no longer the slave quarters of the ship. Not once did they encounter another alien in gold.

They took an elevator up, to the bridge, Travis anticipated, or to some kind of interrogation room. Either way, he could place the slave quarters at the centre and among the lower levels of the ship, which was good – closer to the ground if there was ever a chance to make a break for it. And there *had* to be.

The elevator opened on to another corridor, empty of personnel. Its doors were fewer and spaced out more widely. In front of one of them, Darion stopped. 'Open,' he said.

'Greetings, Lord Darion,' replied the door, obeying dutifully.

'Go in, Earther,' the Scytharene said, more in request than command, Travis thought.

'Where . . .?'

'My private quarters. Please.'

And surprisingly inviting they seemed, too. Travis might have expected spartan decor, the austerity of a barracks, but the room he entered was warm and welcoming. There were comfortable chairs, a table set with food and drink, a desk with a computer inlaid, a floor-to-ceiling tinted window that looked out over the valley – Travis also noted the crescent tip of the ship curling in from the right. Several inner doors led into other rooms, but the most notable feature of this one was its ornamentation. It was crammed with striking and sometimes surreal objects and works of art, most of them small but all of them intricate and delicate, crafted with precision and flair and love. A helmet that Achilles might have worn sculpted from crystal the colour of jade. Miniatures of creatures that no doubt existed somewhere but had never lived on Earth, some of them shimmering as if moulded from insubstantial light. Vases that changed colour and shape, seeking for themselves unattainable perfection. Pictures of distant worlds covering an entire wall, portraying the far-flung planets Travis had briefly and holographically visited during processing, the centrepiece, animate, twin suns arching across a scarlet sky, condensing days into seconds, the landscape teeming with life. None of these artefacts struck Travis as the product of Scytharene creativity, slavers on Earth at least not being renowned for art appreciation; it seemed incongruous that Darion should have transformed his quarters into a gallery. Travis wondered *why* he had.

He turned to the alien. He couldn't be sure, of course, but Lord Darion seemed young, younger than Commander

Shurion, younger than the assessors, in his late twenties, perhaps, if Scytharene years were comparable to humans'. The others Travis would have put ten or fifteen years older than that. Different generations.

'There is a bathroom through there,' the Scytharene indicated. 'You may wish to make use of it. The meal that has been prepared is also for you.'

Travis realised how painfully parched and famished he was, but he regarded the provisions warily nonetheless. 'Why?'

'Are you really in a position to ask such questions, Earther?'

It was a fair point. Travis availed himself of Darion's hospitality. He guzzled the drink, a fruit cordial of some description, and tore into the food, a meat similar to steak. The alien watched him, still pointing the blaster as if the penalty for not clearing his plate might well be severe.

When his prisoner had finished, Darion said: 'What is your name, Earther?'

'You want to know my name?' Travis couldn't help but be defensive.

'I am Darion, born of the bloodline of Ayrion of the Thousand Families.'

'Is this some sort of trick? Why did you bring me here? This meal supposed to be softening me up for something? Where are my friends?'

'Your friends are in the slave quarters,' said Darion, 'and your suspicions are understandable. I had hoped, however, that our conversation might at least be civilised.'

'Civilised? After what you've done to us?' A full belly fuelled Travis's anger. 'Either you're insane, or in Scytharene the word means something different.'

The alien sighed. 'Perhaps, as you're so concerned about your friends, you should rejoin them.'

Idiot, Travis cursed inwardly. He needed to restrain his rage, keep his emotions under control. *Use* this unexpected interview. Darion had to have an agenda. Find out what it is. Listen and learn.

'Travis,' he blurted. 'I'm Travis. Travis Naughton.'

'Travis Naughton.' Darion nodded appreciatively. 'If I put aside my subjugator, Travis' – indicating the energy blaster – 'can you be trusted not to attempt anything intemperate?'

'You mean try and escape?'

'You would fail.'

'I got away from you before. Or someone like you. On the hill.'

'We are not on the hill now,' said Darion. 'Screen: show me the cryo-tubes.'

The room's fourth wall, the one unembellished not only by alien artwork but by any adornment whatsoever, demonstrated why. Suddenly Travis found himself staring into another part of the ship, apparently a storage area. A huge number of long, transparent cylinders were stacked there in horizontal rows, scores if not hundreds of them, connected by narrower tubes to each other and to high walls flickering with instruments, monitoring the cylinders for a reason Travis could not imagine. The receptacles all appeared empty. But *not* all as, at Darion's instruction, the screen like a roving camera guided him among them. Several were occupied.

Now he knew where Giles, Hinkley-Jones, Tolliver and Shearsby had got to.

Wearing a single grey garment like a jumpsuit, they lay on their backs, their hands crossed over their chests, their eyes and mouths closed. They could have been in coffins. But Travis doubted they were dead. In time, he thought grimly, they might prefer to be.

'Screen: pause,' said Darion, almost with pity.

'What have you done to them?'

'Your friends are being stored in the cryo-tubes in a state of suspended animation,' the Scytharene explained, 'ready for transfer to one of our larger slavecraft orbiting the Earth. Once full, those ships will transport them to the slave markets of our homeworld to be sold. That is the final fate awaiting you all. See how many cryo-tubes there are to be filled.'

Travis saw. Travis shuddered. 'Why are you showing me this?'

'It is vital you recognise the hopelessness of your situation, Travis Naughton.'

Who longed to retort that nothing was hopeless. Not only did he suspect that outright defiance would be counterproductive, however, but he'd also have liked to be in a position to at least sound convincing.

'Do I need my subjugator?' The teenager shook his head. 'I am glad.' Darion returned the weapon to its holster.

'They'll be – my friends in the cryo-tubes – they'll be all right?'

'It is as if they were sleeping. No harm will befall them. Scytharene do not like to damage their merchandise.'

'Merchandise?' Travis's tone was bitter. 'We're people, Darion.' Omitting the alien's title intentionally. Darion seemed either not to notice, or not to care.

'To *my* people you are slaves, and slaves are commodities. Valuable commodities, it is true, but in the end, neither more nor less than cargo.'

'You sent the Sickness, didn't you?'

'We did.'

'Then you're bastards. All of you.'

Darion turned his head away, as if his crimson eyes did not wish to enter into debate on that matter with Travis's intense blue stare. 'Screen: off.'

'Do you know how many deaths you've caused? How much grief and misery you're responsible for? How can you . . .? And this isn't even new to you, is it? You've done it before, haven't you?' Travis, temporarily at least, was beyond rage, stricken by horrified disbelief at the scale of it all. 'How many times? How many worlds?'

'Many,' conceded the Scytharene. 'It is the way of my race. We travel the galaxy in search of planets whose inhabitants are suitable for enslavement. Once we have identified our victim, we eliminate the adult population by disease, a means so much more efficient than the open warfare we used to engage in. Our scientists bioengineer the core Scytharene virus – customise it, if you like – in order for its virulence to be confined to the ruling species on each target world; the Sickness, as your kind called it, infects only human physiology.' Darion spoke quietly, without pleasure or pride. 'Thus, when it is deemed appropriate to reveal ourselves and descend from the stars, the only survivors of the indigenous population left to resist us are the young, immature, traumatised, disorganised, powerless. Slaves to be harvested by the Cullers at our leisure. You've already seen a Culler at work. The ship with the tractor beam and the company of battle-pods.'

'Oh yeah, I saw that all right,' said Travis. 'You must be so proud of yourselves.'

Darion returned his gaze to the teenager, and in it there seemed only shame. 'Slavery and death, Travis,' he said wearily. 'It is our way.'

'So what happens when we start developing the Sickness and dying too?' Travis gave a bleak laugh. 'That'll depreciate the value of your merchandise. Or have your wonderful scientists already worked out a way to stop us reaching eighteen? No, they wouldn't have done, would they? That'd be extending life, and they only seem attracted to ending it.'

'There is no need to keep you young,' said Darion. 'The Sickness is not a danger to you.'

'Not even when we're old enough to be infected?'

'You do not understand how it works, Travis. Let me . . . The Sickness is in essence an airborne virus that attaches itself to the cells of a host like any other, like your influenza, for example. However, whereas most viruses do not discriminate between their hosts and attack the cells of all who contract them, the Scytharene virus behaves differently. It has been bioengineered—'

'By your scientists,' Travis interjected sardonically. 'Boy, they like to keep themselves busy, don't they?'

'By our scientists, yes.' If sarcasm was a disease, Darion seemed immune. 'Bioengineered to target only those cells that have attained or exceeded a certain age.'

'And how does it do that? Ask politely how old the cell is?'

'Ageing in any organism is caused by cell deterioration. The Scytharene virus has been programmed via nanotechnology to measure the extent of deterioration in the cells to which it becomes bonded. The chromosomes of your cells, the structures that carry your genes, are protected at the ends by what in your language are called telomeres.'

'This is just like being back at school,' Travis grunted, as if uninterested in what the alien was explaining. 'That was like slavery, too.' But in reality he was listening intently, absorbing every word.

'As time passes, the telomeres fray and become damaged, thus making the cell itself more vulnerable and less healthy – the host organism grows old. The Scytharene virus's initial purpose is to examine the condition of its host's telomeres. The amount of fraying or shortening that the virus finds indicates the age of the host, and if the telomeres have deteriorated beyond a certain point, the virus is programmed then to attack the cell, infecting it, causing the visible symptoms of the Sickness and finally, inevitably, death. Even we do not possess a cure. As you have already learned, the approximate age at which human cells become susceptible to the Sickness is eighteen. But also, as I have told you, Travis, you need not be concerned about reaching eighteen yourself. If the telomeres in a host body are still healthy enough to be resistant to the disease on first contact, its killing potency dissipates, allows the host to build up an immunity to it in the same way that your vaccines work to defend you against the native diseases of your planet.'

'So I can still go ahead and plan my eighteenth birthday party, then,' Travis said. 'Let me tell you, you *won't* be invited.'

'I don't expect you to do anything but despise me, Travis,' said Darion. 'In your position, I would feel the same.'

Which wasn't quite the reaction Travis was expecting. He was still cautious of Darion, but there also seemed to be an increasing possibility that the Scytharene in gold might differ from the rest of his kind in more than the colour of his armour. 'You seem to know a lot about Earth,' he said.

'By necessity. Once an enslavement world has been

selected, it takes years of preparation, years of study and observation from deep space before we are ready to strike. I am fluent in twelve Earth languages, for example.'

'What about the knowledge of human biology? You can't get that from deep space.'

'Abductions,' Darion said. 'And experimentation.'

Travis winced. 'And I guess the Sickness was sent to Earth in cylinders. We found one.'

'That is correct. Devices too small to be noticed or intercepted by your authorities until it is too late.'

'And the flying eyes?' He remembered Linden's claim to have seen a hovering metal globe while they were foraging for supplies in Willowstock, an eyeball in the air, watching her. He hadn't believed her then; he did now. 'One of your surveillance devices?'

Darion appeared puzzled. 'I'm afraid I don't understand you, Travis,' he said blankly.

Leaving the teenager confused, too. So assuming the eye *did* exist, if it wasn't of the Scytharene's manufacture, then whose?

'To what are you referring?' Darion asked.

'It doesn't – it's nothing.' *Change the subject.* 'I don't – I still don't know why I'm here. All these distractions. What do you want from me, Darion?'

'I don't want anything, Travis.' The Scytharene glanced nervously towards the door. 'You're here for the same reason that I deliberately allowed you to elude my battlepod yesterday.'

So it *had* been Darion who'd fired wide. He'd meant to. 'What reason is that?' Travis said, his heart racing.

'Because I want to help you.'

*

'I was born into one of the Thousand Families of the Scytharene race,' said Darion. 'The social and political elite of my people. I was raised in a world of privilege and wealth, entitled to wear the golden armour that is the visible symbol of the ruling class. Position in our society is hereditary, you see, Travis, though not, as among your own aristocracy, simply as a way of selfishly preserving power for a fortunate few. We believe that all the qualities that form our character are inherited, carried in our genes, in our bloodline. We believe not that society shapes us but that we shape society. At least that is what we are taught to believe. These are the orthodoxies which all Scytharene are expected to accept as self-evident and absolute truth.

'In your culture, philosophers debate whether the individual is a product of nature or nurture, do they not? Whether you as a human being have your destiny mapped out for you from the moment of your birth, your future behaviour and personality predetermined by God's plan, or perhaps by your DNA, unchangeable and undeniable; or whether, instead, you are moulded by the myriad random influences to which life subjects you, people, places, events, like a sculpture begun by an artist with no distinct end in mind. Well, in Scytharene culture such discussion would be sacrilegious. It is the first article of our faith that there are superior and inferior people – and *peoples*. We are not created equal. Neither were we intended to be. The universe is one of rulers and ruled, masters and slaves, and birth dictates to which class the individual rightly and properly belongs.

'The Thousand Families are descended from the earliest heroes of our race, the great warriors who founded the Scytharene nation millennia ago. Their strength and nobility and courage live on, flowing through our veins – *these* veins. So it is said. My own revered bloodline is that of Ayrion, of whom the tale is told that, rather than die of sickness or old age, Ayrion rode alone into the camp of our enemies and slew two hundred of the foe before he himself was overwhelmed and put to death. As you can see, Travis, I have a lot to live up to.

'My birth bound me to become a proud and ruthless warrior, but while I have no choice sometimes but to fight, and I have been trained in the arts of battle as all Scytharene are, I do so with neither pride nor, I hope, ruthlessness. I refute the assumptions of my kind. I would sooner live in peace than at war, I prefer to create than to kill, and I have chosen a different course for my life than might have been expected of a descendant of the mighty Ayrion. I am an alienologist, Travis, one dedicated to the study of those cultures conquered by my marauding race. Alienology is not unbiased, of course; it was not established in order to pursue knowledge and understanding for their own sake. My work is political. My findings and researches must conform to the perception we Scytharene have of ourselves relative to other intelligent species. In other words, myself and my fellow alienologists are entrusted with the task of proving scientifically the cultural, social and racial inferiorities of the peoples we enslave, thereby reasserting the Scytharene's right to be considered the one true master race.'

Travis had stayed silent throughout Darion's discourse so far, but he felt compelled to speak up now. 'And you're happy with that?' Disbelievingly.

'No, but were it not for the propaganda applications of alienology, my father would never have allowed me to devote myself to it at all. My father is a Fleet Commander, Travis. He heads our entire slaving operation in this region. He is an important man. Without his permission, I could never have come to know so well the art and literature and the culture, the belief systems, of the worlds I have visited. I could never have learned from them as I have.'

'What have you learned, Darion?' said Travis.

'That all life is beautiful. That all cultures are of worth. That there are no absolutes. That diversity enriches. That exposure to new ideas, new perspectives, new ways of thinking, enhances and improves our understanding of ourselves. All life is precious – it should never be casually or wantonly destroyed.'

Travis studied the Scytharene curiously, thoughtfully. For the first time, skull-white skin and scarlet eyes notwithstanding, Darion born of the bloodline of Ayrion seemed a little less alien, a little more human.

'I have learned to respect and admire our subject peoples,' he was continuing. 'Take this wonderful object, for example.' He lifted the jade crystal that resembled an ancient Greek helmet from its place on a shelf and handed it reverently to the boy.

'Very nice,' Travis thought it politic to say, not that he'd ever been overly interested in art. The piece was light in his grasp.

'It is a memory helm from the planet Lachrima, to be worn during times of meditation and prayer. According to Lachrimese tradition, the wearer is then enabled to commune with the spirits of his deceased loved ones whose souls reside in the crystal.'

'Yeah?' Travis was sceptical. In his experience, the dead

tended to remain where they'd been put, in the ground, in a jar mixed with the ashes of their coffin and the last clothes they'd ever worn. He wouldn't have to go very far to encounter plenty of deceased loved ones lying where the Sickness had left them. 'Each to their own,' he said, returning the artefact to the Scytharene.

'A beautiful creation to symbolise a beautiful belief.' Darion's tone turned to bitterness. 'Yet how many souls have my own people sent screaming into the crystal?' He placed the memory helm back on its shelf. 'But we are not all merciless killers. A dissident movement does exist among us, opposed to slavery and militarism. It is small at the moment, its activities confined to minor acts of protest in the more remote corners of the Scytharene empire, but support for it is growing, among the young, even in influential circles. One day, perhaps, the movement will be strong enough to begin a revolution and bring an end to the injustices and wrongs upon which Scytharene civilisation is founded.'

'So what are you telling me?' Travis was sitting forward. 'You're part of this movement?'

'I wish I was, but . . .' Darion's voice trailed away in shame. 'I sympathise with it. I agree with its avowed aims, the abolition of slavery in particular, but – I am afraid I lack the courage to commit myself fully to the cause. I am not naturally inclined to action, despite my ancestors. I cannot contemplate bringing myself into direct conflict with my own people.'

'So why are we talking?' Travis said in dismay.

'Because neither can I stand by any longer and watch the innocent suffer. Travis, we are talking because I have to help you and your fellow Earthers to escape.'

'I'm listening.'

'I was monitoring the processing data as it was gathered. More than any of the prisoners, Travis, you were identified as possessing leadership potential. That is why I chose you.' Darion began pacing the room as if time was suddenly growing short.

He was racked with nerves, Travis could see, riddled with doubt, and pretty much a self-confessed coward to boot. Yet Lord Darion provided their best – their only – chance of breaking out of here.

The teenager wasn't exactly fired with confidence.

'Once I've explained my plan,' the Scytharene was saying, 'I will conduct you to the main holding cell. The Earthers we captured yesterday were placed in the cryo-tubes immediately after processing to ensure that the life support systems were functioning properly. Shurion won't trouble himself with putting the rest of you into suspended animation until we have more prisoners aboard, which provides us with our opportunity, particularly as surveillance inside the holding cells is not carried out as a matter of routine.'

'You're kidding.' Travis raised his eyebrows in surprise.

'Enslaved races are deemed to be too inferior to be capable of staging a serious escape attempt,' Darion said.

'Excellent. It'll be a pleasure to prove Commander Shurion wrong.'

Darion smiled ruefully. 'The arrogance of my race should work to our advantage. Now, from my quarters here I can hack into the ship's central computer and disengage your cell's security system. The door will open automatically.'

'For how long?'

'Seconds only, I'm afraid, or the source of the interference might be traced. And there'll be a guard outside. You'll need to be ready.'

'Tell me when and we will be,' Travis said determinedly.

'I will. I'll also put the ship's blueprints on screen and show you your best route out. Even so, only the element of surprise gives you any prospect of success at all.'

'That's better than nothing, Darion.'

'And you must tell nobody who I am, Travis, not even your closest friends. In case some of you are recaptured, you understand. Not even my bloodline will save me if I am found guilty of an act of treason.'

'Don't worry. My lips are sealed.'

'Thank you. And if any of – those of you who *do* escape must seek to make contact with what remains of your earth authorities.'

'*What* authorities?' Travis's heart raced again. 'All the adults are dead. Aren't they?'

'Not all, it seems,' Darion revealed. 'We don't know how, but some adult Earthers seem to have survived the Sickness. The slavecraft are encountering small pockets of resistance here and there, sustaining isolated attacks, though my father and his fellow Fleet Commanders are taking steps to eradicate these. Locate any such group still at liberty if you can, Travis. Tell them what I have told you of the Scytharene revolutionaries. If your patriots and our dissidents can somehow come together, perhaps your planet's future might still be secured.'

It sounded good. It sounded hopeful. And hope was something Travis longed to feel. But he needed to be cautious, too. He owed it to the others. Because what if this offer of help turned out to be a trick after all? What if Darion wasn't working against his own people but *for* them? If there were still adults out there capable of retaliation against the invaders, what if he, Travis, and the others were going to be *allowed* to escape? What if they were then going to be followed or tracked somehow so that, eventually and inadvertently, they led the Scytharenes right to the resistance? *What if?* The ultimate question. How could he know for sure?

He couldn't, of course. It had to be a matter of trust. Did he trust Darion or did he not?

'Travis?' The Scytharene was regarding him quizzically. 'Are you all right?'

And Travis thought of the careful, tender way Darion had handled the Lachrimese memory helm, almost like it was a baby, a child. '*All life is precious.*' Trust or no trust?

'Show me the blueprints,' Travis said.

The holding cell was large, and while it still lacked furniture, rectangular sleeping berths were built into two of the walls, in rows extending both horizontally and vertically, the higher units gained by climbing the equivalent of rungs hollowed out of the metal. A third wall, demonstrating unusual Scytharene considerateness, given the teenagers' recent experience of processing, sheltered washroom facilities behind it. It seemed the prisoners were to be incarcerated in this particular cell for a while. But a *shorter* while, Travis hoped, than the slaves expected.

His friends crowded round him, relieved and elated by his reappearance. Linden in his arms again. Mel, Jessica, Richie close by, Antony, too. Everyone in identical grey tunics and trousers. Processed.

'Trav, where have you been?' Mel wanted to know. 'We were worried. We thought they'd done something to you.'

'Not exactly. And I'm here now,' he reassured her, squeezing Linden for good measure as she kissed him warmly. 'Am I the last one?'

'Actually, no.' Antony frowned.

Of course not. 'Simon,' said Travis, appalled with himself that he hadn't registered the other boy's absence immediately.

'Not just Simon,' Antony said. 'Digby. Cunningham. Pates. Altogether there are nine of us still unaccounted for.' His tone was ominous, the voice of a police officer reading out the name of missing persons not expected to be found alive.

'They could just be in another cell, couldn't they?' Jessica experimented with optimism.

'I'm glad *you're* here,' Linden whispered in Travis's ear.

'Why would they do that, though, Jessie?' Mel questioned. 'Put most of us in one cell and a handful in another? There are still beds.'

'I don't know. I'm not one of those monsters, thank God. I don't know how they think.'

'Simes and the others could still be in processing.' Richie's contribution was hesitant and surprisingly sensible.

Travis championed it. 'That's right. They could be. They'll be shoved in here with the rest of us soon, I'm sure. Which'll be good, because you won't believe where I've been, and why.'

'Don't make us guess, Trav,' Mel said impatiently. 'This isn't the place for games. We *are* in a cell.'

'Not for long,' said Travis. 'I know where the corridors outside lead. I know where there's a stairwell that'll take us to the ground level of the ship and out of here.'

'*How* do you know?' Antony demanded.

'Who cares how?' snorted Richie.

'I've made a contact. I've found an ally, a Scytharene we can trust.'

'What's this alien's name?' Antony wanted to know.

'Sorry, Antony, but that's the one thing I can't tell you.' And as Travis eagerly outlined further details of the escape plan, he didn't notice the dark, resentful frown creasing the blond boy's features.

If truth be told, Darion would sooner spend his time aboard ship secluded in his private quarters among the artworks of a dozen foreign planets than fraternise with his own people. At least his rank meant that his general aloofness was not only expected but approved of, which minimised the need to socialise. But he was still obliged to put in regular appearances in the officers' mess and on the bridge, where the elevator took him now. He was still duty-bound to remain on equable terms with the ship's commander.

Shurion was seated in his command chair and attired in full dress uniform as always, the black armour decorated and the ebony robes inlaid with gold. The bridge itself was sickle-shaped to reflect the overall design of the ship, the floor-to-ceiling windows currently offering panoramic vistas of the valley ahead and the hills to right and left. Technicians in red worked at computers; several warriors in black stood by eager to execute any orders Commander Shurion might deign to utter. The command chair itself occupied the very centre of the bridge and could, when required, be raised hydraulically in order to provide the Commander with a better view of bridge operations. This function was only employed by most commanders during battle or at key moments in flight. Shurion kept the chair at maximum height virtually all the time, including the present. Darion suspected he simply liked looking down on people.

'Ah, Lord Darion!' he exclaimed from his vantage point as the alienologist entered. 'There you are.'

'Indeed, Commander Shurion. Here I am.'

'Managed to tear yourself away from the crude, primitive bric-a-brac purporting to be alien cultural artefacts, have you?' He glanced slyly down and sideways to the warriors. 'Alien culture – a contradiction in terms, surely.' The soldiers smiled at their superior's wit.

'Actually, I've been translating a manuscript by the philosopher Tyreetes of the planet Gamelon,' Darion said. 'A particularly difficult passage in which he writes – this is a very loose interpretation, you understand – "O vessel of the greatest noise, how little you know, how empty even your most boastful clamour."'

'Is that supposed to mean something, Lord Darion?' Shurion asked with a scowl.

'Of course not, Commander Shurion.' Darion was all innocence. 'It's nonsense. You're familiar with nonsense, are you not? And how fortunate that most of Tyreetes' works were burned when our crusading Scytharene armies razed the libraries of Gamelon to the ground. But speaking of the ground . . .' Darion looked meaningfully from the command chair to the floor.

'But of course. Forgive me, Lord Darion,' Shurion apologised coldly. At the touch of a button in its arm, the chair descended to its more conventional position. According to

Scytharene tradition, no one, not even a high-ranking commander like Shurion, was permitted to look down on the head of a member of the Thousand Families. 'Tell me, though, where is this Tyreetes now?'

'He died two centuries ago.'

'Did he? A pity. I would have liked to share with him a philosophy of my own.' Shurion stood. 'The only good alien is an enslaved alien.'

The warriors chuckled aloud at that one. The Blackhearts, as the most militant of Scytharene soldiers liked to call themselves, loved Commander Shurion. Which was one reason why Darion despised him. The Blackhearts adored his cruelty, his callousness, and his utter contempt for alien life. Darion loathed him for all three. But he'd never disclosed his true feelings and he never could. While he was Shurion's *social* superior, in the context of the slavecraft's operations, its commander outranked even a member of the Thousand Families. Every ship in the Scytharene fleet bore the name of a hero from the past, selected by its appointed commander. Shurion had chosen to call his domain the *Furion*. Furion, who had led his people's first interplanetary slaving raids, thus setting the course for a thousand years of Scytharene history. That said everything about Commander Shurion. And Darion laboured under no misconception. The unspoken enmity between himself and the Commander was entirely mutual.

'I understand you've been . . . busying yourself, Lord Darion, with one of the Earther slaves,' said Shurion.

'Indeed I have,' the younger Scytharene admitted, as nonchalantly as he could, though avoiding the scrutiny of the Commander's enquiring stare. 'I intend to interview as many of your prisoners as possible, Commander, before you commit them to the cryo-tubes. What I learn from them will assist me in my research into Earther culture.'

'Alienology,' Shurion all but snorted. 'Ah, yes. Your father must be so proud.'

'My father, Fleet Commander Gyrion of the Thousand Families,' Darion dropped in as if by accident, '*is* proud. One can serve our race in a number of ways.'

'I've heard that. But are you not concerned, Lord Darion, that by continually immersing yourself in the products of impure and inferior cultures, by voluntarily associating with primitive and ignorant peoples, you might not, over time, become corrupted by their ridiculous beliefs and discredited creeds? Does not the alienologist risk being tainted by the alien?'

Darion twitched a smile. 'We are what we are by birth, Commander Shurion, as I am sure I have no need to remind you. Nothing can alter that. Those with whom we come into close proximity' – and now he did dare to face Shurion directly – 'influence our true nature not at all. But thank you for your interest in my work. I assume yours is proceeding equally smoothly?'

'It is.' Shurion's pride in his own accomplishments easily exceeded the pleasure he gained from goading Darion. The subject broached, he strode swaggeringly to the windows and gazed outside, the master of all he surveyed. 'Preliminary tests and scans are all but complete. We will have the Cullers operating at full capacity by this time tomorrow. Everything is going to plan.'

'Good,' said Darion. 'May it continue to do so.' But it wasn't Shurion's plan he had in mind.

*

98

They didn't get much sleep, of course, but Travis insisted that they try. It was the same with the food: even though the youngsters' predicament was not conducive to appetite, when their meals arrived, distributed by Scytharene in blue armour with black-clad guards on hand brandishing subjugators, Travis encouraged everyone to force down as much as they could. They'd need their strength when the moment came.

Their watches had gone the same way as their own clothes, and there was nothing like a clock in the cell. They guessed it must be night, however, or at least a sleeping period, when the lighting was extinguished. The only illumination thereafter came from ghostly white strips lining the edge of the ceiling.

Simon and the others who'd not appeared after processing were still missing. Travis had demanded to be told their whereabouts by the guards. He might as well have been talking to the proverbial brick wall.

Worrying about their fate, *Simon's* fate, was one of the factors that kept him awake. Another was the presence of Linden lying on the bed alongside him.

'*Please*,' she'd begged. 'We don't have to – it wouldn't feel right *doing* anything in here, but *because* we're in here I don't want to be without you tonight, Travis. Can we just be together, just, you know, lie together? Can you just hold me? Would that be so bad?'

'Linden.' He'd breathed her name softly. 'I can't think of anything better.'

And they hadn't even undressed – nobody had. And he'd held her and kissed her and eventually she'd fallen asleep and in her dreams she'd whimpered and cried out several times but he'd soothed her and stroked her and she hadn't woken.

And he'd thought of Linden, and Jessica and Mel, undergoing processing, which had been humiliating enough for a boy, but for a girl . . . It sickened him that the girls had been made to endure such an ordeal; it enraged him that he'd been unable to prevent it. Those Scytharene bastards had a lot to answer for.

Lights off to signal night. Lights on, presumably, to indicate day.

Everyone scrambled out of bed quickly, milled around anxiously, looking to Travis and Antony for leadership.

'We just need to keep calm,' Antony advised. 'The guards when they bring us breakfast mustn't suspect anything.'

'Remember what I told you,' Travis added. 'My contact said that after prisoners have been given their breakfast there's a changeover period. With any luck, the guards won't be quite as in place or as organised as at other times. That's when he's going to cut off the security systems. That's when we need to be ready.'

Linden was kneeling beside Juniper and her other four little charges. 'When I tell you,' she explained earnestly, 'I want you to hold my hands and each other's hands and I want you to hold tight and to keep hold whatever happens, do you understand me?'

'Yes, Linden,' said the children dutifully.

'Don't let go of me whatever you do. I won't let go of you. I promise.'

Breakfast came and went. A tasteless, colourless porridge. The catering was certainly superior in Darion's rooms, Travis thought, which was where he hoped to God the descendant of Ayrion was right now, seated at his computer preparing to betray his illustrious ancestor's memory.

The cell was the preserve of the prisoners again. The changeover period had to be imminent. No milling around now. An anxious congregation at the sliding door. Tension crackling in the air like electricity.

And Antony was listening to Travis exhorting everyone to keep together, to follow him. He knew the way out. His new-found, nameless Scytharene ally had shown him the escape route. Only him. Travis would have to lead and it was a situation that shouldn't rankle with the Head Boy of the Harrington School because it was for the good of them all. But it did. A little bit. Boys he'd known for years falling in behind the newcomer. In times of stress, allegiances shifted. Leo Milton caught his eye and gave a thin, bitter smile.

'Naughton.' Richie. 'When we get – when the door opens, you keep going. Don't worry about nothing. I'll watch your back. If you like. I can do that.'

'Thanks, Richie.' Travis nodded appreciatively. 'Make sure you watch your own, too.'

'Jessie,' Mel said as she snatched for her friend's hand, both urgently, 'there's something I need to tell you.'

'When we're out of here, Mel,' Jessica returned. 'When we're safe. Then you can tell me anything.'

'I'll hold you to that.' The black-haired girl embraced the blonde, hugged her tightly.

Travis's eyes were trained on the door, compelling it to yield. He was murmuring: 'Ready. Ready.'

It had to be now. It had to be. Surely Darion must have hacked into the ship's computer by now if he was able to, if he was everything he'd claimed to be, if he'd meant what he said. Because there was always that danger, always that fear that at the last minute, at the very last second, the Scytharene wouldn't be able to find within himself the courage to—

The door slid open, as silent as a secret.

'Trav,' gasped Mel.

And then the alarm went off.

FIVE

The high-pitched siren could be nothing else. The alarm, no doubt reverberating throughout the ship. Travis had a vision of countless Scytharene in black drawing subjugators.

Seemed the element of surprise would be even more short-lived than he'd feared.

Best to make the most of it, then.

'Now! *Now!*' He led the surge into the corridor.

Two guards looking like they'd only just arrived on duty, startled by the strident burst of sound and by the sight of several dozen Earther slaves stampeding towards them. Swarming over them. Travis was on top of the first guard even as the Scytharene's subjugator cleared its holster. He smashed his fist into the sickly white face, the momentum of his body and the hatred in his blow combining to drive the alien backwards and send him crashing to the floor. He pounded the disgustingly pallid flesh again and again, blood the tint of the Scytharene's eyes spouting from the nose, the buttress of the forehead no defence. Rage and loathing made Travis vengeful, made him strong. Part of him longed to carry on hitting the guard for the sheer, satisfying hell of it. The more rational part of him, however, saw that such a prolonged beating would likely prove counterproductive to the kids' chances of escape and was, in any case, unnecessary.

The Scytharene had cracked his head against the metal floor as he'd fallen. He was already unconscious.

His companion, too, bludgeoned into senselessness by a group of Harringtonians. Antony had appropriated this second guard's subjugator. Travis relieved his own victim of the same.

The weapon boosted his confidence. He scrambled to his feet, glanced both ways along the corridor. No Scytharene in sight. But maybe somewhere close by, Simon and the other absentees might be languishing. Or they could be on another level. Had Darion released the doors of all the cells? Maybe Simon was free but frightened in the corridor above their heads or below their feet. There was no way of knowing. There was no way of *helping*. Travis had promised he wouldn't leave Simon behind. '*I never have so far, have I?*'

He had now.

'Travis, which way? We've got to *move*.' Antony, urgent.

There were more people than Simon depending on him, people who right now he had more chance of saving from the cryo-tubes and slavery. Travis hoped that Simon, if he ever found out, would understand, would forgive him. Sometimes, betrayal wasn't a matter of choice.

'Okay, let's go!' Behind him, Travis saw the cell door slide innocently closed again. Darion hadn't lied about being able to disrupt security for seconds only, but that was fine. He'd done his bit. Now it was up to them to do theirs.

The nearest maintenance stairwell was at the end of the cell area to the left.

So were four Scytharene guards. And they weren't standing around in bemusement now. They were racing towards the escapees. They were armed. They were more familiar with the workings of subjugators than Travis and Antony.

Their first blasts decreased the youngsters' number by four. White energy bolts. They still didn't want to damage the merchandise unduly. Maybe that gave the merchandise an advantage, Travis thought grimly. He raised his subjugator, fired. There was no recoil in the weapon at all. His blast stabbed straight and true, struck its black-armoured target. And it appeared the Scytharene were as vulnerable to their own weaponry as any other species.

Antony dropped a guard, too. The survivors retaliated, shot at the two armed teenagers. Travis dived to the floor and the energy bolt flashed above him, rendered unconscious a boy he himself had persuaded to join Harrington a mere week or so ago, a boy who'd trusted him. More guilt to dwell on later. For now, Travis didn't give the Scytharene another opportunity to create casualties.

On the other side of the corridor, Antony was thrust out of the last guard's line of fire by Oliver Dalton-Booth, the Harringtonian who'd wanted to become a doctor. As he collapsed, unaware that his sacrifice had allowed Antony to eliminate their final opposition, it seemed he'd have to content himself with the career of a slave instead.

'*No!*' Antony groaned. '*Oliver.*'

'I know,' Travis said. 'But Antony, we can't help them.'

And the screams and the crackle of subjugator fire began simultaneously from the rear of the group. More Scytharene closing in, cutting down the youngsters. Juniper and the other children squealed. Linden pushed forward with them, expecting any moment to feel the icy, paralysing impact of a blast from a subjugator, as Travis had said the weapons were called. Travis, who was wheeling now and with Antony trying to target the advancing aliens, only they couldn't steady their aim with terrified kids running into them, cannoning off them, blundering past in their panic to get out of the Scytharene's range. Some of them didn't make it.

'Travis, you go!' Antony yelled. 'You have to. I'll hold them back.'

'Don't be stupid, you'll—'

'*Both* of you get out of here.' Leo Milton. He and three other Harringtonians had armed themselves thanks to this second group of fallen guards. 'The others need you.' He fired at the Scytharene. 'You don't need me. We'll hold the line as long as we can.'

'Leo . . .'

'You're Head Boy, Clive,' Leo Milton acknowledged. 'You always were.'

'Thank you. Good luck, Leo,' Antony said.

'Yeah, thanks, Leo,' Travis added. Because it didn't matter now that he'd never liked the ginger-haired boy or vice versa. Leo Milton was making his stand, and that was always admirable. He nodded towards Leo with respect. But only for a moment.

The sounds of subjugator blasts receded as the remaining score or so of escapees sprinted on, rounded the curve of the corridor. What could only be elevators ahead, a door alongside them with Scytharene writing on it.

'The stairwell,' Travis said. 'I hope.' He pressed the button and the door slid open to indeed reveal a metal staircase extending both to lower and upper decks. 'Thank God.' Or Darion. The Scytharene had come good at every stage so far. 'Come on. Inside. Quick. Quick.' Bundling the group through to the landing.

'Wouldn't the lift be quicker?' somebody said.

'Quicker to get caught,' Travis snapped. 'We'll be sitting ducks in there even if we could all cram in, which we can't. We keep to the plan. They won't be expecting us to use the stairs because they won't think we'll know this door *leads* to stairs. The sign's in Scytharene.' Travis closed the door behind them.

'You sure these are the right stairs, though, Trav?' Mel wanted to know. 'Like you said, the sign *is* in Scytharene.'

'I'm sure. Down to the lower maintenance levels. To the stabilisers.'

'The what?'

'The things that keep the ship on an even keel. The technicians have their own access hatches to the outside. They shouldn't be guarded like the main exits.'

'*Shouldn't* be,' repeated Mel, but she didn't sound convinced.

'What,' Commander Shurion demanded from the bridge, 'is happening?' He'd forgone his command chair in order to almost physically menace one of the comscreens. Anger was visible in each deep grove scored across the pugnacious forehead.

The guard reporting to his commanding officer from the slave quarters seemed to wish he was even further away than that, back on the Scytharene homeworld, perhaps. 'The main holding cell's security was compromised, sir. Some kind of temporary power failure. The Earther slaves escaped.'

'I'm aware of that, Clyrion,' Shurion snarled. 'I am also aware that you have yet to return them to safe custody.'

'We've apprehended some . . . many of them, sir,' ventured the guard.

'Neither some nor many is all, Clyrion,' Shurion pointed out acidly. 'I trust the disposal cell remains secure, at least.'

'All systems are back online, sir. It seems the disruption was extremely localised. The disposal cell was never affected.'

'Well, Clyrion,' glowered Shurion, 'unless you wish to join those already incarcerated therein, I suggest you locate and recapture the Earther slaves still at large.'

'Yes, sir. At once, Commander Shurion.' Relieved to end the transmission.

'In the mean time,' Shurion turned from the screen to address the bridge as a whole, 'we will move to defensive alert, level two.' His eyes narrowed into thin blades of blood. 'One thing is certain. The Earthers cannot have acted alone.'

By the time the remaining youngsters had reached the very bottom of the stairwell, the alarm had changed pitch and was blaring out only every five seconds.

'Does that mean something, Travis?' Linden asked.

'Probably,' Travis said. 'Though I don't intend to stop the next Scytharene we see to find out what.' The group pressed nearer together in front of another closed door. Voices were lowered instinctively. 'Listen, we're almost there. The other side of this door should be the stabiliser maintenance area. Techs only, the guys in red. Maybe no guards. Maybe the techs won't even be armed.'

'Maybe they'll just shake us by the hand and show us out,' muttered Mel.

'Well, *we're* armed.' Travis raised his subjugator. 'And all we've got to do is fight our way across the floor. Should be an access hatch no more than thirty yards pretty much directly in front of us, activated just like any of these doors, so whoever reaches it first opens it and we run like hell for the trees. We can do it.'

'Travis and I have done it before,' Antony added by way of encouragement.

Yeah, and you ended up right back here, thought Mel. She glanced at Jessica. That wasn't going to happen to them.

'We'll cover you with the subjugators,' Travis said. 'Ready?'

Jessica gazed up the stairwell. 'I guess there's no point waiting for Leo.'

'You know what I told you about holding hands?' Linden whispered to the children. 'Now is the most important time of all not to let go.'

'Linden, I'm scared,' whimpered Juniper.

Linden smiled sympathetically. So was she.

'Freedom,' Travis said, slamming his palm against the button set into the wall, 'here we come.'

He and Antony opened fire the instant they burst through the doorway, even before they could spot anyone to shoot at. They glimpsed banks of computers, monitoring equipment, hunks of machinery in various states of repair, all by a lurid scarlet light that reminded Travis unpleasantly of processing. Clearly, crewmen were required to operate such instruments, and techs were busy doing so. Lots of techs. Antony practically collided with one as he charged into the room – the force of the subjugator blast on that particular unfortunate knocked him halfway to the access hatch. Which was there as promised. Which was visible. Travis almost *loved* Darion. And the techs were not guards or warriors. They were slow to react to this sudden invasion. Travis and Antony took out a couple more each before the Scytharene responded with equal violence.

Even techs were armed with subjugators.

But the youngsters were all into the maintenance area now and darting towards the exit. Richie paused only to reach down and retrieve a fallen alien's gun; Mel did the same. The escapees' covering fire doubled.

'Stay with me, Jessie,' Mel cried.

As the techs crouched down behind shielding machinery, work stations, computer units. They were more difficult to hit now even if the teenagers had been better shots.

Jodie the musician was first to gain the hatch. She fumbled for the activation mechanism. She didn't find it before a sub-jugator blast found her.

Jessica had better luck – and Mel protecting her back. With a resentful hiss the hatch slid open. Pure, healthy spring sunshine flooded in. Jessica was dazzled. The brightness. The sky. Freedom so close.

'Go, Jess, go!' Mel not just defending her back but shoving it, shoving her. Subjugator bolts flaring past her head and sparking against the wall, the rim of the hatch. Someone went down to her left. Jessica took to her heels.

And the earth felt good beneath her feet again, scorched and bare of grass though it was. It seemed to give her strength and courage and determination, as if it wanted her to escape, wanted all of them free of the Scytharene. Or maybe, it occurred to the hurtling Jessica, and the possibility came as something of a shock, maybe the real strength lay in *her*.

Behind her, Linden was cramming the five small children

through the hatch, Travis, Antony and even Richie forcing the Scytharene techs to keep their distance with a constant spray of subjugator blasts. The children were screaming but they were holding on to her, Juni gripping one hand with Rose and little Willow to her left, the boys River and Fox glued to her right. Travis was yelling for them to run and they did. Linden saw Jessica and Mel racing towards the trees and the slope of Vernham Hill, a handful of Harringtonians between herself and her friends. The boys were on their way now, too, firing behind them to deter pursuit, but fairly wildly, so as not to risk losing their footing and falling.

'Keep going. Everyone.' Travis. 'Almost there.'

But Linden had always been suspicious of almosts. How many times in her life had her mother *almost* been certain they'd found the right place to settle and stay, *almost* fulfilled herself in this New Age community or that? And how many times had she decided sooner or later that the place wasn't *quite* what she'd hoped, that she needed to move on, to drag Linden along with her, leaving the friends she was making, leading her daughter into new uncertainty, new solitude? How many times had Linden *almost* been able to rely on someone, only to lose them one way or another?

She hated bloody *almosts*.

And the Scytharene techs weren't just letting them go. They were spilling out of the ship, not chasing them but continuing to fire their weapons. Not having to run, they could choose their targets, take more careful aim.

A Harrington boy yelped and stiffened as a subjugator blast mocked him with almost. The last girl who wasn't one of Travis's group met the same fate, her paralysed left arm clawing for the forest she would never now reach.

And Linden had been stupid. She should have thought this through. Allowing little Willow, the youngest of her charges – what was she? five? six? – to dangle on the end was asking for trouble. Her little legs. She'd be able to keep up with the others, yeah – almost.

Inevitably, disastrously, Willow tripped. Willow fell. Rose let go of Juniper's hand to keep hold of Willow's. Juniper squealed as if her left arm had been torn from its socket. Linden slowed, not knowing what else to do. 'Willow! Rose!'

Subjugator bolts sent the little girls to sleep.

'Oh, *God.*'

'Lin, you can't . . .' Travis didn't need to tell her what she couldn't do. She already knew.

She couldn't save the children. She could only *almost* save them.

River's hand and Juniper's hand slipped from hers. She was clutching at air. The children were running back towards the girls, towards the guns. The boys were cut down before they'd gone ten yards. Juniper made it, though, and looked like she was about to kneel beside the unconscious bodies of her sister and little Willow before a subjugator blast froze her in white and toppled her over the both of them.

Someone new grabbed Linden's hand. Travis.

'They're gone. We need to be, too.'

And it was as well Travis was leading her, because Linden's eyes were so full of tears she could hardly make out her surroundings. She was only aware of Juniper, Rose, Willow, River, Fox, prostrate on the ground, helpless, lost. And she doubted she'd ever see them again.

'Come on. Come on!' Jessica and Mel yelling animatedly from the cover of the trees. Like it was a race and the forest was the finishing line. Linden didn't feel like a winner when she and Travis sprinted into the wood and the two girls' welcoming arms. Antony wasn't far behind. Richie Coker. But that was all. The six of them. Everyone with a subjugator, herself and Jess.

'We're out of their range,' Mel observed breathlessly. 'And they're not coming after us.'

'Not yet, maybe,' Travis gasped, 'but what if they launch a Culler, those battlepods again? We've got to keep moving.'

Keep moving, Linden thought bitterly. *Almost there.* It was the story of her life.

At first Darion considered it might be wiser for him to remain in his quarters during the defensive alert, out of Shurion's way; he could ascertain via his comscreen whether Travis Naughton was among those Earthers already recaptured and plan accordingly. On reflection, however, he felt it would be safer, more like the behaviour of a member of the Thousand Families with nothing to hide, if he marched on to the bridge and demanded of Commander Shurion an explanation for the unpardonable and unprecedented lapse of security that had resulted in the loss of several valuable items of merchandise.

'My father will be dismayed to hear of it,' he added when, a little later, he stood face to face with Shurion on the bridge. It wouldn't do him any harm to remind the Commander of his irreproachable heritage.

'I will tender my report to Fleet Commander Gyrion in due course, Lord Darion,' Shurion growled. 'Have no fear on that account.'

'Will it contain assurances that all reasonable steps are being taken to reacquire the Earthers still at liberty?' Among whom, Darion had established with significant relief, numbered Travis Naughton.

Shurion regarded the alienologist contemplatively. 'A mere half-dozen slaves are unaccounted for,' he said. 'My priority is to ensure security aboard the *Furion*.'

'I'm pleased to hear it,' said Darion slyly. 'I assume, therefore, that we are not to expect another mass breakout in the near future.'

'That might depend, Lord Darion.'

'Really? On what, Commander Shurion?'

'Scytharene technology does not simply fail,' the Commander asserted. 'Tests have already been carried out on the holding cell's security systems. They are in perfect working order. Which means they were disabled temporarily – and intentionally – by someone aboard this ship. Also, for the slaves to have found their way to the maintenance area by themselves, by chance, defies credibility, does it not, Lord Darion?'

'It might,' Darion conceded, suddenly on the defensive.

'Which suggests that they were afforded assistance. Which implies the presence aboard my ship of a traitor, Lord Darion, a Scytharene who has chosen to side with filthy, stinking slaves against his own people, his own race.' The Commander's eyes burned with crimson rage. 'Who might that be, I wonder?'

'I have no idea, Commander Shurion,' said Darion, as evenly as he could. His heart pounded inside him. With fear, yes, but also strangely, invigoratingly, with pride. 'But I trust you will discover the villain shortly.'

'On that you can rely, Lord Darion.' Shurion turned away. 'And when the traitor's identity is known to me' – casting a baleful glance backwards – 'he will come to wish he had never been born.'

Eventually they could run no further. Adrenalin could delay but not deny the effects of fatigue. 'There's still no sign – I don't think we're being followed,' Antony panted, which seemed generally to be interpreted as permission to sink groaning to the ground.

Not even Travis objected. 'We'll rest up here.' They were in a verdant grove that under pre-Sickness circumstances would have been beautiful. Sunlight played on the teenagers' dejected faces; insects busied themselves about the imperatives of their brief lives, unaware that new masters now trod the Earth. 'We'll just take a . . . not for long, mind. A few minutes. Then we've got to keep moving.'

'Where to, Trav?' Mel lay spreadeagled on her back. 'Where the hell can we go?'

'Back to Harrington, of course.' Propped up against a tree like a wounded soldier, Antony still had the strength to be certain. 'Where else?'

'There's nobody *at* Harrington, Antony,' Mel pointed out. 'Everybody but us is . . .' She failed to complete her sentence. Nobody stepped in to help her.

'Harrington is the last place they'll expect us to go after capturing us there,' Antony said, more to himself than to anyone else. 'So that's where we'll go. We'll be safe at Harrington. We can make decisions, regroup . . .'

Travis found himself more occupied by thoughts of where

the exhausted group had come from than wherever it was they might be heading. The memory of those they'd left behind accused him. He could see it was the same for Linden. The russet-haired girl had all but curled herself into a ball on the forest floor. Like a fragile, frightened animal, Travis thought. He felt a great wave of tenderness for her, maybe more than tenderness. He crawled across and lay beside her, against her, moulded his body to the curve of her back, enfolded her with his arms. Linden snuggled into him. Her cheeks were smeared with the scars of tears. Travis longed to kiss them away.

'I'm sorry about Juniper and the others, Lin,' he consoled her. 'I know how much they meant to you. You couldn't have done more.'

'That doesn't make me feel better, Travis,' she said mournfully, though she was grateful for the sentiment and the physical contact. 'It only makes me realise how useless I am.'

'Not true. Not *true*. But we can't work miracles, however much we might want to. We can only try. If we can't win, we can at least not give up. Six of us escaped. That's six more than it might have been.'

'What'll happen to Juni and Rose and Willow, Travis?' Linden shuddered, not really wanting to think about it. 'They'll be placed in those cryo-tubes you told us about, won't they? If not now, soon. And they'll be blasted into space, condemned to slavery. . .'

'Don't, Linden.' Travis sought to soothe her.

'They might not even be kept together. They may wake up totally alone. And all because I couldn't hold on to them.'

'No.'

'Yes. Because I let go of them.' Linden was absolute in her misery. 'Travis, don't let go of me, will you? Ever.'

'I won't,' he pledged. And he meant it. But then, he'd meant what he'd promised Simon, too.

'What do you reckon happened to Simes and those others?' said Richie, as if he'd just read Travis's mind.

'Like you care,' Mel snorted from the ground. 'You couldn't stand Simon, Richie. You bullied him to within an inch of his life back at school.'

Richie reddened. 'Yeah, but I . . .' He ought to give Morticia a slap, disrespecting him in public like that, reminding the others of what he'd been. The others who were staring at him now with a kind of disgust, like he was a piece of shit or something, like they didn't want him around. For once, even Naughton.

'It's a bit late to make like Mother Teresa now, Big Guy,' Mel taunted. 'You're the wrong sex, for a start.'

'Shut up, Morticia.' He jumped to his feet. He wasn't a piece of shit. He wouldn't be. 'Shut your pissing mouth or . . .' And he didn't consciously intend to, but he kind of jerked his right hand towards her, maybe to jab at her with his finger. He still held the subjugator.

'Or what?' Mel sat up confrontationally. 'You gonna do the Scytharene's job for them and shoot me? That'd be right. Hey, what if I throw my gun down and stick my hands up in the air to make it easier for you?'

'Mel, don't be stupid,' Jessica broke in, much to the black-haired girl's chagrin.

'Jessie's right,' added Travis. 'No squabbling. I don't think Richie meant anything . . .'

'Hey, Naughton,' Richie snapped. 'I don't need you to fight my battles for me.'

And he stalked off, his brow furrowed with frustration.

Why was everything going wrong? He thought he'd done well during the breakout. He'd grabbed a weapon when he could have just fled. He'd fended off the Scytharene techs with Naughton and that posh twat Clive. He'd *helped*. And he'd thought the least the others could do was appreciate that, be grateful to Richie Coker, show him some respect. He'd thought Travis might even thank him. But somehow it wasn't turning out like that. All the good work he'd done in the last few hours was still being outweighed by the Richie Coker he'd been for the past few years. It was Satchwell's fault. Wherever he was right now, old Simes was finally getting some revenge.

Simon heard the alarm, of course, but he had no way of knowing what was going on outside the cell – except that it was almost certainly bad. Several of his companions began to whimper or whine like pets frightened of fireworks; tubby Digby covered his ears. Simon couldn't have felt more alone had he been thrown into solitary confinement.

What if the relentless cacophony *wasn't* an alarm after all? What if it was a signal to carry out the sentence of death upon the occupants of Simon's cell to which the Scytharene had condemned them yesterday? What if it was that? Simon hadn't slept at all during lights-out, hadn't even dared to close his eyes in case the aliens chose that moment to enter the cell with execution in mind. But no Scytharene had appeared then and none did now. Maybe they'd had second thoughts about the disposal of the failures. The fact that neither food nor drink had been provided since processing, however, suggested otherwise.

But they weren't dead yet. Simon knew that if Travis was with them he'd be able to make something inspiring out of that. *They were still alive, and while there was life, there was hope* kind of thing. Travis would believe that implicitly and act on it, but Simon had led a different life to the other boy. He'd *never* had hope.

Where *was* Travis? He ought to be coming to the rescue. He'd *promised* . . .

In time, the note of the alarm changed, resounded less frequently. At last it ceased altogether. The silence was somehow worse than the noise. There was terror in it, and despair, and the shadow of death.

Simon sat against a wall with his knees raised and his arms wrapped round them, hanging his head disconsolately. How long had they got? Would they be killed as a group or one at a time with the others watching and waiting their turn? Maybe the Scytharene were thrifty and were intending to save ammunition as well as food by simply starving their unwanted prisoners to death. In certain cases, Simon thought bleakly, casting his eye over the two scrawny girls, that probably wouldn't take long.

The door opened. Two Scytharene guards entered, their weapons drawn.

Simon moaned in horror, scrambled to his feet, retreated with his fellow captives until their backs struck the far wall of the cell and they could withdraw no further. This was it. The final moment of his life. He thought of the grandparents he'd left dead in their bed, of the parents he'd never really known, the waste and the loneliness of his years. Simon sobbed.

Maybe the Scytharene *should* just open fire and—

'You.' One of them was pointing. '*You*. Slave.' At *him*.

119

'Me?' Simon could scarcely speak.

'Come with us.'

It was going to be one at a time. And elsewhere. Maybe they had a purpose-built execution cell. He'd soon find out.

Simon shuffled forward, his legs locked into near-immobility by fear. His sobbing almost became a dismal laughter. The only time he'd been chosen first for anything in his life and it was to lose that life. Said it all.

He didn't look behind him as the guards prodded him out into the corridor. He didn't know those people in the cell.

'Where are you . . . where are you taking me?' His voice was following the lead of his body and trembling.

The Scytharene didn't deign to answer. Perhaps they thought they were doing him a favour by keeping silent. Perhaps they thought he hadn't already guessed they were escorting him to his death.

Through blue-tinged corridors, blurred without his glasses but still, Simon could tell, different from those housing the cells. Into an elevator, rising towards the higher decks. He'd somehow imagined that executions would be carried out on the lower levels, he didn't know why. Another corridor, slightly different again. A door in front of which Simon was halted.

Did death await him on the other side?

'Warriors Myrion and Varion with the Earther slave, sir,' one of the guards announced, and the door opened.

No instruments of execution beyond. No gallows or electric chair or disintegrator ray. Living quarters, furnished and decorated in a minimalist style, as if their occupant repudiated the very concept of relaxation. Simon thought he recognised the robed Scytharene who stood within. His heart missed a beat.

'Enter, boy,' beckoned Commander Shurion.

An invitation Simon could patently not refuse. The guards did not accompany him inside. The door closed to leave him alone with the Scytharene commander.

Who asked conversationally: 'Do you know who I am?'

'Com . . . you're the . . . Commander Shurion.'

'Exactly.' And bizarrely, the Scytharene smiled, the lipless mouth splitting open, exposing a gash of crimson. 'But I don't know who *you* are.'

'I'm – I'm Simon. Simon Satchwell.'

'Simon Satchwell. Good,' approved Commander Shurion. 'And these are yours, are they not, Simon Satchwell?' He held up Simon's glasses. 'Please, put them on.' Watching as the teenager did so. 'I want you to be able to see things clearly from now on.'

'I don't . . .' Simon was confused, but confused was better than dead.

'You believe me to be your enemy, don't you, Simon?' Shurion said with a disappointed sigh.

'I – I'm not . . .'

'You fear me, don't you? But there is no need to be afraid.' The smile again. The red in the mouth. 'I am not your enemy, Simon. I am your friend.'

The Scytharene had revisited the Harrington School. They must have done. Who else could and would have reduced it to rubble?

They saw the smoke rising from a distance, and empty space where solid stone had stood, the trappings of a castle proclaiming the school's intention to withstand the siege of change and to survive, to endure, the values it nurtured within its walls intact. But the walls had fallen. The stone was smashed. Beyond the hills, the sun was setting.

Antony uttered a strangled cry of shock and disbelief. 'No. *No!*' He broke into a run through what had been the old school's grounds.

'Wait. Antony!' Travis called after him. 'There might still be Scytharene . . .'

The blond boy didn't care. He had no choice but to do what he was doing. The others could stay where they were or follow him.

They followed.

And found the school a smouldering ruin, razed to the ground. Its roof had given way and its sides had buckled under some tremendous pressure from above. Its proud windows had burst. Its mighty entrance arch had cracked and sundered. The books in the library had been incinerated, the beds in the dormitories splintered, the staircases shattered, the Great Hall crushed. In the Headmaster's study, the portraits of the former holders of that office lay charred beyond restoration. Of the Harrington School, nothing salvageable remained.

Antony Clive, its last Head Boy, was rocking on his knees before the wreckage, agonised, punching his helpless fist into the gravel of what had once been a drive. Travis and the others stopped a short distance behind him. Travis could hear Antony groaning as if in mourning for the loss of a parent. Maybe, in a way, that was true. He made towards his friend. Jessica checked him.

'Let me,' she said.

'Jess?' Uncharitably, Mel frowned.

But Jessica had seen Travis comforting Linden while they were resting before. She'd wanted to cross to Antony then, to hold him, to have him hold her, but she'd feared being seen as presumptuous and she'd worried about doing something wrong. None of that seemed an issue now. Even if it was, there were feelings stirring inside her that she'd never experienced before, feelings she couldn't resist, urging her to Antony's side.

She knelt beside him, hugged him, pressed her cheek to his, their blond hair matching. 'Antony, I'm so *sorry*.'

'It's gone, Jess,' the boy said numbly. 'It's all gone. They've destroyed everything.'

'Antony . . .'

'Harrington, it wasn't just a school for me. It wasn't just a building. It was more. It was . . .' Antony struggled to express himself. 'What it meant, what it stood for. A whole way of life. Certainty. Morality. Decency. A vision of the way things should be. And they've taken that away from me, everything I believed in. I've got nothing left.' He sighed. 'I don't expect you to understand.'

'But I do, Antony. More than you think. I felt the same when I saw my mum and dad lying in their . . . when I saw them with the Sickness. The Sickness had violated my home and it had killed them, my mum and dad, and it had stolen the life they'd given me and I felt that I couldn't go on. I felt that *I* had nothing left, too. I felt like you.'

'Did you?' Antony looked to Jessica beseechingly.

'If Travis and Mel hadn't been there for me, I don't know what . . . but they were. And I'm here for you, Antony. I want to help you. Let me help you.' She extended her open palm. Antony took it, squeezed it. The contact felt good. It felt right. ''Cause now I think that nothing we have is ever truly lost. My parents are dead but they're still with me in a way. In here.' She pressed their two hands against her heart.

'You're talking about people, Jessie,' Antony said gently, 'and memories.'

'More than that. I want to carry on living the way my parents taught me. It was a good way. And if you carry on living the way you were taught at Harrington, then Harrington isn't gone either, is it?'

Antony smiled weakly. 'You're very special, Jessica Lane, do you know that?'

While Mel was looking on and thinking, *What?* Jessie with her arms round Antony Clive? Just comforting him, though. Nothing more. Comforting was acceptable. At least they weren't kissing. *Yet.*

Richie was shaking his head perplexedly. He'd never warmed to this poncy bloody school in the first place, all those poncy bloody snobs in their grey blazers, but he felt a weird kind of shame now that it lay in ruins, as if somehow he'd contributed to its destruction. On what had been the sports fields he could see the corpses of the community's livestock, blackened and barbecued. There'd been no need for that. Bastard aliens. And what about the ducks who'd swum in the pond in the inner quadrangle, Romeo and Juliet and their web-footed friends with those dumb fancy names the posh kids had given them? They had to be charcoaled, too. Richie had joked about eating them before. Now he wished he hadn't.

'There's nothing for us here,' Travis said grimly, Linden alongside him. He thought back to all those alien invasion movies he'd seen at the cinema, the annihilation of the White

House, Big Ben and the Houses of Parliament, the Eiffel Tower. Selected by the film's directors for their symbolic value, clearly. But real alien invasion wasn't about symbols, it was about suffering and loss. It was about the devastation of places known and loved, places where previously you'd felt secure. It was about not going home again, never going home again. 'Antony, we can't stay . . .'

'We don't need to stay here, Travis.' Antony rose to his feet with renewed resolution; Jessica stood with him. 'We can take *here* with us.'

'Why don't we make for Willowstock?' Linden suggested, scanning the horizon in the appropriate direction. 'Trav, we could maybe hole up at your grandparents' again while we—' She interrupted her plans with a sudden cry.

'Lin?' Travis followed her gaze. Everyone did.

And Linden certainly hadn't been lying about the flying globe in the shape of an eyeball. They could all see it now.

It was hovering about twelve feet from Linden and eight feet above the ground. A steel sphere the approximate dimensions of a football and gleaming in the last of the day's sunlight. The circular lens returned the teenagers' startled stare precisely as Linden had described.

Travis owed his girlfriend an apology. It might have to wait.

'This unit has been sent to summon you,' the eye said in a robotic female voice. 'Come with this unit if you wish to survive.'

SIX

It was bizarre. Having demonstrated the ability to speak, hitherto unsuspected even by Linden, the eye promptly reverted to muteness again and declined to repeat the feat. It seemed to imagine that drifting away from the teenagers towards the wood before pausing in evident expectation was eloquence enough.

'What do we do, Trav?' Mel wanted to know. 'Do we follow it?'

'Yeah, right. Into a bloody alien trap,' grunted Richie.

'We don't know it's from the Scytharene. Why would they bother to trick us? Why not just attack us if they know where we are?' Linden was puzzled. 'When I saw it before, this one or another identical, when Juni and the kids saw it, it didn't do anything hostile. Just observed.'

'What do you think, Antony?' prompted Jessica.

'I don't know.'

'Well I do,' decided Travis. 'When I mentioned flying eyes to our Scytharene ally he looked like he had no idea what I was talking about. I don't think he did. The eye isn't alien. We ought to do what it wants and follow it.'

'If you say so, Trav,' said Mel. 'But let's keep hold of our subjugator things, yeah?'

Cautiously the little group approached the sphere, and as

they did it moved ahead of them again, luring them on. The teenagers too lapsed into silence as the eye led them through the forest away from the remains of the Harrington School and, more hearteningly, in the opposite direct to Vernham Hill. Time passed. Night fell. The trees became lurking, threatening figures in the darkness, but the orb lit up and glowed with green luminescence, like a star in the sky to guide them.

After several hours and even more miles of weary trekking, the steel globe hesitated before a bare hillside. Unobstructed by foliage, the moonlight here was sufficient to reveal nothing at all extraordinary about the location –

'What the hell have we stopped here for?' grumbled Richie.

'Maybe it's run out of gas,' said Mel.

– until the hillside itself began to split open.

'God.' Travis stepped back involuntarily. An image of graves and Judgement Day had appeared in his head, the earth gaping wide to discharge the dead. There was an over-whelming blackness inside the hill, and for a moment he feared it.

Linden's hand squeezed his as the ground rumbled. King Arthur, she thought. Her mother had told her the legend many times, how Arthur and his glorious Knights of the Round Table were not dead, not lost, but sleeping, slumber-ing, beneath such a hill as this, awaiting Albion's greatest time of trial, at which critical juncture they would awake and ride forth and, shining with the light of righteousness, vanquish all of England's enemies. The way her mother told it, Arthur and his noble company would return as Nature's warriors, to wean men away from the corruption of materialism and reunite them with the purity of the land, and the light which would array them would be green like the soul of the forest.

But when it came, the light within *this* hillside was white, and generated by electricity rather than spirit. Linden felt a pang of disappointment, but she saw relief in Travis's face.

Then all six of them saw the tunnel.

'On our way to Wonderland,' breathed Jessica.

'If I see a bloody white rabbit,' Richie vowed, raising his subjugator, 'I'm going to shoot the sucker.'

'This unit has brought you to the Enclave,' said the eye. 'Follow this unit for decontamination.'

'Enclave?' Travis frowned. 'What's the Enclave?'

But the eye seemed once more to have remembered it was not a mouth.

The teenagers entered the tunnel, a broad ring of concrete and steel ribbed with strip-lighting and thick cables like glistening black anacondas. It burrowed into the earth, sloping gently downwards. Behind them, the entrance was becoming a hillside again. There was no turning back – and little going forward. After a hundred yards or so the passage was blocked by a sheer wall of some kind of reinforced glass or plastic. Its single circular hatch was inhospitably shut.

'When the primary airlock opens, this unit requires you to enter,' said the eye. 'You will then be given further instructions.'

'Sure we will,' Richie snorted. 'Any of the rest of you get the sense that we've been here before?'

'Déjà vu, Richie,' said Jessica.

'Yeah. Up yours, too.'

'Primary airlock. Decontamination. Enclave.' Travis turned excitedly to the others. 'This is a base. One of *our* bases. It has to be. I told you there are still military units out there capable of mounting attacks on the Scytharene. This has got to be one of them.' He grinned. 'A *chance*.'

'The army,' Richie said ruefully. 'The good old British army.' His mum had wanted him to join the army – any of the forces, actually. She'd thought a bit of military discipline might smarten him up, save him from the dead end his life was heading for, booze, violence, drugs. He'd told her what he thought of that particular plan in no uncertain terms. One phrase. Two words. And he'd failed his mum and now, when it was too late, he wished he hadn't. He really wished he hadn't.

Antony and Jessica both seemed to cheer up at the prospect of adult authority being resumed, but Linden remembered the young soldier she and Ash had encountered in the forest while she was still living with the Children of Nature. He'd elected to shoot himself rather than stay alive to face what he'd said was coming – the Sickness, as she now knew. She remembered his fellow troops in gas masks silently taking the body away. It might be premature to expect too much from whoever resided in the Enclave.

Even so, Linden stepped through the hatch gladly enough when it twisted open like the top of a bottle. They all did. More than one of them might have been a little sorry that the eye was accompanying them no further. The voice that bade them enter the secondary airlock – something of a repeat performance – was male, less mechanical, but somehow also less reassuring. Especially when the subject changed to the removal of their clothes.

'Again?' Mel howled furiously. 'Are we living in a world of leches or what?'

But it wasn't so bad this time. Decontamination procedures. Each of the teenagers in turn was to pass from the secondary airlock into the decontamination chambers, where they'd leave all their clothing and personal possessions prior to taking a vigorous shower with chemically treated water. After that, there'd be fresh garments to wear and they'd be safe to enter the Enclave proper. The term *processing* wasn't mentioned once. Mel wasn't happy about giving up their weapons, but there seemed little option. One by one the group went through.

Their new apparel wasn't very different from the old. Boots and combat fatigues in khaki. 'It's like the colour's gone out of the world,' Jessica said sadly.

Mel was sniffing the wet strands of her long black hair. 'I don't know what was in that shampoo they made us use, but it smells like . . .' She wrinkled her nose in disgust. 'Put it this way, they wouldn't have been able to market it pre-Sickness.'

Travis made no comment. There were two doors in the room where they now found themselves, one leading from the decontamination chambers, the other, presumably, accessing the main body of the Enclave. His eyes were fixed on the latter. Darion's words about effecting contact between the human resistance and the Scytharene rebels played on his mind. If he, Travis, could make it happen, his continued freedom would be justified. He would have achieved something, made a difference. And maybe the guilt that tortured him over Simon and the others he'd left behind would come to an end.

The second door opened. Flanked by armed soldiers, a man in the uniform of an army captain walked into the room, slowly, with a stoop. He had to be at least sixty, possibly much older. Thinning iron-grey hair. A moustache like a smear of charcoal. Deep grooves gouged into his face. He reminded Travis of Field-Marshal Montgomery from the Second World War, as if Monty had never died but instead had only aged, kept alive by the dimming, glimmering memories of a distant, glorious past.

'I'm Captain Gerald Taber, military liaison officer,' the man said. 'Welcome to the Enclave.'

And Captain Gerald Taber said: 'We are a high-security military-scientific installation, hermetically sealed and entirely self-sufficient, one of a network of similar bases. We exist in order to provide military and scientific solutions and continuity of administration in the disastrous eventuality of a global catastrophe such as that which has occurred.'

Brochure-speak, Travis suspected. A mission statement memorised for years. Had Captain Taber ever truly imagined the day would come when he'd be compelled to live up to it? In the aftermath of the Sickness, with Scytharene ships thronging the skies above their heads, did he have faith in the answers he and his colleagues were expected to provide?

Because it looked impressive, did the Enclave. Travis had to concede that much as Taber conducted the teenagers through the base. The great domed ceiling where rock and earth had been scooped out. The gleaming steel arches bearing the weight of the hill. The huge glass bubble ensuring that the complex's air supply remained untainted. This upper level was open-plan in design; the group's route along a central walkway enabled them to see prodigious amounts of military hardware on either side, including jeeps, supply trucks and what looked like tanks, though quite how the vehicles had found their way into the Enclave or, indeed, would find their way out again if called upon to do so, seemed something of a mystery. Travis felt as though they'd stumbled on to a set from the latest Bond movie. Yes, it all *looked* impressive.

But looks could be deceptive.

There was plenty of ordnance, plenty of weaponry, but not too many bodies around, it appeared, to put it to use. A handful of soldiers here, another few there, mostly young, mostly unshaven, all intrigued by the new arrivals among them, all affecting nonchalance or inscrutability or confidence. But their eyes betrayed fear. Which Travis could understand. He wasn't criticising. It wasn't as if he was immune to fear himself. Who was? *But* . . . it *was* beginning to occur to him that maybe vanquishing the Scytharene wasn't going to be quite as straightforward as telling the surviving military all they knew and then simply standing back and letting them get on with it. What if they weren't up to the job? Once, he'd been prepared to accept that because an adult was older than him, had greater life experience than him, an adult would necessarily be wiser than he was. To an extent, that might still be true. But Travis also knew now that adults being older didn't make them perfect. It didn't make them infallible. And it certainly didn't make them invulnerable.

The Sickness had proved that. The knife between his father's ribs had proved that.

His eyes met Linden's. He sensed his girlfriend was entertaining similar reservations.

Antony, on the other hand, seemed entirely won over by what Taber was showing them. Maybe he was transferring his allegiance from the Harrington School to the Enclave,

Travis thought. 'And there are other levels besides this, Captain Taber?' the blond boy was asking.

'That is correct, Mr Clive,' said Taber, who after introductions had insisted on retaining a certain formality of address, something else Antony was clearly warming to. 'Two levels besides this. Our arsenal and military training zones here. Immediately below us, the science areas, labs, research facilities, briefing rooms, our monitoring and communications centre. Then finally, below that, accommodation and recreation. We already have rooms prepared for you, but before I take you to them I'd like you to meet our Scientific Director, Dr June Mowatt.'

Who had probably been young in the fifties, bearing in mind the clothes she wore might well have been fashionable then. There was a layer of grey on her hair, like dust, and all the moisture seemed to have been sucked out of her skin over time, giving her a wizened, shrivelled appearance, but the eyes behind her horn-rimmed spectacles were sharp enough, and friendly as she shook the teenagers' hands in the briefing room.

'Sit down, please,' she said, indicating the dozen chairs around a large, circular table. 'Take the weight off your feet. I know you've had a tiring day.'

'And the rest,' muttered Mel.

Dr Mowatt seated herself too, as did Taber. 'Firstly, I must apologise for the rigours and inconvenience of our decontamination procedures. It's not what you want when you first arrive here, is it? I hope, however, you can see why they're necessary. The Sickness is a virus. We have to ensure it does not find its way into the Enclave.'

'Quite right,' agreed Antony with a nod. 'We understand, don't we? Sensible precautions.'

'Are we going to get our guns back, though?' Mel wanted to know.

'The alien weapons are currently being studied by my team of scientists. We obviously need to learn as much as possible about the extraterrestrials' technology so that we can hopefully counteract it.'

'Subjugators,' said Travis – and Dr Mowatt's *hopefully* didn't sound promising. 'The Scytharene call those weapons subjugators.'

'Do they indeed?' The scientist and the soldier exchanged meaningful glances. 'And the Scytharene, you say, Travis. Is that what the aliens call themselves?'

'They speak English.' Hadn't these Enclave people even established that? 'They speak whatever language is native to the part of the world where they've landed, wherever they're carrying out their slaving operations.'

Captain Taber harrumphed and shook his head.

'Slaving?' Dr Mowatt seemed taken aback. 'Oh, my.'

'Slaving, yes,' Travis continued. 'They're *en*slaving every kid on the planet – that's their aim, anyway. I mean, didn't you – haven't you realised?'

'We've seen smaller ships hovering above villages, towns,' Captain Taber said. 'We've seen pods issuing from them and shooting children down.'

'Cullers,' supplied Travis. 'Battlepods.'

'And we've seen the aliens – the Scytharene – take the children's bodies away, but we had no idea to what end. We assumed they were dead.'

'So did we to start with, didn't we, Travis?' Antony charging to Taber's rescue.

'But if you thought they were dead,' reasoned Linden, 'if

you believed the Scytharene were killing kids, why haven't you tried to stop them? You've got the munitions and the men.'

'Lin, we don't know that Dr Mowatt and Captain Taber *haven't* tried to help,' Jessica pointed out.

'Please. Please.' Dr Mowatt raised her hands for quiet.

'Not sure this place is any better than Rich Boy's poncy bloody school,' Richie whispered to Mel.

'You must appreciate our position here,' the Scientific Director said. 'I'm sure Captain Taber has informed you as to our original purpose. The existence of the Enclaves, this and our sister installations across the country, was top secret, of course. The intention was that in response to any disaster of such magnitude that it threatened to fundamentally destabilise society, the various bases would link up and take charge, restore order, prevent anarchy, provide aid. That was the theory.'

'There's a *but* coming, isn't there?' groaned Mel.

'I'm afraid there is, Melanie,' admitted Dr Mowatt candidly. 'I'm afraid, in the event, the panic that afflicted the general population as the Sickness spread infiltrated the Enclaves, too. Not even our decontamination procedures could keep it out. Several of our soldiers lost their nerve. . .'

'I'm ashamed to say,' put in Taber unsympathetically.

'. . . fled the base. To be with their families. To warn the media of what was going on. They must have had their reasons, but however valid they seemed, we couldn't allow our people to reach wider society. We were forced to take steps to bring them back.'

'I *saw* one of those guys!' Linden exclaimed. 'When I was

with . . . I bet it was. I bet he was from here, ranting about what was coming, the end. He killed himself.'

'There was one such unfortunate incident, yes. But thanks to the discipline installed by Captain Taber and the sense of duty among my own scientific team, we coped better than most. At the height of the Sickness, several Enclaves fell subject to outright rebellion. Correct access procedures were not observed. The integrity of those bases was compromised and their personnel became infected by the Sickness. Soon after, communications between ourselves and the other Enclaves broke down. They have yet to be resumed. For all we know, we may be the only Enclave still operational.'

'I can see how that's bad,' Mel accepted. 'Especially as – and I don't want to sound rude – but you don't *seem* very operational to me.'

Dr Mowatt nodded understandingly. 'I'm afraid we have suffered certain . . . depletions of personnel,' she said. 'Patrols that never returned. Individuals leaving the installation secretly and for good – exits are now routinely guarded to prevent further drains on our manpower. The truth is, we number fewer than a hundred now, soldiers and scientists, when our full complement should be nearer a thousand. We have had to limit our ambitions accordingly. And our problems are compounded by the fact that none of us can venture above ground without wearing a protective atmosuit.'

'So instead you choose to stay below ground?' There was a certain accusation in Travis's tone.

Not that Dr Mowatt seemed to detect it. 'Now you see why our intelligence is so partial. If it wasn't for the vigilanteyes—'

'The what?' Mel wasn't sure she'd heard properly.

'The flying eyes. Surveillance drones. Vigilanteyes. It if

wasn't for them, we would have been blind all this time. But now, thanks to the six of you' – Dr Mowatt smiled inclusively – 'we have new ways to see.'

'We watched your capture,' revealed Taber. 'We witnessed your escape.'

'And you didn't kind of think about, I don't know, *helping us out*?' Travis was frankly astonished.

'The vigilanteyes have no offensive capability,' Taber said. 'And we saw no value in committing troops, incurring casualties, alerting the aliens to our presence, not without greater certainty of a successful outcome.'

'You didn't think it might just be the right thing to do to go to the assistance of those who needed help?' Travis pursued.

'An idealistic but naïve position, Mr Naughton,' said Taber with a twitch of the charcoal moustache. 'Right and wrong are not relevant military considerations. Superiority on the field of battle is the only determinant in war.'

'And you might be able to furnish us with that superiority, Travis,' Dr Mowatt broke in. 'All of you. That's why we had the vigilanteye track you and, when we judged it to be safe, approach you and bring you here. You've been inside an alien ship. You have information about these Scytharene that we do not. You can help us *do* the right thing.' Her eyes appealed directly to Travis. 'Will you?'

'But if we hadn't been captured and escaped,' he said, 'if we weren't of immediate use to you, just struggling to survive out there, you'd have ignored us, wouldn't you? You'd have left us to the Scytharene's tender mercies.'

'We would have had no choice,' claimed Dr Mowatt.

There's always a choice, Travis thought.

'Will you help us?' the Scientific Director asked again.

Not that he had much of one now, whatever the deficiencies of the Enclave. Travis hoped he spoke for everyone. 'Of course,' he said.

Simon couldn't believe it. One minute he was languishing in a bare cell, awaiting execution, the next he was here, luxuriating in the lavish kind of accommodation he'd imagined only existed in the Savoy or some other upmarket hotel, certainly not aboard an alien slaveship, certainly not reserved for the sole occupation of someone who hadn't even qualified as one of the slaves. He had to keep putting out his hand to touch everything, the plush chair, the ornate table on which a veritable banquet had been spread for his delectation, just to ensure that his surroundings were solid, substantial, and not an illusion, not an extension of the holograms he'd witnessed during processing. It was all real.

He had Commander Shurion to thank for his sudden change of fortune.

It had been an error on his part to place Simon with the others, Commander Shurion had said. Simon didn't belong in the cells. He hoped that Simon would forgive him his misjudgement and make himself comfortable in the new quarters to which he would be escorted, have something to eat there, relax. Commander Shurion would be along to talk to him again later.

And he'd spoken so reasonably, had Commander Shurion, so amicably, that Simon had begun to think that misjudgements were not confined to Scytharene officers. Maybe Commander Shurion was all right after all.

Simon sat at the table and sampled more of the dishes.

He'd only realised how truly hungry he was when he'd begun to eat. He had plenty of food for thought, too, and an overriding question to answer. *Why?* Why had he been brought here?

Maybe the Scytharene assessed people differently to his own kind. Maybe the aliens weren't so obsessed with superficialities like looks and physical prowess and whether you wore glasses or not and whether you'd ever been kissed by a girl. Or not. Maybe they could see through all that, the shallows of personality, and detect the deeper truth.

Maybe Commander Shurion appreciated Simon more than his fellow teenagers did. Maybe that was why he'd been brought here, to negotiate some kind of deal between human and Scytharene. Maybe the unpleasantness so far had all been a misunderstanding and he'd been chosen to help put things right.

That'd be something, wouldn't it? Simon Satchewell putting things right. Poor old Simes saving the day. Simple Simon elevated from loser to leader. Continuing with his meal, sipping the drink which he thought tasted a little like champagne, Simon began to feel a certain, permissible pride. He'd have Coker eating dirt yet. And Travis, even Travis would have to look up to him in grateful admiration. Because they were all still in the cells but he, Simon, was not. He'd been chosen.

He deserved respect, always had, and at last, it seemed, he was going to get what he deserved.

They'd pretty much been sent to bed, a ritual – 'Isn't it past your bedtime, Melanie?' – Mel had believed lost for ever with the rest of the trappings of the old world. But as soon as Travis had signed them all up to do the right thing and assist the Enclave in whatever way they could – and wasn't *that* a surprise? *Not* – that Dr Mowatt woman had dismissed them all and said there'd be a full debriefing in the morning because '*You could probably all do with a good night's sleep right now.*' Past her bedtime, yeah.

Bet she'd never have a good night's sleep again.

It wasn't that the bed in her little room on level three of the Enclave complex wasn't comfortable. She was lying on it fully clothed now and it was. Her bed back in the dorm at Harrington had been perfectly acceptable, too. It was her mind that wouldn't allow her a peaceful slumber, her memories. One memory.

Herself on the stairs at home. Her father, good old Gerry Patrick, foul, abusive scumbag that he was, gasping with the Sickness. Dad pursuing her upstairs. Him grabbing her wrist – he'd done it many times, grabbed her in lots of places, she'd borne the bruises. Her turning, twisting, flailing to shake herself free. Doing it. And Dad windmilling backwards, losing his balance, losing his grip, falling, crashing to the hall. Breaking his neck. Dying. Dead.

In the real world he was dead. In dreams he still lived, like Freddy Krueger without the finger-knives. But the accusations Dad stabbed her with were sharper than any blade. *You let me die, Melanie. You wanted me to die. You killed me, your own father.* He wouldn't let her rest. She couldn't rest. The more so because, God help her, there was an element of truth in the ghost's denouncing voice. She hadn't deliberately killed him, hadn't actually pushed him. Dad's death had been an accident. *But* . . . she was *glad* he was gone. And the most depressing thing was, while she was still plagued with thoughts of her father, whom she hated, why did her mother, whom she loved, hardly register in her mind at all?

So much was wrong with the world.

Mel rolled on to her side, drew up her knees, clutched them. In the past at times like this, lonely times, she'd have sought solace in the photograph of herself and Jessica that she'd kept hidden and safe in her bedroom, like a love letter. The photograph of them with their arms around each other at a party. The photograph of them smiling, laughing, happy (or in her case, forgetting briefly to be sad). The one that could have been of boyfriend and girlfriend, if either she or Jessie had been a boy. And Mel was thankful Jessie was not.

Boys. Too much like her dad, boys were. Too likely to hurt her. With one or two exceptions, of course. Travis. Because she'd trusted Travis – loved him, really, and still did – she'd *tried* with him. Gone out with him. Kissed him. It hadn't worked. It hadn't felt right. Even *Travis's* hands when they'd been on her had felt like her father's hands. She kind of imagined that if Jessie were to touch her in similar ways, however. . . Jessie didn't have a boyfriend, either, even though . . . even though she was gorgeous. So what did that mean?

If only Mel had the photo with her now, but it was gone. It had been in the pocket of her jeans before processing. It was no doubt still there, unless the Scytharene had burned their captives' clothing, which sounded likely. Incinerated, lost for ever, like the world in which it had been taken. Stolen from her like a last hope of happiness.

But Jessica was still here. Jessica was only yards away, along the corridor in her own room. What was she doing? What would Jessie be doing now, all on her own? Would she be in bed already, asleep? Or would she be awake, lying on her bed as Mel was, or pacing about restlessly, or sitting, staring into space with green and distant eyes? Would she be lonely? Would she be sad? How could she not be?

Would she welcome a knock on the door and a friend?

Maybe the loss of the photograph had done Mel a favour. What, really, had been the point of mooning over a snapshot of the past, a flat, lifeless image made of chemicals and colourings? Jessie, the real her, was nearby. Mel only had to walk, what, a hundred steps to see her, to be with her. Why not? Why wait? It sounded grim, but tomorrow they could all be dead.

Mel swung her legs off the bed and stood. They felt a little weak beneath her.

And Jessie would be glad to see her. Her face would do that kind of lighting-up thing it did whenever she was pleased. And she'd invite Mel in and they'd sit together. On chairs. Or on the bed.

Mel went out into the corridor. The electric light seemed scrutinisingly bright. Mel felt exposed by it.

And Jessie would clearly be unhappy, visibly be upset, and she'd say something like she couldn't carry on, she couldn't cope with this hazardous new life in this harrowing new world alone. And Mel would say she didn't have to. Mel would say she wasn't alone.

The way her pulse was racing, the hundred paces to Jessica's room might have been a hundred thousand.

And she'd put her arm around Jessica and Jessie would let her. And Jessie would rest her head on Mel's shoulder and the black hair and the blonde would look kind of different as their locks commingled but that wouldn't matter. And Mel would say Jessie's name and Jessie would look up into her eyes and they'd see each other clearly then and they'd know. Jessie would know.

Outside Jessica's door Mel paused. Had trouble with her breathing. Knocked and her hand was trembling.

And in her fantasy, Mel would kiss Jessie then. And Jessie would . . .

But of course, she could already be sleeping. The door could be locked.

'Who is it?' She wasn't asleep.

'Mel.'

'Come in.'

And the door wasn't locked.

And Mel went in and Jessie was sitting on the bed alone. 'Mel.' And her face did light up. 'It looks like I'm popular tonight.'

Because she wasn't alone in the room. Someone had taken up residence on a chair.

And Mel felt her heart freeze inside her and the sting of bitter, futile tears.

'Hello, Mel,' said Antony Clive.

Had Mel been in the corridor a few minutes earlier she might have bumped into Linden heading for Travis's room and seen the slightly disconcerted expression on the other girl's face. Linden had taken it upon herself to visit Travis at this late hour, a decision she hadn't actually anticipated being necessary. She'd expected an invitation.

There was still a lot she didn't know – or quite understand –

about her boyfriend. Not surprisingly, really. They'd only met a few weeks ago and, given the hostile nature of life since the Sickness, since the advent of the Scytharene now as well, they hadn't been able to devote a lot of time to long, lingering talks, filling in blanks. When she remembered that Travis's initial reaction on finding her in his grandparents' cottage had been to punch her in the mouth, it was perhaps remarkable that they should be on friendly terms at all, let alone an item. But they were together because, bottom line, Linden knew about Travis all she *needed* to know to want that relationship, to want him.

She did want him. Pretty much immediately.

Back at Harrington he'd said they should wait and she'd agreed (reluctantly). Back at Harrington. Before the aliens came. Before they blasted the school to dust. Linden didn't see much point in waiting now. There was no time to waste. It was what she'd felt during processing, that life was mysterious and wonderful and dear. Life was to be lived, and lived in the moment. She needed to be with Travis now. In every way. Surely he'd feel the same.

All right, she knew Trav could be a little intense. His father's murder had marked him more permanently than any physical wound, she was aware of that, and the Sickness had scarred them all. So Travis saw things in absolutes, in rights and wrongs. So abstract issues like morality mattered to him – she didn't go out of her way to be bad herself. So he had convictions, and the courage to stand up for them. Linden didn't just fancy his bod like mad. It was Travis's sense of purpose, his inner strength, that attracted her to him most of all, the qualities she loved in him. Perhaps because she tended to lack them herself. But she wasn't being weak hurrying to him now, was she? How was this going to be wrong? She'd needed comfort last night in the cell and Travis had given it freely. Tonight she had something she intended to give freely to him in return.

Only there was no response when she knocked at his door. 'Travis, are you in there? It's me, Linden.' She pushed at the door and it opened; Travis hadn't shut it properly. And there was the reason why he hadn't answered her. He couldn't hear her above the hiss of the shower emanating from the bathroom. Smiling, Linden pressed the door home securely, until the lock clicked; interruptions wouldn't be a good idea. Offering her back-scrubbing services to her boyfriend, on the other hand . . .

Even without the cascade of water spurting from the shower-head and drumming against the transparent cubicle walls, however, Travis might not have been aware of Linden's arrival. His mind was focused elsewhere.

On the Scytharene ship. On those he'd left behind. On those he'd failed.

Darion had allegedly picked him out for his leadership potential. Well, maybe the alienologist's judgement was as shaky as his courage. Perhaps he should have searched further afield for an ally to help him successfully execute his own sci-fi version of *The Great Escape*. Antony, possibly, or even Leo Milton. Or Mel: there was no need to impose sexist limitations on the candidates. Someone who might actually get away with more than a pitiful five companions.

Travis thought of the trail of unconscious bodies marking their route from the cell to the woods. He thought of Simon and those others he hadn't even been able to offer a chance of freedom. He ought to have done better. His dad would have

145

done better. He, Travis, had let his father down, his father's memory. He felt ashamed.

Hence the shower. It wasn't that he needed one physically. After the Enclave's decontamination procedures, he could hardly have been cleaner. But there were other kinds of stains that required other kinds of cleansing, and there was guilt that couldn't be washed away with soap and water. Travis was trying. It wasn't working.

But at least, maybe, possibly, he'd be granted an opportunity to redeem himself. The Enclave had the weapons that might hurt the Scytharene. What it didn't seem to have was the will. Taber and Mowatt seemed content merely to cower in their subterranean stronghold, observe the Scytharene's depredations from a safe distance and bemoan their lot. Maybe it was because they were old, their lives lived for more than half a century in a world that had vanished and left them stranded. Time as well as circumstances was curtailing their future. But Travis had decades ahead of him yet – so did the others – and he wasn't prepared to give those years up or spend them in slavery. He'd fight for them. Let the Enclave provide the weapons; *he'd* supply the will to use them.

And there was somebody in the bathroom. A shadow against the cubicle wall.

'Who the . . .?' Travis slid the door back violently.

'Room for one more in there?' grinned Linden.

'Lin, what . . .?' Aware of her eyes on him.

'I realise I'm kind of overdressed, but we can soon sort that.' She began to unbutton her tunic.

'Lin, what the hell do you think you're doing?'

And when she saw Travis grab a towel and wrap it round

his waist, Linden knew things weren't going to go as planned. She'd rather hoped he'd be grabbing her.

He turned the shower off.

'What the hell do I think I'm doing? Hmm, that's not quite the welcome I expected, Travis.'

'Come on, into the other room.' Dripping wet, Travis ushered her through. 'How did you get in?'

'Door was open. You want me to go out again?'

'No, of course not.' Travis heard the displeasure in Linden's voice, which wasn't fair. She shouldn't have surprised him like that. He had things on his mind. 'I just wasn't expecting . . . it's late.'

'Bedtime,' said Linden. 'I know. You want me to help dry you off, Trav?'

She reached out her hand to stroke his bare chest. Travis seized her wrist before it could get there.

'Tempting offer, Lin, but now is not the time.'

'Now is not the time?' She was doing a good line in repeating Travis's words tonight. 'It never is with you, though, Travis, is it? When would be a good time for you and me? Should I make an appointment?'

'Don't be infantile, Linden.' Travis's turn with the displeasure.

'Don't be infantile? I seem to remember you promising you'd never let go of me.' She wrenched her hand free. 'What happened to that, then, huh? It's like you don't even want us to touch now.'

'That's not true.'

'And just at the moment when we can, just when the moment's right—'

'But that's exactly it, Lin,' Travis objected. 'The moment

147

isn't right. Not while we've still got friends imprisoned aboard the Scytharene ship. Not while we still might be able to save them if we work quickly. They might not have been put in the cryo-tubes yet. I let them down before, but—'

Linden shook her head emphatically. 'You didn't let anybody down, Travis. You did the best you could.'

'Yeah? A shit kind of best, then.'

'Shit is what you're talking. Without you, Trav, none of us would have made it. Come on, you mustn't agonise so much. It's not healthy. Here, let me . . .' She tried with both hands this time, found his shoulders with them and squeezed, pressed herself against him, brushed his lips with hers.

He stepped away.

'I can't, Linden. Not now. Not yet. We shouldn't . . . how can we think about ourselves when the Scytharene are out there capturing, enslaving kids just like us? We've got to fight them. We've got to stop them.'

'I agree with you, but—'

'We can't afford personal distractions, Lin. I – we have to focus all our energies on the bigger picture.'

'Saving the world, huh?' Linden gave a hollow laugh. 'Is that it, Travis? Saving the world? I guess you can't get a much bigger picture than that. Oh, I know all about saving the world. I've lived with people wanting to do that most of my life. The Children of Nature, for a start. Mostly they wanted to do it by sitting on their arses in the middle of a forest growing beards, eating berries and claiming benefits. They didn't change anything and they weren't ever going to, but one thing I will say for them, Trav, at least they knew what they wanted to save the world *for.*'

'I don't—'

'People, Travis. They cared about people. People *are* the world. And what people feel for each other when they're in love, what two people do together out of love, that's what makes the world good, what makes it *worth* saving. Love – you and me, Trav, being together tonight, which is what I want, which is why I'm here – I think that's kind of more than a personal distraction, don't you? I mean, don't turn your back on it, Travis. If you do, what's the *point* of fighting the Scytharene? Please, Trav, I want to stay with you. Don't make me go.'

His brow creased but his voice was firm enough, inflexible. 'It wouldn't be right, Lin. It wouldn't *feel* . . . I'm sorry.'

'Sorry?' she sighed, rebuttoning her tunic. 'Yeah. Me too. See you in the morning, Travis.'

He didn't want her to leave like that, not understanding. He wanted to call out to her, to make her see. He had to think about others besides himself, before himself. He had responsibilities. He had to lead. It was a matter of priorities. He did love her, but . . .

She wasn't there to hear.

When the door opened, Simon expected his caller to be a member of the ship's crew bringing him breakfast. It wasn't. It was Commander Shurion.

'Good morning, Simon,' the Scytharene said. 'I trust you slept well.'

'Yes, sir, thank you, sir.' Simon blinked behind his glasses. Shurion was still maintaining a veneer of politeness, but there was something different about him this morning, a colder undertone in the voice, a steelier glint in the scarlet eyes.

'If you're expecting breakfast, I have something to show you first. I thought it might not be sensible for you to eat until you have seen it.'

Which didn't sound particularly encouraging. Simon gulped.

'Screen: disposal cell, one minute prior to disposal.'

He gulped again as at Shurion's instruction one of the walls revealed the interior of Simon's previous accommodation. The *disposal* cell? Digby was still there, wandering in a kind of weary circle. The boy in the corner was still coughing – Simon could hear as well as see. The two scrawny girls still clung to each other. Though not, perhaps, for long. *One minute prior to disposal?*

'You are about to witness what happened last evening,' Shurion said. 'While you were eating your fill here. Be grateful, my young friend, that you were not *there.'* Jabbing a bone-white finger at the screen.

'I am grateful, Commander Shurion, sir.' Simon nodded as vigorously as if he was trying to shake his glasses off. 'Very, very grateful.' Nervously beginning to rub his thumbs and forefingers together. Silently, fearfully, counting down the seconds from a minute. 'What – can I ask? – what did happen last evening?' Thinking he might want to be prepared.

'Watch,' ordered Commander Shurion.

As, within the disposal cell, a droning hum commenced. The sudden sound surprised the eight inmates as much as it did Simon, who was reminded of an engine warming up. Its volume increased, steadily, in an ominous crescendo.

Words were exchanged in the cell. Simon couldn't catch the syllables but he could assess the tone. Anxious. Panicky. Alarmed. Digby paced more quickly, more agitatedly in his

150

perpetual circle. The boy in the corner staggered to his feet. The girls embraced more tightly still.

'What's – what's . . .?' Simon's mouth was dry with fear.

As every panel in the ceiling of the cell began to glow, began to colour, blushing the modest pink of a girl on her first date. And it seemed to Simon now that the incessant, intensifying hum was concentrated in these panels, generated by them.

And their pinkness deepened into red, into scarlet, as though something inside them was bleeding.

The prisoners were shouting. They were having to. And even then they were dumb to Simon. They were like mime artists, playing terror, performing despair. Only none of it was pretence. And they were . . . perspiring, it appeared. Sweating as if the panels were suns. Dark patches dampened their clothes. And the boy who'd been coughing was gasping now. And Digby had taken to pounding his plump fists against the door.

His clothes were smouldering.

The hum beat at Simon's ears like an endless sequence of blows, deafening him. He glanced across to Commander Shurion. The alien was observing the events in the disposal cell with total emotional detachment, as one might look on having dusted an ants' nest with insecticide.

Digby, Simon thought. *Oh, God.* Because he kind of knew what was coming. The crimson panels, blindingly bright, scalding the retina. The tumultuous din of the energy imminently to be unleashed. They were dead in the disposal cell. They'd been dead for hours, all the while he, Simon, had been sleeping. But, and this thought did occur to him, though he wished it hadn't, *better them than him.*

And on the screen Digby died again, the moment of his immolation immortalised. As the grey tunic and the grey trousers spontaneously combusted, whooshed with flame, and as his hair ignited and his limbs and his head. Digby was burning. The coughing boy, too. The girls, crackling together like twin guys on a bonfire. All of them ablaze. And if they were screaming until their vocal cords were incinerated, Simon was grateful he couldn't hear them.

His stomach heaved. Shurion had been wise to keep breakfast back for the moment.

But at least he was spared the grisly spectacle of eight charred corpses. Hardly had they erupted than the shooting flames were dissipating, seeming to dissolve into nothingness, disintegrating, and with them the bodies. Digby and the others, they were dark smudges in space, they were the merest shapes of human beings, shadows and smoke. They were atoms in the air.

They were gone.

Simon stared at the empty disposal cell. The panels' colour faded. He could hear his own laboured breathing and thumping heartbeat: the hum had ended now that its work was done. Simon had thought he knew what horror was already, but like everything terrible in life, horror was chillingly versatile and paralysingly ingenious: the forms it could take were infinite. Every one was too much to bear for Simon Satchwell.

'Disposal,' Commander Shurion summarised. 'This is what happens to those aliens for which we can find no use. I thought it best for you to be aware of that before our little talk, Simon. Screen: off.'

'What – Commander Shurion, sir – what about my other

friends?' Simon ventured. If the same thing happened to *Travis* . . .

'Your other . . . friends?' In a tone that suggested Shurion knew something he was not yet prepared to divulge. 'Sit down, Simon. And do not be afraid. The fate suffered by your former companions will not befall you.'

Thank God, Simon thought. Thank *God*. He'd do anything not to die like that. Anything at all.

'You are probably thinking that we Scytharene are cruel, heartless, even evil. Yes?'

'Uh . . .' How to answer *that* so you'd still be breathing tomorrow?

Fortunately, the Scytharene seemed to have been speaking rhetorically. 'If so, you mistake the nature of the universe. Belief systems that have come to be called moralities, concepts of right and wrong, good and evil, are irrelevant to life. They are delusions, philosophical affectations, more often than not used as spurious justifications for one group to impose itself upon another – this has been so on countless occasions on your own planet, has it not, Simon? It is the same throughout the galaxy. The reality is, however, that only one quality matters if one's people are to survive and prosper, and that quality is *strength*. The only true division in all of creation is that between the weak and the strong. Every species, every race, every living being is born to be one or the other, hunter or prey, leader or led, master or slave. We Scytharene recognised that inescapable and incontrovertible truth early in our history and made ourselves strong. We accepted reality and made ourselves masters. We are *your* masters, Simon.'

Who bowed his head. He was in no position to contradict

the alien. He'd never been in much of a position to contradict anyone.

'The human race has shown itself to be innately, genetically inferior to ourselves. You are a weak and conquered people. You have proven yourselves suited only to be slaves, and slaves you shall become. With certain exceptions. Such as those who are too puny even to function profitably *as* slaves – they will be disposed of as you have seen. But others will prosper, those in whom we sense potential, those in whom our instruments detect characteristics that find favour with us, qualities that might in time convince us to number their possessors not among the weak, but among the strong, at our side. Only a fortunate few find themselves in that privileged position, my young friend, and you are one of them.'

'What?' Was that good? It sounded good. *Privileged* always sounded good. Did it mean he was going to live? What did he have to do to live?

Shurion smiled faintly. 'Processing taught us much about you, Simon. I suspect your life has been difficult, has it not? I suspect your peers have never fully appreciated you or understood you, have they? I can see the struggle of your life, Simon. Undervalued. Underestimated. Victimised unfairly? Tormented? The object of derision. The butt of jokes.'

All true, of course. And Simon didn't want to cry, not here, not now, in front of Commander Shurion, but even his own tears treated him with contempt.

'You have been forced to walk a lonely path, my young friend, have you not? And for so many years. They excluded you, didn't they, the others? They turned you into an outsider, spurned you, your own kind, never knowing your true worth.

But *I* know your true worth, Simon Satchwell, and I am offering you the chance to belong.'

'With . . . you?' Simon was confused. His mind was a maelstrom of emotions, bitterness, sorrow, hate, companions who never strayed far from him. 'I don't understand.'

'Demonstrate your loyalty to us, Simon, and we will be loyal to you.'

'How? I mean . . .' It was a trick. Had to be. Shurion was attempting to take advantage of his weakness, to deceive him. Travis would refuse to listen to any more. He ought to do what Travis would do. Travis had never let him down. It was *Travis* who deserved his allegiance. Simon whimpered: 'I can't . . .' But what if the only alternative was the disposal cell?

'Ah, how brave of you to say *can't*, Simon,' acknowledged Shurion with an admiring nod of his ghost-white head. 'How noble. I chose wisely when I chose you. You believe you should be loyal to those whom earlier you called your friends, don't you?'

'Yes.'

'You believe that if you ally yourself with us you would be betraying those friends, don't you?'

'Y-yes.'

'But they are not your friends, Simon. And they have already betrayed *you*.'

Simon didn't believe it. What Commander Shurion went on to tell him, he didn't want to believe it. The others engineering an escape, that wasn't the issue. It was what he would have expected – no doubt Travis was its instigator and its inspiration. But that they should seek freedom for themselves and simply abandon him, Digby and the rest, run out on them, *that* was what he couldn't accept. At first. But Commander Shurion insisted it was so. They'd had help, he told Simon. A Scytharene traitor had shown them how to break out of their cell. Equipped with such knowledge, they could have searched the other cells until they'd located Simon and his late companions. If they'd wanted to. If they could have been bothered. But they hadn't. They'd fled at once to save their own skins. They didn't care about Simon. They'd proved that.

'N-no.' Simon fought to be sure. 'I don't . . . believe it.' Travis wouldn't just leave him behind. He'd promised he wouldn't. And if he'd broken his promise, well, that would make Travis no better than the others. No better than Coker. Where could Simon go if that were true?

And Shurion was showing him glimpses of the escape on the screen, people he recognised, Mel, Jessica, Travis, that Linden and Antony Clive – *Coker* – outside the ship and racing for the woods. Others falling by the wayside, but those he'd fooled himself into considering his friends, his only friends, making it. And Travis and Mel, Coker, Clive, they were armed. They *could* have tried to find him. The subjugators would have bought them time enough for that. Commander Shurion said so.

'Or perhaps the traitor among my own crew suggested liberating those of you in the disposal cell and your' – a pause – 'friends declined. Perhaps they thought you would only slow them down. Whatever the exact course of events, actions speak louder than protestations of loyalty, my young friend. The truth is, they deserted you. You owe them nothing.'

Yet Travis had taken Richie Coker with him. Again he'd

valued Coker above Simon. That was bad. It was wrong (unforgivable). Travis ought to be shown *how* wrong.

'The Scytharene traitor I spoke of has still to be captured,' said Shurion with anger in his eyes. 'My interrogations of the Earthers we recaptured have revealed that only the one called Travis Naughton knows his identity.'

Of course, Simon thought, and bitterly. Travis knew everything. Including how to act like your friend – all the while it suited him. (Unforgivable.)

'This is how you can help me, Simon.' Shurion's voice insinuated itself into Simon's consciousness like a serpent. 'And help yourself, too. This is how you can prove you are strong enough to be the Scytharene's friend. I need to know the name of the traitor.'

'But how can I find it out if—'

'I am going to set you free, Simon. Find this Travis Naughton. Learn the name from him. Your reward for carrying out this small task will be great, for completing it successfully will spare you the captivity that awaits your kind and mark your transition from slave to master.'

And that'd be something, wouldn't it? Slave to master? That'd show Travis, all right. That'd show them all. He'd been right last evening. Commander Shurion *did* see him for what he was.

And yet . . . 'You want me to be your spy,' Simon said. It sounded wrong put like that.

'Our *agent*,' Shurion revised, which sounded better. '*My* agent. Nobody knows about our little arrangement but you and me, so young Travis cannot possibly be warned. I am placing my trust in you, Simon. When was the last time any of your so-called friends did that?'

It was a fair point. They'd left him to die. (Unforgivable.) They must have known, must have guessed his likely fate. *Bastards.* Coker. Clive. The girls. Girls had never liked him, not really, not even Jessica Lane. *Bastards.*

'What do you say, Simon?'

And Travis. Travis most of all. Travis more than any of them. Said one thing. Did another. Made promises he never intended to keep, promises that were lies. *Bastard bloody bastard.*

'Will you accept a new allegiance? Will you become a Scytharene agent?'

Simon had endured enough misery and suffering in his life. It was someone else's turn now. *Travis's* turn. He didn't want to die and he wouldn't. (Unforgivable.) He looked Commander Shurion squarely in the eye, finding a kind of fearlessness in his own sense of hurt and rage and injustice. And with a single, simple nod of the head, he consented.

From now on, Simon Satchwell would side with the Scytharene.

SEVEN

The missiles appeared from nowhere.

One moment there was a cloudless sky and the Scytharene ship basking in the sun as if it belonged here in England on the outskirts of an empty town. The next, the peacefulness of the morning was shattered by the scream of the missiles searing into view and streaking groundwards.

They had only one target.

But the Scytharene ship appeared entirely unperturbed by its potential destruction. It maintained a lofty silence while the hail of missiles shrieked ever nearer, disdaining – it seemed – even to defend itself. It glistened silver in the sunlight and it waited.

Whoever had programmed the missiles had done their job well. Not one of them was going to miss their mark.

None of them did. The salvo struck the ship in a barrage of detonations of such tremendous power that the earth shook and the buildings in the immediate vicinity exploded, as if expressing solidarity with the alien craft. An unnecessary gesture as it turned out.

The missiles, full of sound and fury, had signified nothing. They'd caused not a dent of damage to the mighty scythe of the Scytharene ship, not a blemish, not a scratch. Perhaps the shimmering, crackling blue sheath which now entirely coated its surface had something to do with it.

'An energy shield,' said Dr June Mowatt, though the six teenagers had already guessed that. 'Rendering the ship impervious to harm, immune to attack.' They'd pretty much seen that for themselves as well. Dr Mowatt tapped her knuckles against the large screen in the briefing room in front of which the seven of them and Captain Taber were gathered. 'Not long after this bombardment failed, the Scytharene launched several of their – Cullers, did you call them? – their Cullers. We must assume they traced the origin of the missiles and retaliated. We must also assume, given that similar assaults on the aliens are almost nonexistent now, that their offensives have proven rather more effective than those of our countrymen.' She switched the screen off and returned to her seat at the table. 'When I told you yesterday that communications had not been resumed between Enclaves, I neglected to explain that the reasons for this are not wholly technical. We're reluctant to even attempt to restore communications in case the Enclave we contact is overrun by Scytharene, who may then learn of our existence. We're not ready to fight them yet.'

'Well you'd better *get* ready – with respect,' said Travis, who seemed to the others tetchier this morning than usual. 'And soon. Or there won't be any point. It'll be too late. The cryotubes will be full.'

'It would be madness to engage the enemy when our weapons cannot penetrate their defensive shield, Mr Naughton,' said Captain Taber. 'It would be a waste of men and munitions. Purposeless sacrifice does not win wars.'

'Neither does sitting around doing nothing,' snapped Travis.

'Easy, Trav.' Mel stroked his back. She was surprised

Linden wasn't sitting beside Travis, but the girl with russet hair had opted to occupy a place next to Richie on the opposite side of the table. 'Captain Taber's got a point, hasn't he?'

'Haven't *I*?' Travis retorted. 'That footage was of a different ship to where we were held. How do we know Shurion's ship is also equipped with shields like that?'

'I think Captain Taber's response would be, if I may, Travis,' intervened Antony, 'how do we know it *isn't*? What sense would it make for some ships to have shields and others not? They must all be anticipating an attack somewhere down the line.'

Travis grunted sceptically. 'Well the way things are going here, Commander Shurion's going to be disappointed.'

'I understand your feelings, Mr Naughton,' said Taber, 'but I cannot authorise action and jeopardise the lives of my troops without at least first knowing how to neutralise the aliens' shields.'

'I imagine that's something your scientists are working on, isn't it, Dr Mowatt?' assumed Antony.

'My scientists are working on many things,' Dr Mowatt said with pride. 'In shifts, twenty-four hours a day. Attempting to identify the nature of the energy employed by the Scytharene in their shields, yes. Looking for ways to strike back at them.' With a sidelong glance at Travis. 'Trying to find a cure for the Sickness itself. We have information sent to us by colleagues who were working at a research establishment in the desert – before they died. One of the cylinders that we now know brought the virus to Earth was discovered nearby. Their findings are proving to be of some assistance to us, but – Archimedes' eureka moment aside – progress in science takes time.'

'Time the Scytharene are spending harvesting slaves,' Travis scowled. 'Listen, you may be right about not mounting any kind of full-scale operation just yet – I'll accept that – but there are other things we can do in the mean time, aren't there? Look at all the space we've got down here, corridors of empty rooms on the accommodation level. Why don't we fill them? Why don't we get your vigilanteyes to lead kids here and then they can be looked after. Save them from being rounded up. We can do that, can't we?'

'That's a great idea, Trav.' Mel patted his arm.

'It really is,' enthused Jessica. 'Even if we end up having to share our rooms.'

'No one's sharing *my* room,' grumbled Richie, arms folded defensively.

'Who would want to?' said Mel.

Antony said nothing.

Linden glanced at Travis with an expression that mixed disappointment and resentment with grudging admiration and sheer physical desire, but she looked at him only for a second before her eyes were drawn by a spot on the tabletop that apparently merited the most intense study.

'We *could* do as you propose, Mr Naughton,' admitted Taber reluctantly, though when the *but* came nobody was surprised, least of all Travis, 'but the Enclave is not geared to cope with a steady – effectively endless – influx of what would really be refugees, many of whom would be very young, requiring the kind of care and attention we could not possibly provide—'

'So it's a no, then,' Travis interrupted. 'You're in charge, Captain Taber. You can say it. You don't have to go on. No to saving kids from the Scytharene.'

'We will save children when we can *defeat* the Scytharene,' responded Taber. 'Not before. The presence of children here at this time will be a distraction that we cannot afford.'

Linden laughed aloud at that, briefly and bitterly. 'Sorry,' she said. 'I have a thing about the word distraction.'

'Are you all right, Linden?' Jessica asked, and apparently she was, though the blonde girl wasn't so sure. She was sensing a lot of tension around the table today, within the group. Travis was behaving a little out of character, for a start. What he was saying was still very Trav, but he wasn't normally so confrontational. And he and Linden were barely looking at each other. Had they fallen out or something? And Mel, she seemed uncomfortable, too, like she had something on her mind. Jessica doubted her friend would even have sat with herself and Antony at breakfast had she not called her over. And Mel had left her room last night only minutes after arriving, just before Antony did, too, as it happened. Maybe she'd wanted to talk or something then. Further round the table, Richie was his usual sullen self, though Jessica felt that even the one-time bully's mood was exaggerated somewhat this morning. Maybe Richie had hoped that someone might have come knocking on his door for a chat last night and no one had.

Only Antony seemed the same as ever. Or did he? Was she imagining it, or did there seem to be a rift opening between Antony and Travis that hadn't been there before? She hoped she was wrong. Travis and Antony were the two most important boys in her life. One she loved like a brother. The other – Antony – how did she feel about Antony Clive? With the slightest of smiles that hinted at previously unadmitted possibilities, Jessica thought it safer to snap out of her reverie and focus again on what was being said around the table.

'I promised I wouldn't reveal his name.' Travis.

'Not even to us.' Antony, with a hint of criticism.

'But that was so anyone recaptured during the escape wouldn't be able to give him away to Shurion. Situation's changed since then. I guess it's more important that you do know who helped us. His name's Darion and he could be our only hope.'

'Darion,' Antony said. 'Your new best friend, Travis?'

'Lord Darion, born of the bloodline of Ayrion of the Thousand Families,' Travis expanded, 'to give him his full title. And he might well turn out to be the best friend any of us have got, Antony.'

'We clearly need to hear all you know about this Lord Darion, Travis, don't we, Captain Taber?'

'We do, Dr Mowatt,' Taber agreed. 'I suggest we therefore commence the young people's individual debriefing with Mr Naughton.'

'That'd be right,' hooted Richie. 'First in line again, leader-man.'

And Jessica noticed Antony frown.

'Everyone else,' said Dr Mowatt, 'you may leave. Take the opportunity to rest some more, why not? Relax. Or make use of the recreational facilities, if you wish.'

'Is this a military-scientific installation or a glorified gym?' Mel muttered to Linden on their way out.

'You'll be called when we need you,' Dr Mowatt assured them.

'In that case, take your time, Trav.' Mel waved.

He intended to. It was probably wrong of him, cowardly, but given the rather fraught nature of their parting last night, Travis felt he'd sooner delay the moment of finding himself alone again with Linden for as long as possible. 'So, Captain Taber, Dr Mowatt,' he said. 'Where would you like me to start?'

Shurion reported to Fleet Commander Gyrion from the privacy of his quarters. Ordinarily, he liked to be ensconced high in his command chair and arrayed in full ceremonial robes when conferring with those who had chanced to acquire a superior rank to himself. He liked to think he was making a kind of statement to his bridge crew by doing so, proving that Shurion of the bloodline of Tyrion was intimidated by nobody and had by his own efforts made himself at least the equal of anybody, accidents of birth notwithstanding. On this occasion, however, he thought it advisable to keep what might pass between himself and the Fleet Commander a matter for the two of them alone. If he was to be upbraided, Shurion had no desire for his crew to witness it.

His decision was a wise one. Fleet Commander Gyrion was not happy. His golden cloak and armour shone as his image filled the wallscreen; Shurion's largely black uniform looked common and dowdy in comparison.

'An escape? From our custody?' Gyrion's eyes blazed with crimson fire.

'Attempted escape, Fleet Commander,' Shurion moderated. 'All but six of the Earther slaves were immediately recaptured and have now been committed to the cryo-tubes in preparation for trans—'

'Then six of the aliens are still at large, Shurion, is that what you're telling me?' pressed Gyrion unsympathetically. 'Six sources of shame for yourself and the *Furion*.'

'They were aided, Lord Gyrion, by one of our kind, a reprehensible traitor who—'

'And by your own incompetence, too, Shurion, no?'

'I refute the accusation of incompetence, my lord.' As humbly as he could manage.

'Why? You are the *Furion*'s commander, are you not?' Gyrion established. 'For the time being, at least.' And Shurion seethed at the implications of that casual aside. 'The responsibility of crew selection is yours, with the exception of anyone belong to the Thousand Families, of course, such as my son. As commander, therefore, you *allowed* a traitor aboard your ship, Shurion. You are accountable.'

'Yes,' Shurion was forced to concede, unwillingly, through gritted teeth, 'my lord.'

'Whoever this vermin is,' Gyrion muttered in a voice as cold as a razor blade, 'he must have contacts in the dissident movement. Weak, lamentable bleeding hearts, all of them. Criminals and cowards. They ought to have their hearts cut out and bleeding for real.' His white fingers twitched as if willing and eager to offer their services in that direction. 'What measures have you taken to apprehend this villain, Shurion?'

'I have recruited one of the Earthers to our cause, my lord, as a spy. He'll discover the traitor's name from the only slave who knows it, one of the few still at liberty. They are acquaintances, it seems. Our informant will be trusted. I have also—'

'Enough,' snarled Gyrion. 'Enough. You have *recruited* one of the Earthers? Is the pure and proud Scytharene race now dependent upon filthy aliens to expose our own criminals? By the gods of the Thousand Families . . .'

166

'Perhaps it takes a traitor to catch a traitor, Fleet Commander,' suggested Shurion.

Gyrion snorted sardonically. 'Perhaps it does, Shurion. You had better hope so.'

'My lord?'

'A commander of true honour would already have resigned his position after the debacle that has befallen the *Furion*. Even an officer selected from outside the Thousand Families should be aware of that, *Commander* Shurion.'

'I am aware of my duty, my lord.' And even though respect for superior officers was generally accepted to be part of it, Shurion could barely contain his contempt for the arrogant, complacent, patronising Fleet Commander. 'I believe my duty is to put right what has gone wrong aboard my ship. I appeal to you, permit me to remain at my post in order to do so.'

'Hmm.' Gyrion grunted, unimpressed. 'There was a time in my youth when the command of slavecraft was awarded only to members of the Thousand Families. In those days, standards could be guaranteed. We didn't have mass alien breakouts then, or traitors in our midst. This is what happens when we are persuaded to relax the rightful rigidity of our social hierarchy even by a little.'

Shurion's fists were clenched. He hoped Gyrion couldn't see or wouldn't register that fact.

'But it would perhaps be premature to dismiss you now, Shurion,' the Fleet Commander granted, though with a degree of reluctance. 'Even so, consider yourself on trial. I want the traitor caught. We must make an example of him so bloody that we will strike fear into the cowardly, corrupt hearts of his fellow dissidents. Succeed in finding the deviant, Shurion, and all will be well for you.'

'I pledge I will send you the traitor's head if you desire it, my lord.'

'Ensure you are in a position to do so, Shurion, for if you fail, I will certainly be sending for yours.'

Shurion waited – prudently – until the Fleet Commander had brought their interview to an end before venting his spleen. Then he didn't hold back. He howled in fury, smashed his fists against the table. It was white. It could substitute for Gyrion's puffy, pampered face. How dare anyone speak to him like that! How dare even a member of the Thousand Families belittle and berate him in such a manner! He, Shurion of the bloodline of Tyrion, who'd fought and battled and clawed his way up from the ranks to gain the lofty prominence he occupied now. He hadn't been gifted his status like the Fleet Commander. He'd earned it, by blood and sweat and toil, sacrificed for it, dedicated every fibre of his being to his advancement. And he knew his own worth, did Shurion. He *deserved* to be where he was. In fact, he deserved more. He deserved to be Fleet Commander in Gyrion's place, to have at his bidding not just one slavecraft but ten, a hundred, a thousand. What right did a moribund fool like Gyrion have to deny him the final fulfilment of his ambitions?

Every right, of course, according to Scytharene law. The right of birth. The right of blood. The right that all elites on every world Shurion had ever visited insisted was theirs to perpetuate their own power and to prevent others from sharing it, whatever their personal merits. Shurion looked down at himself, at his armour, at his robes, the uniform that conveyed to his fellow Scytharenes who and what he was. Once he'd been proud that his black warrior's garb had been supplemented by a commander's cloak, and both adorned with gold, the colour of the Thousand Families, to symbolise the high esteem in which his people held him. Now the glittering embellishments seemed to mock him, and wrapped around his body like chains. Because they indicated that he had reached the summit of his career; he was allowed to rise no higher. Above him only the Thousand Families remained, unreachable, their power and influence forever unattainable for one not born to wear armour of purest gold.

It wasn't fair. It wasn't just. And now, thanks to the treacherous antics of one cursed dissident, all that Shurion *had* achieved might be taken away from him. Well, he would ensure that did not happen. One way or another, he would track the traitor down.

And make him pay.

'You seem troubled, son,' Gyrion observed from the wallscreen. 'Is anything wrong?'

'No, Father, of course not,' Darion lied. 'It's simply . . . I'm concerned about the incident with the Earthers, and with a traitor still at large . . . What else did Commander Shurion say about his Earther spy?'

It was fast turning into an afternoon of unpleasant surprises for Darion. First, his father seeing fit to be sociable, having finished with Shurion, thus interrupting Darion's studies in his quarters. Second, learning that the *Furion*'s commander was sending one of Travis's acquaintances after him on a mission to learn the Scytharene traitor's name. Well, it was a name with which Darion was already rather familiar. As, indeed, if he only knew it, was his father.

Darion shuddered inwardly at the news. Here was a development he hadn't foreseen and didn't appreciate. It was probably unlikely, but what if Shurion's informant *did* manage to catch up with Travis Naughton and glean from him the name? It would mean torture. It would mean death. Yet, somehow, though he was afraid, Darion didn't repent of what he'd done. He was still glad.

'Father? Did Commander Shurion provide any details about this spy?'

Gyrion shrugged. 'Just an Earther. Isn't that detail enough? Why would you want to know more, Darion?'

'No reason.' Composedly. 'I just hope the Commander has chosen his agent well, that's all.'

'I imagine Shurion hopes the same,' Gyrion said with a cryptic chuckle. 'Are you certain nothing else is disturbing you?' Apparently Darion *was* sure. 'Hmm.' The father inclined his head as if he knew his son a little better than that. 'I'm not convinced you're being quite frank with me, Darion. I suspect I know what the real matter is.'

'You do?' Darion doubted that. If only his father would get to goodbye so he could *think*.

'Lack of companionship, is it not? Being forced to live apart for so long from those of your own class.'

'You're right, Father,' Darion flattered with a wondering smile. 'You're absolutely right. However did you guess?'

'I'm your father, Darion. You can hide nothing from me. I told you it would be difficult for you, the only representative of the Thousand Families living among our inferiors for months on end.'

'You did, yes, Father,' remembered Darion. 'I should have listened to you.' Only he'd been too desperate at the time to leave every last representative of the Thousand Families (save one) behind him, preferably for ever. A fact he judged it impolitic to mention to his father now. 'Perhaps if I transferred to the *Ayrion III* . . .'

'No, no.' Gyrion dismissed the idea of his son joining him aboard his flagship out of hand. 'That wouldn't do in the middle of an enslavement. But I think I can help. The *Ayrion III* is stationed outside the Earther city of Oxford as you know. The city is in the process of being harvested at the moment, so alienological operations have yet to begin. Which means . . .'

Despite the dangers of his present situation, Darion's heart leapt in anticipation.

'. . . I can spare a certain alienologist for a short period, I imagine, someone who might be persuaded to pay you a brief visit during that time, remind you of the civilised society you've been missing.' Gyrion spoke with a father's indulgence. 'Would you like me to arrange that for you, son?'

'Oh, yes,' said Darion.

And soon. Too much of a delay and Darion might be receiving visitors in a cell.

She had to act quickly. While Travis was still being debriefed. Before anyone else was summoned by Mowatt and Taber. While she could rely on Antony and Jessica both being around.

Mel wasn't proud of what she was planning to do, but she felt she had little choice. She couldn't allow Jessie to get involved with the former Head Boy of the Harrington School, not in the kind of way that seemed to be threatening to happen, the relationships kind of way, *romantically.*

She hated that word – *romantic*. It was such a fraud, such a lie. Romance these days – pre-Sickness days, at any rate – meant a couple of bottles of cheap cider and a spotty, drooling lad pawing about inside your top or under your skirt – and you *letting* him. Romance meant forgetting who you really were, abdicating your independence to pander to the whims and fantasies of someone else. Romance meant heartbreak and unhappiness. But Mel was losing her thread.

It wasn't that Antony was a bad person. She hadn't known him long (though, of course, neither had Jessie), but he did seem nice enough, decent enough. He wasn't going to go out and deliberately hurt Jessica, even Mel had to concede that much. But he was still male. He was still a boy. And boys became men and men became fathers, fathers like hers, and when it came to relationships with girls, boys had bad news ingrained in their DNA. Mel was really only trying to do Jessica a favour, to save her from herself. She just hoped she wasn't too late. What if Antony had stayed in Jessie's room last night, *all* night, taken advantage of her best friend's sweet, trusting nature? Nah. She doubted that. From her acquaintance with girls who had Done It with their boyfriends (and all too often, shortly after *having* Done It, *ex*-boyfriends), they kind of gave off different signals afterwards, were kind of smugger than they'd been before, like they knew a secret that you didn't. Jessie wasn't behaving anything like that this morning. Mel still had a chance to ensure her friend wouldn't be behaving like that *any* morning in the foreseeable future.

She just had to act quickly.

'Hey, Jessie!' Catching up with the blonde girl as they returned to the accommodation level from the briefing room.

'Can I' – whispering – 'have a word' – then mouthing the syllables silently – 'in private?'

'Sure.' Jessie had clearly been right that something was bothering Mel. 'See you in a bit, Antony.' Who'd been keeping in step alongside her so precisely they could have been competing in a three-legged race. When the two girls were alone, Jessica asked: 'What's up?'

'Nothing, really. I . . . can we talk?' Mel adopted her little-girl-lost expression, the one she'd developed for her male teachers on days when she hadn't done her homework. 'We just – we haven't talked since Harrington and I really need to get my head around a few things.'

'You and me both,' Jessica sympathised. 'You want to go to your room?'

She squeezed her friend's hand and Mel felt both exhilarated and disgusted with herself, in pretty much equal measure. 'Yeah, but listen, I really should . . . I didn't get to shower this morning before breakfast.'

Jessica sniffed. 'And I thought it was just the recycled air in the Enclave,' she joked.

'Well can you give me time for a shower first? Come along in, say, fifteen, twenty minutes?'

Jessica was fine with fifteen, twenty minutes, but of course Mel had no intention of showering in the mean time. Instead, as soon as she'd closed her door behind her, she was on the comlink to Antony. Thank God for the complex's internal communications system. And thank God Antony was in his room although, given the reason for Mel's gratitude, perhaps God didn't have much to do with it.

Antony listened intently. Mel had something important to tell him? But not over the comlink? It was too sensitive? It concerned Jessica? Could he maybe come to Mel's room right away?

He was on his way already. Because, Mel realised with a sinking heart, he genuinely cared for Jessie. But so did she.

'What is it? Where's Jess?' the blond boy demanded the instant Mel let him in. He was anxious, which was helpful. It meant he didn't notice in the slightest that his hostess had not closed the door properly, had left it ajar.

Jessica would be along shortly.

'Come and sit down, Antony.' Mel led him by the hand. 'On the bed. Next to me.'

'Is Jessica all right? I wouldn't want her to be . . . not all right. What's this something important all about, Mel?'

'It's something that happened at Harrington, Antony,' Mel said, producing a frown of confusion on the boy's face. 'The party we had? The night the Scytharene came?'

'Obviously I remember it, yes, but I don't . . .' *Feel right*, he might have said. He didn't feel right sitting on a bed with Melanie Patrick, their knees touching, even though Mel's hair was as luxuriantly long and black as ever and her eyes as captivatingly blue and her tunic rather undone and baring quite a lot of pale, creamy flesh, and at one time, not so long ago, he'd have given his right arm – or his left, he was open to negotiation – to find himself in this position . . . *like* at the party . . .

'You asked me to dance, remember that?' Mel prompted. 'I turned you down.'

And Antony did remember that, of course – most boys reserved a whole frontal lobe in which to catalogue their rejections – but the recollection only bewildered him more. 'I thought this was supposed to be about Jessica?'

'I lied,' Mel admitted. 'It's about me. And you, Antony.'

'But I didn't think . . . what are you talking about?' Feeling uncomfortable now.

'I should have danced with you before. I was stupid to turn you down. I realise that now. I realise lots of things.'

'You do?' And *very* uncomfortable as Mel squeezed his knee and ran her hand up and over his thigh, as she leaned towards him and her breath was warm on his skin, her eyes filling his vision.

'I want you, Antony.'

'But . . .' Flinching back. 'I'm flattered, Mel, but . . .'

'Has anyone ever told you you have very kissable lips, Antony?'

'You're too late, Mel.'

'To tell you you have kissable lips?'

'Too late' – grabbing her hand, lifting it from his leg – 'for anything like *this*. Sorry. I'm really sorry, but I don't – I don't feel about you now the way I might have done then.'

'You don't?' Mel echoed lamely. Of *course* he didn't. And she knew why.

'No. You're a great girl, Mel, really attractive and everything, but . . .' And he might have dreamed of being in this situation once, but now the girl he wanted to be with was blonde and green-eyed, and there was more to her than looks anyway, a lot more, and he longed to explore and discover it all. So Mel hadn't actually lied. This *was* about Jessica. 'Look, I think I'd better go.' He started to get to his feet.

'You can't. Not yet.' Mel jumped to hers first, seized his shoulders. 'Not until—'

A knock at the door. 'Mel? It's me.' A voice at the door. The fifteen, twenty minutes were up.

And it was too late to turn back now. Mel was committed. She clasped Antony in a bear-hug of suffocating proportions, glued her lips to his as if they were made of Araldite and toppled the astonished boy on to the bed. And she closed her eyes so she wouldn't have to see her best friend's expression of hurt and dismay when Jessica pushed the door open.

Pity Mel couldn't have blocked up her ears somehow as well. The blonde girl's startled cry did nothing for her self-esteem.

'Mel, what are you doing?' Neither did her words. Mel had hoped they'd begin with '*Antony*, what are you doing?' There was a difference. 'What's going on?'

Antony pushed her away and Mel rolled on to her back on the bed. He tried to get to his feet a second time and on this occasion made it. 'Jessica . . .'

'Jessie, it's not my fault.' Mel adopted an attitude of injured innocence. 'He just turned up, out of the blue, said he had something important to tell me . . .'

'What?' Antony gaped incredulously. 'That's what you told *me*.'

'And then he jumped me, Jess. He was all over me.'

'You drew me here under false pretences and then you threw yourself at *me* . . .'

'He's lying, Jessie. You can't trust him.' Mel sat forward on the bed. 'You saw for yourself what was happening, didn't you?'

Jessica shook her head, blinked as if seeking to clear a speck from her eye. 'I wish I hadn't.'

Antony glared at Mel with both fury and pain. 'What are you up to, Mel? What sort of game . . .?' He turned pleadingly to Jessica. 'This is all . . . I don't understand what Mel's

176

playing at, Jessica, but I promise you I didn't come on to her. I wouldn't.'

'He would. He's a boy, isn't he?' Mel sprang up too. 'They're all the same. Anything in a skirt . . . or trousers, as long as she's female. You can't trust any of them, Jess. You know how he's always fancied me.'

'I thought,' Jessica said evenly, switching her gaze from Mel to Antony, 'that you might be beginning to have feelings for me.'

'I am,' the blond boy declared. 'I *am*. And I'd hoped you were feeling the same way, so why would I go and spoil something like that with something like this, Jessica, a cheap, cheating grope with somebody who ought to be your friend.' Snapping the last accusingly at Mel. 'I'd never do anything to hurt you. This is some kind of twisted set-up. You didn't come by this minute by accident, did you? Tell me.'

'Don't listen to him, Jess,' Mel said scornfully. 'He's full of it. You don't need him or any boy . . .'

'Jessica, *believe* me—'

'Enough! Both of you.' Jessica's raised voice cracked like the lash of a whip. It was decisive, authoritative. It sounded like it knew what it wanted. To Mel, it didn't sound like Jessica at all. Her eyes, there was confidence burning in them that hadn't even been a flicker in the old days, when Jessie had lived in her nice, safe house with her nice, protective parents. Her circumstances had changed and Jessica Lane was changing with them. 'It's all right, Antony. I *do* believe you.'

And Mel felt chilled to the heart. 'You believe *him*? Jessica, over *me*? But that's . . . you can't. We've been friends for years.'

'Which is how I know when you're lying, Mel,' said Jessica

gravely. 'Which is why I don't understand what you were trying to do here. Drive a wedge between me and Antony? Why would you want to do that? Why would one friend not want to see another friend happy?'

'I *do* want you to be happy, Jessie.' Tears stung Mel's eyes. 'That's why . . . you can't be happy with Antony. It's not his fault. Boys . . .'

'Mel.' Jessica spoke her name as if it belonged to someone who'd recently passed away. 'So many terrible things have happened. So much has changed. But I never thought you would. I thought you'd always be there for me. I thought we were going to be friends for ever. Seems forever doesn't last quite as long as you might expect.'

'Don't say that, Jess. I'm sorry . . .'

'Antony, I don't think either of us ought to be here.' The two of them moved to the door. Together.

'You need to sort yourself out, Mel,' Antony recommended, but there was no hatred in his voice. Mel wished there had been. She deserved it.

'Jessie, please, don't go. Don't leave with him . . .'

But she did.

Mel lay stretched out numbly on her bed for what might have been hours. Her grand scheme had resulted in total and absolute failure. Rather than split Jessica and Antony up, she'd inadvertently brought them closer together. Irony was such a bitch. She, Mel, was the one on whom Jessica had turned her back, and she wasn't sure how she could handle that. Without Jessica in her life, she had to look hard for reasons to go on at all.

When the door shook beneath a flurry of excited knocks, she hoped the source was a repentant Jess. It wasn't. It was Linden. 'Mel, are you in there?'

'No.'

'Come on. Get your arse in gear. You'll never guess who's here.'

'Winston sodding Churchill.'

'Simon escaped-from-the-Scytharene-spaceship-after-all Satchwell.'

So Mel got up, went out, accompanied Linden to the briefing room where the others were already waiting for Simon to navigate decontamination. She couldn't hide away in her room indefinitely, no matter that she might want to, and at least for the moment the focus of attention would be on Simon and not her. She wondered if she'd be able to look Jessica in the eye. She wondered if Jessica would even glance at her, and if she did, whether it would be with revulsion.

Linden was jabbering as they walked: 'Yeah, so the vigilanteye spots this boy hanging around Harrington's ruins and transmits pictures back to the monitoring centre and they see he's wearing the same clothes we were before we got here, the Scytharenes' standard slave-issue grey. So Mowatt and Taber get interested and show the footage to Travis who's still being debriefed and Trav says it's Simon and they've got to let him into the Enclave because he's one of us and might have valuable information. But Taber isn't convinced so Travis says either Simon's allowed in or *he* walks out, and he's pretty sure that most of us will follow him. A little presumptuous there, maybe.'

'I doubt it,' said Mel.

'Anyway, so Taber gives in and the vigilanteye does its

thing and guides Simon here. Looks like we'll all be together again.'

'I'm so pleased for us.'

'Mel, can I ask you something? You've known Travis a long time, haven't you?'

'Longer than I've known anybody left alive,' Mel realised, 'except for Jessica.'

'Have you ever been mad at him?'

'Loads of times.'

'And stayed mad?'

Mel smiled in spite of her troubles. 'Never.'

Linden sighed, as if admitting some kind of defeat. 'No, I thought not.'

Simon looked well, Travis thought, everyone gathered delightedly around their reunited friend in the briefing room. It was more than good to see him. It was a weight lifted, a prayer answered.

'After I was processed,' Simon recounted, 'they gave me my glasses back and put me in a cell on my own, I don't know why. It wasn't pleasant, though, I can tell you, being alone. Then, when the door just suddenly opened and that alarm sound started, I didn't know what to do. I crept out into the corridor. Nobody. No guards. No Scytharene in sight. No sign of any of you.'

'We must have been kept on a different level or something,' Travis said. 'Our Scytharene friend Darion disrupted the security systems.'

Simon smiled faintly. 'Useful to have friends in high places, Travis. Darion, hmm?'

'We wanted to find you and the others, Simon, we really did. But like I've already told you, there wasn't time. I've regretted not being able to search for you every minute since. I don't know if you can ever forgive me . . .'

Travis sounded quite desperate, Simon thought. Must be harbouring a lot of guilt. *Deserved* to be harbouring a lot of guilt. (Unforgivable.) But 'I understand, Travis,' he said graciously. 'We all have to make choices, don't we, and sometimes those choices are difficult. I don't think there's any need to talk about forgiveness. I got out in the end anyway, didn't I? Here I am.'

'Yeah.' Richie had stared at Simon throughout with a kind of disbelief, a dawning and until now inconceivable admiration. 'How *did* you manage to escape, Simes? On your own as well. I don't reckon I'd have made it.'

That's because you're a brainless piece of shit, Coker, Simon thought. 'I'm sure you would have done, Richie,' he said, 'if you put your mind to it.' *If you had a mind, you bloody moron.* 'I just kept out of the Scytharene's way. I'm good at keeping out of people's way. Had a lot of practice at school. I must admit I expected more guards to be around. They were probably all chasing after you. So in a sense you did help me to escape, Travis.'

'It's generous of you to see it that way, Simon.' Travis nodded appreciatively.

'I hid in some kind of storeroom,' said Simon, continuing his lie. 'There was a plan on the wall – of the ship. I used it to help me find my way out. It took time. I obviously didn't want to risk getting caught again. Luckily it was dark when I finally found an exit hatch or whatever it was. I made my way back to Harrington. You know the rest.'

'Outstanding,' Richie grinned. 'Simes, I never thought I'd say this, but you is the man.'

Coker, shut your stinking mouth. 'All the time,' Simon said, 'I was thinking of all of you, hoping I'd see you again.' And he was grateful now that Commander Shurion hadn't given him that comdisk gadget thing in order to contact him as he'd originally intended. The device would have been discovered at decontamination, as therefore would his true loyalties. But he had a name already. *Darion.* He'd learn more if there was more to learn, then all he needed to do was find a way to get in touch with the Scytharene commander. That shouldn't be too hard. After all . . .

'Simon, you're so brave.' Jessica hugged him, kissed him, though not on the lips. 'I didn't *know* . . .'

'Ah, Jessica,' Simon winked behind his glasses, 'there's a lot about me you don't know.'

EIGHT

He'd spent most of a sleepless night coming to his decision, but by morning Darion had resolved to do absolutely nothing. Which might have been seen as ironic by some people, hours of deliberation expended and only inaction at the end of them. But those people wouldn't have been familiar with Darion, born of the bloodline of Ayrion of the Thousand Families. The young alienologist was by nature deeply conservative and a thinker, not a doer; his entire upbringing had been geared to teaching him to value and preserve the way things were and never to question them or contemplate change. It had cost Darion a monumental effort of will to help the Earthers in the first place. To alter his habitual patterns of behaviour again was probably beyond his ability.

Besides, sitting tight and carrying on as usual made good tactical sense. Any sudden departure from his established routines Shurion might interpret as incriminating – Darion was sure the Commander suspected him of being the traitor, *wanted* it to be so. Remaining aboard the *Furion* also enabled him to monitor the slaving operations closely, to check as carefully as he could whether the scores of Earthers harvested by the Cullers included one Travis Naughton.

It was helpful that Earthers grew hair, unlike his own race, whose orthodox opinion was that hirsuteness was an indicator of savagery and therefore inferiority. It was also a boon that Earther hair sprouted in a range of colours, otherwise Darion would hardly have been able to tell the aliens apart. He hadn't spotted the brown-haired Travis yet, though that didn't necessarily mean the boy hadn't been recaptured, with or without his fellow escapees. Scores of prisoners was well on its way to becoming hundreds. Processing was continuing nonstop, the information gathered feeding the *Furion*'s voracious data banks. The cryo-tubes were filling and the cells were full. A compound was already being constructed nearby where Earthers could be held securely until it was their turn for processing. For all Darion knew, Travis could be languishing there.

But he doubted it. He believed the processing data. If Scytharene technology judged that Travis Naughton was a leader, then he accepted without question the truth of that estimation. Not that he was reliant on the computers alone. His own impressions of the Earther youth supported their assessment. Even in captivity, Travis had demonstrated certain qualities, defiance, self-belief, inner strength, which Darion knew leaders required. They were qualities he envied, qualities he was afraid he himself lacked. So he had faith that Travis would not have been apprehended again, trusted that he'd even outwit Shurion's agent, if the spy did ever manage to catch up with him. Darion had nothing to fear from that direction. If he simply brazened this traitor alert out, he had nothing to fear at all. Shurion –

– was at the door, activating the intercom and requesting entrance.

All the alienologist's confidence evaporated like moisture in a desert. Shurion had never been near his private quarters before. It could hardly be a social call now. If he appeared flanked by guards then it was all over for Darion.

Yet he could hardly leave the Commander standing in the corridor. He instructed the door to open.

'Commander Shurion. What a surprise.' And Darion laughed with a kind of nervous relief. Shurion was alone.

'Not a pleasant one, though, Lord Darion, hmm?' The black-garbed Scytharene strode in, his frown nearly as dark as his armour.

Evidently Darion still had to be cautious. He felt his muscles tensing, his fingers trembling. 'I don't know what you mean.'

'You were expecting perhaps a different visitor? The guest I was informed this morning we will shortly be welcoming aboard the *Furion* from the *Ayrion III*.'

'Really?' Shortly couldn't come quickly enough. 'Well, in that case, Commander Shurion, if you'd be so good as to explain why you are here, I do have preparations to make.'

'I'll be brief, Lord Darion,' said Shurion tersely, 'and I'll be frank. I do not approve of the presence aboard any slavecraft, least of all my own command, of a visitor of the kind you are about to receive. I do not deem it to be appropriate, and if I had any authority in the matter I would prevent it from happening.'

'But my father outranks you.'

'It is my duty and my honour to follow Fleet Commander Gyrion's orders,' Shurion said, as if the words had been extracted from him under torture. 'However, it occurs to me that both yourself, Lord Darion, and your companion might prefer to spend your time together somewhere other than aboard this ship.'

They might indeed, Darion thought. This could be an unexpected bonus.

'Do you have a location in mind, Commander Shurion?' he wondered.

'There is an Earther dwelling of considerable scale and size – by this planet's primitive standards – adjoining the slave camp. It belonged to a family of Earther aristocrats, so I understand. We have removed the corpses. You could go there,' Shurion said with as much of a sneer as he dared. 'No decent Scytharene would care to reside among the shabby, squalid trappings of a backward culture, of course, but somehow I doubt two alienologists such as yourselves will be unduly concerned about that. In fact, I imagine you'll feel right at home' – casting a contemptuous eye around him at the alien artworks, the miniatures of non-Scytharene lifeforms, the protean vases – 'given the unwholesome ornamentation you seem to find acceptable even here.'

'These artefacts are integral to my studies,' Darion defended himself, 'as you well know, Commander Shurion.'

The Commander's gaze settled on the Lachrimese memory helm. He crossed the room towards it. 'These *profanities*,' he reworded, 'are the foul and unclean scraps of conquered and impure societies. It offends me to look at them. To touch them' – lifting the glittering green crystal with disgust – 'makes me almost physically sick.'

Alarmed, Darion raised his hands in warning. 'Please, Commander Shurion, that object is very rare.'

'Rare? Atrocities such as this should be extinct. How can you bear to surround yourself with such corruption, Lord Darion? It could be argued that to do so almost qualifies as a criminal offence, as an anti-Scytharene act.'

'Nonsense, Commander Shurion. I told you, my work as an alienologist requires—'

'It does not require you to store such vile trash in your private quarters, Lord Darion, I know that.' Shurion's scarlet eyes narrowed and gleamed slyly. 'You *choose* to keep them here. It could be argued that anyone doing so must be motivated by a twisted admiration for these poor and ugly baubles . . .'

'Nonsense. Now please, Commander Shurion, the memory helm . . .'

Shurion smiled humourlessly. 'Of course it's nonsense, Lord Darion, because if it was not, it might also follow that their owner might in time become foolish and misguided enough actually to sympathise with impure, inferior slave races such as the Earthers. And if I were to believe *that* . . .'

'Be careful what you say, Commander Shurion,' Darion protested a little desperately, his heart battering his ribs in fear. 'Remember who I am. I belong to the Thousand Families. I share the bloodline of Ayrion the Fearless. Do not forget your place.'

'Oh, I never forget my place, Lord Darion,' said Shurion cryptically. 'And forgive my speculations. They were not intended to impugn you personally, of course. I know as well as anyone that the Thousand Families are beyond criticism.'

'Yes, well, your apology is accepted. But the memory helm, please, commander, if you could put it down, please . . .'

'This? Down? Of course, Lord Darion,' obliged Shurion, and released the crystal helmet from his grasp.

'No!' cried Darion.

But the laws of gravity were beyond the command of even

a descendant of the great Ayrion. The Lachrimese memory helm dropped to the metal floor, struck it and shattered into a thousand pieces, a thousand crystal shards like tears of jade.

'*No*,' Darion groaned.

'How clumsy of me.' Shurion shook his head with mock regret. 'But at least you have something to occupy you until your visitor arrives, Lord Darion. Putting it back together. Excuse me.'

The Commander whisked out but Darion scarcely noticed. He'd cherished the memory helm. He'd worn it himself on many occasions and had hoped the souls of the departed Lachrimese would speak to him through the shining crystal. Thus far, they never had. Now they never would.

He sank to his knees on the floor. He felt himself shaking uncontrollably, with helpless fury at Shurion's arrogance and ignorance, with panic at the Commander's hostility and vengefulness. There could be no doubt. Shurion would never have dared speak to him as he had done unless he seriously suspected Darion of being the traitor. Only the younger Scytharene's social rank was protecting him from formal interrogation. But his antagonist had no proof. All the while that remained the case, Darion was safe. Not that he felt secure just now, virtually grovelling on the floor in his own quarters with the splinters of the memory helm scattered around him.

The intercom buzzed again. Someone was outside. Shurion, returned with proof and guards and an arrest warrant? Shurion, who'd only been toying with him before?

Darion staggered to his feet. His throat dry, he croaked, 'Door: open,' and when it did he cried out. But not with dread. With joy. Because the figure in the doorway was not

Commander Shurion but somebody else, the one he'd been yearning to see.

Dyona.

In the Enclave, Jessica's response to finding Mel at her door was somewhat less enthusiastic.

'Oh. It's you. I didn't expect . . . after yesterday . . . what do you want?'

'To talk. To explain, hopefully.' Good things and bad things. Good: Antony wasn't in Jessica's room with her; she was alone. Bad: the expression on Jessie's face, guarded, defensive, closed against Mel. The black-haired girl could hardly bear it. 'Please?'

'There isn't any time. Mowatt and Taber want us in the briefing room.'

'In half an hour. That sounds like time to me.'

'It might do to you, but you have some strange ideas about some things lately, don't you, Mel? Like friendship, for instance.'

'Please. Jessie. *Because* we're friends.'

'Or were,' Jessie revised. She sighed. 'Okay, you can come in, but this had better be good, Mel.'

It would at least be the truth. Scheming and deception had failed. Mel had agonised about it, but she felt her only recourse now was honesty. Total honesty. Whatever the consequences. 'Thanks, Jessie,' she said, entering the blonde girl's room. How could her situation be worse than it was already? And maybe, if Jessica knew how she felt, really knew . . .

'So?'

'I'm sorry. About yesterday. Me and Antony. It was – it was

189

nothing to do with him. What he said was all true. I tricked him into my room. I came on to him. I arranged it so you'd come in and find us together.'

Which admission baffled rather than shocked Jessica. She'd thought she knew Mel, better than anyone did with the possible exception of Travis, but the girl she'd seen on the bed with Antony yesterday, the girl who stood pleadingly before her now, physically it was Mel, but what she was saying, how she was behaving . . . Jessica didn't understand. 'Why?' she said. 'Why did you do that? Do you fancy Antony after all?'

Mel laughed hollowly. 'It wouldn't matter if I did. He wasn't interested in me. There's only one girl he's interested in, Jess, though she *is* in this room. But I don't fancy him anyway, no. What happened, it was never about me and Antony. It was about me and you.'

'Us?' And at the back of Jessica's mind, the tiniest of alarm bells began to ring.

'Yeah. I kind of wanted to split you and Antony up before you ever really got started as a couple.'

'Because you think he'll hurt me? That's what you said . . .' And if it was as simple as that, an example of misjudged overprotectiveness on Mel's part, then they could maybe get through it, move on, pretty much forget yesterday's tawdry little scene. Jessica hoped it would be so, but . . .

'That's what I said, yeah, and I meant it,' Mel acknowledged. 'But that's not the main reason I couldn't bear to see you and Antony together, Jessie, or even think about you and him like girlfriend and boyfriend. Or you and anybody. Any boy.'

'I don't . . . follow.'

'Don't you? You must do.' The moment of crisis was upon

190

her. The next minute, Mel knew, would shape her life for ever. 'I'm jealous, Jessie. Jealous when I think of you with anyone else.'

'Why?' Not necessarily wanting to know but *having* to know.

'Isn't it obvious? Haven't you always, deep down . . . Because *I* want to be with you, Jessie. Because you're in my head all the time. Because I'm always thinking about you. Because when I go to bed I want to dream about you. Because I adore you. Because I love you. Because – I don't just want to be a friend, Jess, not even your best friend. I want to be more than that. I want to . . .' And she took a tentative step forward.

Jessica took two back.

'Jessie?'

'No, Mel.'

'No?'

And Jessica was remembering being at home, in the days when people still had homes, and parents, and family evenings shared in front of the telly. And in the programme they were watching, two girls kissing, and Dad shaking his head disapprovingly and saying that it shouldn't be allowed, it was wrong, it was unnatural. Lesbianism, he'd said, and homosexuality, he'd said, whenever you switched on the box these days, even before the watershed, thrust in front of your face by liberal TV programme-makers who clearly didn't believe in family values and were probably gay themselves, sexual immorality presented as if it was normal, as if it was something to be proud of. Well it wasn't, Dad had said. Same-sex couples, same-sex relationships, they were something to be ashamed of; the people in them should be ashamed. It was deliberate government policy, Mum had added, to corrupt young minds, to erode standards and to attack the concept of decency, and wouldn't it be better to change channels so Jessica didn't have to see it?

'Don't say no, Jessie.' In the present, Mel was still hoping. 'I love you.'

'You ought to be' – as sixteen years of upbringing asserted their authority – 'ashamed, Mel.'

'What?' Mel seemed to bend, to crumple, as if a knife had been stabbed into her heart and twisted.

Jessica did not bend. 'Why did you say those things? Why did you have to say them?'

'Because they're true, Jessie.'

'That's irrelevant. I don't care about that. I didn't know and it was better not knowing. But now you've forced me to hear those things and I can't *un*hear them and they change us, Mel. They change you and me. I have to make a decision on them. We can't be to each other what we were any more. I wish you'd never opened your mouth.'

'Please, don't just . . . don't look at me like that.'

'How am I supposed to look at you?' Jessica objected. 'How *should* I look at you after what you've just told me?'

'I'm not ashamed, Jessie.' Even though, well, at dark moments in the night, awake and alone . . . 'Why should I be? What I feel for you, it's amazing, exciting, it's . . .'

'Wrong,' Jessica concluded for her. 'It's wrong, Mel.' Even though, well, in the great scheme of things, if there was one, would it truly be a crime if . . . 'You looked after me, didn't you? When I was in that trance?'

'Of course I did. Jessie, listen to me . . .'

'Travis said you never let me out of your sight, wouldn't let anyone else . . . Why, Mel? You wanted to keep me to yourself? Like your doll? Like your plaything?'

192

'Jess, it wasn't like that . . .'

'I never thought so, but after this little revelation you've let slip, it sort of puts a whole different kind of gloss on the matter, doesn't it, Mel? Gives you a bit of a new agenda. You fed me, didn't you? You attended to my needs. Did you put me to bed at night? Next to you?'

'Jessie, please . . .'

'Did you undress me?'

'Jess . . .'

'No, I don't want to know. I don't want to think about it. It's . . . dirty.'

'It's not dirty.'

'I think it is. I think' – and for a moment, the agony of loss contorted Jessica's features – 'why did you have to spoil our friendship, Mel? You've ruined it, just when we needed each other more than ever. You – *idiot*.'

'No. Jess. Listen.' Panicking. Events slipping out of control. 'I'm sorry if you . . . I'm sorry. Don't . . . forget I said anything. I didn't say anything. I didn't mean . . . it was a joke. I'm glad you like Antony. I like boys, too. I'll never mention this again. Just . . . don't hate me, Jessie. Don't hate me.'

But whatever her feelings, Jessica was turning away, shielding them from Mel. Her voice was stony. 'I *can't* look at you right now. I'm going to the meeting.' She made for the door.

'Please, Jessie, you mustn't go like this. Don't leave me . . .'

Alone. In the silence of Jessica's room. Mel closed her eyes but tears still squeezed out. Her heart ached. Every breath she drew was a struggle that at this precise moment she wasn't sure was worth the effort. All finished. All over. She'd sent Jessica scurrying for the briefing room when she'd wanted her falling into her arms. That would never happen now. Never. If she couldn't hold Jessie, she'd never hold anyone.

And perhaps it wasn't so silent in the room, after all. From somewhere, at least, Mel was certain she could hear her dead father chuckling.

When Mel failed to appear in the briefing room on time, and when Captain Taber's comlink to her quarters went unanswered, Jessica said that she might be asleep. Apparently, Mel hadn't looked too good earlier when Jessica had last seen her. Stress, probably. Or time of the month.

Taber harrumphed. Wherever Miss Patrick was, and for whatever reason, they would have to carry on without her. He and Dr Mowatt had something to show the youngsters, something in which Mr Naughton, with his impatience to strike back at the Scytharene, might be particularly interested.

Joshuas.

'Maybe I ought to go and check Mel's all right,' Travis suggested to Jessica on their way up to the higher level.

'She'll be fine,' the blonde girl said, resentful that Mel's confession, obviously the reason for her absence, had pretty much forced her to lie to her friends. Mel had a lot to answer for. 'Let's see what these Joshua things are.'

'Tanks!' Richie for one seemed buoyed by the fact. 'They're bloody well tanks.'

The six teenagers stood with Mowatt and Taber alongside two rows of identical vehicles. 'The Joshua Assault Vehicle,' Captain Taber declared with pride, 'is considerably more than any tank you might be familiar with, Mr Coker.'

'Bloody great,' enthused Richie. 'Give those bloody aliens a bloody nose.'

'Why are they called *Joshua* Assault Vehicles, Captain Taber?' enquired Antony politely.

'You know your Bible, don't you?' the military man replied. 'Thanks to God, Joshua brought the walls of Jericho crashing down. Thanks to British weapons technology, *our* Joshuas can bring crashing down the walls of *anywhere*, smash any defence, break any barrier, cripple any opposition, including those damned Scytharene spaceships.'

Really? Simon thought. Then this might be a little bonus for Commander Shurion.

'Including the shields protecting the Scytharene ships?' Travis asked pointedly.

Which remark Taber ignored, equally pointedly. And there were only twelve of the Joshuas, Travis counted, arrayed against maybe hundreds of slavecraft. How were these glorified tanks going to make a difference? Taber was deluding himself if he imagined they could defeat the Scytharene with a few oversized popguns. But then Travis remembered another Bible story. David and Goliath. Maybe he should have a bit of faith. Maybe the Joshuas could be their slingshot.

'You will notice' – Taber was well into his salesman routine – 'the JAVs' wheels turn on a caterpillar track like previous models of tank, though you will also observe that the wheels themselves are all but concealed by the vehicle's reinforced-steel skirts – to render them less vulnerable to disablement. The tracks are fitted with retractable diamond spikes so that the Joshuas' grip on the earth is guaranteed however difficult or treacherous the terrain. The main body' – Taber patted it with an affection usually reserved for a beloved pet dog – 'is cast from a molybdenum steel alloy, almost impossible to penetrate with conventional weaponry.'

But what about the battlepods' destructive yellow blasts, Travis wondered, or whatever decimating missile or ray had levelled Harrington, or any other nasty and potentially terminal surprises the aliens might still have lurking in their arsenal? The Josuas' sleek and gleaming grey armour appeared formidable enough, the assault vehicles' design more streamlined, less angular than the machines he'd seen flattening French towns in old war movies, each central domed turret equipped with dual long-barrelled guns of considerable diameter, one mounted above the other. Even so, how would Taber's pride and joy hold up in action? Travis supposed that in the end there was only one way to find out.

'The Joshuas can be operated by a single man,' Taber said, 'though there is room for three in the control cabin within, accessed through hatches fore and rear. A battery of cameras and sensors relays a constant stream of information to the operators, becoming their eyes and ears and avoiding the need for viewpoints which might allow an enemy to target members of the crew. These gun ports you can see, again at front and rear as well as along the flanks, when the Joshuas' assault systems are activated they can function as rocket-launchers, flame-throwers or machine-guns at the operator's choice. The turret rotates a full three hundred and sixty degrees and both of its guns' – the twin barrels at present pointing forwards in perfect harmony – 'can be moved and positioned independently as well. They can even be elevated to a height capable of dealing with an aerial attack, a useful capacity given the likelihood of an engagement with the aliens' so-called battlepods, hmm?'

'Impressive stuff, Captain Taber,' Travis accepted. 'I wonder why you haven't committed the Joshuas already.'

Taber bridled slightly at the implied criticism. 'For two perfectly valid military reasons, Mr Naughton.'

'The first of which my scientists and I have successfully addressed,' broke in Dr Mowatt. 'For a Joshua crew to have to wear atmosuits during operations would be cumbersome and possibly even impair their efficiency, endangering their lives, yet all the while the air is carrying the Sickness virus, any adult venturing topside would have no alternative but to suit up. What we've done, therefore, is to design and fit the JAVs' cabins with a miniature version of the environmental system that protects the Enclave itself from biological attack. The control cabins are now totally self-contained, recycling their own oxygen and impervious to biological agents. In other words, our crews will be able to operate above ground in safety, which is why we've waited until this point to introduce you to the Joshuas, now that theoretically they can be deployed.'

'Theoretically?' Travis picked up on the word at once.

'Our second problem,' Taber said. 'The aliens' shields. I cannot in conscience commit the Joshuas while those shields are still in place.'

Travis shook his head frustratedly. 'But what about the kids we might be able to save? If your Joshuas are so wonderful . . . What about *them*?'

Simon watched Travis intently, listened to his words. Because oh, he was good, was Travis Naughton. Oh, he was convincing. Hear that moral indignation in his voice! No wonder he, Simon, had been taken in by the teenager's line in *looking out for others*, deceived by his *doing the right thing*. Travis should have been an actor. Because it *was* an act. Simon was sure it was. It had to be, didn't it? Because hadn't the same blue-eyed boy who was haranguing Taber to save kids now – kids he didn't know, mind, had never met, never promised anything, not to their faces – hadn't he, Travis, run out on Simon, his supposed friend, deserted him aboard the Scytharene ship, left him alone again?

Oh, yes.

And he'd *trusted* Travis. He'd trusted him more than anyone. That was what hurt. And Travis had let him down like everyone had let him down, like life had let him down, and Travis ought to suffer for that, he ought to be punished for that and made to see. Pretty Jessica, too, and Mel, wherever she was, and Linden, and Clive and Coker, especially Coker, they all ought to be made to see and understand that Simon Satchwell was not just the wimp with the glasses, the useless weakling, the victim. He could do things. He wasn't to be sneered at, not any more. He had powerful new friends. They needed to see that. They needed to be shown.

And yet – what if he was wrong about Travis?

His supposed protector's own version of events aboard the Scytharene ship, of the escape, well, it *could* be true. It wasn't *impossible* that Travis had wanted to search for him but that others had been depending on him, too. It wasn't *implausible* that he'd been compelled to put those others first and that he'd suffered because of it, endured real guilt and regret at having to leave Simon behind. Travis's relief and gladness when he'd seen Simon again, it wasn't *inconceivable* that they were genuine.

198

Simon was muddled, confused. Back on the Scytharene ship, he'd been sure. When Commander Shurion had been explaining what had happened he'd been persuaded, utterly, entirely; everything must have been as the Scytharene described and for Simon to turn against Travis and the others was all they deserved. You couldn't betray a betrayer. (Unforgivable.) But now, with Shurion's influence removed, with everyone around him again, with Travis here, saying Travis things, behaving in Travis ways, being himself, Simon doubted. In spite of the brush with death his abandonment had led to, part of him wanted to believe in Travis again and belong with his own kind. Part of him wanted to forgive.

It was a battle waged inside him. On the one hand, bitterness at his treatment both recently and in years gone by; on the other, the feelings of loyalty Travis had inspired in him since before the Sickness came. Who truly deserved his trust, Travis or Commander Shurion? Whose side should he really be on? He had to be certain, resolved, before he did anything that could not be undone. So he watched Travis intently, listened to his words.

'Then I guess there's only one thing to do, isn't there?' the brown-haired boy was saying. 'It's so obvious I'm surprised we haven't already done it.' Everyone, including Mowatt and Taber, looked at him in puzzlement. 'We want to put the Scytharene's shields out of action, don't we? Give the Joshuas a crack at the ship? Simple. I'll just have to get myself recaptured . . .'

NINE

'I don't like it,' said Captain Taber, once everyone had reconvened in the briefing room.

Everyone now included Mel, whose appearance was so pale and wan that it was easy for the others to suppose she was unwell, as Jessica had led them to believe. The black-haired girl did nothing to contradict this assumption. She responded to her friends' concern about her health with an assertion that she was fine really and an apology that she'd missed the meeting so far – she'd just sit and listen and soon catch up with what had been happening in her absence. She settled herself as far from Jessica as was physically possible while remaining at the same table. Jessica had *not* asked how she was. Nobody seemed to notice the tension between them, however. There were other matters of greater urgency.

'I don't like the idea at all,' Taber reiterated.

'With respect, sir, liking it isn't the issue,' Travis pointed out. 'The issue is whether the plan can work or not, and I think it can. I head for Vernham Hill, deliberately put myself in the way of the Cullers, get taken back inside the Scytharene ship, contact Darion again and persuade him to sabotage or disable their shields somehow.'

'*Somehow*,' Linden emphasised. '*Somehow* you'll convince this Darion to help us again. From what you've already told us, Travis, he was hardly a happy revolutionary before. What makes you think he'll find the courage to put his life on the line for inferior Earthers a second time? You could end up in a cryo-tube – and for nothing.' Spoken as if she cared what happened to Travis, even though she was avoiding his gaze.

'Linden's right, Travis,' agreed Jessica. 'For a start, how can you be sure you'll even be taken to the same ship? And even if you are, we don't know that Darion's treason wasn't found out after we escaped. He could be in a cell himself by now, and the only thing he'll be able to sabotage from there is your plan. It's too dangerous. It's too . . . uncertain.'

'What isn't these days?' said Travis.

'What if Commander Shurion or an assessor or somebody recognises you before you can reach Darion?' Antony backed Jessica up. 'How are you going to contact Darion anyway?'

'Well the short answer is I don't know.' Travis gave a helpless laugh. 'I don't know. I don't know. I don't know. But I *do* know we need to do something, and this qualifies as a pretty positive something.' He glanced around the table in appeal. 'I mean, what if I *can* find Darion? What if he does neutralise the shields? The Joshuas can blow their bloody ship to kingdom come and kickstart the comeback for the whole human race. That's worth a few risks, isn't it? Dr Mowatt? Captain Taber?'

The Scientific Director turned to her army colleague. 'We could send a vigilanteye with him, monitor the situation as best we can.'

Behind rheumy eyes, Taber seemed to be making calculations. 'One life weighed against the opportunity for a significant victory. Perhaps you have a point, Mr Naughton.

Militarily, your plan might make sense. But what if you *are* discovered, recognised? Might you not be tortured into revealing the location of the Enclave?'

Linden shuddered at the juxtaposition of Travis and torture.

'They're not even aware this place exists,' Travis said. 'How is anyone going to try to force me into betraying it?'

Taber deliberated. 'It would be good to fight again, to engage the enemy at last.'

'Then you know what to say,' pressed Travis.

'You ought not to undertake this mission alone,' Taber said. 'In case anything should happen to you . . .'

'Is that a yes, though?'

'I'll go with Travis.' Antony. 'I volunteer.'

Mel read admiration and adoration in Jessica's face as she gazed at the former Head Boy of the Harrington School and squeezed his hand. Another knife in her heart.

'Thanks, Antony,' nodded Travis.

'I can't let you hog all the glory, can I?' Antony laughed a little nervously.

'I'd like to go too,' requested a new voice, causing six pairs of teenage eyebrows to be raised in simultaneous surprise. Offering to place himself in certain danger was something nobody really expected of Simon Satchwell. 'What are you looking at me like that for?' *If they only knew.*

'No. No reason, Simon. It's good you're putting yourself forward,' Travis said.

'Don't you think I'm up to it?'

'Sure. I mean, of course. We'd love to have you with us, wouldn't we, Antony?' Antony certainly would. Love to. 'But you've only just escaped from the Scytharene ship. Maybe you should rest up a bit before . . . maybe that'd be better, Simon. What do you think, Captain Taber?'

Publicly, Captain Taber thought Mr Satchwell would indeed benefit from a longer recovery period. Privately, Captain Taber thought that he wouldn't want a weakling like Mr Satchwell anywhere near an operation with which he was involved.

'If you're sure, Travis,' said Simon. So, if he was going to contact Commander Shurion at all, he'd have to find another way. 'Maybe Richie can go with you instead.'

For whom volunteering was also an alien concept. But he ought to say yes now. 'Uh, I . . .' With everyone's eyes on him. Naughton's. Morticia's. Poncy bloody Tony Clive's. He *wanted* to say yes – part of him did. The part of him his mum had believed would benefit from joining the forces. The part that was capable of feeling pride and courage, that suspected that there were some things that were right and some things that were wrong. The part he'd kept hidden away for years, like a prisoner in a dungeon, a cell to which he couldn't yet find the key. Maybe it was lost. And Richie shrugged, clamped his lips shut, wrinkled his brow and peered down at the table. Damn Satchwell for exposing his cowardice.

He heard the disappointment in Naughton's voice. 'Okay, well, that's just the two of us, then.'

'Perhaps one of the girls should accompany you as well,' Dr Mowatt suggested. 'The Scytharene sound rather a sexist culture. Perhaps they'll pay less attention to a female.'

'I'll go.' Linden and Jessica spoke as one.

'No you won't.' So did Travis and Antony, and for the same reasons. Mel saw their respective gazes lock on to their girlfriends'. Nobody was looking at her.

'But Travis . . .'

'But Antony . . .'

'*I'll* go.' Then everyone was looking at her, Mel had spoken with such finality. 'I *want* to go. I don't want to stay here.' Not with Jessica. She wanted to be far away from Jessica.

'But Mel, are you sure you're up to . . .?'

'I'm fine, Trav. There's nothing wrong with me. I can do this. Let me do this. Let me be the girl on the team. *Please.*'

Travis seemed a little puzzled by her vehemence, but, 'Okay, Mel. Far as I'm concerned, you want it, you've got it. Antony?'

The Harringtonian approved of Mel's participation in the mission too. As did Dr Mowatt and Captain Taber. Mel was in. She'd be leaving the Enclave tomorrow early with the two boys, which was good.

If she never returned, she thought, that would be even better.

'So what's this about, Simon?' Travis said, the boy in glasses ushering him into his room and closing the door kind of surreptitiously behind them. 'If you're still upset over not coming with Antony and Mel and me tomorrow, don't be. You do need time to recover from the ordeal you've already been through. We all did, and we at least had each other. You know I'd want you in my corner otherwise, don't you?'

'It's not about that,' Simon said tersely. 'It's about Coker.'

'Richie?'

And it's about you, Travis, Simon thought grimly. *About whether I trust you or whether I throw in my lot finally and decisively with*

Commander Shurion. So I suppose it's about me, too. All of us. What you say in the next few minutes will decide the future for all of us. This is your test.

'Richie how?'

'Coker doesn't deserve to be here with us, in the Enclave, Travis. He doesn't deserve to be one of us.'

Travis winced. He'd thought – hoped – that Simon had got over his Richie fixation. 'Didn't we sort this out when we first left Wayvale?' Though it was probably easy for Travis to say. Richie Coker hadn't been making *his* life a misery for years. He ought to be fair to Simon.

'You said, Travis, I remember what you said, when you and Mel voted for Coker to join up with us, you said we needed him – in case there was fighting to be done. Well, we don't need him for that now, do we? Not with all the weapons the Enclave's got two floors above our heads.'

'Well, no, in that sense I guess you're right, but . . .'

'And Mel said, if he stepped out of line once, we'd ditch him, and you didn't disagree, Travis. We have to have people around us we can trust, don't we?'

Travis frowned. 'You're leading up to something, Simon. Why don't you just tell me what it is.'

'You *can't* trust Coker, Travis. None of us can.' And whatever the more covert purpose of this conversation, Simon truly believed that. 'You said he'd change but he hasn't changed. You reckoned he'd reform but he's the same bastard piece of shit he always was.'

'Simon.' Travis recoiled as if he'd been physically struck. He didn't think he'd ever heard the bespectacled boy swear before. It didn't seem right. It didn't sound like Simon.

'He beat me up, Travis.'

'What? When?' Not that Travis didn't believe Simon, but . . .

'At Harrington. At the party. The night the Scytharene came. Coker beat me to the floor and threatened there'd be more of that, lots more, if I ever told you or Antony or anyone what I knew about him.'

'What . . . do you know about him?'

'During the battle with Rev and his bikers, I was posted to the first floor with Giles to monitor and report on Rev's strength, his plan of attack . . .'

'I remember.'

'Well, later on, I was making my way down to the quad – you saw me there – but not before I saw Richie.' Hatred distorted Simon's features. 'Running *up* the stairs. Away from the fighting. Leaving the rest of us to risk our lives while he fled and hid himself in the dorms. You see what I mean, Travis? Coker's a coward. He's only interested in saving his own skin. If he had to betray us to the Scytharene or something to do that, he would. Without a thought. You can't trust him.'

Travis frowned. Simon's depiction of Richie behaving less than heroically had a ring of truth about it. 'That's bad, Simon, what Richie did. It's bad. No doubt about it.'

'It's unforgivable, Travis.'

'Well, unforgivable . . . Maybe he's just taking longer to change than we'd hoped. But I think he *is* learning. I mean, I know you weren't there, but when we broke out of the ship, Richie grabbed a subjugator and stood by our side. That wasn't the action of a total coward.'

Simon snorted cynically. 'I suppose neither was his absolute refusal to accompany you and Antony tomorrow. He can pick and choose when to do the right thing, can he, Travis? I wouldn't have thought you'd be a fan of that. Coker cannot be relied on.'

'All right. For the sake of argument, let's assume he can't. What are you proposing we do about it, Simon? Kick him out of the Enclave now? Take him back to Harrington or somewhere and just abandon him there?'

Like you abandoned me, Simon thought. '*Exactly,*' he said.

'We can't.' Travis gave a simple shrug. 'We can't do that. Even if Richie's conduct was entirely beyond the pale, and like I said, I think he's gradually becoming less selfish, less of a thug, we couldn't just throw him out. The Scytharene'll pick him up, pack him in a cryo-tube, make him a slave for the rest of his life. No one deserves that.'

'Coker does,' Simon snarled.

'I know the two of you still have issues, Simon, but if you can find it in you to give Richie another chance . . . It'd show you're more of a man than he is, for a start.'

Simon pressed his lips together in a thin, bitter smile. 'So you're telling me Coker stays. Regardless.'

'We have to pull together, Simon. We're in this to—'

'No. Travis. Spare me the speeches. Just – That's what you're telling me, is it? Despite what I've told you, despite what I want, Coker stays. I wouldn't like there to be any scope for misunderstanding.'

Travis regarded his friend curiously. 'Richie stays,' he said.

'Fine. Fine. Thanks for clarifying matters.' Simon turned away so Travis could not possibly see the tears in his eyes, like drops of acid. 'I know where I stand now.'

And who with, Simon brooded. Since Travis insisted on valuing scum like Coker over and above Simon himself, the bespectacled boy was left with only one course of action. *And on Travis's own head be it.*

History, Jessica reflected. Mr Franks had told them that those who failed to learn from the mistakes of the past would be condemned to repeat them. He'd been a gloomy sort of teacher, Mr Franks; Jessica had always imagined he'd chosen to immerse himself in years gone by because he couldn't bring himself to face what was happening today – she'd always kind of sympathised. And he'd told them that nobody ever really learned anything, that the human race never truly improved or advanced, not where it mattered, in hearts, in minds, and that therefore history was in essence an endless cycle of repetition. Different times, yes. Different names. 'Same old shit,' as Mel had whispered in her ear – when Jessica had been happy to allow Mel that close to her.

Repetition.

Dawn at Harrington, mere days ago, Travis and Antony had set out to locate and make contact with an alien spacecraft. Now, today, another dawn – according to the clocks – in another place, but the two teenagers were preparing to journey again to the Scytharene ship. They had a slightly different intention in mind on this occasion, true, and their previous companions being unavailable, only one other person was joining them, but for Jessica there was still a sense that all this had happened before. The cycle of history.

How she prayed that for once it could be broken, that they'd learned enough from their last encounter with the Scytharene to outwit and defeat the aliens this time.

The seven teenagers were gathered in the recreation room

prior to the expedition's departure. Travis, Antony and Mel had dressed in jeans and sweatshirts supplied to them by Captain Taber – it obviously wouldn't do for them to be captured wearing either regulation Enclave fatigues or the grey uniform of the processed Scytharene slave.

Jessica would have hugged Travis whatever he'd been wearing, and begged him to stay safe, to come back safe. He was like family. As for Antony, 'You know,' she said as they embraced, 'I think I could get used to your arms around me. I want to get used to it, Antony. Don't let this be the last time you hold me. Don't take any stupid chances out there.'

'You needn't worry about me,' Antony said staunchly.

'I can't help it. And you know what? I don't want to help it. What I want is this.' And before the Sickness, Jessica would never have dreamed of being so forward with a boy. She draped her arms around Antony's neck and pressed herself against him, lifted her mouth up to his. Their lips touched, tasted. They lingered. They parted. For now, Jessica pledged silently. Only for now. 'Be careful, Antony.'

And she should have said the same kind of thing to Mel, Mel who was hanging around looking pained and isolated but restless, too, like she couldn't wait to be on her way. Mel who was her best friend – or had been. But Jessica didn't know how to speak to Mel now, how to approach her, how to put things right between them, if that was even possible. It was easier pretty much to ignore her. And it was simpler and safer to keep her feelings for Mel inside, unspoken, sheltered from misinterpretation. Because Jessica still loved Mel, as a friend. She still prayed that no harm would come to her, today or any day. And really, she longed to hug Mel, too. Only she didn't dare.

Linden crept up on Travis from behind. He felt her breath, warm, tickling, thrilling, on the nape of his neck. 'Jessica and Antony, then,' she observed.

'It certainly looks that way.'

'What do you think?'

'Good luck to them. I think they make a great couple.'

'I used to think the same about Travis and Linden.'

'Used to?' Travis turned to look at her. There was hurt etched on both their faces.

'Well, they just seem to keep getting things wrong, don't they?'

'I blame him. He can be a real idiot sometimes. Drones on about the big picture, not that that's wrong in itself, but sometimes he forgets that the beauty of a picture is in the detail.'

'No, I think she's at fault. She can just be too damned impatient. Rushes into things. Doesn't think. Especially physical things. She likes – she needs physical things. That's her.'

'It's not a crime. But him, he's got a few hang-ups, I think. In that direction. I happen to know he's not exactly what you'd call experienced. Actually, he's never, well, I know it's hard to believe, but he's never actually been with a girl, slept with – you know.'

'I don't think she'll care about that in the slightest. I know she doesn't. And I know she's sorry if he thinks she's trying to force him into something he's not ready for. Thing is, she kind of gets confused about sex and love. Thinks they're the same thing.'

'They can be. They ought to be.'

'Only sometimes they're not. She's found that out to her cost.'

'And sometimes they are. Maybe for Linden and Travis they will be. I kind of think they will – soon.'

'I think she'll be prepared to wait. She'll want to do that. Good things are worth waiting for.'

'Still, she shouldn't have to wait for ever. I think he'll want to talk things through when all this business with the Scytharene ship is done. I think, then, Linden and Travis can be together. For real.'

'God, I hope so, Trav.'

She placed her hand on his chest as she'd longed to do when his skin had been bare. He raised it to his lips and kissed her fingers, drawing her to him.

'Me too. I've missed you, Linden. I'm sorry what happened the other night.'

And she felt his body beneath his clothes, and soon there'd be nothing to keep them apart. 'Trav,' she said as he graduated from fingers to neck to mouth, 'I don't know what I'd do without you. You're the only boy for me, Travis, the only boy in the world.'

So Naughton and Hippie Chick were getting into the tonsil hockey. So were Tony Clive and Barbie. Maybe he should have volunteered for their stupid bloody suicide mission after all, Richie thought ruefully. Might have earned him some lip action himself. He could always have done a runner soon as they sniffed trouble. At least Morticia looked miserable, though he doubted she could be feeling as bad as he was.

Bloody Simes. Just when Richie had been starting to change his mind about the four-eyed little twerp, just when – almost – he was beginning to regard Satchwell with something close to respect, Simes had to go and spoil it by putting him, Richie, on the spot like that, humiliating him in front of the others, proving he'd deserved all the beatings Richie and his cronies had lavished on him over the years. *Deserved* them.

Because the way the others had looked at him since. Not like they hated his guts or something, not like they were suspicious of him, the way Morticia for one had looked at him even after he'd saved their arses from Jester's mob back in Wayvale before they knew of the Scytharene's existence. They weren't *hostile* to him any more. It was more like they couldn't care less what he did or who he was. They were past caring. Like they didn't expect anything good from him. Like he'd let them down once too often. He'd had his chance – blown it.

Unlike Naughton, of course. Not only was Naughton volunteering to be dragged back to that nightmare bloody Scytharene ship, but the whole hare-brained scheme was his idea. Finding this Darion geezer, trusting an alien. Richie trusted no one. Actually, that wasn't entirely true.

He trusted Naughton, damn it.

And he wanted what Naughton had. He wondered what that would be like, not to be Richie Coker for a bit, to forget being Richie Coker. To be Travis. To have people respond to him as if he was Travis Naughton. Hippie Chick, for example, *Linden*, the way she was clinging on to Naughton now, tearfully, her tears on his skin, the way she was kind of rubbing up against him, like he could have her if he felt like it, whenever he wanted to, just say the word. Bit of a turn-on, that. If Richie was Travis, she'd be like that for him. If only.

And while the couples said their goodbyes and Richie and Mel kept their own counsel, Simon regarded the whole group with increasing disdain. Their sordid little relationships. Their pathetic little plan. Did Travis really believe it was going to work? He probably did. He thought he knew everything. But he didn't. Simon knew things, too.

That the time for him to reveal his new loyalties was near. That the traitor Darion and all of them were doomed.

Last spring it would have been a pleasant day for a stroll. Warm, bright, peaceful among the trees and the drowse of Nature. Context was everything, though, Travis reflected. Last spring there'd been no Sickness, no Scytharene. Today there was, and the surroundings could not provide him with comfort, however hard they tried.

The three teenagers had left the Enclave several hours ago. Keeping a discreet distance behind them, a vigilanteye floated in pursuit, relaying every detail of their trek back to the Enclave's monitoring and communications centre. Travis and Antony were not exactly slacking, but Mel was striding out in the general direction of Vernham Hill so swiftly she was almost at a run, as if she was being chased.

'Mel, slow down,' Travis called after her. 'We need to keep together. The idea's to get captured, not separated.'

'Yeah, if I meet a Scytharene I'll scream,' Mel retorted, turning to face her companions and walking backwards. 'Only I thought you two Romeos might want to be alone to swap notes about your Juliets.'

'We've got more important things to think about than relationships right now,' Travis said – then hoped Linden wasn't sitting in the monitoring and communications centre listening to him.

'Relationships are all boys *ever* want to think about, if you know what I mean.'

'Actually, I don't and I'm not sure I want to.' Travis was beginning to wonder whether bringing Mel with them was a mistake. She was behaving oddly, kind of recklessly. 'Just don't get too far ahead of us, Mel.'

'Don't worry. I'm only a girl. I'm bound to need you two hunks to protect me sooner or later.' Sarcastically.

'I must admit,' said Antony, 'I'd feel safer myself if we'd come equipped with the subjugators or a selection of Captain Taber's army-issue goodies.'

'What, and put the Scytharene on to us right away?' Travis's eyes flashed. 'Great idea, Antony.'

'I was joking, Travis,' Antony said with a sense of grievance.

'Oh.' *Obviously.*

'You *can* assume a certain amount of common sense in others, you know, Travis. You're not the only one capable of rational thought.'

'Of course not. I'm sorry, Antony. I didn't mean to sound so . . . stress, I guess. Some of those what ifs that didn't seem much to worry about when we were back in the Enclave – not finding Darion at all comes to mind – out here now, when a Culler or a battlepod could appear any minute, they kind of loom a little larger, don't they?'

'We'll be all right. If we keep our heads. If we remember what we're doing this for. At Harrington we were taught that good always triumphs in the end.'

'Let's hope so.' Travis thought it politic not to undermine Antony's sentiment by mentioning the end that had befallen the Harrington School itself. Besides, his friend's certainty heartened him. 'I *am* sorry if I put your back up before, Antony. I'm glad you're here. Not just anyone. You. I think we've proved already we make a good team.'

'A team, yes,' Antony said pointedly. 'Equal partners.'

'The only kind worth having.' Travis glanced ahead. 'As for Mel – I don't know what's got into Mel lately, but something has.'

Antony thought he might have an idea but elected to preserve a diplomatic silence. He ought to have a little chat with the black-haired girl himself first, but as Travis had said, now was not the time to become sidetracked.

Particularly not as Mel was suddenly hailing them, gesticulating frenziedly for them to join her. 'Trav! Antony! Take a look at this!'

The boys pelted to her side, the vigilanteye hovering at theirs. 'Oh my God,' breathed Travis.

The teenagers found themselves on the fringe of the forest. From here the ground sloped gently downwards to make a broad trough of grass before it rose towards woodland once more, a couple of hundred metres opposite them. A long way to their left, thicker undergrowth grew, clumps of sheltering trees. Even further to their right, steeper ground, higher hills. But the immediate object of their attention, straggling over the expanse below them, was children. Scores of children, maybe hundreds, a great multitude. Of every age. From teenagers of sixteen and seventeen to infants of four and five. The older ones in many cases carrying the younger. Others holding hands, strung out in lines, several dozen children linked together. Hair wild. Clothes crumpled. Expressions glazed and eyes staring, fixed on a point somewhere ahead of them, somewhere above them. Moving as silently and unthinkingly as a breeze across a field of harvest wheat. In unison. As one. All of them. From left to right in the same, single direction.

'Refugees,' Mel murmured, her brow furrowed, 'and no one to save them. *Trav* . . .' As if Travis might.

'No. This is not good,' Antony moaned. 'This is not good at all. You know where they're heading?' Pointing to the most prominent rise in sight. 'Vernham Hill. They'll blunder straight into the Scytharene!'

'They can't do that. They mustn't,' Mel declared agitatedly. 'We have to stop them, Trav.'

'I know. We will.' He addressed the vigilanteye. 'You heard all that? You can see? Stay here so you don't frighten any of the kids. We're going to warn them away. Come on,' he urged Antony and Mel.

Perhaps for the first time since they left the Enclave, the three teenagers acted in complete concert. 'Stop! Wait! Hey!' Racing down the slope towards the children.

There were so many of them, though. Mel's heart sank. What could be done for so many? And maybe they couldn't all hear. Maybe none of them could. Because they weren't stopping and they weren't waiting. They were surging on, as if driven by some inner compulsion that could not be denied. They didn't even seem to register the newcomers' arrival, not even when Mel and the boys charged out directly in front of them.

'You've got to stop! You've got to go back! Listen to us. The aliens are this way.' Travis and Antony were throwing their arms wide, confronting the crowd with brutal reality, yelling out like prophets in the wilderness. 'They're Scytharene. They're slavers. Go back. Go on and the aliens will make you slaves. Stop. Wait. Listen to us.'

This wasn't going to work.

Canute, Mel thought, trying to hold back the tide. Antony and Trav, they had the right idea but they also had limits. It was easier to sway one than a hundred and one.

The crowd didn't look like it had leaders as such any more than a flock of sheep does, but there were several older teenagers marching out a little further ahead of the others. Maybe they had influence. Mel dashed to one of them, a girl with tangled auburn hair and a bloody lip, a girl carrying a sobbing little boy with several other sobbing little boys trailing behind her. Mel made herself an obstacle.

'Listen to us. You can't go this way. It's dangerous. The aliens . . .' Her blood froze. On the other girl's face, blankness. In the other girl's eyes, deadness. No sign of caring or spark of life. She was a zombie, an automaton. Glancing at the kids around her, Mel saw that they all were. Like Jessica had been after the Sickness. And Jessica had been brought back. 'We can help you if you *listen* to us,' Mel cried, grabbing the girl's shoulders. But the girl shrugged out of Mel's grasp, continued on her way, like a machine subject to an overriding program.

Further along the line, Travis and Antony were similarly failing to check the remorseless advance. The throng of youths was like a body of water flooding past them that they had no power either to arrest or divert. They were reduced to shouting, waving, darting between one youngster and another, seizing arms, shaking shoulders. None of it did any good. It was like trying to wake the dead.

In the midst of the multitude, the three teenagers came together again.

'Travis, it's horrible.' Mel shuddered. 'It's like their minds are shot.'

'Their spirits are broken.' Travis's tone was bleak. 'They don't have the strength to stand. They don't have the will to fight. They've given up already. It's not just down to the Sickness or the Scytharene. These are the kids our society has produced.'

'Travis, what if' – and Antony appeared shocked by the thought – 'what if they *know* where they're heading?'

And above Vernham Hill, rising into the cloudless sky, the glittering silver sickle of first one Culler, then another. Soaring over thick forest towards the open ground, towards the mass of young people. Twin scythes preparing for a slave harvest.

Battlepods billowed from the ships' underbellies like bubbles blown by children on a summer afternoon.

'No,' Mel cried in futile denial. 'No!'

And at last a sound from the children surrounding her. Mel remembered it from the captured Harringtonians in the cell aboard the Scytharene ship and condemned to slavery, the groaning anguish of the soul. Here it loudened, escalated, crescendoed into the shrillness of a scream of fear, the scream of prey when it knows the predator is poised to pounce.

Yet even now there were dissenters. Some of the youngsters thrust their arms up and open-palmed, lifted their faces imploringly, their eyes half closed, like worshippers of a god who had finally come to Earth. Some even ran forward with a manic desperation that suggested they regarded the aliens as a source of comfort and help.

When they were within range, the battlepods shot those down first.

Most of the children, however, fled.

Bodies buffeted Mel now as panic took hold and the youths stampeded. She couldn't stand against them, could hardly keep her balance. They were going to knock her to the ground, trample her into the soil. Or they were going to bear her away with them as helplessly as a straw on an ocean and she would never see Travis again or Jessica to explain and to beg for another—

Travis gripped her hand, held her fast.

'Let's keep together, huh?' His eyes like blue stars.

Firework flashes from the battlepods. White lightning forking to earth. The cold crackle of the energy bolts. The glass and silver spheres swooped over the scattering mass of youngsters, firing at will, rarely missing. Children frozen in their moments of terror but briefly before slumping to the ground and into blessed unconsciousness.

Mel saw the armoured Scytharene in the pods, their black animal masks disguising their true features which, while white in hue, seemed to Mel in essence blacker still. 'Bastards,' she spat.

'What do we do?' Antony, as a ten-year-old boy who'd been running at full tilt crashed to the ground beside him, the energy blast still flickering across his body as though encasing him in ice. 'Try to stay out of their way or . . . we want to get caught, don't we?' He didn't sound too enthusiastic now that their opportunity had arrived.

'What about the kids, Trav?' Mel demanded.

Travis's decision was delayed. Suddenly and startlingly, in a whoosh of smoke, from the cover of the trees on the far side of the grassy strip, a rocket shot into the air. Like a shell from a bazooka, Travis had time to think, before it struck an astonished and unprepared battlepod and blew it to pieces. Shards of twisted, smouldering metal fell from the sky. The craft's pilot had to have been killed. *Good*. And better, it seemed the battlepods weren't protected from attack by the same shields as the mother ship. Maybe they required more power to function than the man-sized spheres could generate.

Captain Taber would be interested in that.

'Trav!' Mel, pointing, as with a revving of engines and whoops of bravado, the source of the rocket assault became clear. Motorbikes, roaring out of the forest, numbering well into double figures, leather-clad teenagers at the handlebars. A Charge of the Light Brigade with a post-Victorian kind of horsepower. Several cars tore into sight as well, battered four-by-fours, one with its roof somehow ripped off. A guy with a hand-held rocket launcher in the back, firing again at the pods. Many of his comrades were also armed. Shotguns. Rifles. Was that the rattle of machine-guns? But Travis doubted that bullets would trouble the battlepods. 'Who the hell . . .?' Mel cried.

Some of the pods sheared off from the main focus of the Scytharene's onslaught to counter this new enemy. Energy bolts stabbed at the fast-moving vehicles, found them more difficult targets to pick off. Bikes wove crazily between the blasts.

They zipped among the fleeing children, too, adopting the same direction, and where they could, their riders braked, scooped a youngster up and perched him or her on the bike behind them before screeching away again over the grass. The cars were attempting the same thing, slowing with drivers bellowing at kids to pile in, the terrified youngsters cramming on to the back seats.

'It's a rescue mission,' Travis realised.

As a trio of Harleys scorched up alongside them, a vacancy on each for a pillion passenger.

And, 'I don't believe it,' he gaped.

'Well you'd *better* believe it. We meet again, kiddo,' said Rev.

TEN

It was him, beyond a doubt. The pockmarked, unhealthy skin. The vaguely lupine features.

'Get on. You're wasting time.' Rev thumbed to the seat behind him. ''Less you *want* to get zapped by those damn things.'

'Trav?' As Mel and Antony were issued identical invitations by Rev's companions.

This wasn't the moment to explain that actually, yes, they *did* want the Scytharene to abduct them. Every second the three bikers expended on his own group jeopardised their continued freedom. Travis couldn't have that.

'Let's go,' he said.

'More like it.' Rev nodded as Travis mounted up behind him, Mel and Antony following suit on the other bikes. 'Go's the word.' He gunned the engine.

Travis lurched back in the seat as the Harley accelerated, grabbed hold of Rev's leather jacket to steady himself. And Rev yelling for him to hang on. Not so long ago, Travis might have expected the biker not only to relish the chance to push him off himself but also to take great pleasure in then running over his head while he lay on the ground. From the roadblock where they'd first encountered each other to the storming of the Harrington School, there'd never been much love lost between Travis and Rev.

Maybe things had changed.

With Rev threading his expert way between sprinting, squealing children, Travis glanced to the rear. The guy with the rocket-launcher was still in action, only now the battle-pods, wise to the weapon, flitted out of the missiles' range. The rockets' impotent parabolas plunged them into the ground instead, where their final detonations meant nothing.

The teenager firing them must have realised his number was up. He was barking something to the driver of one of the four-by fours, probably along the lines of 'Let's get the hell out of here,' given the sudden burst of speed the driver applied to the vehicle. He'd have needed Concorde velocity to escape the battlepods now, however. Half a dozen bolts of yellow energy seared from the sky, any one of them destructive enough to obliterate the car and all within. They struck together.

The explosion signalled the end of even token resistance. Rev's forces were now in full retreat, augmented by as many kids as the various vehicles could carry. The hapless youngsters still on foot had to seek safety as best they could. Very few reached the trees whichever way they fled. The Scytharene's blasts cut swathes through them, effortlessly, ruthlessly.

And the Cullers were commencing their operations too, now, hovering above the ground where the fallen children lay, activating their tractor beams. In the white light's embrace the youths were lifted carefully, almost paternally into the bodies of the ships. Dozens of them rising together, like souls ascending to Heaven. Only they'd wake in the cells of the slavecraft.

'Poor bastards, huh, kiddo?' Rev called back over the roar of the engine. 'Well, we'll make these aliens suffer soon enough.'

Travis would have liked to ask exactly what Rev meant, but the biker was abruptly compelled into taking immediate and extreme evasive action. Battlepods above them to right and left, establishing a crossfire of energy rays directly in their path. Rev swung the Harley hectically from left to right, the machine obeying its rider with almost psychic precision but its tyres slipping dangerously on the grass. One slip too far, one slight and single lapse of concentration on Rev's part, and there'd be two more slaves for the Cullers to collect. A bolt lancing blindingly close to Travis's right shoulder. More spearing to the left like railings in a deadly kind of fence. Rev undeterred. Rev whooping defiance and reckless joy.

And punching the air with his fist, flipping the bird to the battlepods as the Harley raced between trees at the far end of the stretch of open ground. Most of the other bikes had made it too. With relief, Travis saw Mel, saw Antony. The battlepods reared higher again and wheeled above the wood, seemed to be returning to finish off the children still caught in plain sight.

Travis breathed more easily. Not for the first time, the forest had saved them.

'What do you mean, lost them?' Linden rose from her seat in the monitoring and communications centre in sheer disbelief. 'The vigilanteye get a speck of dirt in its lens or something?'

'The vigilanteye is operating perfectly,' Dr Mowatt said as

though to suggest otherwise was tantamount to a personal insult. 'You can see that, surely?'

Linden could. So could everyone else in the moncom centre, Jessica, Simon and Richie, Dr Mowatt and Captain Taber, a quartet of techs working at the control panels and the screens. The screens that provided them with the vigilanteye's view – from a safe distance among the trees – of a kind of field littered with unconscious children, Cullers tractor-beaming them into captivity.

'Unfortunately,' the Scientific Director conceded, 'we can only see what the vigilanteye can see.'

'Well if it got nearer,' protested Jessica, 'we might be able to see a bit more.'

'Increase magnification to maximum, Stephen,' Mowatt instructed one of the techs. 'This is the best we can do. We can't allow the vigilanteye to be spotted and then perhaps appropriated by the Scytharene. It might lead them to us.'

'This place is just full of the spirit of self-sacrifice, isn't it?' muttered Linden.

At least now she could make out the faces of the casualties, faces of little boys and girls who, when sleeping like this, should be doing so in their own beds in their own homes, not sprawled on the grass beneath the pitiless gaze of alien warriors. Linden scanned many faces, too many, but she didn't recognise a single one. Travis was not among them (neither were Antony or Mel). She wasn't sure whether she should feel delight or dismay.

'The Cullers could already have them,' observed Simon dispassionately.

'Maybe, but I thought I saw Mel at least on a motorbike,' Jessica said. Certainly there'd been a girl being driven off, her long black hair streaming out behind her. It *could* have been Mel. 'I can't be sure. All those *children* . . .'

'The plan was to get themselves captured.' Simon again. 'Why would they even try to get away?'

'If we hadn't lost sight of them in the crowd in the first place,' Linden cursed.

'Don't worry about it, Linden.' Comfort from an unlikely source: Richie. 'Naughton knows what he's doing. He'll be fine. Trust me.'

'Trust you?' said Linden.

'Say they're not there,' Jessica was assuming. 'Say they were picked up by those bikers . . .'

'Doubt our old mate Rev's one of them,' Richie grunted. 'Tosser.'

'Can't we program the vigilanteye to search for them, Dr Mowatt?'

'We could,' said the Scientific Director.

'But we won't,' refused Captain Taber. 'There's too much alien activity at present to justify the risk to our own security that the loss of a vigilanteye might incur, as Dr Mowatt has already pointed out. Program the unit to return to the Enclave, Mr Macy. Mr Naughton, Mr Clive and Miss Patrick understood what the mission entailed before they took it on. We have no choice but to wait to hear from them and to hope that we do. Whether they are prisoners of the Scytharene or not . . .'

'*From now on,*' Jessica replayed Taber's final words in her mind, '*they're on their own.*'

As was she.

226

They'd left the moncom centre a while ago on the understanding that if there was any news, they were to be informed immediately, whatever the hour. Linden had looked like she could do with some company, hadn't wanted to let Jessica out of her sight, in actual fact, but the blonde girl had excused herself anyway. She preferred to be alone just now.

Getting used to it, maybe.

The three people who were closest to her, the three people who meant the most to her in the world, they were gone. Whether their absence was likely to be as dark and as permanent as her parents' remained to be seen – God, and she prayed *not* – but she had no guarantee. She might never see Travis or Antony again. Or Mel. As she wandered the empty corridors of the Enclave, Jessica had to acknowledge that possibility, prepare for it, mentally and physically.

There was an old saying she remembered. She thought a philosopher might have coined it, that one with the German name that sounded like somebody sneezing. *That which does not destroy us makes us stronger.* Yeah, well, Herr German Philosopher hadn't had to contend with the Sickness and the Scytharene in swift succession. But he was right. It was astonishing what you could cope with in the end, sort of unreasonable, frightening. Even her. Even Ken Lane's little princess, pretty little Jessie with her hair in bows who was going to marry a prince dressed in pink (her, not the prince) and live happily ever after – in a world that no longer existed. She almost hadn't made it, of course. Her parents' deaths had almost crushed her spirit. But thanks to Travis (and Mel), thanks to their love for her, she'd survived. She'd lived. And her spirit was strong inside her, maybe stronger than it had ever been.

But could she go on without those *she* loved? That would be hard. Who would fight for her then?

She would have to fight for herself.

The sound of gunshots alerted her to where her random course had brought her. Perhaps not so random. The shooting range on the upper level. A handful of soldiers in combats practising their skills, imagining no doubt that their targets were not humans in wood and paint but Scytharene in flesh and blood.

One of the soldiers, a young man who seemed to have been born without a neck, called to her. 'Hey, girlie, how'd you like to get your hands on my weapon?' Maybe he had *some* neck, after all.

Jessica paused, considered. Once she'd have simpered or blushed at a boy's innuendo, been embarrassed. Now, though, 'If you mean, would I like you to teach me how to shoot that rifle you're holding, I think I would.'

'Now you're talking,' laughed the soldier. 'Come over here. What's your name?'

'Jessica,' she said, taking the offered gun and weighing it in her hands as if reaching a judgement.

She would have to fight for herself.

They picked up a road and followed it several miles before pulling into a layby where once families might have stopped to picnic. No such thing as picnics any more, Travis reflected, or, indeed, families. Enemies, on the other hand . . . At least there was no sign of Scytharene pursuit.

'So how you doing, kiddo?' Rev enquired affably once they'd both dismounted the bike.

'I've been worse,' Travis responded cautiously, 'though I've been better, too.'

'Haven't we all?' Rev guffawed. 'Bastard aliens.' He surveyed the layby. 'Still, not bad. We lost some, we gained some.' The biker's original force was certainly depleted; although the smaller and more manoeuvrable motorbikes had generally evaded the battlepods' blasts and were parked up alongside their leader, only two of the cars had made it, from which sniffling younger children now spilled. 'That makes it . . . what's the word?' – glancing around as if expecting someone to be there to assist him with his vocabulary, but nobody was – 'well, who cares? We kicked alien arse, didn't we?'

Antony and Mel joined Travis. 'Are you both all right?' he asked them.

'Sure,' Mel said. 'You?'

'Jury's out on that one,' Travis muttered, remembering being surrounded by goons and guns in Rev's company before.

'What are you looking so down about, kiddo? We're still breathing, aren't we? I know why.' Rev grinned. 'You don't trust me, do you?'

'Given our previous meetings, that can't come as a surprise, can it?'

'S'pose not. I've held a gun to your guts. You've held one to my head.' He turned his attention to Mel and Antony. 'I recognise you two. You' – Mel – 'were with kiddo here at the roadblock, weren't you, and you' – Antony – 'you're Head Prefect or whatever at that poxy bloody school we tried to take. Not sure I caught your names then.' They were supplied now. 'Yeah, well you don't have to look like the end is nigh, either. It ain't. All that bad blood between us, forget it. What's the word? Water under the bridge. Yesterday's news. What I'm saying is, you can trust me now.'

'So what's changed, Rev?' Travis said.

'Everything. The aliens have come and they've changed everything – ain't you noticed?' Rev laughed hollowly. 'You and me, kiddo, all of us, we're on the same side now. It's us against them. No more of that custodians of the Queen's highway crap. Now we're the human resistance movement, like the Froggies in the war.'

'I'm pleased to hear it, Rev,' approved Travis. Because of course, he wanted to believe that people could change for the better, that people were capable of redeeming themselves. He'd hoped to see it with Richie, and still did. But he liked to think he wasn't naïve. Some people never altered. Others, it was depressing to acknowledge, maybe others changed for the worse. 'You've acquired some new weaponry, I see.'

'Yeah, I'll tell you all about that when we get back to base, kiddo. Don't you just love the way that sounds, *back to base*? But what are you three doing out here anyway? Thought you'd be cowering behind the walls at that school.'

'Harrington,' bridled Antony. 'The Harrington School, and we never cowered anywhere, as you well know.'

'The school's gone, Rev,' said Mel. 'Its walls are rubble. The Scytharene destroyed it.'

'The who?'

'The aliens.'

'Bastards. I mean, if we'd burned it down back when we were . . . well, that would have been different, but *this*.' Rev's eyes suddenly narrowed. 'How do you know they're called Scytharene?'

Travis explained. About the fall of Harrington and the teenagers' capture. About their ally and escape, though he didn't mention Darion by name – best to err on the safe side. About the Enclave. About their plan for *re*capture.

'No wonder you didn't look too keen to hop up on the bike,' Rev said. 'But you're thinking the wrong way, kiddo. I'm disappointed in you. You're trusting the wrong people.'

'If you mean Captain Taber and Dr Mowatt,' objected Antony, 'may I remind you that they're rather older than us, they have experience . . .'

'Of what?' countered Rev. 'Alien invasions? Any kid who reads comics or watches *Star Trek* or *Dr Who* knows more about aliens than a bunch of senile old gits in uniforms or white coats or whatever. They're adults. They screwed up the world in the first place. They knew shit before the Sickness and they know shit now. Don't put your faith in them.'

'Ludicrous,' huffed Antony.

'As for trusting an *alien*? You need your bloody head examined, kiddo,' recommended Rev, shaking his own in disbelief. 'Maybe you took a knock during our little disagreement before. It's them against us, and that ain't open to – what's the word? – negotiation.'

'Well if you're right,' warned Travis, 'it's going to be a pretty one-sided battle, and not in our favour.'

'Don't you believe it, kiddo, my man.' Rev tapped the side of his nose slyly. 'Come and see what *we* found. Those alien bastards are in for a shock.'

Simon waited with the indefatigable patience of the victim. How often had he spent breaktimes, entire lunch hours at school squatting under stairwells or beneath the stage (his favourite hiding place if the door wasn't locked), concealing himself in store cupboards among the cleaners' mops and disinfectants, silent, still, scarcely even breathing, prepared to stay there for the rest of the day, the rest of his life if to do so meant avoiding Richie Coker and his ilk, the extortion and the threats, the bullying, the blows.

It was a small matter for him to watch the moncom centre from a discreet distance until the duty operator finally sidled out of the room for an unscheduled and illicit break.

Nobody did their duty the way they should, Simon had always known that. People's indifference to their duty was what *created* victims, allowed bullying. For once, though, he was grateful for another's laxity. As soon as the operator had disappeared along the corridor, Simon was slinking into the moncom centre, like a rat in search of food.

He closed the door behind him and wondered where to start. The screens, which at present showed only views of the immediate above-ground vicinity of the Enclave, were irrelevant. It wasn't the monitoring capacity of the facilities that Simon needed to access, but the communications.

Specifically, he had to contact Commander Shurion.

But it had seemed more straightforward in theory. He'd anticipated simply sitting at a console, as he did now, and just pressing a button to open a channel that could be heard by the Scytharene ship. In reality, however, there seemed so many buttons *to* press, and if he made a mistake, he'd be found out. Simon's hands hovered over the console's control panel, like a magician's about to perform a trick. And if he was found out, then—

'Simon? What are you doing here?'

He was on his feet, whirling towards the door, almost sending his chair flying. 'I . . . ah . . . Dr Mowatt . . .'

Entering the room, the Scientific Director regarded him sympathetically. 'You don't need to look so troubled, Simon. I understand.'

'You do?' Simon gulped.

'Of course. You're worried about your friends, aren't you? But there's no need for you to come to moncom to check what's happening. Captain Taber and I told you, as soon as *we* have any news, you'll have news.'

'Sure. That makes me feel . . . thanks, Dr Mowatt.' *Thanks indeed, you stupid cow*, Simon thought, breathing a sigh of deep relief. 'I'd better just . . .' He indicated the door.

'Why don't you find your other friends?' Dr Mowatt suggested. 'And Simon, take heart. I'm sure everything will turn out just the way you want it to.'

Before the Sickness it had been a restaurant, one of a chain to tempt hungry motorists on long journeys. Travis had eaten in several himself in the old days, first with both parents and later just with Mum. The waitresses had been in the habit of plying him with pieces of moulded plastic they rather optimistically called toys – to begin with he'd imagined it was because they liked him, and it made him like them back. Eventually, though, he'd discovered that the distribution of toys to children was only company policy, a commercial device to lure in the lucrative family market. The food had never tasted quite as good again.

This particular restaurant came with a garage and a small hotel attached. It looked busy. Several dozen motorbikes, the latest, largest and fastest models, were parked around, as were army trucks, jeeps and four-by-four vehicles numbering well into double figures.

'Looks like Rev and his mates have moved in big-time,' observed Mel.

It seemed they had. Travis had never had the biker down as a Pied Piper type, but plenty of kids had followed him here one way or another: the new arrivals joined a mob of young-sters already resident in the hotel and quickly made themselves at home, gaining confidence from the company. Soon they were charging up and down the stairs, hooting at the tops of their voices.

'You seem to be allowing the younger members of your community to run riot,' Antony sniffed. 'That's not the way we did things at Harrington.'

Rev shrugged. 'It's the way we do things here, Ant.'

'Ony. Antony.'

'I think it's good,' said Mel, and not only to annoy her blond companion. 'Let the kids play. Let them forget for a while.'

A boy of nine or ten collapsed groaning and writhing with melodramatic zest at Mel's feet, clutching his stomach as if his innards were about to make a sudden, painful exit. His playmate, a girl of the same age, darted up and stood over him, pointing at him with fingers in the shape of a gun. 'Got you. You're dead, you alien bastard,' she squeaked.

'I'm an alien bastard,' the boy moaned. 'And I'm dead. Urgh!' Throwing his hands above his head as if surrendering to the inevitable.

'That'll teach you for killing my mummy,' the girl cried, kicking her little friend's leg. 'That'll teach you for killing my daddy. Alien bastard.'

'Good, Olivia,' approved Rev. 'Good.'

And Antony's expression communicated more effectively than telepathy that this *very* definitely was not how things had been done at Harrington.

Among the older teenagers in Rev's band, Travis was looking for two faces he'd have known had they been present. 'What happened to Ash?' he asked in the end. 'Is he still with you?'

'Who? Oh yeah. Ash.' Rev grinned mischievously. 'The guy who had your girlfriend before you did, kiddo, that who you mean? Never saw him again after you gave us a kicking at Ant's school. Thought he was dead.'

'No. We let him leave like we let you,' Travis said.

'Dunno, then.' Rev appeared not to care, either. 'Maybe the aliens got him.'

'And what about . . . I was expecting to see a certain girl in leather . . .'

'Stevie.' Rev's brow wrinkled in what might have been pain. 'Oh, Stevie, yeah.' But his voice retained a tone of dismissiveness. 'She's gone for sure. The aliens did get her. I saw it. She fell off the bike. We were outrunning them and I told her to hold on to me, but . . . Stevie, yeah. Won't see her no more.'

'I'm sorry,' said Travis, as much for having doubted Rev's conversion to the side of the good guys as for the loss of the girl in leather. Maybe the two things went together.

'Yeah, well, what the hell, Stevie who? Come on.' Briskly, Rev led the three teenagers out of the hotel and into the restaurant itself. 'This is what I really want you to see. This'll impress you. Even you, Ant.'

The restaurant was offering a different menu post-Sickness. Fare with the potential to strike the recipient down with considerably more than a touch of indigestion. Machine-guns and other types of automatic weapons. Ammunition for the same. Grenades packed in boxes like eggs. More of the hand-held rocket-launchers Travis, Mel and Antony had already seen in action. Shells in plentiful supply. A virtual armoury where travellers had once savoured all-day breakfasts.

Mel whistled. 'I guess nobody smokes in here, huh?'

Antony was thinking, if Harrington had been equipped with this kind of hardware, maybe it would still be standing. Maybe his title of Head Boy would still have meaning.

Travis was thinking, not enough. Still not enough. Not against the battlepods and the shields. Rev was just another David when it came down to it, only in leather instead of a loincloth.

But the biker himself obviously reckoned his arsenal made him a Goliath. 'Pretty damn good, huh? Kiddo? We found an army depot the other side of Willowstock. Looked kind of makeshift. Lot of dead soldiers – from the Sickness. All this stuff was in it. Loads more as well but this is all we've got room for right now. Best not to keep all our stores in one place anyway, and this is enough for what we've got in mind.'

'You've got something in mind, Rev?' Travis asked.

'You bet, kiddo. We're gonna wipe out a few aliens *and* free some of our own kind.'

'You don't intend to attack the Scytharene ship, surely?' said Antony.

'Not yet,' said Rev. 'We've got a better target first, easier. There's one of those posh old stately homes not too far from here, the kind your granny probably used to like visiting in case she saw the Queen or some lord or somebody having

236

tea – Clarebrook House. The aliens have set up a prison camp in its grounds, a concentration camp. It's filled with kids. Only not after tonight it won't be. Not after we've put this little lot to use.'

'You're gonna break the kids out?' Mel said.

'In one, babe.' Rev winked. 'You want a piece of the action? You look like you do. I've got a seat going spare on the back of my bike.'

'Trav?' Mel seemed eager. Her eyes were bright. Disconcertingly bright, Travis thought, like Mel wasn't entirely in control of herself.

'Won't the camp be guarded?' he said.

'Probably, kiddo,' Rev conceded with good humour, 'but that's okay. Gives us someone to shoot.'

'It's not okay if there are way more of them than there are of you.' Travis frowned. 'You need to plan your operation, Rev, find out as much as you can about the Scytharene's numbers, defences, all that. You don't want this to turn into a suicide attack, do you?'

And Rev's eyes were shining too, and there was something irrational in them, and there was something glazed and distant about the biker as well, now that Travis thought about it. He'd seen the same aspect in the faces of the children marching willingly towards the Cullers. It was a kind of madness, an inability to cope with the nightmare of reality. It occurred to Travis that Rev didn't care whether his proposed raid on the prison camp was successful or not. It was going to be loud and violent, and that was enough.

'It's all right, kiddo,' Rev chuckled. 'You worry too much. We've got plans of the place if you want to see 'em. We know how it's laid out. Listen, this is your chance, though. Are you in or not? You've fought against me. Why not prove there's no hard feelings and fight *with* me for a change?'

'Come on, Trav,' encouraged Mel.

'If it works, we will be saving children from the cells,' Antony observed, though he was more concerned by the *if* than Mel appeared to be.

'You can still get yourself caught if you feel like it,' Rev said. 'Just stay behind when the rest of us leave. But you'll have helped liberate other kids. You can't lose.'

Travis wasn't so certain about that, but both Rev and Antony did have a point. And after all, *he'd* been the one urging Captain Taber to take direct action against the Scytharene. It was a risk, but 'All right, Rev,' he decided. 'Count us in.'

He only hoped Linden would understand.

She'd eaten little at lunchtime and less for dinner. Not that Richie normally paid much attention to Linden's dietary habits, but appetite, he knew, often signified a person's state of mind, and how Hippie Chick was feeling today was kind of important to him. If he was going to go through with his plans.

If he was going to seduce her.

She stayed in the canteen, too, long after everyone else had gone. Except himself, of course. She sat kind of hunched over the table with her arms folded and her fingers plucking at the elbows of her tunic, her shoulders rounded, her stare lowered and unreadable. Not happy, though. Kind of mournful. She didn't even seem to notice Richie was still there, at the other end of the table.

He'd been worried about Jessica. He'd felt certain that the two remaining girls, both their boyfriends lost in hostile territory, would want to cling together until there was news, support each other, the way the chicks always used to scamper off to the bogs together at clubs and discos to witter on about who they fancied and who they didn't. If Jessica had been around, that would have been a problem for Richie, but for some reason she'd been off doing her own thing most of the day, leaving little Linden all alone. Like now, for example.

Now was a good time.

He got up. First choice: should he sit opposite her or next to her? Opposite he'd be able to look her in the eye more easily. Next to and the comforting arm around the shoulder was in range. Richie didn't kid himself that Linden would ever be up for gazing longingly into his eyes, which were a muddyish sort of brown and might with some justification be called piggy. Next to sounded more promising.

'Hey, Linden,' he said.

She glanced up at him reluctantly. 'Richie?'

'How you holding up?' Sliding on to the chair to her right.

'I don't think I am.' She edged away from him a little. 'Sorry, Richie, I'm not very good company at the moment. I think I'd sooner be on my own if that's all right with you.'

Oh no. On her own, no. That wasn't all right with him. And he knew she didn't mean it. Hippie Chick wasn't one who did on her own.

'Naught— Travis is going to be okay, you know.'

'Is he?' Gloomily.

'Course he is. He won't let anything bad happen to him. Not with a gorgeous chick like you back here waiting for him.'

Linden smiled thinly. 'Compliments don't suit you, Richie.' But they sounded nice, even if they did include the word *chick*. Compliments were caresses without touch. If Travis had called her gorgeous . . .

'Course, if I was Travis,' Richie said, 'I wouldn't have left a girl like you in the first place, not even to save the whole bloody world.'

'I believe you, Richie. That's why you're not Travis. He's not selfish like you . . . like that. He puts other people first.'

'He ought to put you first. I would. If I was, like, you know, him.'

'Why are you talking like this, Richie?' Linden said quietly. Her voice didn't carry a lot of protest.

Richie's brow creased as he looked at her, and she seemed helpless, and she seemed vulnerable, and she seemed very, very desirable – but he didn't want to seduce her now. *Seduction* seemed kind of cold, calculating, cynical, kind of like bullying. He couldn't do that to Linden.

Yet he did still want her. Not just to have what Naughton had, not only that. For himself. For Richie Coker.

'I don't like to see you looking sad,' he said. 'A girl like you . . .'

Linden turned to him quizzically, uncertainly.

'You should never be sad. Or lonely.'

'I'm *not* . . .' Linden began. Then gave up. Because she was. Where was Travis? God, why wasn't Travis here? She wanted, *needed* him to hold her, to kiss her, to make her feel important and alive. But there was only Richie, and 'I don't know what you think you're playing at, Richie, but I'd sooner you didn't say things like that. I'm with Travis. You know. I'm with Travis.'

240

'Travis isn't here.'

'Well that doesn't mean you can just move in and try to take advantage of me when I'm . . . not feeling good.' As Ash had done. Ash had fooled her, exploited her, got his grubby hands on her. She'd vowed never to make the same mistake again. It ought to be easy not to repeat your mistakes.

'He could be here, though. Travis could.'

'I don't . . .' *Ought* to be easy.

'Close your eyes. Just . . . close your eyes.'

'What do you mean? I'm not just closing my eyes for you, Richie. This is ridiculous. Why . . .?'

'Close them,' Richie said. 'Imagine Travis is here.'

'He isn't.'

'Then you've got nothing to lose, have you? Eyes,' coaxed Richie. Linden's deep hazel eyes.

Closed. 'I'm going to regret this. I'm regretting this al—'

'Ssh,' Richie whispered. None of this was what he'd planned, what he'd expected, but he was in the moment now and he could pretend for a little while, he could be who he wanted to be, who Linden wanted him to be. 'Travis is here.'

'Richie, you . . .'

'Don't talk. Don't open your eyes. Don't nothing. Just imagine. Just feel. A hand.' He pressed the flat of his left palm against Linden's back. The girl shivered, uttered a little sigh, but she didn't draw away, not now. Instead, she sat up and arched her back, and Richie stroked the shape of her shoulder-blade, squeezed her left shoulder. 'Another hand.' His fingers inserting themselves between her own, easing her right hand away from its unnecessary business at her tunic's elbow. Her eyes were still shut. Linden was dreaming. 'They

241

could be Travis's hands, couldn't they? You can't feel the difference, can you?'

'But there is one.'

'But you can't feel it. It's not physical. A hand's a hand. It's the same with other . . . if Travis was here he wouldn't be able to resist doing this.'

Richie leaned in and kissed Linden on the lips. Overeagerly. Tongue like a battering ram. And this time Linden did pull away, and for a moment Richie thought he'd blown his chance and if he had he didn't know what he'd do – but the girl's eyes didn't open, her spell didn't break.

'No. Not like that. Gently. Slowly. Travis kisses—'

'Show me. Show me how Travis kisses. I'll be Travis for you, Linden, if you'll let me.'

And she showed him. And she let him. Because strong hands *were* strong hands, and she was weak, and human contact, human warmth, they were what she needed. And she could almost imagine – almost – that Richie was Travis if she kept her eyes closed. Which she did in the canteen.

But they were open when Richie led her to his room.

Rev showed them a rough scrawl purporting to be an accurate representation of the prison camp's layout. The design did indeed remind Travis of prisoner-of-war or concentration camps he'd seen in movies and documentary footage, a square compound containing ranks of long huts for accommodating the inmates, the incarcerating fence studded in the corners and halfway along each of its four sides by raised sentry posts, like watchtowers, Rev said.

'One or two differences, mind,' he added. 'The huts –

I've called them that but they look more like they're made of some crap alien plastic than good old English timber – they look like mounds, curved, no sharp edges. The sentry posts are all enclosed but they've got glass or perspex or something windows around the top so you can see the aliens inside – four or five on duty at a time. And the fence, it's not barbed wire, kiddo. It's a force-field thing, controlled from the sentry posts. Jez' – one of Rev's lieutenants who was standing by nodding his head – 'has seen them turn it on and off to let foot patrols in and out. Yeah, foot patrols. Plenty of aliens in armour but I'm reckoning we can deal with those. *No* pods.'

'At all?' Travis queried. 'The Scytharene don't seem big on road transport. How do they deliver the kids to the camp?'

'Your Culler things land up nearer to the house, Jez says,' Rev explained. 'Then the kids are marched down. Clarebrook House is a bloody large estate and the camp's out on open ground. That's another good thing. The aliens' barracks are at the house itself, so if we hit the bastards hard and fast we should be out of there before they can even think reinforcements.'

'What kind of scale is the camp on?' asked Antony.

'Jez reckons each side's a couple of hundred metres long,' said Rev.

'And how do we plan on getting through the force-field?' Travis wanted to know. He thought of missiles failing to penetrate the shields of a Scytharene ship.

'Don't panic, kiddo,' Rev soothed confidently. 'I've got it sussed. We attack the corner sentry posts, give 'em everything we've got. Smash them and we disrupt the force-field. Disrupt the force-field and we nip in and start liberating. Happy?'

'Not entirely,' Travis said. 'What if there's an override control for the force-field somewhere else?'

Rev considered Travis for a moment. 'You know, kiddo, on the quiet you're a real killjoy.'

'Trav,' Mel exhorted, 'we can only try.'

'In one, babe. You should listen to the babe in black, kiddo,' Rev admired. 'That's a girl who knows how to have fun. Now you wanted a plan and you've got one. Soon as it's dark enough, let's get *on* with it.'

Though Rev had worked himself up almost into a frenzy well by then. He was circling his bike restlessly, kicking at the road with his boots, wielding a machine-gun as if glimpsing Scytharene in the night before the rest of the grandiosely titled assault team had even emerged from restaurant and hotel. With one exception. Mel was trying out the pillion position on Rev's machine in advance.

Travis hadn't liked the idea of Mel riding with the biker. He'd told her so when she'd informed him that Rev had been serious in suggesting the arrangement. 'You'll be safer with Antony or me,' he'd advised. 'Rev's likely to take too many needless chances. You've seen the way he is now. Reckless. Like he's into the danger for its own sake.'

'You mean like he doesn't care what happens to him?' Mel had said.

'Exactly.'

'Then thanks, Trav. You've decided me. I'm with Rev.' And Mel had left to let the biker in on the good news before Travis could ask her what the heck she'd meant by *that*.

With departure for the prison camp imminent, however, perhaps she'd changed her mind. Travis crossed to Mel hoping so. She was wearing a long black leather coat that Rev had loaned her. Travis wondered if it had belonged to Stevie. He didn't want Mel going the same way as Rev's previous companion.

'You're not armed yet, Trav,' she tutted playfully, wagging a finger. 'Better hurry. You're gonna get left behind if you're not careful and miss all the excitement. This party is gonna go with a bang. I guarantee it.' Producing grenades in each hand from the coat's evidently voluminous pockets.

'Mel, I'm not sure loading yourself up with those is sensible.'

'Sensible, Trav?' She laughed humourlessly. 'There's no more time for sensible. I'm gonna take down those alien scumbags or . . .'

'Or what?' Travis felt his concern for her growing with every moment. 'Mel, or what?' He clasped her elbow. 'What's the matter with you?'

'What's the matter with *you*?' The girl reacted with another laugh, which some might have interpreted as a sob. 'Let go of me, Trav. Please. You know I don't like boys touching me.'

'I'm not just a boy. I'm your friend. Come with me and Antony, Mel . . .'

'Sorry, kiddo.' Rev grabbed both Travis's hand *and* Mel's elbow, parted them. 'Three's definitely a crowd on a bike, and Mel's already made her choice, clever girl. Get yourself tooled up. We're moving out.'

'Mel . . .' A final appeal.

Falling on deaf ears. 'Take care, Trav.'

And then everyone's ears might as well have been deaf as dozens of engines revved riotously, proudly to life, the outburst of sound defiant, like a challenge, the roar of a lion. Travis had little option but to back away reluctantly from Mel and Rev. He all but collided with Antony.

'She didn't listen,' the blond boy remarked.

'We shouldn't have brought her,' Travis said ruefully. 'I should have said no, insisted no.'

'This isn't your fault.' Antony frowned in Mel's direction, remembering the taste of false kisses. 'She doesn't know what she's doing.' And the pain in Mel's eyes when he and Jessica walked out on her. 'We need to help her.'

'With Rev doing a real fine impression of Custer at the Little Big Horn, you're too damn right we do. Let's go.'

Travis and Antony ran to their allocated motorbike. Around them the other vehicles were beginning to move off, their outlines spiky with the barrels of automatic weapons, stabbing the night with their headlights, the bikes racing ahead already, the jeeps and four-by-fours in pursuit, more than one carrying teenagers with rocket-launchers, and finally a pair of tarpaulin-tented army trucks into which the intention was to pack the liberated children once the force-field had been breached.

Antony clambered awkwardly behind the handlebars, his authority to drive based on his experience of riding quad-bikes and the like over his family's ten acres. Travis swung on behind him.

'You're not taking a gun or anything?' Antony asked in surprise.

'It's not the Scytharene I'm worried about tonight, Antony,' Travis gritted. 'It's Mel.'

'You and me both.' Kickstarting the bike.

Which lurched into sudden acceleration. Maybe he should have told Travis about the number of times he'd crashed the quadbikes in the old days. But his friend would no doubt have seen that as an excuse to swap places and relegate him,

Antony, to being a passenger again. Head Boys of the Harrington School did not ride pillion.

He could do this, even though the bike was rather more powerful than anything he'd handled before. He could do it, even though speed was okay on its own, or direction if he only had to concentrate on that, but speed and direction *together* . . . As they nearly ran a fellow biker off the road and only just avoided clipping the rear of an army truck.

'Antony!' Travis yelled in his ear. 'The Scytharene might want to kill us. I'd kind of hoped you didn't.'

'Sorry!' he yelled back. 'I, uh – I'm not used to riding without a helmet.'

But gradually he exerted control over the machine. The only thing was, to do so he had to reduce their speed slightly. Which meant Rev and the leading bikes gained their first view of the prison compound significantly ahead of them.

Mel saw it over Rev's shoulder. It looked pretty much as described, except that she'd envisaged it in daylight. By night there was something eerie, ghostly about the camp. Both the accommodation blocks and the sentry posts, circular and towering high on poles like stilts, had been constructed from materials with the quality of luminescence: they glowed blue in the black. As did the pulsing, intricately latticed force-field that strung the sentry posts together. Mel imagined she could hear its hum of energy from their shelter among the trees, still several hundred metres from the camp itself.

'Look at that light. Bloody perfect. We'll be able to see just who we're firing at,' Rev anticipated gleefully.

Their own vehicles' headlights had been extinguished when they'd left the road to drive through the woodland on the fringe of the Clarebrook estate. So the aliens wouldn't see them coming. That had been the plan. The headlights were to remain turned off during the initial stages of the assault, to disguise the attackers' numbers, to use the darkness as camouflage. That had been the plan, too.

Rev was improvising.

'Lights *on!*' he bellowed. 'Stick all your lights on! Let the bastards see who's firing at *them!*'

And beams of brightness thrust towards the camp like assassins' blades. In the sudden dazzle Mel could see Rev's features more clearly than she had all day. Lit up, they were lunatic. He was laughing and he'd lost it and he was leading them to disaster, and that frightened her. But not as much as something else.

She couldn't find it in herself to *care*.

Rev brandished his machine-gun, loosed a burst of bullets into the treetops. 'Attack!' he screamed. '*Attack!*'

ELEVEN

The raid started well. Mel thought so.

At Rev's command a blistering salvo of gunfire blazed from the undergrowth – maybe too far away from the camp to do any actual damage, but as a statement of intent it couldn't really have been improved. The first of the rockets whistled into the air, landed and exploded several metres short of the central sentry post. But its red flame was like fury.

Rev's forces streamed forward, tearing up the open ground. The hysterical clatter of gunfire, the whoosh of further missiles, the shouts of the attackers and the petrol cries of the engines, a cacophonous barrage of noise that alone deserved to claim victory. The wind gusted in Mel's face, her hair streaking behind her as Rev raced the bike towards the camp. Her arms were clinging on to him, her senses alive, alert. The chaos, the violence, the anarchy of sound raging around her, they were her thoughts, her mood, her being. And when a rocket smashed into the force-field and shook the blue screen with thunderous white, the Scytharene's defence trembling vulnerably, she truly did think things were going well.

By now, however, the Scytharene were aware of what was happening.

Spotlights of scorching intensity jabbed from the sentry

posts and swept the open expanse in front of them. Mel was blinded, Rev, too, given the sudden tirade of expletives. She felt the light almost burning into her. She felt exposed and helpless, like an insect under a microscope.

The yellow rays followed.

And shouts became screams. The Scytharene's energy weapon was not deployed in intermittent bolts here, but as a continuous, raking beam, and fired from each of the three sentry posts along the camp's perimeter facing Rev's band it created havoc. Bikes too slow to react, vehicles too cumbersome to veer out of their path, the yellow rays cremated in incendiary eruptions. Motorbikes bursting like firecrackers, their riders briefly transformed into bright beings of flame, almost beautiful but for the shrieking, and then the charred and blackened remains, the tender flesh melted on the bone.

God, if it touched them, if the yellow ray touched them. One moment of excruciating agony, and then . . . Did the dead feel pain, Mel wondered, or only peace? If she was dead, would she still dream of Jessica?

'Shit!' Rev was gunning the engine and they were spurting beneath the deadly gesture of the energy beam. They were close to the camp now, but what good was that? The force-field shimmered impregnable before them. Rev's bullets were being absorbed by the blue as if he was shooting into water. Mel felt that she could measure the rest of her life in moments, but she'd have liked to give some captive children a chance for a little longer first.

The central sentry post exploded.

Sheer luck, of course. A rocket-launcher aimed with good intentions rather than pinpoint accuracy. Somehow the shell's trajectory had been straight and true. The boy who'd fired it even had time for a yell of triumph before the yellow rays from the corner towers fried him to a crisp. But at least his final act had been a positive one.

The sentry post burned. Inside it, Scytharene in black armour writhed and screamed as they burned too. Better still from the point of view of the surviving attackers, almost unbelievably the force-field along the entire perimeter of the compound vanished.

Travis and Antony saw it flicker and fail as they hurtled across the field, not quite so open now, strewn with burning wreckage like funeral pyres. An army truck, tarpaulin blazing, a corpse at the wheel. A bike exploding to their left, its riders thrown alight into the air. But others of Rev's followers were already in headlong retreat.

'Don't look at them, Antony,' Travis urged. 'Look at Rev. Look at Mel.' Who were leading the ragged remains of the charge and who were through, past the sentry posts, into the compound itself. 'We have to be with *them*.'

'I know,' Antony scowled. 'We will be.' He knew time was of the essence. The Scytharene could repair the force-field any second.

Ahead of them, 'Yeah, yeah, yeah!' Rev was howling as he and Mel screeched into the compound. They were met not by imprisoned children grateful for rescue, however. Scytharene warriors, armoured in black, ran to join the fray firing subjugators and some other kind of blaster. Rev returned fire with his machine-gun. 'Yeah? You want some? You want some of what I've got, you alien bastards?'

Heart pounding, Mel rummaged in her pocket, found and flung her grenades. The ground erupted where the

251

Scytharene stood. The aliens scattered, those who still had their legs.

But they regrouped. And they were reinforced. And the handful of bikers that had made it into the compound with Rev and Mel were reduced to circling impotently, no room to do much else. They were becoming targets. Where they could, they were withdrawing.

And then they couldn't. Hardly had one last machine sped into the compound than with an electric crackle the force-field became active again, a blue barrier now stranding the few remaining teenagers inside the camp.

It was the end, Mel realised.

So she wasn't surprised when a Scytharene blast struck the front of the bike and suddenly she wasn't holding Rev any more but she was flying, she was falling. The impact with hard soil knocked most of the breath out of her, but not all. She still had enough to live on and, miraculously, no bones broken. Rev, on the other hand . . .

It was the end, and she wasn't surprised he was dying.

Blood bubbled from his mouth as he lay on his shattered spine. He reminded her of how her dad had been when his time had come.

'We did it . . . didn't we, babe?' Rev coughed feebly. 'We gave those alien . . . bastards hell, didn't we?'

'In one,' said Mel, and her eyes filled with tears.

He was gone. He was dead. The living didn't stare like that. Rev. She wondered what his real name had been.

And bastards. He'd been right. Alien bastards. In her pocket, one final grenade. One final chance to go out in a blaze of glory – not that she deserved to. *Okay, Melanie,* she berated herself. *On your feet.*

Scytharene advancing towards her, still twenty metres away. She could reach them with the grenade. They could reach her with their subjugators. But who'd be first? She drew back her arm to hurl the explosive, groped for its pin.

Travis thudded into her, bore her to the ground. 'No. *No.*' Wresting the grenade from her and tossing it harmlessly aside. 'You're not getting yourself killed.'

And she was crying openly now, the tears welling from her eyes like blood from a deep and fatal wound. 'Trav, please. Let me go. Let me – I'm not worth it. I'm not worth saving.'

'Mel, you are. Of course you are. I love you.'

'No, don't say that. I don't deserve to be loved. You don't know, Trav . . .'

'Uh, Travis . . .' Antony was standing alongside them. His hands were raised in surrender, as were those of the few other survivors.

Travis glanced up at the Scytharene warriors now surrounding them. He sighed. Rev was dead and his attack had failed – on every count save one. Travis, Antony and Mel found themselves again in the custody of the Scytharene.

Simon was beginning to think he was a natural spy. Being the butt of bullies had plenty in common with being a secret agent. You learned the value of silence, the trick of invisibility. You planned ahead and you took nothing for granted.

So even now, in the middle of the night, he knew he had to keep his wits about him. He *shouldn't* encounter anyone between his room and the Enclave's exit zone, but he couldn't be sure. Coker and his cronies had always had the habit of appearing at unexpected moments, and here only the clocks betrayed the actual hour: the Enclave's lighting was constant whatever the time.

He'd decided, after that idiot Dr Mowatt had found him in the moncom centre, that the only way of contacting Commander Shurion was to pretty much follow Travis's example – no change there, then – and *physically* get to the Scytharene ship. The first alien he met, all Simon would have to do was to tell him who he was, send his name to the Commander, and that would be that. Mission successfully accomplished, this Darion person dumped comprehensively in the *shit*, and Simon himself spared the slavery that would be promptly imposed on his former friends – oh, and the death and destruction that Shurion would no doubt mete out to the Enclave, too. The base's existence Simon would reveal as a kind of bonus. To prove what a really, really valuable asset he was.

In case Commander Shurion might start thinking otherwise.

Because there was a little more urgency about his task now. It wasn't beyond the realms of likelihood that Shurion might find Travis before Travis found Darion, or might locate the Enclave independently before either. He might then be persuaded that Simon had reverted to his former loyalties, his human loyalties. He might consider Simon to be an enemy of the Scytharene rather than a friend.

The disposal cell still weighed on his mind.

But Simon had seen nobody who might feel inclined to ask him inconvenient questions as to his reasons for wandering the Enclave's corridors at one in the morning. A couple of soldiers had passed by, but he'd ducked out of their way and they hadn't noticed him. The same with one of Dr Mowatt's scientists, who seemed so distracted by his own thoughts he probably wouldn't have registered Simon's presence if the teenager had greeted him at the top of his voice. All this was good. Nobody would realise he was gone until maybe lunchtime. Simon felt he was virtually home free.

There were guards at the exit zone.

They were ambling about in front of the first of the hatches, laughing, joking. Simon hoped the Scytharene would slaughter them horribly.

Because of course. Linden or Jessica or somebody had jabbered on about it and he hadn't really been listening. The exits were guarded as a matter of routine to prevent personnel from running away. Damn. *Damn.* Simon clenched his fists in frustration. He was as trapped below ground as the rest of them. But he couldn't afford to panic. He didn't dare. There still had to be a way for him to communicate with Commander Shurion.

There *had* to be.

The Warrior-Prime in command of the Scytharene garrison at Clarebrook House wouldn't even consider permitting such an illustrious personage as a member of the Thousand Families anywhere near the slave compound until the Earthers' attack on it had been utterly repulsed, security restored. Even then he was reluctant to consent to his superior's whim to inspect the site and the captured Earther survivors personally. The Warrior-Prime did not believe it to be seemly for a scion of such a pure and blessed bloodline to be brought into close physical proximity with unclean and degenerate alien specimens.

But Darion insisted.

The Warrior-Prime himself thus accompanied the heir of Ayrion to the camp, along with a guard of vigilant Scytharene soldiers. The wearing of helmets was insisted upon. The officer intended to take no chances with the safety of the Fleet Commander's son, for his own self-preservation as much as for any reason to do with professional competence.

'My warriors are already clearing away the Earthers' vehicles and remains, Lord Darion,' said the Warrior-Prime as the group approached the camp. 'I have dispatched patrols into the surrounding woodland to ensure that no aliens are still hiding there, and I have requested a unit of battlepods from the *Furion* in order to search the wider area for the raiders' base of operations.'

'You have done well, Prime,' flattered Darion, knowing that praise was what the soldier wanted to hear. 'Very well indeed.' In a darker undertone as they passed a huge bonfire blistering the night sky, and on to which the already carbonised bodies of the Earther attackers were being tossed, casually, like logs for fuel, like waste to be disposed of. All young, Darion noted grimly. Obviously. There were only the young left for his people to kill.

He wondered whether any of the unrecognisable corpses had in life been Travis Naughton.

He sincerely prayed not, but whether he was equally desirous to find Travis among the prisoners was another matter. Darion felt certain somehow that his Earther friend was involved in this abortive raid on the slave camp. When news of the attack had first been broken to himself and Dyona in their temporary apartments in Clarebrook House, he hoped it signified the actions of an organised Earther resistance. Perhaps Travis Naughton had followed his advice and made contact with the rump of the human military which evidence suggested did still exist. But it had quickly become apparent that this ill-planned escapade was the work of a ramshackle and poorly organised mob of teenage Earthers; it had been dealt with expeditiously.

If only the adult members of the human race had placed greater trust in their youth in the time before the Sickness, Darion reflected, given them more responsibility, challenged them to question their society and its orthodoxies, to foster real, attainable ambitions, to aim high with their lives, to develop as genuine individuals and to recognise their own special potential, their uniqueness. Then the younger generation might find a way to avoid becoming slaves, a strength to resist and ultimately throw off the oppression of the Scytharene.

But the little Darion had so far learned of Earther society intimated that such an enlightened attitude had not been prevalent during the last days of humankind's tenure as rulers of their planet. The governing adults had seemed to be in the process of dismantling the bloodline structures – the family – that bound the generations together and that existed in any healthy culture to guide the young towards independence and a positive maturity. How foolish and misguided those so-called leaders had been. It seemed to Darion that Earther society had come to classify the teenager as a kind of sub-species, and either regarded teenagers with suspicion and fear or sought to exploit them by marketing products and images at them, imposing upon them a conformity only masquerading as individuality. Small wonder, Darion thought, that he'd been hearing from assessors aboard the *Furion* that the general quality of the slaves was not as high as they'd hoped. Stifled initiative. Spoon-fed lives. The Earther child was, at present, a rather disappointing commodity.

There were not many like Travis Naughton.

And if Travis *was* among these latest prisoners, what did he, Darion, intend to do about it? Help the boy – again – or ignore him? Consign the teenager to slavery for good this time or endanger himself – again – by protecting him from such a fate? Shurion already half suspected his involvement in the escape aboard the *Furion* – besides Dyona, that was probably another reason for the Commander wanting him off the ship. Perhaps Darion was secretly under surveillance. Perhaps, if he acknowledged Travis in any way, his treachery would be discovered. What should he do?

The force-field flickered off to allow the Scytharene entry to the compound. The Warrior-Prime said, 'This way, Lord Darion,' and led him towards the hut where the captives were kept.

Travis had been sitting on a bench doing his best to comfort a sobbing Mel, Antony anxious the other side of her, but he riveted his attention on the door immediately it opened.

'On your feet, slaves,' snapped the Scytharene in black, and the dozen or so survivors of Rev's band obeyed at once.

Then Travis saw the Scytharene in gold.

'Darion?' mouthed Antony.

As the Scytharene removed their helmets, Travis nodded. Darion. Maybe their luck was changing. *God, it needed to.*

But Travis made no direct eye contact with the Scytharene

lord. He didn't dare do anything that might compromise his ally. If, indeed, Darion was still an ally.

It wasn't looking good in either respect. 'Such an unsavoury odour in here,' Darion was observing, wrinkling his nose distastefully. 'I'm sure these Earthers have no concept of personal hygiene. You ought to have had them washed before my visit, Prime.'

'Yes, Lord Darion. My humblest apologies.'

'And how ugly they are. I'm surprised our assessors can bear to touch them.' Darion walked the line of prisoners, studying each in turn as if examining a display of disgusting yet fascinating insects. He paused by Antony. 'All this hair. Primitive. Degenerate. Look at this female, for example.' Mel. 'Such savage locks.'

'Shall I tear her mane out by the roots, Lord Darion?' offered the Warrior-Prime.

'No, no. Let her new owners decide once she is sold.' And Darion sighed as he stood in front of Travis. 'Perhaps I should have stayed at the house as you advised, Prime. There is nothing of interest for me here among the Earthers.' He turned his back, and strode towards the door. 'Let us go.'

'As you wish, Lord Darion.'

And Travis was aware of Antony's alarmed gaze on him, and Mel's. Darion was leaving, abandoning them. Travis's plan was disintegrating. All he'd done was to condemn himself and his two friends to captivity and slavery. He'd failed. Just when he couldn't *afford* to fail.

And Darion was at the door.

'On second thoughts' – he hesitated – 'perhaps I ought to conduct at least a token interview for my studies. Have . . . oh' – glancing back at the prisoners as if about to choose a flavour of ice-cream – 'have that male with the brown hair and the blue eyes brought to my apartments first thing in the morning.'

Linden woke up hating herself. She'd probably hated herself all night in her sleep as well, but that wasn't so bad because she hadn't been aware of it. Now she was, and conscious too that self-loathing was the least she deserved to feel. Shame should also be in the mix – and was. Bitter regret. All boxes she could tick. At least, when she sat up, she found herself back in her own room and alone. Richie wasn't in bed with her now, which was a relief as far as it went. Still, though, the damage was already done.

She slid from under her sheets. A shower might be a good idea. Some stain of Richie Coker might yet linger on her skin.

Prior even to that necessity, however, she used the comlink to contact the moncom centre. Fruitlessly. There was no news of Travis or the others. 'No news is good news,' the duty operator said, in an attempt to boost her spirits, no doubt detecting the dejection in her voice. Linden might have retaliated that no news could just as easily be bad news delayed, but the root cause of her gloom was nothing to do with the moncom operator. It was nobody's fault but her own.

'Damn it, Lin, you idiot.' In the bathroom she pulled her nightdress over her head, glimpsed her face in the full-length mirror. Her features had the contrition of the repentant sinner about them, but their expression failed to soften her heart. 'You *idiot*,' Linden condemned her reflection. She'd sooner have had nothing to be penitent about.

And the mirror presented her too with the cold details of

her naked form. Her mother, Deborah Darroway by birth, Fen by choice, had told her never to be ashamed of her body. That had been the central theme of her Facts of Life talk to Linden when the girl had been eleven or twelve. 'And really, love, I don't like to think of any of this as the *Facts* of Life, more the *Beauty* of Life. Facts aren't about feelings, and what you do with your body and with boys certainly should be.' So never be ashamed of her body, and never be afraid of it, either. Or what it needed. Or what it desired. Or where it wanted to take her – or with whom. The body was always right, her mother had assured her, because what it felt was natural, and natural was good. Nature was good.

Linden wasn't sure she agreed with her mother on that score now (though she wished Fen was still alive to discuss it). Her body, it seemed to her, so often let her down, too often turned traitor to what she *truly* wanted, played her into the hands – literally – of sleazes like Ash and Richie when she knew in her head – *and* in her heart – that she only wanted Travis. Some of her other parts seemed slow to realise this. And how did she feel now? Not good. A little bit dirty. A little bit cheap – a lot cheap, actually. After you'd slept with a boy, you shouldn't wish you hadn't slept with him. You should want to sleep with him, be with him, again.

She didn't even want to *see* Richie Coker again.

If Fen was here, Linden would tell her that she was wrong. Physical love, sex, it might be natural and it was certainly nothing to be ashamed of, but on its own it wasn't the answer. It didn't make you happy. It didn't fulfil you. You had to love with the mind and the body together for that, to think *and* feel. You had to wait for somebody to appear in your life who attracted you on both those levels, who both stirred your emotions and stimulated your brain, and if that meant waiting a while, then you should do it and be patient. Superficial relationships produced only superficial pleasures. Linden had probably always, deep down, known that. Probably everyone did. But now she *believed* it.

Ash and Richie, maybe, in the long term, they'd done her a favour.

Travis, she thought. *He mustn't find out about Richie.*

Which was why, after her shower – in *very* hot water – but before breakfast, Linden was knocking on Richie's door, praying that no one would come by to see her there.

'Linden. Hey.' Richie was already dressed (thank God), though he seemed disturbingly prepared to adjust that condition. 'You come back for a repeat performance?'

'Not exactly, Richie.' She winced. 'Can we talk?'

'Sure. Talking was one thing we didn't do last night.' He grinned weakly. Richie Coker had not been blessed with an inordinate amount of imagination, but he kind of knew what the subject of their conversation would be. Linden's pained expression kind of gave it away.

He'd hoped she'd have been glad to see him again. After what they'd done.

'What happened last night, Richie . . .'

He'd been different with Linden than with the other chicks, the slappers who'd hung around him and Russ and Terry Niles. He'd tried harder with her. He'd wanted to give Linden pleasure.

'What happened . . . I don't quite know how to put this, Richie, because I don't want to hurt your feelings or anything, not more than . . . you have to believe me on that, but what happened last night shouldn't have.'

262

'Shouldn't have,' Richie repeated dully.

'It – us – was a mistake, a stupid . . . it was my fault, Richie, my fault. I should have known better but I let myself get caught up in my worries over Travis and kind of emotional, and I needed . . . I thought I needed comfort, someone to hold me, and you were there and . . . it shouldn't have happened. I should have controlled myself.'

'Yeah, maybe you should have,' Richie said ruefully. Though he couldn't help but be glad she hadn't.

'I'm sorry.'

'You're not the only one.'

'So what I'm saying is, last night, it can't happen again. It mustn't. You and me, we can't . . .'

Course not, Richie thought bleakly. 'Cause he'd given it his best shot but he still wasn't Travis. Never would be. Naughton was too good for him. *Linden* was too good for him.

'I love Travis, Richie.'

Course she did. How could she not? *Shit.*

'I forgot that for a moment, but I know it now.'

'So call me next time you get amnesia, Lin.' Richie laughed hollowly.

'So what I'm saying, Richie, I've come to ask you a favour, a really big favour, kind of an unfair favour, really, but I'm hoping . . .'

'You're hoping I'm not the total bastard you think I am,' Richie anticipated. 'The bastard everyone thinks I am.'

'Richie, I wouldn't . . .'

'The kind of sleaze who's gonna blab to Travis soon as he gets back 'bout what he's been getting up to with his girlfriend while he's been out trying to save the world. You don't want Travis knowing about last night, do you, Lin, and you're shit scared I'll tell him. To get my own back, stir trouble, break you and him up. Hurt Travis. Hurt you. Things a total bastard would do without a second thought.'

Linden shrugged. 'You're right. I don't want Travis to know. I don't want you to tell him – I know I won't. I'm not sure he'd forgive me.'

'Not even if you strung him that moment-of-weakness kind of crap?'

'Travis and moments of weakness, they don't get on so well. He can't know, so . . . I'm at your mercy, Richie.'

Who laughed again, as emptily as the first time. 'You never knew me before, Lin. In Wayvale. When Trav and Morticia and Simes all knew me. And you know what? I'm glad you didn't. Back then I *was* a bastard. Totally. Back then I'd have told Travis what we'd done in gory detail, with sound effects. Shit, I'd have told everyone, just to make you squirm, just to make me feel – powerful. But you're all right, Linden. We're not back then. Times have changed. Richie Coker – he's trying to change. I don't want to hurt you. I'd *never* . . . So our little secret's safe. Travis won't hear anything about it from me.'

'Do you promise?' Linden said, her expression torn between doubt and relief.

'You wish last night hadn't happened?' said Richie. 'It never did.'

'Thank you, Richie. *Thank* you.' She hugged him. 'I'll see you at breakfast.'

'Yeah, I'll be along.' He watched her leave, and in one respect he was glad that she'd gone. Richie Coker didn't do blubbing in front of *anyone*.

*

It was the second time Travis had found himself in Darion's private quarters. Unlike the first, however, his surroundings in the Georgian-style Clarebrook House came with the reassurance of cultural familiarity. Elegant Regency furniture in the rooms, portraits of ladies and gentlemen who'd once been alive on the walls, books and ornaments and the trappings of the past. A past that had belonged to the people of Earth.

Travis wished he could be as sure about the future.

Darion stood gold-armoured before the fireplace. He dismissed the warrior escort, and only then did Travis dare to speak. 'Darion, am I glad to see *you* . . .'

'I am pleased also to see that you are well, Travis Naughton,' reciprocated the Scytharene, which, sincerely and perhaps a little surprisingly, he was. 'Though I'd hoped never to find you a prisoner again . . .'

'Well, there's a story to that,' Travis said. 'But listen, first, two of my friends were captured with me. I realise it's asking a lot, but is it possible to have them brought here as well? I'd be happier if we weren't sepa—' The teenager's words froze in his mouth. Another Scytharene swept briskly into the room. A kind of alien he'd not seen until now.

The female of the species.

He supposed. The new arrival's curves suggested so, though precious little else differentiated her from Darion. Their shimmering golden garb was identical – which meant, Travis assumed, that the newcomer also belonged to the Thousand Families – and the two of them were equally bereft of hair. The lack of lines or wrinkles on the female's skull-white skin made her a similar age to Darion, while the gristly ears, the flat pugilist's nose, the crimson eyes and the slash of scarlet mouth did not depart from the features of the male

Scytharene. Unlucky, that, Travis thought. Scytharene women must have *bloody* good make-up (or Scytharene men little by way of aesthetic appreciation, which was probably likelier). In fact, about the only facial distinction between the two sexes seemed to be the decoration to the hard buttress of bone along the forehead which the female Scytharene had applied, the protrusion tattooed with various arcane symbols that reminded Travis of the sigils employed in witchcraft.

He looked smartly to Darion for guidance, tensed his body again to resume the pose of prisoner.

'Standing firmly to attention, hmm?' the female said with a sly smile. 'I have that effect on men.'

'Dyona,' Darion tutted indulgently. 'It's all right, Travis. You can relax. I have told Dyona all about you.'

Travis was more confused than relaxed. 'Who . . .?'

'Yes, Darion,' scolded the female, casting an appraising eye over Travis. 'Where are your manners? Introduce me to your Earther friend properly.'

'Travis Naughton,' Darion obliged, 'it is my honour to introduce you to Dyona, born of the bloodline of Lyrion of the Thousand Families. My betrothed.'

'Your what?' Travis blurted.

'His betrothed,' Dyona repeated more slowly. 'His intended. His fiancée. His significant other. His wife-to-be. The light of his life. Are any of these terms known to you or are our translators inaccurate?'

'No, they . . . Congratulations,' stumbled Travis.

'Thank you so much,' Dyona said, 'though sometimes I wonder whether Darion deserves me. I notice you can't take your eyes off my bellineum, Travis.'

'I beg your pardon?' With a gulp.

'My bellineum. The anatomical term for the ridge of bone above our eyes.' Dyona tapped it for illustration. 'You will not have seen one embellished like this, of course. Only females of our race are entitled to beautify themselves so.'

'It's – um – very nice,' said Travis.

'He has more social graces than a Blackheart,' Dyona observed to Darion. 'Yet such as he are cast as slaves while such as Shurion delude themselves that they are masters.'

'Please, can we . . . my two friends. . .' reminded Travis.

Darion introduced their existence to his betrothed, then Travis named and described them.

'I know Darion explained to you that he is an alienologist, Travis,' Dyona said. 'So am I. I'll send Etrion to fetch your friends here on the pretext of assisting me with *my* work. We can trust Etrion. His bloodline has served mine for centuries.'

'Thanks,' said Travis earnestly. 'Thank you. Dyona.'

'You might have more to thank my fiancée for yet, Travis,' Darion said with pride. The teenager looked quizzical. 'Dyona is a member of the Scytharene dissident movement.'

Mel and Antony huddled in the hut with the remnants of Rev's band. Travis had been led away by a Scytharene guard a while ago, and since then, nothing.

'Maybe they've forgotten us,' Antony submitted to a morose, dishevelled Mel.

'I wish we could forget them,' the black-haired girl responded. She might have added, *I wish I could forget everything.*

'Travis'll be bringing Darion up to speed on what's been happening,' Antony theorised. *'He'* won't forget us. We'll be

267

sent for or something, too. I'd put money on it. If I was carrying any. And if my parents hadn't disapproved of gambling.'

'Your parents own stocks and shares, Antony?' Mel asked.

'Of course.'

'So what's – what *was* – the stock market but gambling in suits? And gambling with other people's money as well. You get more honesty in the local bookie's or a Las Vegas casino than you do in the whole of the City of London. But of course, it's all right for you upper classes to make money without earning it. If a working man wants to chance his arm, it's a vice. Sheer hypocrisy. Investment bankers? I've got a better word for them – and it rhymes.'

Antony smiled. 'That's more like it.'

'What? The word? I'm surprised somebody with your refined background can even guess it.'

'No. Getting angry. Being outspoken. Standing up for what you believe. That's more like you, Mel.'

The girl grunted. 'Temporary relapse.'

'You know Travis is worried about you.'

'I didn't ask him to be.'

'When does one friend have to be asked to be concerned about another?' Antony said. 'He can see you're different – all that senseless risk-taking with Rev, almost as if you were trying to get yourself killed.' Mel shifted her weight on the bench guiltily, avoided looking Antony in the eye. 'He doesn't know why, though. Neither Jessica nor I have told him.' He paused. 'What was that all about the other night, Mel?'

'Me being a prat,' she said, heartily relieved that Jessica evidently hadn't shared with Antony the dismal rest of the story. Mel herself wasn't about to do so, either. There was only one boy she might possibly confess her weakness to, and he wasn't here.

'I didn't deserve to be used like that,' Antony criticised gently.

'I know.'

'Jessica didn't deserve to be put in that kind of awkward situation, either.'

'I *know*. I know I know I know, all right? I'm sorry.' Mel turned to Antony now, imploringly. 'I am sorry.'

'Did you think I'd cheat on Jessica or something, Mel, is that why you did it? To prove I would?' Antony clearly wanted to understand. 'Because I wouldn't. I won't. I have . . . strong feelings for Jessica.'

Yeah? Mel thought bitterly. *Strong feelings? What the hell does that mean?* Couldn't he say it? Had Antony's upper-middle-class public-school life of respectability and reserve removed the word from his careful and neatly cultivated vocabulary? Did he love Jessica? Because Mel did. Did he ache in his soul when she wasn't in sight? Because Mel did. Would he die for her?

Because Mel would.

'I know you like her, Antony,' she conceded, though, with a sigh as of defeat. 'I won't be messing you about any more.'

'We both want Jessica to be happy, don't we?' Antony pursued. 'So we ought to get along together. We ought to be friends.'

'We *are* friends, Antony,' said Mel, managing a weak smile of confirmation.

'I'm glad. Jessica will be, too. So no more wild escapades on the backs of motorbikes, Mel. We've all got to stay alive. Then, when we return to the Enclave, you and Jessica can sit down together and you can talk your differences through, make up.'

Like that was going to happen. 'Ever the diplomat, hey, Antony?' She shook her head bleakly.

'Is there something you're not telling me, Mel?'

'So we sit down and we make up and it's happy endings all round.' She didn't sound convinced. 'I'm going to tell you a joke, Antony. It sums up the way I'm feeling. A man goes to the doctor's, says, "Doctor, I don't know what to do. I look at the world around me and it seems a dark, depressing place and I don't seem to belong anywhere in it. I look at the people around me and I feel I don't know them. I'm in despair, Doctor. Life's lost its meaning for me and I'm not sure I'll ever get it back." And the doctor says, "You need your spirits lifted, that's all. You need to remember that life can be fun. I happen to know that the great clown Grimaldi is in town today, and tonight he's putting on a show in the theatre. Go and see Grimaldi the clown. If anyone can remind you of what life's about, he can." And the man says . . . the man says, "That's just it, Doctor. I *am* Grimaldi."' Mel's eyes brimmed with tears. 'I am Grimaldi.'

'I'm not sure,' said Antony, 'I under . . .'

The door of the hut opened. Silhouetted in the doorway stood the black figure of a Scytharene guard.

'. . . So if the Enclave can link up with your organisation's leaders,' Travis concluded, 'maybe we can finally fight back.'

'I wouldn't raise your hopes prematurely, Travis,' cautioned Dyona, pacing the room where she, Darion and the teenager were awaiting the reappearance of Etrion with Mel and Antony in tow. 'I'm afraid the dissident movement is not structured quite like that. We do not have a single leader or leadership group for us to contact, with lieutenants below them and activists below *them*. There is no chain of command as such. We work as equals, with individuals coming together wherever and whenever possible in order to make our protests. Do you know how liberating that is, by the way, the freedom to operate on the basis of equality when every aspect of our society is so rigidly ordered and uncompromisingly hierarchical? Of course you don't. Be glad you don't, Travis. But I'm afraid the truth is that at present you are looking at the sum total of the dissident movement's representation on Earth.'

Travis glanced between the Scytharene. 'Is that one or two?' Appealing to Darion.

'I don't know, Travis. I can't promise . . .' He wriggled uncomfortably. 'I helped you escape before. I'll help you and your friends to get away again now, but more than that . . .'

'It's two, Travis,' Dyona answered him, throwing her arms around Darion's neck. 'I'll persuade him.' And if Scytharene had lips, Dyona's kiss would have smacked wetly against those of her betrothed. 'My darling fiancé is braver than he thinks.'

Let's hope so, Travis thought. And where were Antony and Mel?

'Our union was arranged while we were both still infants, do you remember, my love?' Dyona said friskily. 'Members of the Thousand Families can only marry *other* members of the Thousand Families, of course. To keep the ruling bloodlines pure. And Travis, it was thought that a match between the bloodlines of Ayrion and Lyrion would serve to strengthen the Families' pre-eminence. We share the same totem, you see.'

Travis didn't see.

'Every Scytharene bloodline long ago in our history adopted an animal native to our homeworld as their totem,' Darion explained. 'A kind of household god, if you will. From each bloodline's chosen beast or bird, it is said, the power of tooth and claw flows forth and all the courage and ferocity of nature passes into the Scytharene's warrior hearts.'

'Those ridiculous helmets our soldiers wear in battle,' Dyona added, 'they're fashioned after each warrior's animal totem to provide a form of spiritual protection. Thicker armour might be a little more effective, if you ask me.'

'The totem of the bloodline of Ayrion is a scarath,' Darion said. 'A feline beast akin to the sabre-toothed tigers of your prehistoric period. Dyona's bloodline reveres the scarath also.'

Dyona growled playfully and made claws of her fingers, scratched them down Darion's chest. 'A mating of two tigers,' she explained. 'You can see why they thought it'd be a winner. If only they knew how much we both despise their whole sick system.'

And her snarl, an amusement just seconds before, now became edged with genuine menace, and there was a loathing in her voice for her own race that was almost palpable. Travis was taken aback. There was something perhaps a little unbalanced about Dyona of the bloodline of Lyrion.

'Travis,' she said, 'did you know that in our language the word for alien and slave is the same? You do now. My people founded our entire civilisation on two beliefs, that the species of the universe can be divided into the strong and the weak, and that it is the right of the strong to dominate and exploit the weak. *Three* beliefs. I apologise. The third is that the

Scytharene are strong, the mightiest race of all.' She snorted contemptuously. 'You begin to see how countless generations of our people have justified the practice of slavery and contributed wholeheartedly to the expansion of the interstellar slave trade. When technology permitted, we didn't just reach for the stars, Travis. We crushed them in our gauntleted fists.

'But what began as a statement of Scytharene power and cultural superiority has now become an economic necessity. Our race depends on the wealth generated by the slave trade – without it our society would collapse – and so the need to enslave further planets, such as Earth, is perpetuated. The Scytharene will never stop until they are forced to stop, Travis, and though to my shame I am Scytharene-born, I will do whatever is in *my* power to stop them.'

Dyona's fists were clenched. Darion raised them to his mouth and kissed them. 'My love,' he said.

'You see, we are of the same mind, Darion and I.' The female alienologist smiled. 'Our love has grown because of our beliefs, not our bloodlines. We share the view which I have no doubt my beloved has already expressed to you, Travis, that all cultures are valuable and that all races are equal. That slavery is an abomination. Which is why you can rely on us both to help you and your people.'

'That's good to hear,' said Travis.

But Darion winced. Dyona noticed. 'Is it not so?'

'We are of one mind, Dyona, yes,' her partner allowed, 'but two voices. Yours condemns our people utterly, mercilessly and to a man. Mine – I would prefer to use mine to persuade. Surely our people can be made to realise the wrongs they have perpetrated and to change. Surely, if we grant that goodness exists in alien hearts, we cannot in conscience refuse to accept its presence in our own kind. It is our society that has made us what we are, not ourselves.'

A diplomat. Where was Antony? Travis wondered with a half-smile. He and Darion should get on well. And then no smile. Yeah, where *was* Antony?

'You think goodness exists in Shurion's heart, my love?' Dyona was establishing sceptically.

'Somewhere. Perhaps. It has to, doesn't it?'

But before Dyona could respond or Travis interrupt to ask whether it should really be taking so long for Etrion to hurry to and from the prison camp, a knock rapped at the door. Travis needn't have begun fretting. Here was Etrion back again.

Alone.

Oh God. Travis's blood froze in his veins. *Alone.*

'I'm afraid we were too late,' the Scytharene servant said. 'Commander Shurion has apparently already given orders for the Earther survivors of the raid to be transported to the *Furion*. The prisoners are no longer in the compound.' He turned to Travis. 'Your friends are lost.'

TWELVE

'Where's Travis? What's happened to Travis?' The fact that she, Antony and the other ten or so unfortunates who'd fought with Rev were being at this moment unceremoniously bundled through the corridors of a Culler, no doubt to resume their acquaintance with a Scytharene cell, seemed of lesser consequence to Mel than the location of her oldest friend. Travis had to be all right. He *had* to be. All the while he was, Mel felt, there was hope, maybe even for her. 'Antony?'

'I don't know, Mel. I can't . . .' *Think*, what with a Scytharene warrior amusing himself by jabbing Antony frequently and unnecessarily with the nozzle of his subjugator. But he *must* think. Travis hadn't sent for them. They'd been marched instead to this Culler on a cleared landing area nearer the house. It didn't take a genius to work out their ultimate destination and its purpose – processing had been humiliating enough the first time. But did this mean that Darion had refused his aid? Or was Travis himself at fault somehow? A Harrington student, particularly a Head Boy, would never leave his friends in jeopardy.

There *was* a cell. Bare, metal, the usual. The teenagers were thrust inside to rue their fate.

'I half expected to find Trav here ahead of us,' Mel said.

'I'm glad he's not.' She crossed to the viewing panel and peered out. The Culler seemed to be undergoing the final preparations before take-off.

'Your first question was a good one, though,' Antony said. 'Where is he? I think we might have to consider the possibility that Travis has failed to accomplish his mission.'

Mel regarded the blond boy pityingly. 'Travis never fails.'

'Well, your loyalty is commendable, Mel' – if only he could command it in the same way – 'but I do think we might need to rely on our own wits to escape rather than wait for either Travis or this Darion to turn up.'

He was right in relation to the latter. It was neither Travis nor Darion who entered the cell minutes later. But the Scytharene female in the gold armour and with the black-clad warriors toadying in attendance still insisted that Antony and Mel go with her.

'It's what I've always said,' Mel enthused. 'You want a job done properly, get a woman to do it. She – Dyona – was magnificent, Trav.'

Who had his arm round Mel, one arm, leaving the other free to shake a secretly chastened Antony by the hand. Darion and Dyona's private accommodation in Clarebrook House was becoming a popular venue.

The Culler had departed for the *Furion* two potential slaves light.

'The manner in which Dyona handled the Culler's captain was certainly impressive, Travis,' confirmed Antony.

'I try,' Dyona said with mock modesty. 'Don't I, my love?'

'Indeed,' agreed Darion with rather less humour. 'You can be very trying sometimes.'

'This captain guy, Trav,' Mel grinned, 'he says to Dyona it's against regulations to disembark slave cargo once loaded without written permission from a slavecraft commander. And Dyona says regulations are for lesser beings than the Thousand Families, and what Commander Shurion doesn't know can't hurt him, and what difference will two slaves more or less make anyway, and she needs a male and a female for her alienological studies, and she'd take it as a personal favour if the Captain would let her have them. "We of the Thousand Families make valuable friends, Captain," she says, "but dangerous enemies." And this captain guy, he kind of looks this small' – about a centimetre, if the gap between Mel's thumb and forefinger was to any extent accurate – 'so Dyona gets her way and here we are.'

'Dyona,' said Travis, 'I don't know how to thank you.'

'I trust you're not considering a kiss,' the Scytharene demurred, fluttering her fingers protectively at her lipless mouth. 'The equality of races I can accept, but it has to be said you Earthers are ugly.'

'I guess that's in the eye of the beholder,' Travis laughed. 'Beauty, I mean.'

'Not according to Scytharene tradition,' Dyona returned. 'Our people have a saying, beauty is in the blood.'

'Please,' complained Darion, 'I am delighted the three of you are reunited, but this is still hardly the time for banter.' He left his companions and paced almost petulantly to the window.

'Are you sulking because I acted while you were only con-templating action, my love?' Dyona teased, and confidentially to the teenagers: 'He's always been a dreadful sulk, you know.'

Travis didn't care about that. But he did care about Darion's usefulness as an ally. Because the truth was, while Antony and Mel were being forced aboard the Culler, Darion of the bloodline of Ayrion *had* been agonising over what to do about it, how to minimise risk, how to maximise the chance of success. Fair enough if you had the luxury of time to make your plans, but every second had been vital, every moment precious. Only Dyona had realised that and left for the Culler despite her partner's protests. She might well be erratic but at least she seemed to be resolute and determined when it mattered. Could Travis guarantee the same would be true of Darion?

'I'm not . . . don't be so childish, Dyona,' chided Darion from the window, surveying the visible grounds of Clarebrook House as if fearing immediate reprisals for his fiancée's crime in the form of Commander Shurion and a Scytharene guard unit advancing upon them. 'It may seem heroic and exciting to act in haste, but actions have consequences, and when what we've done constitutes a betrayal of every principle our people hold dear, the consequences for us could be severe.'

'So had you rather I left Antony and Mel in the cells of the Culler?' Dyona retorted indignantly.

'I simply think . . . it might have been more sensible to wait until they'd reached the *Furion* before removing them. Two Earthers subtracted from the hundreds aboard the ship would have been less noticeable than two from twelve. Now, if the Culler's captain thinks twice and informs Shurion of your intervention, my love . . .'

'He won't.' Dyona dismissed the idea out of hand. 'I belong to the bloodline of Lyrion.'

'All I am suggesting' – Darion addressed the teenagers as much as his betrothed – 'is that sometimes it is wiser to wait.'

'With respect, Darion,' said Travis, 'we can't wait. As far as the freedom of our people is concerned, the clock is already ticking. We need to strike a blow against your forces, make them at least think twice about their occupation of Earth, and we need to do it now.'

'We're listening,' said Dyona, and Darion did not contradict her.

'I told you about the Enclave,' Travis continued. 'Well, there's a specific reason we needed to find you again, Darion. I guess you must have researched our major religions before you began the enslavement. What do you know about Joshua?'

A little, it turned out. But the two alienologists soon knew plenty about the Joshua*s*. *And* what Captain Taber believed they could achieve if it wasn't for the Scytharene ship's shields. *And* exactly how Travis, Antony and Mel hoped Darion would be able to assist them.

'Sabotage the shields?' the Scytharene repeated unenthusiastically when Travis had finished.

'Is it possible?' the teenager pressed.

'It's possible.'

'Will you do it?'

'And allow your tanks – your Joshuas – to destroy the *Furion*. With me still aboard.'

Travis's brow creased. He hadn't actually thought of that.

'Hah! Don't worry about the little details.' Dyona crossed to her partner and draped her arms around his shoulders. 'Darion's clever enough to avoid going down with the ship, aren't you, my love? There are emergency evacuation procedures, for a start.'

'For us,' Darion reminded her. 'Not for the Earthers in the cryo-tubes and the cells. You could end up killing more of your own kind than mine, Travis.'

'Damn.' Because that terrible and ironic possibility hadn't occurred to him, either. Maybe Darion had a point about the value of patience.

'There's a solution to every problem,' interjected Antony. 'We were taught that at Harrington.'

'Of course!' Dyona exclaimed. 'The cryo-tubes will soon be full, won't they, Darion?'

'If they're not already,' her partner replied.

'And that's good news why?' said Mel.

'Because then the whole batch is extracted from the *Furion* and transported to a cryo-ship currently orbiting your planet, to be replaced by a fresh stock of unoccupied tubes. But in the interim period, there'll scarcely be any Earthers aboard the *Furion*, possibly none.'

'So if we mount our attack then . . .' In Travis's mind's eye, the Scytharene ship was already in flames. 'Darion, you've got to help us.'

'I don't know, Travis.' The Scytharene shook his head. 'If I do as you ask, many of my people will die. Because of me.'

'They'll deserve to, my love,' Dyona said with casual cruelty.

'You only see them as slavers, Dyona,' Darion pointed out. 'And as such, as beyond redemption. You, Travis, and Antony and Mel, you only see them as aliens, as enemies – not that I blame you. But they are also fathers and they are also sons. Husbands. Brothers. They are not monsters. There has to be another way to resolve this conflict between our races apart from bloodshed.'

'I hoped that once,' said Antony dismally.

'There isn't,' said Travis. '*Darion.*'

'Darion, please.' Mel thought the addition of a female voice might help.

'I am sympathetic to your cause, my friends, you know that,' sighed Darion, 'but I need time. I need—'

Etrion again, practically bursting into the room. His bloodline may have been in the service of Dyona's since time immemorial, Travis thought, but he seemed to have gained certain privileges thereby. Like the right to cut off a member of the Thousand Families in mid-sentence without punishment.

When he explained why, of course, in hushed and horrified tones, punishment for his impertinence was the furthest thing from anyone's mind.

'He's executed them,' Etrion revealed. 'Commander Shurion. He's executed the rest of the Earthers who were captured with . . .' Nodding towards Travis, Antony and Mel. 'The Earthers responsible for the raid on the compound. They weren't being taken to the *Furion* for processing but for the disposal cell. As soon as they arrived they were killed.'

'God.' Travis had only ever really hated one person in his life before – *hated*, not simply disliked or despised, but abhorred with a black, almost self-destructive intensity – and that person had been the junkie who'd murdered his father. Now the objects of his hatred doubled.

'We' – a fearful realisation dawned on Antony's face – 'if we'd still been on the Culler . . .'

'We'd be dead too.' Mel's expression was unreadable. 'Really dead.'

Darion sank into a three-hundred-year-old chair as if he was suddenly of similar age. He lowered his head into his hands.

'There's more,' said Etrion. 'Shurion's broadcasting the execution on all channels in the hope that any Earther resistance fighters might pick it up and learn the consequences of daring to defy the will of their new masters. His words. He's taped a commentary.' Etrion glanced apologetically around the room. 'I thought you'd want to know.'

'You acted correctly, Etrion. Thank you,' said Dyona. 'You may leave us now.' Which the servant did. Dyona turned to her betrothed. 'Darion?' Reaching out to touch him.

'No.' Darion sprang to his feet. The set of his features was suddenly harder, harsher, his bellineum like the knuckles of a fist clenched in anger – in hatred, Travis recognised – and his eyes like lava. This was a Darion the teenagers had never seen before.

Neither, apparently, had Dyona. 'Darion? My love? Where are you going?'

He was striding purposefully towards the door. 'Wait here, Dyona. All of you.'

'I'll come with—'

'Wait *here*.' As he left alone.

Dyona attempted to cover her astonishment and dismay with a laugh. 'He can be so masterful when he wants to be, can't he?' She disguised nothing.

Travis, Antony and Mel supported her with weak smiles. The room lapsed into a silence that was clearly destined to last as long as Darion's absence. The alienologist, however, was gone only a few minutes.

He returned holding a slim disk the size of a hand.

'I'm sorry about that,' he said. 'Etrion's news . . . I'm sorry about a lot of things. Principally, my cowardice.'

'Cowardice? What are you talking about, my love?' Dyona frowned.

'My indecision, then. My reluctance to act. My obsession with caution. It all amounts to the same thing. If you'd listened to me, Dyona, if we'd delayed liberating Antony and Mel until they'd boarded the *Furion* as I thought best, our friends would now no longer be with us. My cravenness would have condemned them to death. Innocent lives would have been lost and I would have been to blame. I'm sorry. To all of you, I'm deeply sorry.'

'It's all right, Darion,' said Mel sympathetically. 'We're here. We're alive.'

'But many are not,' said Darion, 'and many more may not be soon unless those of us who believe in freedom and brotherhood and the equality of all races find within themselves – at last, in some cases – the courage to stand against the evil of slavery and to oppose those who advocate it, whoever they may be, whatever the cost. Dyona, I said before that we were of one mind but two voices. Now let us also speak in unison. From this moment on, I swear to be a dissident in deed as well as thought.'

'Darion.' Dyona embraced her husband-to-be.

Travis exchanged pointed glances with Antony and Mel. Darion's conversion to direct action was dramatic and brave – he felt *proud* of the alienologist – but what precisely might the Scytharene's new-found commitment to the dissident cause mean for them?

He soon found out.

'I will do as you wish, Travis. I will resume my place

aboard the *Furion* as promptly as possible so that we can co-ordinate your Joshuas' assault with the time when the cryo-tubes have been removed. Then, at the right moment, I will disable all of the ship's primary systems – defence, flight, communications. I know how. There will be no shields, no escape for the *Furion,* and Commander Shurion will be unable to summon help.' Darion smiled grimly. 'We have a saying on our homeworld: a scarath without claws is soon without life. I think we can ensure the first victory in your people's war against the Scytharene.'

'How will we know when to attack, though?' The prospect of victory was inspiring, but practicalities, Travis knew, still had to be sorted.

'You can contact me with this comdisk.' Darion showed what he'd fetched to the three teenagers. 'It's a communica-tions device, not unlike your mobile phones.'

'Terrific,' Mel said. 'Does that mean we can download clips from crap Scytharene TV shows, too?'

'You hold it by placing your fingers in these indentations here.' Five of them, appropriately spaced out on the reverse side of the comdisk. Darion demonstrated. 'You operate it by utilising the keyboard here.' A miniature computer system inlaid into the business face of the object, complete with mouth- and earpiece. 'I'll show you what to do, but there's something else I should mention first, a possible danger to us all.'

'Go on,' said Travis. They were having to cope with plenty of *actual* danger in their lives since the Sickness. He doubted any threat that was only *possible* would trouble him unduly.

Of course he was wrong.

'Shurion has recruited a spy to try to find you, Travis. I

don't know who, but one of your own kind. Shurion knows a Scytharene aboard the *Furion* helped you to escape. He knows *you* know the traitor's identity and he hopes his informant will learn it from you.'

Travis shrugged nonchalantly. 'Well I don't think we need to lose any sleep over that. How is this spy guy going to find me? How can he even know who I am? Travis Naughton wasn't exactly a household name before the Sickness.'

'He is already an acquaintance,' said Darion. 'Shurion's agent was captured with the rest of you from your Harrington School.'

'What?' Antony objected. 'A Harringtonian turned traitor? Impossible.' But he wondered – what about Leo Milton?

Travis said nothing, fought for his features to reveal nothing. But he knew.

'Has anyone joined you since you broke free of captivity?' Darion pursued. 'Anyone claiming that they too, independently, escaped from the *Furion*?'

'No,' Travis declared emphatically, a denial that earned puzzled stares from his two companions. Antony and Mel's memory of recent events evidently diverged from Travis's. But they did not contradict him. His warning glare ensured their silence – for now.

'Well,' Darion was adding, 'if somebody does appear out of the blue, someone you know, Travis, with a tale like that, don't believe him. He'll be your traitor.'

They'd shaken hands with Darion and Dyona – and Scytharene flesh, it seemed, differed from its human counterpart in nothing but pigmentation – thanked them, wished

Darion in particular luck for the task he had undertaken. Heartfelt wishes, because their lives would soon depend on the young male alienologist, and sentiments which had been sincerely reciprocated. Then, under cover of darkness, they'd been smuggled from Clarebrook House and into the surrounding grounds.

Only when they'd put several miles between themselves and the Scytharene, with the night as thick as the forest around them, did Antony demand they pause.

'What for?' Travis scowled. 'We should push on. We need to get back to the Enclave as quickly as—'

'Possible,' Antony accepted. 'I'm aware of that, and I don't know about Mel, but there's a certain matter *I* think we need to discuss before we get there. In a word, Simon.'

'What about Simon?' Travis was grateful his companions couldn't see his face too clearly in the dark, the pain and disbelief, the crushing disillusionment in his eyes.

'Trav, Antony's right,' said Mel. 'You *know* what about Simon. Why didn't you tell Darion he fits the bill for the spy?'

'One, because I didn't want to say anything that might give Darion second thoughts about putting his neck on the line for us. Two, because I don't think it's true. Simon – he can't be a traitor.'

'Why not?' Antony wanted to know. 'Because you say so, Travis? Because you don't want him to be? Not everyone turns out the way you'd like. This is life, not a novel where you can create and control your own characters, and—'

'All right, Antony,' Mel cut in sharply. 'Thanks for the intertextual analysis.' She turned more tenderly to Travis. 'I know it's going to be hard for you to accept, Trav, Simon of all people, when he owes you so much, when if it wasn't for you he'd probably be rotting away in Wayvale or packed into a cryo-tube, but you have to he honest with yourself. You have to admit, it looks bad for Simon. When you think of his story, I mean on reflection, think critically, him hiding aboard the ship for hours without being discovered, just happening to find an exit hatch . . .'

'It wasn't quite as coincidental as that, Mel,' Travis resisted, but tamely. 'Simon said he found a plan of the ship on the wall . . .'

'Hmm. Still dodgy. Sorry, Trav.'

'Perhaps Travis is more concerned that it'll look bad for him,' commented Antony acidly. 'But this is not about you, Travis. The presence of a traitor in our midst endangers us all. Simon might have found a means of contacting his Scytharene masters already . . .'

'If he had, do you think Darion would still be walking around free?' disputed Mel.

'No. Fair enough. But my general point still stands,' Antony insisted. 'You must view this dispassionately, Travis, not emotionally. Leo Milton turned against me when I believed I could trust him. Why shouldn't Simon Satchwell turn against you?'

Because, Travis thought, remembering the cringing, cowering Simon of Wayvale Comp. The victim. The loser. Friendless and vulnerable. And hc remembered what he'd promised Simon, before the Sickness, before the Scytharene: '*If you ever want help . . . If you ever need a friend, you've got one.*' Hadn't Simon believed that? Why couldn't he have been stronger?

'Okay,' Travis conceded with a struggle. 'It's possible.' The words like lead in his mouth. 'Simon could be Shurion's agent. But I'm not going to convict him out of hand. He's still Simon. Mel, he's still the Simon we've known for years. We started school together. I won't just ... I will give him a chance to defend himself.'

'But Trav' – Mel didn't appear so keen – 'he could just deny everything. We've no *proof* . . .'

'I know how we can secure proof,' said Antony.

While the former Head Boy of the Harrington School outlined his scheme, several miles away Darion and Dyona of the bloodline of Ayrion and Lyrion respectively were sitting for the last time in the room where long-dead generations of Clarebrooks had gathered. They sipped wine from crystal glasses, having found both to their taste during their brief sojourn here.

'I'd hoped we might have been able to spend longer together,' said Dyona regretfully.

'Events seem to be conspiring against us,' acknowledged Darion. 'Forcing us apart.'

'Bringing us closer, too.' Dyona smiled. 'In ways that matter more.'

Her partner sighed. 'Everything seems so clear in my mind when I'm with you, my love. What will I do when you are gone?'

'The right thing, Darion,' Dyona said.

'Whatever I do when I return to the *Furion* tomorrow,' he mused, 'people will die because of it. Earthers or Scytharene. Aliens or our own people.'

'The innocent or the guilty, Darion,' said Dyona. 'Those are the terms that signify.'

'I know. Here, tonight, with you, I know. I hope I can find the strength to know the same when I am alone again. *You* give me that strength, Dyona.'

'No.' She moved nearer to him. 'You may think I do, but I am only your mirror, Darion. What you see in me are simply your own qualities reflected back at you. True strength, true resolve, my love, comes only from within, from will and determination and self-belief.' She pressed her palm against his chest. 'From the impulse of a noble heart. When the time arrives, you will not be found wanting.'

And Darion held his betrothed. And he prayed that she was right.

Travis kept smiling. Which was easy when he, Antony and Mel found their way back to the Enclave without incident and the hillside opened wide to welcome them. Which was a natural and sincere response when reunited with certain people who rushed to greet the homecomers after decontamination. Linden in his arms once more, her lips fastening themselves to his with the frequency of the addicted. Jessica, their close embrace and single kiss rather less sexual but no less loving. He was genuinely glad to see Captain Taber and Dr Mowatt again, even Richie, who shook his hand with uncharacteristic humility and mumbled that it was good to have him back without actually looking Travis directly in the eye.

With Simon, though, his smile was fixed, false, frozen. A lie.

'I knew you'd be all right,' the bespectacled teenager rejoiced, pumping Travis's hand, slapping him on the back. 'I told the others. I told them, Travis'll be all right, no worries.' And smiling, too, and if Antony and Mel's suspicions turned out to be truths, with equal spuriousness.

'Sounds like you've got a lot of faith in me, Simon,' Travis said. 'I don't know whether I deserve it.'

'Sure you do,' declared Simon.

And all the while, no sign on his face that he might have been plotting with Commander Shurion against his own kind. No hint in his manner or expression that he was a traitor. *Could* be a traitor, Travis sought to cheer himself. Even post-Sickness, the accused was innocent until proven guilty. If Antony's plan worked, they'd know for certain soon enough, and then Travis could allow the set of his features to reflect his true feelings, the relief of vindicated trust or . . . But he didn't want to think about *or*.

For the time being, Travis kept smiling.

He was so intent on Simon, he missed the occasional guilty glance that passed between Richie and Linden.

However, 'I've missed you,' Linden assured him. 'I mean, really, *really* missed you.'

'Ditto.'

'Don't go anywhere without me again, Travis, will you? I need you. I'm not . . . strong without you.'

'Looks like you're stuck with me, then,' Travis said, 'and you know what? I wouldn't want it any other way.' Because he could rely on Linden. There was no question of *Linden* being a traitor.

While alongside them, Jessica faced Mel with the security of Antony's arm around her shoulders. 'So you're still in one piece, then?' Awkwardly.

'Just about,' Mel said. 'On the outside, anyway.'

'Mel's fine. Mel did just fine, didn't you, Mel?' said Antony.

'I'm glad,' said Jessica. 'Honestly.' And here was the opening for reconciliation, for a forgiving hug or even just a hand offered in renewed friendship. Jessica knew it was her move to make and she wanted to make it, part of her was so happy to see Mel again, safe and sound. She wanted to throw her arms around her friend and tell her that everything was all right, that everything was good between them.

But she couldn't.

In the briefing room, Travis and Antony recounted their recent adventures, Mel providing an accompaniment of caustic comments. Rev and the attack on the prison camp. Dyona. Darion agreeing unreservedly to throw in his lot with the Earthers. The comdisk. Surprisingly, all three teenagers seemed to have forgotten Darion's warning of a Scytharene agent among them.

Jessica was amazed by the biker's sudden change in character. 'I suppose you can never really know what somebody's capable of,' she remarked.

Mel grunted. 'Ain't that the truth.'

Taber and Mowatt were more interested in the comdisk, which, having been sterilised to avoid the risk of contamination, was now being handed round the table for everyone to study like a variation on Pass the Parcel.

'It gives us a direct line to Darion,' Travis said. 'Totally secure, as well.'

'Actually,' Antony put in, 'I imagine we could contact the Scytharene ship itself with the comdisk if we wanted to.'

'Not that anyone in their right mind would want to,' added Mel.

'Absolutely not,' came a voice that Travis would rather not have heard.

'Given its importance,' he said, 'we reckon you ought to keep it in the moncom centre until we're ready to get in touch with Darion, Captain Taber.'

'A sensible idea,' Taber approved. He extended his hand. 'If I might take charge of the device, Mr Satchwell?'

'Oh,' said Simon. 'Sure.'

How obliging of this Lord Darion character, Simon mused, to supply him with the means by which he would prove his loyalty to Commander Shurion and save himself from a painful demise. Sadly, in Darion's case, of course, the opposite would be true. He'd have to drop by the disposal cell in the fullness of time to thank the Scytharene personally.

Perhaps Travis merited his gratitude too for placing the comdisk so nearly within his grasp, importing it into the Enclave with all the innocent idiocy of the Trojans wheeling the Wooden Horse inside their impregnable walls. On the other hand, though, he doubted Travis would consider thanks appropriate under the circumstances. Simon smiled thinly, the kind of smile he'd seen Commander Shurion give during their last interview, anticipating triumph. The smile of someone who was strong, Simon considered.

He ghosted through unpopulated corridors towards the moncom centre. Above ground it was black with night. Below ground, darkness had been banished, but those he was about to betray were sleeping nonetheless. *The fools. And they thought they were so clever. They didn't know.*

He'd recognised the comdisk for what it was immediately.

Commander Shurion had shown him one, instructed him in its operation before deciding that possession of the device if discovered might be a little difficult for his agent to explain. Even so, all Simon had to do now was to send the moncom centre's duty operator off on the wild goose chase he'd already concocted – if he was even there in the first place – and he could contact the *Furion* at his leisure. Not only one traitor's name to offer up as a kind of sacrifice, but two. Darion *and* Dyona.

A female Scytharene. Except for those specifically womanly parts, it seemed, looking exactly like the male of the species. Simon wrinkled his nose in disgust. He hoped Commander Shurion harboured no plans to pair him off with a Scytharene girl as an element of the reward he imagined he could expect for his imminent services to the slavers' cause. The girls of his own race were bad enough – though at least they tended not to be physically repellent – always laughing at him behind his back and stuff. Actually, half the time they were laughing at him in front of his face as well. Mocking him. Scorning his approaches. Humiliating him. Making him feel small and wretched and less than a boy. Demonstrating their woeful and inexcusable lack of discrimination as a sex by slobbering over Neanderthals like Coker and never even giving him, Simon, a chance. Tarts like Cheryl Stone, they deserved to be punished for that, put in their place. Mel and Linden, too. Even Jessica. They were all the same. It was them against him, always.

But things were going to change, very soon, with a single use of the comdisk, and then, when Simon was walking with the Scytharene, he suspected girls would begin to regard him a little bit differently, that they'd be begging for *him* to condescend to notice *them*. They'd be on their knees and at his feet. And *then* the tables would be turned. Then they'd be sorry they'd spurned Simon Satchwell.

They'd all be sorry. All of them. Sorry they'd laughed at him, the bullies and tormentors. Because Simon's years of persecution were almost over.

Ahead of him, moncom.

Which was empty. Perfect. Nobody around to see him slip inside and close the door. Nobody around to hear his voice – or his heart, which hammered against his chest like a man trapped and pounding on a door for release. Like a warning.

Which Simon ignored. There was no going back now. He'd made his choice. Commander Shurion had been right in dividing all living creatures into the weak and the strong. For too long Simon had been content to languish with the weak.

Locating the comdisk on a console. Slotting his fingers into the depressions. Picking it up. Turning it on.

In seconds only, finally, irrevocably, Simon Satchwell would be joining the strong.

THIRTEEN

'I'd put that down if I were you, Simon.'

'What?' Simon blanched.

'Preferably now.' Travis. Grim-faced. Somehow, he was standing in the doorway. Entering the room. With Antony Clive behind him. And Captain Taber. And Dr Mowatt.

And a couple of soldiers bearing arms.

'I don't understand,' Simon bluffed with a laugh. 'What's going on, Travis?'

'This is a monitoring centre, Satchwell,' reminded Captain Taber, the omission of the *Mr* hardly accidental. 'Its cameras can be trained inwards as well as out. We've been waiting for you to give yourself away.'

'Give myself . . .?' Simon felt himself trembling. 'I don't know what you mean.'

'Darion knew that Shurion had recruited an informant, Simon,' said Antony, 'a spy, but he didn't know who. We did. Commander Shurion let you have his number, did he?'

'No.' Simon shook his head in frantic denial. 'No no no. This isn't what it looks like. I was worried . . . it suddenly . . . I suddenly thought, what if this comdisk thing is actually a signal beacon or something, letting the Scytharene know our position? I mean, you can't trust a bloody alien to tell the truth, can you? This thing could bring the Scytharene down right on top of us.'

'Would have done if we'd left you alone with it five minutes longer, I'm sure.' Antony regarded Simon with a mixture of pity and scorn. 'Betraying your friends. You'd never have made a Harringtonian, Simon.'

Who switched his appeal more directly to 'Travis, you know me better than that, don't you? You believe me, don't you? I wasn't betraying anybody. I was just checking the comdisk in case—'

'Simon,' Travis interrupted, his voice heavy with disappointment. 'No more lies. It's too late for lies.'

But for a second, Simon toyed with the idea of continuing to protest his innocence. 'I'm not lying, Travis, you have to' – with the soldiers advancing towards him, flanking him – 'believe me, you have to' – and Dr Mowatt easing the comdisk from his hand with the gentleness of a mother retrieving a dangerous implement from a child – 'believe . . .'

'I'm sorry, Simon.' Not a trace of a smile on Travis's face now. Weariness and bafflement. A troubled frown of failure. 'I wish I could believe you.'

'Well if you did you'd be as much of an imbecile as that bastard retard Coker.'

'Huh?' The sudden hardening of Simon's voice startled Travis.

The boy with glasses laughed. Coldly. His one-time protector's discomposure delighted him. Because there was no point now in further pretence. Contacting Commander Shurion was impossible. He'd have to settle for making his so-called friends realise how he'd deceived them, how he, Simon Satchwell, had at last got the better of them. 'Of *course* I'm the Scytharene's spy, Travis. Of *course* I was about to betray you. Why else would I be creeping about in the middle of the night? Hunting for a midnight snack?'

'*Simon!*'

There was anguish in Travis's voice and Simon relished it. He'd suffered from that emotion often enough himself. To make another experience the same pain he felt was a kind of victory, a kind of strength. 'I was chosen, Travis. Commander Shurion chose *me* to be his agent.' Unrepentant, even proud. 'And I'll be his agent again when the Scytharene smash your Joshuas and kill your Darion and find this stinking hole in the ground and destroy it. When you're all slaves, I'll be free. When you're all packed into cryo-tubes, I'll be living in luxury. When you're nothing, I'll be *somebody*.'

Just not Simon, Travis thought. Not the Simon he knew anyway. Already the teenager in glasses seemed to be altering, his features twisting, contorting, becoming ugly and cruel, his mouth a rictus of contempt. Whatever had actually happened to Simon aboard the *Furion* had changed him, crushed and then reshaped him into someone new, something Scytharene. A figure consumed with hatred for everyone around him. Or – and the possibility made Travis feel sick inside – maybe all the aliens had done was expose the true Simon Satchwell. 'I'm somebody now, Travis. I was chosen.'

'Take him away,' snapped Captain Taber.

Travis looked on in dismay as the soldiers escorted Simon from the room. He felt Antony's hand squeezing his shoulder. Heard his words: 'I'm sorry, Travis.'

Nodded ruefully. 'You and me both, Antony. You and me both.'

*

'I can't believe it. It can't be true.' Jessica's glance flitted between Antony and Mel as if expecting one or the other of them to crack any second and admit that the revelation that Simon was a traitor in the employ of the Scytharene was some kind of warped, unfunny joke. She'd realised Antony must have a good reason for mustering them all in his room before breakfast, but she hadn't anticipated anything like this. Only Travis had not appeared. Apparently, he was otherwise engaged.

'There's no mistake,' Antony sighed. 'We caught him red-handed with the comdisk and he confessed. Worse than that, he didn't even show any remorse. Pretty much the opposite, in fact. It was like he was revelling in his treachery. It shook Travis up a bit, I can tell you.'

Jessica could understand that, at least. 'But this is Simon we're talking about. Simon Satchwell. I *know* him.'

'Truth can be a bugger when it's not what we want it to be, hey, Jess?' observed Mel.

Jessica sought support from either Linden or Richie, but the russet-haired girl simply shrugged, while Richie, sitting on the bed, seemed to be finding staring at the wall preferable to making eye contact with any of his companions.

'But I've known Simon since we were five years old. We started school together.' Jessica grew wistful. 'I remember Mum telling me, whispering to me, that I had to be kind to poor little Simon because he didn't have a mummy or daddy, and I tried to be kind to him but I liked to be happy and Simon always seemed so sad. Maybe he could see what was in the future.'

'Doubt that,' Mel said. 'If he could have seen the Sickness coming he'd probably have gone out and hanged himself. He wouldn't have been the only one.'

'But what can have driven him to it? Betraying us, I mean,' Jessica said. 'His friends.'

'Maybe he never really believed that that was what we were,' offered Mel. 'I don't think Simon was too familiar with the concept of friends.' Her tone darkened. 'What do you reckon, Richie?'

'Get stuffed, Morticia.' Without turning from the wall, his powerful shoulders sagging.

'Are you blaming Richie, Mel?' Linden said. 'For what Simon did by himself? That doesn't seem very fair.'

'Oh, I think it's more than fair,' Mel retorted. ''Cause Simon *didn't* betray us just by himself, not really. Richie was there giving him a helping hand every step of the way – so to speak.'

'What are you talking about, Mel?' Even Antony seemed confused now. 'Richie wasn't on board the *Furion* when Simon completed his Judas deal with Commander Shurion.'

'Not physically, no,' Mel conceded. 'Not literally. But he was there in spirit, weren't you, Big Guy? You were there in poor Simon's head like you've always been. You want me to let Linden and Antony into the details of your scumbag, bullying past? How you made Simon's life a misery at school, extorting money from him, humiliating him, victimising him until he was terrified of his own shadow, suspicious and distrustful of everyone and everything . . .'

'Is this true, Richie?' Linden said, shocked. 'I could see there was bad blood between you and Simon, but something like *this* . . .'

'Even so,' protested Antony, 'I don't see the relevance.'

'Don't you?' Mel cocked her head to one side. 'Then your parents wasted their money sending you to Posh School,

Antony. It's all relevant. It all turned Simon into a traitor. Every time someone yelled Four-Eyes at him, or Simple Simon, or any of the other names he was christened in the corridors, in the playground. You know the kind of thing. Not very inventive, but you don't need to be a creative genius to hurt someone. Which is probably why most bullies tend to be cretins. Yeah, and every time Simon was picked on, every time he was clouted or kicked or tripped or taunted – by Richie over there and his moronic mates – every time he cried and wondered why him and maybe, yeah, every time he wished he was dead, they all turned him into a guy with the potential to side with the Scytharene. Because what happens to us in our lives makes us who we are. You made Simon who he is, Richie. Are you listening to me, Big Guy?' Two strides across the room and she was slapping Richie round the back of his head, the close-cropped, bristly black hair.

'*Mel!*' Jessica's eyes widened.

'Can you hear me?' Because there'd been no reaction from the bully. 'You made Simon believe the whole world hated him. So now Simon hates the whole world. That's why he betrayed us. It's *your* fault, you bloody great shithead. I hope you're proud of yourself.' Mel gave a brief, bitter laugh. 'Only it's our fault too, of course. Because we stood by. Because we let the bullying go on. Because maybe, sometimes, we even joined in. It was easier that way, easier to mock and abuse and not to get involved.'

Richie mumbled something.

'It speaks,' Mel sneered.

'Richie?' Linden was a little more encouraging.

'Not proud.' Like a radio station gradually tuning itself into clarity. 'I'm not proud.' Richie stood to confront his companions. His face was ashen and his eyes . . . well, if they weren't Richie Coker's eyes, their redness might even have been put down to tears. 'Of anything I did before the Sickness. I know you won't believe me – at least not you two who knew me then – but if I could change things now I would. I *would*. But when we were back at school, what I did to Simes, it seemed harmless, you know, a good laugh. I didn't think of the effects on him. He was easy pickings and it was, like, the way things were, the weak and the strong, and it didn't feel . . . it never felt like it was wrong.'

'Would you have stopped if it had?'

Richie hung his head. Tony Clive's question wasn't the issue. The past was the past and you couldn't go back there. It was over and done with. God, but if Morticia was right and he was to blame for Simon's treachery . . . He could have got them all killed or enslaved, Jessica, Naughton, *Linden*. How could he make up for that? How could he put things right in the future, tomorrow or the day after, when he possessed the power to choose his own course of action? That was what mattered. Richie would do anything not to have to endure again the cold condemnation in the eyes of those around him, the hostility he was suffering now.

And Simes, his own life marred, ruined beyond repair even before the Sickness and the Scytharene. By *him*.

Before her death his mother had been ashamed of him. Perhaps, for the first time, he understood why. For the first time, Richie Coker was ashamed of himself.

One last try, had been Travis's thinking. One final attempt to reach the old, familiar Simon. Antony and Mel could tell the others what they needed to know without Travis being present. It was more important that he endeavour to make Simon see sense, come back to them of his own free will. If he failed, then they'd do things Captain Taber's way. But he'd do all he could to succeed.

He owed Simon that.

'Whatever you want, Travis,' the bespectacled boy chuckled, hands behind his head as he lay on his bed in the room that had become his cell, 'you're wasting your time.'

Seemed it wasn't going to be easy.

'Am I?' Travis leaned his back against the door, arms folded. 'If you didn't want to talk at all, you could have refused to see me.'

'I was under the impression I was a prisoner now. Until my new friends find their way here and release me, at any rate. Prisoners aren't usually in a position to refuse their jailers anything. A bit like victims and bullies actually, Travis, not that you'd know about that. You could always ask Coker, though, seeing as you two are so close nowadays.'

'They're not your friends, Simon.'

'Definition of friend: someone you can rely on, someone you can trust, someone who'll stand by you. Someone who's there when you need them.'

'You think you can trust Commander Shurion, Simon?' Travis kept his voice calm, reasonable. 'You can't. He's using you. Deep down, surely you must know that.'

'I don't know that.'

'We're your friends.'

'Oh, right. Of *course*.' Simon sat up, clicked his fingers. 'How stupid of me. And that's *we* including Richie Coker, is it, the kind of friend everybody wants, as long as they're keen

302

on physical assault and endless years of persecution. *We* including Jessica and Mel, who could barely *look* at, scarcely *speak* to me back at school, who at best only ever tolerated me. I'm *convinced*, Travis. Oh yes indeedy. Fine chums they are one and all.'

'I'm your friend, Simon.'

'Yes, and I've heard that one before, too.'

'I am. You can trust me.' His blue gaze searching, urgent. He turned his open palms to the other boy. 'We can get past this. We can sort things out with Richie, whatever you want. Just don't cut yourself off from us, Simon. You don't belong with the Scytharene.'

And for a moment Travis believed his appeal was working. 'I did trust you, Travis. Before the Sickness. And afterwards, for a while.' And in that moment, Simon seemed to be relenting, his features softening, reminding Travis of the boy he'd been. 'When you said I could rely on you. When you said you'd be there when I needed you. Definition of a friend. That's what I thought you were.'

Definition of a moment: a period of time that passes swiftly and can never return. Travis groaned inwardly.

'But then you put Coker's interests ahead of mine.' Simon's face closing against him. 'More than once, and I gave you every opportunity to put that right, Travis, and you chose not to take it. But then you deserted me aboard the *Furion* when I was alone, and afraid, and they were going to kill me' – leaping to his feet in his anger and his fear – 'they were going to dispose of me like I was nothing, like I was shit on their shoes, and where were you when I needed you, Travis? Where were you then?' Advancing on the other boy, yelling in his face. 'Snogging Linden or backslapping with Antony,

303

taking all the credit for your own escape, who cares about those you left behind?'

'Don't, Simon. It wasn't like that.'

'No? Not good old Travis? He's so *brave*. He's so *strong*. You can trust old Travis to stand up for good and do what's right. Yeah, yeah. When it bloody suits him.'

'You're wrong, Simon. I tried . . .' Guilt crashing into him again like a wave. He'd failed Simon. He was a failure. 'I wanted to help you . . .'

'So you could look good. So you could look noble, impress the chicks . . .'

'No.'

'Well it worked with Linden, unless it was the smack in the mouth that won her over. Maybe she likes a bit of rough. I'd watch out for Linden and Richie if I were you, Trav.'

'Don't say any more, Simon.' His fists clenching almost of their own accord.

'Why not? A bruise to the ego, is it, a blow to the old self-esteem? 'Cause that's what it all is to you, isn't it, Travis, the reason for your posing and your posturing and your high-and-mighty moral stands. It's to make yourself feel *good* about yourself. You don't really mean any of it. You suckered me in once but I can see clearly now. I can see right through you. It's all vanity, isn't it? You're on an ego trip and we've all got tickets to ride along.'

'That's not true.'

'You don't give a shit about anybody but yourself, nobody.'

'Simon, don't . . .'

In a hiss of poison. 'Not even your dead dad.'

And Travis had lashed out before he knew it, and Simon's

blood was on his knuckles and Simon was on the floor dabbing at more of the same trickling from his nose like scarlet snot and gazing up in a kind of amusement at the boy who'd hit him.

'That's better, Trav. Can't persuade me to shut up, so you force me to by half breaking my nose.'

'Simon, I'm sorry. I didn't mean to . . .' He took a step forward to help the other teenager stand, but Simon was waving him back, refusing assistance.

'Nah, nah. Of course you *meant* to, Travis, and you've proved my final point. Power. Strength. That's what you can trust. That's what you can rely on to protect you – not people. And the Scytharene wield more power than you can imagine. I want a bit of that, Travis. I deserve a bit of that after being shat on all my life, don't you think?'

Travis closed his eyes. He didn't want to think. If he did he'd have to acknowledge that his efforts had been useless. Simon had moved beyond redemption. He was lost to them.

'That's why you're wasting your time here, Travis. I'm with the Scytharene now.'

Okay. Captain Taber's turn. Travis sighed. 'Then you won't mind helping them out, will you?'

Even over the comdisk, Commander Shurion sounded surprised to hear him. *Because* of the comdisk.

The traitor had given it to Travis so that they could maintain communications, Simon explained. It was scarcely ever left unguarded, which accounted for Simon's delay in contacting the Commander, and the necessary brevity of their exchange now that he had. There wasn't much time. A pity the Scytharene communications officer who'd picked up his transmission hadn't patched him through to Commander Shurion sooner.

Shurion wasn't interested in details. Only names. One in particular.

He didn't seem too happy to learn that the Scytharene traitor was called Tyrion. There was no Tyrion serving aboard the *Furion*. The traitor had given his Earther ally a false name in order to protect himself.

Actually, to say that Commander Shurion didn't seem too happy was an understatement.

But Simon hoped he could still redeem himself. After all, he was presently hiding out with Travis Naughton and a whole load of potential slaves – maybe a hundred teenagers, good condition. If Travis Naughton was captured, he could be *persuaded* to point out the traitor personally and then the Commander's troubles would be over. Simon could help the Scytharene apprehend Travis, direct a Culler to the teenagers' lair. It would be a simple matter to—

Curiously, Commander Shurion didn't appear overly keen. Simon got the impression that Culler availability was limited at the moment. But in the end the temptation to unmask the traitor proved too great.

Where? The village of Otterham.

When? (It would have to be soon because Travis was talking about relocating.) Tomorrow. First light.

The Culler would be dispatched at dawn.

And someone was coming now so Simon had better end his transmission. He hoped he'd justified Commander Shurion's faith in him.

'You've done well, Simon,' approved the Scytharene.

A verdict confirmed by Captain Taber as the bespectacled boy placed the comdisk on the table in front of him.

'Your little ruse won't save you,' Simon glowered. 'Even without Cullers or battlepods, even if Darion disables every computer on the entire ship, the Scytharene will be too strong for you. You'll be crushed.'

'Let us worry about that,' Taber said tersely. 'Mr Naughton' – who was standing alongside the officer – 'let Lord Darion know that our attack will commence at dawn. Advise him to be ready.'

'Before you do, though,' Simon broke in, glaring up to his left and right, to the soldiers there, into the barrels of their rifles, 'do you think you could get these bloody guns out of my face?'

When Darion made his obligatory appearance on the bridge that evening, he found Commander Shurion not ensconced in his command chair but standing imperiously before the floor-to-ceiling windows, gazing outside with a smirk of satisfaction on his face.

Which was fine by Darion. Let Shurion smile while he could. Tomorrow the Commander would be wearing a rather different expression. Earlier today the alienologist had been conspiring with Travis.

'Ah, Lord Darion,' greeted Shurion with uncustomary bonhomie.

'Commander.' Darion joined him. 'You seem to be in good humour tonight.'

'Indeed. I enjoy the nightfall on this otherwise tawdry little backwater of a planet.' Shurion savoured the sight of the valley ahead of them sinking into a well of blackness, the tops of the trees like the rigid fingers of drowning men. 'I like to watch the darkness extinguish the light and cover all the Earth. It puts me in mind of our own inevitable victory over the inferior races who were born to be enslaved.'

'Operations are proceeding smoothly then, I take it?'

'But of course.' Shurion seemed affronted that Darion could even imagine otherwise. 'Our first consignment of slaves is being delivered to the cryo-ship as we speak. As soon as the Cullers have returned, we can begin harvesting anew.'

'Excellent.' Darion thought it incumbent on him to approve.

Shurion chuckled. 'Further subjects for your studies, hmm, Lord Darion?' The alienologist instinctively opened his mouth to defend his discipline, but a gesture from the Commander rendered protest unnecessary. 'I meant no disrespect, my lord. It's a pleasure to have you back with us, as I hope to prove shortly. Why, the way I feel tonight I could even be persuaded to permit the beautiful Dyona of the bloodline of Lyrion to stay aboard the *Furion*. What a privilege it would be for my humble self to host not one but two members of our blessed Thousand Families.' The sarcasm was almost palpable.

'I sense there is more to your mood than the time of day and the successful completion of the cryo-tube transfer, Commander,' Darion said. 'Perhaps you have also unmasked the traitor among your crew.' He couldn't resist the goad.

But Shurion's smugness seemed impregnable. 'Soon, Lord Darion. Very soon.'

'I'm gratified to hear it.' And what was that colourful and expressive word the Earthers had for someone they didn't like? Its origin lay in illegitimacy, bloodlines, an issue never far from Scytharene hearts. Oh, yes. 'I would be even more impressed to see it, Commander Shurion,' said Darion. *Bastard*.

The two Scytharene faced each other on the bridge overlooking the dark valley, and smiled at each other, hating each other, and each secretly felt that tomorrow would be the making of him.

Dr Mowatt's techs swarmed over the Joshuas. Every one of the dozen assault vehicles needed its systems to be checked, rechecked, then checked again. Nothing could be allowed to go wrong when dawn came and the machines closed in on the Scytharene ship. A loose wire here or a faulty circuit there could result in the death of a Joshua operator and the failure of the mission. 'Malfunctions mean murder,' was Captain Taber's motto.

The techs were assisted by the Joshua operators themselves. Travis, who together with the rest of his group was following the activity alongside Mowatt and Taber and despite the late hour, counted them. Twenty. When maximum occupancy for the JAVs at three men per vehicle would require thirty-six. It wasn't the machinery that was likely to be the problem, but the manpower.

Maybe he could do something about that.

'Captain Taber. Sir? I want to go with them,' he announced suddenly. 'Be one of the team that attacks the *Furion*.'

'Travis, no.' Linden tugged at his arm as if expecting him to leap into one of the open-hatched control cabins this very minute.

'Lin, yes. This is something I want to do.' He squeezed her hand, he hoped reassuringly. 'It's something I *have* to do.' His confrontation with Simon had hurt him, more than he'd disclosed to Linden or anyone. It had sown seeds of self-doubt in his mind. Was Simon right – even slightly? Could his, Travis's, leadership of the group be interpreted as an exercise in vanity? Was even the tiniest part of him more interested in looking good than doing good? 'Captain Taber, please, let me ride with the Joshuas.' Because fighting the Scytharene, that was indisputably the right thing to do. No questionable motivation there. No shades of light and dark. No doubts.

'Mr Naughton, I applaud your courage,' said Captain Taber, 'but you are neither a trained JAV operator nor, indeed, a soldier.'

'We're all soldiers now,' Travis responded. 'All of us. And haven't I proved already I can fight? And I don't know, I might come in useful. There might be a situation where someone needs to climb out of the Joshua or something, I don't know why, but . . . and I don't need an atmosuit or anything so I could do it. Give me this chance, Captain Taber,' the teenager implored. '*Please.*'

And Taber's mind roamed back over his forty years of military service, and he remembered other young men who'd been desperate to prove themselves on the field of battle, determined to confront themselves and learn who they truly were, because in war there were always two potential enemies, the man in the uniform of another country and the man inside yourself, inside your heart, inside your soul. And Taber envied Travis Naughton his passion and his youth; his own he'd lost many years ago. He'd lived too long. He couldn't stand in the boy's way. He couldn't deny him his chance to know himself.

'Very well, Mr Naughton,' he acceded. 'You may accompany Parry in Joshua Seven.'

'Are you sure that's a good idea, Captain Taber?' objected Dr Mowatt.

'You are the Enclave's Scientific Director,' Taber said. 'The deployment of the Joshuas is a military matter.'

'As you wish.' The woman shrugged. 'I hope you know what you're doing.'

'Well *I* do, and you're not leaving me behind again, Travis.' Which would be difficult with Linden clamping her arms around the brown-haired boy's body. 'I'm coming in the damned tank with you. Don't even *think* of saying no.'

'I'm not sure I can say anything, Lin. You're cutting off my circulation.' But inside Travis was shouting, *yes, yes, yes.*

'Captain Taber?' Linden said. 'If Travis can join the assault team, I can too, can't I? This *is* supposed to be the age of sexual equality, isn't it?'

Certainly, it appeared to Taber, it wasn't only males who had something to prove. He inclined his head.

'I don't think it would be appropriate for me to stay behind while Travis and Linden are risking their lives.' Antony now stepped forward.

'Brandon, Mr Clive,' said Taber. 'Joshua Nine.'

'And if Linden can go with Travis, I can—'

Jessica was interrupted. 'It can't be wise for all the youngsters to be part of the assault team, surely,' Dr Mowatt ventured to her military liaison officer. 'Bearing in mind their freedom of movement above ground, it might be more desirable if at least somebody remained here in the Enclave.'

Antony held Jessica's shoulders, peered earnestly into her eyes. 'Dr Mowatt's right, Jessie. It's better if you stay here. Someone needs to. And there's someone *else* you need to sit down and sort things out with.' His gaze directed Jessica's pointedly to Mel.

'I'm coming with you, Antony,' Mel said, raising her hands to fend off the possibility of being left behind. 'Or with Trav. Or with a Joshua that isn't Seven or Nine.'

'Not this time, Mel,' Antony said and, disappointingly, Travis didn't overrule him. She should be mad with Antony – she could never be mad with Trav – but somehow she wasn't. Mel sensed a warmth and even a tenderness in the blond boy's tone. With a start, she realised that she trusted him, almost as much as she trusted Trav. 'I think I've finally worked out the punchline of that joke you told me in the prison camp. You don't have to be Grimaldi. You can choose not to be.' Antony took Jessica's left hand, Mel's right. He forced them together and their fingers brushed. 'Jessica – Mel. Mel – Jessica. There. Reintroduced. Now whatever's gone wrong between you, you can put it right. Before we get back, you understand me?'

If they did, neither girl looked as if she was keen to commence the process any time soon.

'Who's Grimaldi?' said Jessica.

'Well if you two are staying, you don't need me here as well.' Richie spoke with his usual sullenness, but his face was crimson as the others turned to him in frank astonishment. Astonishment? It was an improvement over sheer bloody hatred. 'I s'pose I could sit in one of those bloody tin cans with Tony – if it's all right with you, like.' Addressing his prospective companion.

'You call me Antony, Richie,' said the Head Boy of the Harrington School, 'and it certainly is.'

'What do you know?' Travis said quietly to Linden. 'Richie Coker volunteering to put himself in harm's way. Maybe he does have some decency in him after all.'

'I wouldn't,' said Linden, 'be too sure of that, Travis.'

Captain Taber called the teenagers together. They'd better snatch a few hours' sleep, particularly those who were supplementing the assault team. The Joshuas' departure for the *Furion* was scheduled for 0500 and it could not be delayed.

At first light, the human race's fightback against the Scytharene would begin.

FOURTEEN

The sky was like stone, the light of the reluctant dawn as slow and heavy and grey as granite interring the Earth. In his private quarters, a sleepless Darion thought of the moon orbiting the Scytharene homeworld which was reserved for the tombs of the Thousand Families, his society's elite differentiated from the common herd in death as in life. Mile upon mile of silent mausoleums, the satellite inhabited only by the keepers of the crypts and visited from time to time by grieving members of a noble bloodline depleted by one, a new addition to the keepers' care. The tomb complex devoted to the heirs of Ayrion alone was built over an area the size of a city. Darion himself would increase its population one day.

If he survived this first.

He voice-activated the wallscreen in his rooms and was shocked by his dry and faltering croak. He looked down at his hands: his fingers were trembling like an old man's. In Earther culture, he knew, the colour white was often associated with cowardice or fear. This morning Darion felt his skin to be of a suitably symbolic tint. He clenched his fingers into fists. Now was not the time to be afraid.

He ought not to entertain recollections of his ancestors' resting-places; he ought to banish such morbidity from his mind. His people had a saying: 'The thought of death brings death to pass.' Better to dwell on Dyona, a reason for living. Better still, perhaps, not to think of anyone at all but to focus totally and absolutely on the work that needed to be done.

On the wallscreen Darion watched the final Culler aboard the *Furion* rise from its berth and leave the ship. Shurion had taken the bait. By the time the Culler reached Otterham and found no Travis Naughton or Scytharene spy there, it would be too late. The Earthers' attack would already have been launched.

Its success, however, still lay largely in his quaking hands.

Darion seated himself before his computer. Scytharene custom was to call upon the spirits of one's ancestors and the courage of one's animal totem before commencing any undertaking which would place one's life in jeopardy. Somehow, though, Darion doubted that either would be very sympathetic to his present cause.

Instead, 'May the right keep me strong,' he murmured.

No warrior by nature, Darion nevertheless set about killing the *Furion*.

Several decks away, on the bridge, Commander Shurion too spectated as the Culler took to the quarried skies. His heart – what there was of it – soared with the ship. His moment of redemption, of vindication, was upon him. Shurion's habit of draping himself in full ceremonial robes seemed particularly appropriate today. Black and gold. His subservience and his ambition dramatised side by side.

He sat forward eagerly, expectantly in his raised command chair and, though he didn't know it, of course, his fists were clenched as Darion's also were at the same instant. If the

Culler was successful in its mission, if that wretched slave he'd duped into betraying his own kind had told the truth – and Shurion didn't doubt that – then the traitor would be his within hours.

Even if the Culler failed somehow, Shurion would not be foiled. A good commander always had a contingency plan.

Any attempt by the renegade to repeat his treachery would bring him down once and for all . . .

The hatches of the Joshuas rotated and locked into place. 'Control cabin sealed,' said Parry, a dark-haired man of about thirty with a head like a bullet and eyes that never seemed to blink. 'Activating enviro-systems now.' A green light appearing on the console at which he sat. 'Enviro-systems fully operational. Running final checks on propulsion, surveillance and weapons systems.'

At least this guy Parry seemed to know what he was doing, Travis thought, which was encouraging, bearing in mind that his and Linden's lives depended on him. It seemed to have been a long time since he'd even been able – let alone willing – to place his faith in an adult.

But he kept a close and studious eye on what Parry was doing, absorbing, recording. The Sickness and the Scytharene both had taught him to take nothing for granted.

Linden's hand grasped his. 'You okay?' he smiled, turning to her in the frosty blue light of the control cabin. 'It's not too late to stay with Jessie and Mel, if, you know . . .'

'I'm afraid it is too late,' said Parry, without a great deal of sympathy. 'All systems are fully operational. We're ready to move out.'

'That's fine. *I'm* fine. Honestly, Travis. I want to be here.' Squeezing his hand.

'Hmm.' Parry sniffed. 'No intimacy in the vehicle, please. Are you both strapped in?' As if half suspecting the teenagers would be all over each other if not.

The seatbelt was so tight, actually, that Linden could scarcely move at all. The control cabin of the Joshua was circular at the floor and conical as it rose towards the claustrophobically low ceiling directly beneath the twin-gunned turret. That ceiling and every square centimetre of wall were studded with lights, switches, gauges and other instrumentation. Around the perimeter of the cabin, at equal distance from each other, three consoles were positioned with an array of screens above providing visual access to the assault vehicle's immediate surroundings, at present its fellow Joshuas and some fussing technicians. The idea, Linden supposed, with a full complement of trained crew, at any rate, was for each operator to sit at his own console. The chairs were all fixed to a circular runner on the floor, however, and so could slide to the right or left as required. She'd shifted hers to be as close to Travis as possible. That, after all, was the object of the exercise.

But though the enviro-systems kept the air purified and cool, Linden felt herself perspiring, her palms clammy. Enclosed spaces didn't bother her as such, but she'd been so used to living outdoors – 'What do we need tiles and plaster for?' Oak used to say. 'The sky is Nature's ceiling' – that finding herself crammed into the coffin dimensions of a Joshua control cabin came necessarily as something of a culture shock.

'Final checks completed, Joshua crews.' Dr Mowatt's voice crackled over the comlink. 'We are opening the primary exit hatch. Proceed in formation, and good luck to you.'

'You two ready?' said Parry.

'Because here,' said Brandon in Joshua Nine, 'we go.'

And Richie was surprised how quietly. He could hardly hear the vehicle's engine.

'Magnetic,' Antony reminded him. 'Weren't you listening to Brandon just now?'

The Joshua operator, nearer forty than thirty, nearer baldness than not, glanced over his shoulder at Richie and laughed. 'I think Coker's got other things on his mind than this baby's propulsion units, that right, Coker?'

Kind of. Like the fact that he was more scared at this moment than he'd ever been in his life before, more scared than anybody had a right to be who hadn't yet collapsed in a quivering, blubbering mound of jelly. *Shit*-scared, not to put too fine a point on it. Not that Richie could admit that to Tony Clive. Not that he could allow it to deter him from remaining part of the assault team.

'Hadn't you,' he stammered, 'aren't you better off watching where you're bloody well going?'

Brandon laughed again. 'There's no bog on board, Coker. You throw up or you piss your pants, you're gonna have to sit in it. Either that or aim it at the enemy first.'

'Guy's a comedian,' Richie grumbled. 'We have to get lumbered with a comedian.'

'Ah, Richie,' Antony ventured, 'you aren't *going* to throw up, are you?'

In the moncom centre, a dozen screens followed the progress of a dozen Joshuas. Captain Taber and Dr Mowatt divided their attention between all twelve of them.

Jessica and Mel were interested in only two.

The assault vehicles had rumbled out of the tunnel, out of the hill that hid the Enclave. Their squat grey molybdenum alloy forms bore towards the forest like a faster, larger and more aggressive species of tortoise, the metal gleaming dully in the dawning light. They spread out into an extended line. When the moment finally came, the plan was to encircle the Scytharene ship and blast it from all sides.

They looked powerful, Jessica thought. By themselves, anyhow. As they smashed into the woodland, splintering those trees that foolishly stood in their way, it was possible to imagine the Joshuas overwhelming any resistance, grinding remorselessly over any foe. But how would they appear next to the towering Scytharene slavecraft, the skyscraper decks of the *Furion*? How would they compare when their target came into view? Like Gulliver in the land of the giants, she feared. Like beetles to be crushed underfoot.

Antony. Travis. They'd left her alone again, and . . .

A hand snatched hold of hers. Surreptitiously. Guiltily.

And she wasn't alone. Not entirely. Not if she didn't want to be.

'It'll be all right, Jess,' said Mel with a weak, apologetic smile.

And Jessica didn't wrest her hand away, though that was her first, cruel instinct. She couldn't hurt Mel like that under present circumstances. In fact, she realised with a stab of wonder in her heart, she was glad to have Mel with her after all.

When Mel dared to squeeze the blonde girl's hand, Jessica squeezed back.

*

On the bridge of the *Furion*, the Scytharene tech couldn't believe what his instruments were indicating, and with a remarkable lack of alarm. His own response was rather more anxious, particularly as it was his duty to report the same inexplicable information to Commander Shurion.

'Commander, sir?'

'Technician.' Shurion gazed down at the crewman from his elevated command chair with the generous toleration of a god.

'It appears . . . we seem to be experiencing a certain degree of systems failure, Commander.'

'Indeed?' His expression inscrutable, Shurion lowered his chair.

'Weapons. Shields. Communications. Even our flight systems. They appear to be, ah, temporarily offline.'

'What are you telling me, technician?' Shurion said quietly. 'Are you telling me my ship is effectively crippled?'

'Ah . . .' A bead of sweat on the Scytharene's bony brow.

'Do you know why this unpardonable situation has arisen?'

'N-not at the present moment, Commander Shurion, sir.' Anticipating the disposal cell.

But Shurion's mouth split into a scarlet grin. He threw his head back and laughed. 'Then it's as well that I do. Blackhearts, to my side.' The several Scytharene warriors present on the bridge hastened to comply. Shurion stood imposingly, and now not humour but hatred occupied his features, burned crimson in his eyes. 'At last. At *last*. The traitor is ours.'

The Joshuas bulldozed through the forest. Their armour shouldered aside any natural obstacle without visible effort;

their tracks turned relentlessly, compensating automatically for the rise and fall of the terrain so that the assault vehicles' speed never once slowed. The machines advanced like warriors towards their destiny.

In Joshua Nine, Richie could see from the viewing screen that the vehicle was snapping tree-trunks like matchsticks as it drove its way towards Vernham Hill, but the impact of collision wasn't felt within the control cabin. There was neither sense nor sound of the buffeting where Richie sat frozen in his chair. Which was just as well. A less than smooth ride and his already queasy stomach might indeed have thrown in the towel and heaved up his breakfast. He became suddenly aware that he was gripping the arms of the chair so tightly his knuckles were bulging like a Scytharene bellineum. He glanced sideways. Tony Clive was aware of it, too – and how come the posh kid still looked like they were out for a spin in Daddy's motor on a Sunday afternoon?

'What's the matter with you?' Richie growled defensively.

'Nothing,' said Antony. 'You?'

'Nothing.'

'Good. Then we're even.'

Though Antony registered his companion's terror, of course, he didn't think any less of Richie Coker because of it. In a strange way, he felt himself beginning to admire the bully-that-was, to be sympathetic. Here was Richie, slick with fear, yet struggling to suppress that emotion and overcome it. Whether he achieved his aim or not, the attempt alone was worthy of credit. And this grand effort, Antony reflected, from a feckless lout whose middle name before the Sickness had probably been Asbo.

Antony was afraid, too, but his education both at

Harrington and at home had taught him to control his feelings, to keep them hidden like secrets. Reason was what mattered, not emotion. Yet many times Antony had lingered beneath the roll of honour in the Great Hall at Harrington and gazed up at the names immortalised thereon, their owners having perished in the mud of Passchendaele or the Somme, in the deserts of North Africa or the jungles of Burma, on the long, bloody march to Berlin. '*Dedicated to the memory of those Harringtonians who paid the supreme sacrifice fighting for justice and truth in two world wars. May they sleep in peace and wake to glory.*' He'd worshipped those names of long-dead men who, while boys, had stood where he stood and worn the same uniform, he'd recited their names like prayers, and he'd wondered how they'd *felt* when their moment of reckoning had come upon them, when the shells screamed and the machine-guns spat. And he'd wondered how *he* would feel in the same deadly situation, in battle, in war.

He'd soon know.

For the ground was rising now, steadily, steeply, and the diamond-spiked tracks of the Joshuas were working harder to maintain progress, and the relief-map displayed on the screens noted and represented graphically the slopes of Vernham Hill.

'One minute to visual contact with target,' Brandon said, as much to the scientists back at the Enclave as to the teenagers with him in the JAV.

The screen showed Joshua Eight to their left, Joshua Ten to their right, surging forward, climbing higher in perfect synchronisation. Antony felt his heart thudding. He felt a kind of crazy exhilaration, a reeling wildness. He wanted to shout and sob and laugh and embrace somebody, embrace Jessica, though the rush in his heart was about more than sex. He yearned to embrace life itself, to grasp it tightly, to hold it to him like a cherished child and keep it safe. Because life was the most precious and important thing of all.

And worth fighting for. Worth dying for.

The names on the roll of honour. Antony remembered them. *Adams, J.C.*, he repeated silently. *Addison, C.L.K. Amory, D.E.*

The Joshuas breasted Vernham Hill. They ranged along the ridge, their guns towards the enemy at last. The colossus that was the *Furion* awaited them below.

'My God,' breathed Brandon. 'Let's hope your alien mate's done his job.'

'Shit. Antony,' gritted Richie. 'This is it. This is bloody it.'

'I know,' the blond boy said. *Brumby-Ellis, G.W. Caversham, T.*

Clive, A.R.?

'Advance and engage.' Captain Taber snapping orders from miles away. 'Joshua assault team, engage at will.'

The door protested – 'Entry to Lord Darion's quarters has not been granted' – but to no avail. The intruders had employed an overrider. Shurion and his Blackhearts were through before the door had even slid fully open. The warriors' subjugators were drawn.

Darion at his computer shot to his feet. 'What . . .?' But it was obvious what. 'Computer . . .'

Shurion's hand clamped around the alienologist's throat, cutting off his speech. 'I don't think so, *Lord* Darion' – sarcasm reducing the rank to meaninglessness – 'do you?'

'Get your . . . unhand me at once.' Because two warriors were grabbing his arms, forcing them behind his back. 'I belong to the Thousand Families. I'll have your flesh peeled from your bones for this outrage.'

'Again, my lord,' Shurion grinned darkly, 'I don't think so.' But he removed his own hand and gestured for his underlings to do likewise.

'When my father hears of this assault against my person, Shurion . . .' Darion strove to sound authoritative, in control, but it was difficult. *Shurion knew. He'd suspected, yes, but now, somehow he was sure.* Difficult simply to stand with his bones liquefying with fear.

'Your father will hear of it,' Shurion assured him. 'Fleet Commander Gyrion will hear of everything pertaining to this deplorable incident, particularly its most relevant, shocking and unhappy detail, Lord Darion. The fact that you, his son, are a traitor to the Scytharene race.'

'Pre-preposterous,' Darion stammered. 'Computer: delete program.'

'It's too late, Darion,' Shurion chuckled. 'You weak, puling boy. You *betrayer.* You could wipe your computer clean of memory but we would still know what you have had it do. Disable the *Furion*'s weapons systems? Render our shields inoperative? Deny us the power of flight? Leave us mute and helpless? I assume this means your filthy slave friends are preparing to attack us, hmm? With our last Culler conveniently absent?'

By all the Scytharene gods, Darion hoped so, prayed so. Let the onslaught begin now. It had to be now. Why were Travis's people delaying? Where were they?

Had he sacrificed himself for nothing?

'Sabotage and conspiracy, Lord Darion,' Shurion listed. 'To add to your litany of crimes. *Capital* crimes.'

'I don't know' – with a last attempt at defiance – 'what you're talking about. It is you who are reserving a place in the disposal cell, Commander Shurion. Do you truly believe that my father or the tribunal of the Thousand Families will value the testimony of a commoner such as yourself above that of one of their own kind?' Ironic it would be, however, if the system Darion despised saved him from execution.

'Perhaps not testimony,' Shurion allowed, 'but I have cold, objective and incontrovertible evidence to submit before their honours of the tribunal when your sad, sorry case comes to trial.'

'Perhaps you sent a spy among the Earthers to learn this alleged traitor's name,' Darion theorised. 'If you did, I doubt you'll find him reliable – or even find him at all.'

'You learned of that, did you?' Shurion nodded. 'Then our Culler is wasting its time, is it? Well, and were you also aware that after the slaves' escape I had installed in the ship's mainframe a tracer program, so that any future interference with the *Furion*'s computer systems would be tracked back to its point of origin and to the foul criminal responsible. To this computer here, Darion. To *you*.'

Darion's mouth made motions to speak, but there was nothing he could say. It was finished. *He* was finished.

'What's the matter, Lord Darion?' Shurion sneered. 'Scarath got your tongue?' He thrust his face closer to the alienologist's, his expression seething with hatred. 'I'm so glad you *are* the traitor as I suspected all along. It proves I was *right* to despise you. I ought to have you killed now. I ought to do it myself. It would give me the most profound personal satisfaction to take your life with my own hands and watch you die – after the trouble, the humiliation your pathetic acts of treachery have caused me. But' – restraining himself from carrying out his desire only with difficulty – 'your privileged position still protects you. For now. We must ensure that due process is observed for a member of the Thousand Families. You'll have to be tried according to the ancient laws of our people, but have no doubt, Darion, you will be found guilty and your worthless life *will* be terminated. And I will be there watching in jubilation.'

'You're sick, Shurion,' Darion grimaced. 'Sick in the soul.'

Shurion seemed amused rather than offended by this assessment of his character. 'An insult without a blow raises no welts,' he said. 'But perhaps I ought to thank you, Darion. You may not realise this, but you have actually *helped* me. You and your contemptible dissident friends seek to overturn our social system for the benefit of alien scum, to save the slaves. I too want our government revolutionised, heir of Ayrion, but for myself, to fulfil my own ambitions and to finally become what and who I deserve to be, first among the Scytharene. It will not be yourself alone on trial when the time comes, Darion. It will be the entire social class you represent, the decadent, moribund, incompetent Thousand Families. For what rational Scytharene in future will be prepared to toler- ate or accept a ruling elite which claims to be incorruptible but which in reality spawns traitors? The right of the Thousand Families to wield authority without question will at last be challenged, the tyranny of bloodlines exposed. Your father and his kind will fall, and those who think like me will seize the reins of power and usher in a new golden age for the Scytharene. And then the galaxy will groan beneath the yoke of slavery. Your Thousand Families are obsolete, Darion: a man is what he makes himself, and I will make myself great.'

'Are you finished now? If not, Commander, I was going to ask if I could sit down. I find listening to insane rants so wearing.'

Shurion chuckled. 'Then I'll send you where you can rest. Take him to the cells.' Exultantly, he watched his warriors remove Darion from the room. If he believed in the gods, which he did not, Shurion would have thanked them for this moment. His heart swelled within him. He felt strong, supreme. There was nothing he could not do.

A communication from the bridge. A phalanx of Earther tanks had apparently crested the hill on their left flank.

'And?' snorted Shurion.

'Our weapons and defence systems are offline, Commander. What if the Earthers attack?'

And nothing could harm him. 'Then let them.'

The next few seconds would tell, Travis knew, as the Joshua powered down the side of Vernham Hill. Whether Darion had come through for them. Whether they even had a chance. Whether there was hope.

As one the assault vehicles burst from the final cover the wood could offer. At once they opened fire. In turn, along the line, the turret cannon thundered, the higher gun first, followed by the lower like the most violent of echoes. A twenty-four-shell salvo and within the Joshuas the control cabins shuddered.

Instinctively, Linden cried out. Instinctively, Travis reached for her.

The missiles struck the *Furion*.

And immediately their grey casing disintegrated and became orange flame and yellow fire, but the colour Travis was scouring the ship for was blue, the ethereal but invulnerable blue of the Scytharene shields.

It didn't appear.

The shields were down.

'Yes! *Yes!*' Travis whooped. Linden whooped. Parry whooped.

The *Furion* shook under the impact of the shells, its silver hull scorched, blistered, scarred. Blackened. The black of burned metal was a good colour today.

Travis's heart leapt. His body would have done the same had it not been for the seatbelt. At least he was able to throw his arms around his girlfriend. 'Darion did it. He *did* it.'

'I love him!' Linden rejoiced. 'Well, not actually. I just mean . . .'

Celebration as well in the Enclave, the screens in the moncom centre lighting up with the flares of exploding missiles. Technicians cheering at their consoles. Dr Mowatt clapping, seeming suddenly younger by twenty years, eyes bright behind her horn-rimmed spectacles.

Mel and Jessica hugging.

'It's going to be all right. It *is.*' Jessica's voice choked with emotion.

'I told you.' Mel's too.

Captain Taber the only one exercising restraint, his Montgomery moustache twitching nervously. Captain Taber knowing that the last shot in a battle counted for more than the first. Noting that the damage caused to the Scytharene ship was superficial only, aware that the absence of shields did not automatically remove the possibility of retaliation. Barking further orders: 'All Joshua operators, press home the assault. Now, while the advantage lies with us. But stay alert. The aliens may still be able to deploy their weapons.'

Travis heard Taber's voice and the soldier was right. But whatever offensive capability the *Furion* normally possessed it seemed unable to bring to bear now. Darion's work again.

A second barrage from the Joshuas bombarded the ship unchallenged, the explosions reverberating through the valley and smoke and flame pluming into the sky. The silver hull battered and buckling but not breached. Stubborn. Despite the heritage of the assault vehicles' name, the walls still stood.

'Looks like if we want to punch a hole in that big bastard we're gonna have to get even closer,' muttered Parry. 'Well, we can do even closer. You kids hold on.'

'Advance and encircle,' Captain Taber instructed. 'Use every means at your disposal. Bring this battle to an end.'

The bridge trembled as the *Furion* was blasted by missile fire, but Commander Shurion did not. He sprawled in his fully raised command chair like a king, almost laughing out loud at the hapless red-armoured techs scurrying chaotically from one computer bank to another, desperately monitoring the slavecraft's status, frantically struggling to restore its sabotaged systems. Not for the slightest second did Shurion fear that this might prove impossible. Not once did he doubt his eventual and total victory over this feeble Earther force in their tiny tanks.

He felt himself to be invincible, chosen. It seemed the fates themselves were bending to his will. The traitor Darion exposed would further his political ambitions, while an Earther incursion crushed would reinforce his military reputation.

Perhaps it had been worthwhile coming to this godforsaken mudball after all.

'The tensile integrity of the hull in sectors one, three, four and seven is only sixty per cent, Commander.' An anxious tech addressing him. 'Tensile integrity in sectors two, five and six is down to fifty-four per cent. Commander?'

'In other words,' Shurion deigned to respond, 'the hull remains intact.'

A second tech joined his comrade. 'Commander, all systems online. It'll take a little while to reboot fully, but—'

'At what capacity can we operate now?'

'Perhaps fifty per cent, Commander, but any major expenditure of energy may delay—'

Shurion dismissed the tech's reservation with his hand. 'Half our strength is more than sufficient. One Scytharene is worth ten slaves.'

The bridge rocked as a missile detonated a deck or two below it. Fire washed across the windows. The first tech gulped. 'Shall I activate the shields, Commander Shurion?' As if he really *wanted* to.

'Commander, sir, the Earthers' vehicles.' The intrusion of an eager third tech postponed Shurion's reply. 'Our instruments indicate that their power source is magnetic.'

'So?'

'Our instruments can lock on to the residual magnetic energy left in the vehicles' wake and trace their journey back to its starting point.'

So indeed, gloated Shurion. 'To the Earthers' base, whatever that may be.' He switched his attention to the first tech again. 'Contact the Culler we sent to the Earther village. Inform Captain Myrion that his orders have changed.'

'Of course, Commander.' The tech's spirits rose. 'He is to return here at once?' And fell again.

'Of course *not*,' Shurion scoffed. 'He is to follow the co-ordinates that will be sent to him, locate this Earther base and utterly destroy it.'

'Yes, Commander,' said the tech, dismayed, an attitude to which Shurion, fortunately for the tech, was oblivious.

'We have no need of assistance. We have no desire for rein-forcement. We will smash these impudent slaves ourselves. The wrath of the Scytharene roused is awesome to behold – as the Earthers will discover.'

Blue.

A startling, sparkling sheen of blue, strangely serene.

'Shit,' observed Richie in Joshua Nine. 'They've got their bloody shields back.'

As the missiles found, their detonations now just as loud, their bursts of flame as hot, but their effectiveness as weapons designed to cripple an enemy craft reduced to zero. They might as well have been eggs hurled against a wall.

'What now? What now?' Richie was thinking maybe back to the Enclave. Actually, he was thinking back to pretty much anywhere.

'Let's see how those suckers like our rocket-launchers,' Brandon said, activating the gun ports on the Joshua's wings. Twin rockets screeched into the fray.

Absorbed by the Scytharene shields.

'We've got other weapons too, right?' Richie hoped.

'And time,' Antony added. 'At least they're not returning fire.'

He could have bitten off his tongue.

With an ozone crackle and a blinding yellow flash, energy bolts seared from the *Furion*, dozens of them, unleashed from rows of apertures suddenly opening up between certain decks and extending along both sides of the ship's sickle structure. It was an onslaught of lightning, the soil sizzling, erupting around the Joshuas, the field torched into an inferno, flat ground fissuring into pits of fire.

In Joshua Seven, Travis was quick to assess their chances. Under these revised circumstances, they had none. 'Withdraw. Parry, we've got to withdraw. When those beams find their range . . .' And the shields were functioning. Weapons systems were operational. What had happened to Darion?

Was he discovered? Was he dead?

'Can't run without orders, kid,' Parry said, swinging the Joshua sharply to the left to avoid a lancing energy bolt. The control cabin lurched violently.

'We're too exposed here. We need cover so we can regroup. Forget orders,' Travis snapped. 'What about common sense?'

'Trav! My God!'

Linden was still half-watching the screens, so she saw the end of Joshua Six. The Scytharene energy beams had blasted a blazing trench in the earth and the Joshua had tipped into it. The diamond spikes on its tracks were digging into the dirt, clawing towards a more navigable surface. The vehicle might have been able to save itself had the next bolt not scored a direct hit. Joshua Six's magnetic propulsion units exploded.

Its armour shattered. Its exit hatches popped like champagne corks. Its proud turret was consumed in flame. No one could have survived.

'*Travis*.' And Linden clutched his hand with both of hers, imploring him to put her mind at rest, to assure her that they'd get out of this, escape the conflagration raging around them. That they'd survive. That they'd live. She wanted to live.

Travis felt her fear. Somehow the knowledge that she was looking to him for comfort helped him master his own. 'Linden, nothing's going to happen to you. I won't let it. I promise.' Though he'd said much the same thing to Simon, who'd betrayed him.

'Taber!' Parry was screaming into the comlink. 'Captain Taber, are you getting this? Come in, for God's sake. What the hell do we do now?'

But only silence in the moncom centre, the grim and awful hush that comes with the realisation of disaster. The burning wreckage of Joshua Six was on screen. Life-support readings for its two operators had flatlined.

At least it wasn't the occupants of Joshuas Seven and Nine who were dead, Mel found herself thinking, and was immediately ashamed. As if Travis and Linden's lives, Antony and Richie's were worth more than other people's. To *her*, though . . . She glanced at Jessica. The blonde girl wore a guilty expression, too.

And the years that had vanished from Dr Mowatt with the prospect of victory, in the shadow of defeat were returned to her and more. Taber too, who physically seemed to shrink in his uniform. Neither appeared able to cope with this sudden reversal of fortune.

Not good enough. 'Captain Taber,' Mel demanded. The voices of the still-living Joshua operators, Parry, Brandon, clamoured over the comlink for direction. 'Do something. We've got to help them. You've got to tell them what to do.' The military liaison officer stood slack-jawed like a zombie. Not *good* enough. Mel grabbed his shoulders and shook him. *'Captain Taber.'*

His eyes frightened her. They were the empty eyes of a dead man. They were her father's eyes. 'There's nothing we can do to help them,' Taber said brokenly. 'Or us. There's nothing we can do.'

Jessica joined Mel. 'Then order them to get out of there. Retreat. Withdraw. Whatever the word is. They have to get away or they're all going to die.'

'Sir,' reported one of the techs. 'Joshua Two.'

In flames. A hatch unscrewing. A man emerging. Burns made it difficult to recognise who. No voice to scream. No eyes to see. No breath. He pitched forward over the body of his Joshua and was dead.

'Well if you won't tell them, I will.' Mel darted to the comlink.

Dr Mowatt reached it first. 'All Joshuas, abandon mission. Retreat. Save yourselves.'

Which was something. The two girls' pulses raced as the remaining vehicles wheeled and accelerated towards the refuge of the woods, Seven and Nine streaked with smoke but otherwise undamaged. 'Come on, Trav,' Mel murmured urgently. 'All of you, come on.'

'Dr Mowatt, Captain Taber.' They knew it was bad news

334

from the tone of the tech's voice. 'On the radar – a large unidentified flying object rapidly approaching. In visual range now. I'll switch it to screen.'

A Culler, like a steel and silver bird of prey.

'Is it from the *Furion*?' Jessica frowned. 'How?'

'Must be the one we diverted to Otterham,' guessed Mel. 'Didn't find Travis or Simon there. Got pissed off. Coming to look for them here instead.'

'How does it know we're here?' Jessica looked nervously to Dr Mowatt.

'It doesn't,' the woman decreed. 'It can't.'

'Is that your considered scientific opinion, Dr Mowatt,' asked Mel, 'or plain, good old wishful thinking? 'Cause it looks like it knows where it's going to me.'

'And why,' whispered Jessica.

From each tip of the Culler's scimitar curve, missiles flamed.

'Incoming!' the tech declared unnecessarily.

On the screen, the group in the moncom centre saw projectiles rip holes in the hill above them like wounds in flesh. The Enclave shook. There was a rumble like a distant landslide.

Battlepods spilled from the Culler's innards like paratroopers on D-Day.

'Oh. My. God.' It was immaterial to Mel how the Scytharene had learned of either the base's existence or its location. The relevant fact was clear enough.

The Enclave was under attack.

FIFTEEN

Even from his cell, Darion could hear the sounds of combat. Even when he covered his ears and groaned aloud.

The sounds of his friends' slaughter.

Because they'd have restored the shields by now, and the weapons systems. Scytharene techs were nothing if not efficient. Travis's small unit of assault vehicles would be no match for a fully operational *Furion*. Joshuas, hadn't Travis called them? After the Joshua in the Christian Bible whom God had assisted in bringing down the walls of Jericho. No wonder the forces of the Enclave were doomed. They had no God to call on to engineer their victory, only he, Darion of the bloodline of Ayrion.

Darion the failure.

He'd failed Travis. He'd failed Dyona. He'd failed himself.

On the bridge, supervising the destruction of the Earthers, Shurion would be laughing. At *him*.

Darion trudged the floor in slow despair. And why shouldn't Shurion exult? He'd won. Darion had lost. A 'weak, puling boy', the Commander had called him, and he'd been right. *Weak*. All that lay ahead for him was to be dragged before the tribunal of the Thousand Families, a trial, the inevitable verdict and then death. A lonely, pitiful end, execution. A coward's end. It would be better to die as Travis and his comrades were possibly dying at this moment, bravely, defiantly, fighting for a noble cause, making their stand.

If he ended his life like that, Dyona could at least be proud of him.

And his pacing of the cell became quicker, more purposeful. He thought of his great ancestor Ayrion riding to face certain death in the camp of his enemies rather than expire naturally of old age, a manner of passing that he would have considered weak, shameful. Darion had never understood his forebear's philosophy before. He did now. Ironic that he should find succour in his bloodline at this late stage.

But perhaps not *too* late. Perhaps he had not yet failed. Travis could still be alive, and even if not, he could certainly still be avenged.

There remained a way for Darion to thwart Commander Shurion and strike against his people. One simple thing for him to do. Darion, born of the bloodline of Ayrion of the Thousand Families, would have to die.

The screens told the story. The Culler's missiles had torn gaping lacerations in the hillside, stripped away the soil like flesh to expose, like bone, the metal shell of the Enclave beneath. Another strike and even that would be punctured, the installation and its pitifully few defenders laid bare.

The battlepods were landing nearby. Night-armoured Scytharene warriors in snarling, bestial helmets were clambering out, brandishing black guns the length of rifles. Mel imagined they might be a little more high-tech than that, however: their barrels were tipped laser-white. She kind of hoped she could avoid making closer acquaintance with the weapons, but she doubted it.

Joining up in disciplined ranks, the Scytharene bore down on the Enclave.

Inside the base, the general alarm jangled like a terrified child.

'All personnel to defence positions. Code: Rorke's Drift.' Dr Mowatt sounded confident over the comlink. 'The Scytharene must be repelled at all costs.' Her eyes, however, betrayed the truth. She turned to one of the techs: 'We'd better get into our atmosuits, too.'

'Yes, Dr Mowatt.' The tech flipped a switch and a panel in the wall slid open revealing a science-fiction writer's wardrobe. Racks of futuristic silver suits designed to encase the whole body, including the head, a visor stripped across the eyes, filters at the nose and mouth. The techs began hauling them on. Hastily.

'Should we . . .?' Jessica indicated the new clothing.

'The atmosuits are to protect us from the Sickness virus should the Enclave's seals become compromised,' Dr Mowatt said. 'You girls don't need to worry about that. And I'm afraid they won't stop a Scytharene energy blast.'

'No, but maybe a subjugator can,' Mel said. 'Where are you keeping them? Come on, tool us up. Jessie and I can do our bit.'

'Your "bit",' Dr Mowatt said, 'is to stay here with us – at least for now.' She addressed her colleague: 'Captain Taber.'

The military man was staring dully, mystifiedly at the screens. He couldn't believe the pictures they were transmitting. An alien craft pulverising the Enclave's outer entrance.

Alien soldiers swarming through and surging down the tunnel towards the primary airlock.

They were under siege. The enemy was here. The enemy was coming for him.

'Taber, snap out of it. You shouldn't be here. Your men need you.'

'Like a hole in the head,' muttered Mel.

A new note added to the alarm, and a flashing red light above the moncom centre's door.

'Fire?' worried Jessica.

'Worse,' Dr Mowatt said. 'Fires can be put out. The seals have been breached. The Enclave is open to the outside. I have to get' – struggling into her atmosuit – 'this *on*.'

'The enemy is here,' Captain Taber breathed.

'That's right.' Mel divided her gaze between the officer and the screens. Soldiers were engaging Scytharene at the airlock. Machine-gun fire from the former; laser hisses from the latter. Screams and cries universal. 'See that? Use your bleary old eyes, Taber. Take a good look. The enemy is here in huge bloody numbers and what are you going to *do* about it?'

It was coming for him, he realised. The enemy. Death. He'd eluded it for half a century while others had fallen, at first, before he'd scaled the ranks, men older than himself, but for so long now the casualties had been younger than he, boys who should have had their whole lives before them, boys almost too young to shave, teenagers barely out of school. He'd seen them taken by the enemy and it had been wrong, *unnatural* for the young to perish while the old sat in their command headquarters or at home in their gentlemen's clubs or the Houses of Parliament, committing innocents to front lines without recognising the cost. Perhaps that was why the

Sickness had only done for the old and spared the young, to redress the balance of history. And now, finally, the enemy had come for him. He could only meet it like a man.

'What am I going to *do*, Miss Patrick?' he said, taking his pistol from its holster. 'I'm going to face the enemy and fight. Good day to you.'

He saluted, turned smartly on his heel and strode towards the door.

'Captain Taber!' Dr Mowatt called after him. 'An atmosuit.'

Taber paused and glanced back. 'No thank you, Dr Mowatt,' he said.

The far-off thunder. The alarm. The flashing red light above the door. Simon may have been locked in his room with a guard outside, but he still knew what was going on.

The Scytharene were invading the Enclave.

He tittered a little idiotically, clenched his fists in front of him and shook them up and down like an armchair football fan whose team had just scored. He was at the door. 'You hear that, soldier boy?' Yelling to the guard. 'You know what that is, what it means? You might as well let me out now and maybe I'll put in a good word for you with Commander Shurion. When my new friends get here I'll be released anyway. They're coming for me.'

When the guard duly opened the door, however, Simon couldn't hide his surprise.

'Don't get excited,' the soldier said, barging in. 'You're not going anywhere. Back off. Right to the wall.' Simon obeyed, hands above his head for good measure, keeping well out of his jailer's way. Because the soldier wasn't much older than he was, and didn't look all that stable, and the automatic rifle he was pointing at him was kind of quivering. 'I just want . . .' A switch on the wall Simon hadn't really noticed before, opening a compartment in which hung some sort of protective suit.

To prevent infection from the Sickness. Which meant the Enclave was no longer secure. Simon's allies were already *inside*.

He had to go to them. He had only to make himself known to them and all would be well. A new life for him would begin.

'That's fine, that's fine,' Simon said slyly to the trooper. 'You take whatever you want.'

The door was only metres away. The soldier would never pursue him without the suit on.

'Don't move.'

'I'm not moving.'

Not until the guard was reaching for the atmosuit, lowering his gun for a second, switching his attention from Simon to the garment just for a moment. *Then* he was moving. Lunging for the door with frantic speed.

The soldier swore after him, probably raised his rifle again, might even have fired a shot. Simon didn't know. Simon didn't care. No one was better than Simon Satchwell at doing a runner when threatened. He was through the door and down the corridor and he'd been right about the guard's priorities.

Simon was free.

*

It was as bad as Captain Taber had feared. His handful of men were struggling to hold the line on the upper level, but the Scytharene had secured a bridgehead at the airlocks and their numbers were overwhelming. Air corrupted by the Sickness was gushing into the Enclave but the soldiers might as well have followed their commanding officer's lead and dispensed with atmosuits. It wasn't disease that was going to kill them.

Energy bolts scorched from the alien weapons, slicing with equal efficiency through flesh, fabric, even the metal of the machinery and the electronic equipment behind which the defenders sought to shelter. Consoles exploded in spumes of sparks; severed cables writhed. Taber saw an amputated arm on the floor, the wound cauterised and virtually bloodless, the hand clinging valiantly to a machine-gun. The arm's former owner lay a short distance away, smoke rising from a fiery hole through his heart.

Taber checked his pistol. Six bullets. He hoped he'd have time to fire them all.

Several young soldiers screeching incomprehensible words as they scurried past him in retreat. Their eyes behind the visors didn't register Taber's presence, only the enemy's. An energy bolt speared to Taber's right and cut the spine of a fleeing soldier in two. He didn't flee much further after that.

The position was being abandoned, overrun. The Enclave troops were scattering in headlong flight.

But not Captain Taber. He was pressing on. He pointed his pistol and it was remarkable. How *steady* his hand was. How *sure* his advancing feet. How *calm* he felt. Like a soldier should when all his campaigns were over.

He fired one bullet, two, as his men floundered around him howling with terror.

He fired a third, a fourth, not aiming, unconcerned whether he hit a Scytharene or not. It was the firing that was important. The marching towards the enemy. The facing of the fear.

A fifth shot. And he was alone now, only a pack of beasts before him.

A sixth. The enemy had come for Captain Taber.

Out of ammunition, which was fine. He wouldn't have had time to reload in any case.

Retreat too on the slopes of Vernham Hill.

The Joshuas' offensive had been ordered and well drilled, the assault vehicles advancing as one. Now they were reduced to ragged, ramshackle, reckless flight, and one *by* one they were falling victim to the energy weapons of the Scytharene. If Brandon's performance was anything to go by, Antony thought, it was easy to see why.

The operator of Joshua Nine was in a state approaching blind panic, fumbling at his instruments, one moment gazing at them in bewilderment as if he'd never seen them before, the next swearing at the controls as if they were involved in some kind of conspiracy against him. It seemed he was quickly losing faith in the machine he drove.

Brandon would not have excelled at Harrington, Antony thought. 'Calm down, man,' he urged. 'Focus on what you're doing. Give us some covering fire.'

'What the hell are you talking about, kid, covering fire?'

'Swivel the turret. The guns can fire to the rear as well as ahead of us, can't they?'

'Yeah, yeah.' A capability which seemed to have slipped

Brandon's mind. 'But what the hell do we want to do that for? They won't penetrate those shields.'

'Because we *can*,' said Antony.

And did. Richie saw on the screen the turret rotate and more missiles pepper the *Furion*. Like spit in the wind, he thought. A futile gesture. Tony Clive was big on futile gestures. Like Naughton. This whole trying to do the right thing crock was the biggest futile gesture of all time. Richie preferred to clench his teeth and clench his fists and hope to God they outran the range of those bloody energy bolts before one crisped them to a cinder like those other poor suckers.

And Joshua Twelve, crippled, its left track snapped and useless, firing both guns nevertheless until the Scytharene weapons struck again. And Joshua Five, aflame, its two operators scrambling from its hatches, leaping to the ground, flinging up their arms to shield their faces and screaming at the injustice of it all as the energy bolts obliterated them.

In Joshua Seven, Travis's tactic was the same as Richie's if he only knew it. The woodland on the higher hill itself probably wouldn't offer much defence, but distance was their friend. Already the *Furion*'s blasts were tending to drop short. The crunch of uprooted trees as the Joshua rammed into and past them was almost comforting.

'Damn,' Parry growled. 'We've lost contact with Taber and Mowatt. Comlink must have taken a hit.'

'Don't worry about it,' said Travis. 'We'll be back at the Enclave ourselves soon enough.'

'You think so, Travis?' Linden brightened.

Sure he thought so. 'They've got nothing to come after us with, Lin.' Once safely out of the slavecraft's range, they

344

could return to base, make new plans, attack again. *Never give up.*

There was a sudden, mighty, deafening whoosh of engines. The earth quaked beneath the Joshua's tracks.

What now? What the hell *now*?

It was all on the screens. They'd *never* be out of range.

Behind them, from the valley floor, the *Furion* rose into the air.

Lord Darion was ranting. Clyrion, the guard posted outside his cell, could hear every single word of the alienologist's bellowed tirade, and every single word disturbed him deeply. Clyrion's parents had been conventional, law-abiding members of his race; their son had been raised to revere the Thousand Families of the Scytharene.

'How dare you incarcerate one who belongs to the Thousand Families? How dare you treat your superior as if he was a common criminal? You'll pay for this outrage, you realise that, don't you, warrior?' Targeting him directly through the steel of the door. 'Shurion will pay and *you* will pay and not only you. Your entire bloodline. Can you hear me, warrior? Are you attending? Your entire wretched bloodline will suffer for your affront this day to the heir of Ayrion.'

There was more, too, considerably more, generally concerning the absolute certainty that Lord Darion would be exonerated of the heinous crime of treason of which he was accused and that then the bloodline of Ayrion would exact a terrible revenge on those party to the charge. Clyrion could certainly imagine Lord Darion's first assertion coming to pass. It was unprecedented enough for one of the

Scytharene's elite to be placed in custody at all; it was simply inconceivable for him to be found guilty of wrongdoing. Which meant that the threats against Clyrion's own bloodline also had to be taken seriously. He felt himself slipping towards panic.

'Whatever happens to me now, on your own head be it. Do you hear me, warrior? On your own . . .'

Silence. Sudden. Deathly.

In need of investigation. Clyrion activated the viewscreen into the cell. He saw the body of Lord Darion of the Thousand Families lying crumpled on the floor, not moving. Not breathing? Clyrion almost joined him. Had his prisoner suffered a fit? Committed suicide somehow to avoid further disgrace? While he, Clyrion, was supposed to be keeping watch. If so, it would be the end for him.

Clyrion thrust his subjugator into its holster and pounded the door mechanism. In a blur he was inside the cell, kneeling by his prostrate charge, lifting Lord Darion's head to check for signs of life.

There were some. Eyes snapping open. Mouth peeling back in grim determination.

Hand darting out, plucking the warrior's subjugator from his side.

'What . . .?' Clyrion had been tricked, but even now he might still have salvaged the situation. If he'd grappled with Darion, overpowered him. He should have been strong enough for that. Perhaps he was handicapped by an inbred deference towards any member of the Thousand Families. Because he hesitated.

And Darion shot him.

The guard slumped forward over his prisoner, dead – his

weapon had obviously been set to fatality mode. Darion heaved the body off in revulsion and sprang to his feet. So he was capable of killing after all; perhaps he *was* a true descendant of Ayrion. Though his legs seemed weak, a little shaky even. But there was little time left to worry about that.

The *Furion* was lifting off.

Simon was running, while the Enclave's corridors seemed to shudder around him, violent conflict raging on the levels above. He tried to order the gunfire and screams and explosions into a narrative, as if he might glean from the clamour alone which side was winning and which was doomed to lose, his old friends or his new. The proximity of battle suggested the Scytharene were in the ascendancy, marauding deep into the base. He was glad. His emancipation was near.

Despite the burning in his out-of-condition lungs, Simon smiled.

He took one of the stairways to the science and research level two metal stairs at a time. At the top, he was almost sent tumbling back down again.

'Kid, what the hell . . .?' One of three soldiers, all young, all with desperate fear widening their eyes. 'You're going the wrong way. The *aliens*.'

'Come with us. Come on with us. We'll get you out.' A second trooper grabbing Simon by the arm.

'Get off me.' Shaking himself free and earning a bewildered frown because of it.

The third soldier: 'Wait, isn't this the traitor kid Taber—'
'Aliens!'

The first man's observation was correct. Scytharene

teeming towards them, attacking with a blinding fusillade of energy blasts.

Cravenly, Simon threw himself to one side. The soldiers, having been trained to respond rather more forthrightly to danger, returned their assailants' fire. Or tried to. The soldier who'd wanted to help Simon didn't even manage to loose a shot before half a dozen new orifices inimical to life gaped in his body. His comrades at least discharged their weapons. One black-clad Scytharene warrior with a helmet like a hawk even collapsed clutching at wounds in his chest, but neither soldier saw it. The dead are blind.

But Simon was laughing in relief. 'Thank God. Thank God.' Lifting his hands to show he wasn't armed. 'Don't shoot. You don't need to hurt me. I'm on your side. I'm one of you.'

The Scytharene warriors didn't shoot. They were too amused by the young Earther's antics.

'You all speak English, don't you? Well I'm Simon Satchwell. I'm Commander Shurion's agent. I work for you.'

The concept of which the warriors first seemed to find ludicrous, then actually a little offensive. Their good humour faded.

Simon sensed it. His own laughter died in his throat and his tone became pleading. 'You believe me, don't you? You've got to . . . Just call Commander Shurion. He'll vouch for me. I'm on your side.' Silence among the Scytharene, sceptical, hostile. 'Listen to me. Listen. Commander Shurion said I was strong enough to side with you, that I'm a master, not a slave. Don't . . . you mustn't . . .'

A line of energy weapons rose and aimed. Like a firing squad for traitors.

Simon's eyes behind his glasses brimmed with futile, helpless tears, the tears he'd shed so many times at school, the tears of a weak, miserable and frightened boy. A victim's tears.

'I turned against my friends for you!'

The Scytharene didn't care. They killed him anyway.

Above Vernham Hill the silver scythe of the *Furion* hovered, and from its belly lightning stormed to ravage the hillside. The earth was flung up like spray, in great, black geysers, trees torn asunder. The land thrashed and heaved at the torture wreaked upon it.

Joshua One, erupting into a blaze of tangled, twisted metal. Joshua Ten, dropping aflame into a dark crevasse. Joshua Four, stabbed to death by bright blades of energy.

The screams of the dying amplified over the comlink in the surviving vehicles.

Not to Richie's taste. 'God, can't we turn that *off*?'

Antony sympathised. 'Brandon? What about it?'

'What about what?' The operator's eyes ranged wildly over the instrument panels in front of him. Nothing seemed to make sense. Nothing seemed to work. 'This is no good. We can't stay here. We're sitting ducks here. We've got to get out.'

Brandon braked the Joshua sharply, fumbled with his seatbelt.

'What the hell do you think you're doing?' yelled Richie.

'I've got to get out!'

While in Joshua Seven, Travis had rarely ever felt so helpless. Above them the titanic curve of the *Furion* almost blotted out the sun, like an eclipse, a chariot of the gods. He was so insignificant compared to the Scytharene. To try to resist the aliens was like attempting to stem the tide of history. How could he ever have believed he could make a difference? Maybe Simon was right and it had been vanity all along.

As an energy blast lashed from the sky and rocked the Joshua, instrument panels exploding in cascades of sparks, Parry crying out and clutching at his bleeding face.

As the control cabin was plunged into darkness.

They'd lost contact with the Joshuas, and that was worrying enough. Worse, the disruption of communications allowed all the screens in the moncom centre to switch their attention to the fall of the Enclave. On each one, Scytharene forces overwhelming the paltry human defenders, driving them back into the very heart of the complex.

They'd be here soon.

Mel wasn't prepared to wait for that. 'Listen,' she confided to Jessica, 'I'm easy whether we take these bastards on or cut and run, but either way I'm not staying here. You with me?'

Jessica, like the techs, was nervously watching the door through which Dr Mowatt had exited minutes before accompanied by one of her scientists and with a promise to return. 'I guess so . . .'

'You guess so? We twiddle our thumbs here any longer and the Scytharene'll be so close we'll be able to see the reds of their eyes.'

'Dr Mowatt told us to wait,' Jessica pointed out.

'Dr Mowatt could be dead by now,' Mel retorted, not unreasonably in her opinion. 'If this is about you and me, Jess, now is not the time . . .'

But Dr Mowatt wasn't dead. She was rushing back into the room, her arms laden with weapons; the scientist behind her was similarly burdened. 'Our science can't help us now,' she said wryly. 'We must become soldiers, too.'

Everyone grabbed a gun.

'Yours,' the Scientific Director said, handing subjugators to Jessica and Mel. 'I think you have more of a right to these than the rest of us.'

'Thanks,' said Jessica.

Mel was surprised at how expertly the blonde girl seemed to be handling her subjugator. For herself, pointing and firing would have to be sufficient. 'Now let's do some damage.'

'No.' And Dr Mowatt removed the helmet of her atmosuit.

'What are you doing?' Jessica cried, appalled.

'And what do you mean, no?'

'I want to breathe my last air through my nose and mouth, not a filter,' Dr Mowatt said. 'We can't stop the Scytharene, and even if I could escape the Enclave, there's no future for an adult on the surface, not with the Sickness in the atmosphere. It's best if I . . . remain at my post. For you two, though, it's different. You mustn't fight. You have to get out.'

Inexplicably, Mowatt crossed to a computer and began to key in instructions.

'All right, so we make a break for it. That's good,' Mel said. 'I mean, somehow we need to find out what's happened to Travis and the others. They *could* still—'

'*Are* still alive,' insisted Jessica.

'Yeah. Are. But how do we reach the airlock without running slap-bang into half the Scytharene army?'

'You don't. There's another exit, Melanie,' revealed Dr

Mowatt. 'A secret exit, if you like, designed for just this eventuality. A tunnel that brings you out in the woods.'

'Yeah? How do we get in in the first place?'

'Access is from the accommodation level. I'll tell you in a moment.' She was printing something off, a piece of densely worded A4 she thrust into Jessica's free hand.

'What's this?' The teenager scanned a long list of what seemed to be map co-ordinates and directions.

'The locations of the other Enclaves, the ones we never dared to contact. Perhaps we should have done but we didn't. Perhaps they're all gone but they may not be. In one of them, perhaps scientists are searching for a cure to the Sickness, and that might give us a chance against the Scytharene. Find that Enclave, Melanie, Jessica. Seek it out.'

'We will, Dr Mowatt,' Jessica promised, tucking the paper into a pocket.

'And survive. Live on. That most importantly of all. My generation is lost but yours must not be. You have to grow and flourish and be strong. You're the future. Melanie. Jessica.' Touching each girl tenderly on the arm as she spoke their names for the final time. 'Now I'll direct you to the secondary exit and then my techs and I will delay the Scytharene for as long as possible. Good luck to you both. Our prayers go with you.'

And it looked like they were going to make it. The Scytharene semed to be occupying themselves with the elimination of any further resistance on the base's upper floors before venturing lower; they didn't appear to have any presence at all on the accommodation level.

That didn't stop Jessica's pulse from racing as fast as her feet. 'Almost there, Mel. Corridor 12A then . . . Mel, keep up.'

The girl with the black hair smiled to herself. Bit of a role reversal going on, she thought, remembering their flight from Wayvale with her having to drag a catatonic Jessica along. Not that she'd minded, even if by doing so she'd been increasing the risk to her own safety. She'd have done anything for Jessie then, given her life for Jessie because she'd loved her and, before she'd ruined everything by confessing the truth, had dreamed that one day Jessie might even love her in return.

'Mel, what are you slowing down for? Come on.'

Actually, Mel felt the same way now. Which was why: 'I'm not coming with you, Jess.'

'*What?*'

Stopping in the middle of the corridor. 'You'll have a better chance if I try to keep the Scytharene back with Dr Mowatt.'

'But we're nearly there. We can *both* make it.'

'No. You go on. I'll follow when I can.'

'Mel, what are you . . .? You won't be *able* to follow. They'll kill you.'

And Mel thought of Rev at the end, resigned somehow, even peaceful, despite lying broken in the prison compound. Peace would be good. A little bit of peace. 'It doesn't matter. My life doesn't mean very much.'

'It does!' Jessica protested. 'To me it does. You matter to me. *Mel.*'

'You must hate me, though. What I told you. I shouldn't have. I'm sorry.'

'Mel, I don't care about that now. I should never have cared about it.' Jessica saw herself as petty and small-minded. However their relationship might evolve, she realised now she couldn't cope without Melanie Patrick in her life. 'And I don't hate you – I couldn't ever. I overreacted, Mel. *I'm* sorry. I behaved like a little girl. Don't make me regret it more than I already do. Don't give up on yourself. You're my best friend. I need you.'

'For real?'

'More than any— Mel!' Thrusting her companion out of the way as a Scytharene warrior appeared at the far end of the corridor. Dispatching him with one perfectly placed blast of her subjugator.

'Bloody hell,' Mel gaped. 'Lara Croft, what have you done with Jessica?'

'It's me. I've been practising,' said Jessica modestly.

'That's just as well.'

Another Scytharene, a couple more behind him, suddenly aware that in this part of the Enclave at least the battle was not yet over.

And wouldn't be, Mel felt with a surge of love and pride for her friend. Not now that she'd rediscovered the reason to fight on. Not now that, after all, she wanted to live.

Mel fired her subjugator, too. Side by side with Jessica. As it should be.

Stand or fall, they'd do so together.

There was always a guard posted outside the ship's armoury. Slavecraft regulations. Darion expected to encounter one. The guard himself was probably less prepared to see Lord

Darion of the Thousand Families charging towards him with a subjugator drawn.

And shooting him dead.

The duty armourer might have heard the guard's cry. He was halfway off his chair within the circular control console as Darion burst in, fired again. He never made it fully to his feet.

Darion closed the door, fused its activation circuits with a blast from his subjugator. Nobody was getting into the armoury for a while now.

Or out.

Which wasn't the way he'd necessarily wanted it, but it was the way things had to be. The engine of revolution was sacrifice.

The alienologist gazed around at the stocks of military hardware, the racks of weapons, hundreds of weapons, not just firearms like subjugators and suppressers but mines, siege launchers, laser packs.

Grenades.

In the sudden blackness Travis felt Linden's arms around him, her burning cheek against his. 'Hold me, Travis.' Tears coursing down that cheek. 'If this is it, I need to know you're here.'

His heart wrenched. 'We're not finished yet,' he vowed. 'Not yet.' As the Joshua's emergency power reserves kicked in and the control cabin was illuminated once more.

Parry's eyes were open but they weren't seeing anything. They were daubs of white paint in a palette of red, his head thrown back, arms thrown wide and hanging. There was nothing Travis could do for Parry.

But he could still save Linden. *That* was the difference he could make, here and now. If he could save one person, keep one precious person alive, it would be worth the struggle, worth the stand. His father would be proud.

Travis examined his own instrument panel, fought to recall which controls did what, drawing on his observation of Parry. Made a decision and grabbed a lever. 'Hold on, Lin.'

'To you?'

'To everything. We're getting out of here.'

He shoved the lever forward and the Joshua lurched into motion, jolting the teenagers with it. The tracks tore into the already churned hillside, heaved the vehicle higher. Travis gritted his teeth and prayed he'd only need to perform basic manoeuvres.

'Keep watching the screens, Lin. I need to concentrate on . . . tell me where the *Furion* is.'

'Trav, it's right above us.'

'Oh, great. That's just bloody great.' Wrestling with recalcitrant controls. A battery of red lights flashing. The Joshua was damaged more grievously than Travis had thought.

'I can't see the others, Trav. Antony and Richie . . .' Linden's voice was icy with horror. 'We're all that's left . . .'

'And we're not giving up,' Travis swore, forcing the Joshua on as much with the power of his will as with instruments and propulsion units. Faith had brought down the walls of Jericho. Faith would keep them from harm now. 'We're. Not. Giving. Up.'

'Travis!'

Linden recoiled from the screens with a cry, dazzled by the brightness each of them blazed into the control cabin, the searing brilliance of a Scytharene energy bolt.

The ground was suddenly gone beneath the Joshua's

tracks, diamond spikes losing their value. The vehicle was a tin can kicked by the boot of a giant. The teenagers grasped for each other but their limbs couldn't obey. Their straining seatbelts sliced into their chests as gravity jerked them cruelly back and forth. And they weren't falling so much as rolling, twisting, crashing down the hillside, floor and ceiling flipping over in crazed cartwheels, the Joshua's armour battered at every impact, its instrument panels erupting anew, even the red warning lights bursting under the stress. Their function was obsolete anyway.

And this time, when the main light went out, it wasn't restored.

But Linden had been mistaken in her belief that Joshua Seven was alone.

'Brandon, no!' Antony cried. 'We go outside we're dead.' He meant due to the firepower of the *Furion*. He didn't even think about the Scytharene virus and the Joshua operator's lack of an atmosuit.

Brandon wasn't concerning himself with such matters either. Panic, not reason, was spurring him to release the access hatches, sheer, stark panic. He was out of his seat, darting for the ring of daylight nearest him. 'Stay *here* we're dead. I'm not waiting – you kids do what the hell you like.'

Brandon scurried through the hatch.

'We've got to go. He's right.' Richie had already unbuckled his seatbelt and was standing. ''Sides, neither of us can drive this thing. Come on, Tony.' At the three-runged ladder to the hatch. 'We bloody well *are* sitting ducks now.'

He hauled himself up, poked his head into a scalding

landscape of carnage and chaos. The *Furion* still above them, approaching in a new destructive sweep across the slopes, a curtain of flame advancing inexorably towards the motionless Joshua. Richie quailed.

'Tony, *now*. What the hell are you doing?'

The answer chilled Richie's blood even in the midst of the conflagration. 'I can't – my seatbelt's damaged. Stuck. I can't get out. Richie!'

Dipped his head back inside the Joshua. Saw Antony struggling to free himself. The seatbelt, from safety feature to effective cause of death. If Richie did irony, he could have quoted this as a prime example.

But generally speaking, Richie Coker only did self-preservation.

'Richie, help me.' The Head Boy of the Harrington School pleading, to him. 'For God's sake.'

What about Richie's sake? He bobbed his head above the hatch again. The *Furion* was closer. Death was bearing down on him in a barrage of energy bolts. If he fled now, he might have a chance, find refuge somewhere, might escape notice being nothing but a worthless bully.

If he stayed, however . . .

'Richie, are you running out on me? Richie!'

When the screen in the arm of his command chair flashed that a viewlink to the armoury was opening, Shurion was irritated rather than concerned. What did that damned armourer think he was playing at, interrupting his commander's moment of glory? The final Earther assault vehicle was there to be destroyed.

358

'What is it?' Shurion snapped.

It was Darion, grinning in a nervous kind of way, Darion escaped from his cell and for some reason inhabiting the armoury instead. Holding a grenade. In front of him so Shurion could clearly see it, a deadly, gleaming egg.

'I thought I'd better warn you, Shurion, if you were thinking of celebrating victory,' Darion said, 'I wouldn't start just yet.'

'What are you . . . how did you . . .?' Shurion's mind raced. 'Don't do anything rash, Darion.'

'Clarify rash. Do you mean something like pulling the pin of this grenade? Hmm. Yes, the amount of potentially explosive material in here, I can see that might qualify. A little accident with a grenade would turn the ship into a fireball and your sick ambitions into ashes, Shurion.' Darion considered. 'You know, I'm liking the sound of rash.'

As the alienologist was speaking, Shurion's fingers were flying across the control panel in his chair. The viewlink to the armoury also appeared on the bridge's main screen. The command chair descended from the heights. Security was alerted.

'I admire your resourcefulness, Lord Darion.' Who was still a weakling at heart, Shurion reasoned. Whose evident intention could still be thwarted. The Commander strode to confront the larger image of his enemy. 'Overpowering your guard somehow, the armourer too, obviously, as you're in the armoury. Did you kill them?'

'I'm afraid I did. And the security team you've no doubt dispatched to kill *me*, Shurion, I'm afraid they'll not break through the door in time.'

'Oh, I think they will, Darion.' Shurion was aware of the

bridge crew gathering horrifiedly around the viewscreen. 'While I might have underestimated your cleverness, I have certainly not misjudged your courage – or should I say, your lack of it. You don't have the strength of will to blow yourself up.'

'Do you not think so, Shurion?'

Contempt and loathing contorted Shurion's face. 'I *know* you don't. Not a slave-lover like you, pampered, privileged, leading a life you haven't earned, wielding power you don't deserve. You're too soft, Darion. To kill requires a warrior.'

'Then perhaps we have more in common than you ever imagined, Shurion.'

Suddenly Darion was alerted by a furore in the corridor outside the armoury. The security team trying to force an entry. He could afford to delay no longer. His heart thumped in his chest even as his limbs began to tremble.

His final moments were upon him.

'What I do,' he began, 'I do for the cause of the equality of all races . . .' And it was going to be worth it just to witness the dawning realisation on Shurion's face that he too was facing imminent death.

'Wait. Darion, wait.' In rising panic.

'. . . I do because slavery must end, because our people must change.'

'You can't . . . you mustn't . . .' Shurion couldn't *die*. He was immortal, invincible. He didn't deserve to die. It wasn't fair.

'The flame I light here is the flame of freedom.' The last thing Darion saw before closing his eyes was Commander Shurion pounding his helpless fists against the viewscreen. *Travis, I hope I'm in time.*

'Darion, no. Think of Dyona.'

He *was* thinking of Dyona. Her hand was on his as he pulled out the pin. She was with him, he felt.

He heard Shurion scream.

The detonation came.

SIXTEEN

Somehow, the buckle snapped open. Richie didn't know whether his frantic tugging at the seatbelt in conjunction with Antony had anything to do with it or not and he didn't care. The other boy was free. It was kind of urgent they should be elsewhere now.

Before Joshua Nine became their tomb.

'Richie, thanks,' Antony gasped. 'You stayed.'

'More fool me,' Richie observed over his shoulder, already lunging for and scaling the ladder to the hatch. 'And I'm out of here for sure now whether you can make it or not.'

Antony smiled wryly. 'Oh, I can make it.'

Richie was waiting on the shell of the Joshua to help him up in any case. 'Did you do athletics at that poncy bloody school of yours, Tony?' he asked. 'Hope you were good at the hundred metres.'

'Actually, I was senior school champion at the hundred metres.'

'Should have known. Wish I could say the same.'

The *Furion* was almost directly above them, the heat radiating from its energy bolts of roasting intensity. The teenagers leapt to the ground. It was probably at *least* a hundred metres to any kind of cover.

Richie swore at himself for not being closer to it by now. 'Get out of this we'll need a miracle,' he groaned.

The *Furion* exploded.

They heard the blast first, a rumbling boom from somewhere within the heart of the ship, and the sound seemed to roll towards them like thunder, rising in volume. The slavecraft shook. The energy bolts ceased. And then fire like gouts of blood spouted from every window on every deck, its tremendous destructive force tearing away huge chunks of the body of the ship, the shockwave driven before it swatting Richie and Antony to the soil. They cried out, shielding their eyes from the atom-bomb flare of immolation. A second eruption followed, volcanic, consuming, engulfing. The *Furion* flamed like a sun, or like a burning meteor.

And there was one key property of meteors . . .

'Richie, on your feet!' Antony was scrambling to his, hauling at his companion's jacket. The Scytharene could finish them off even though they were dead. Or at least, their ship could.

The *Furion* wobbled in the air, tilted, plunged.

'Bloody hell!' Richie gaped.

He and Antony broke into a desperate sprint, bounded down the hill, hurtling with such giddy, unbridled speed that even to stay upright was a challenge and each time their feet pounded the earth pain jolted through their muscles. There were ruts and fissures in the ground that had to be avoided, scattered burning debris, and no time, no chance to pick a careful path. Instinct alone was going to have to save them, instinct and luck.

While in the sky the *Furion* was screaming, its agony expressed in a screech of tortured metal that filled the world. A tail of flame spewed out behind it as it plummeted.

And crashed into the slopes of Vernham Hill.

Richie whooped, looked back. Almost stopped. Until he realised the Scytharene hadn't quite given up trying to kill him.

The slavecraft's sickle hull bit deep into the earth on impact, gouging out an instant crater and hurling up tons of dirt and rock mixed with uprooted trees and the shattered remains of Joshuas. Worse still, the ship's momentum was bringing it ploughing down the hillside like a blazing avalanche, as if it was taking pursuit of the two teenagers personally.

Running was still a good idea.

And Richie did the best he could. He didn't even glance behind him again. He gazed ahead. The grinding, rending death throes of the *Furion* he fought to ignore, but they battered at him physically, overwhelming, disorienting. He tried not to trip and fall.

Trying and succeeding are not always the same.

The wildly racing Richie felt his foot snag on something, tipped forward, slammed into the ground himself, rolled over and over, kind of bouncing, blood in his mouth, air punched painfully from his lungs. Eyes jammed shut. He couldn't get up again now. If the *Furion* was going to slide over him and squash him, he didn't want to see it. Or maybe the black cascade of soil would bury him first. Every fibre of his body tensed.

When Antony tapped his shoulder he screamed.

'Actually, Richie, I think three cheers might be more in order.'

'What?' Embarrassed now.

'Look.'

Richie did. And the tears of relief that stung his eyes he'd also have preferred to hide. The ship had finally come to rest still dozens of metres behind them, its wake a dark scar on the land, the nearest of its crescent tips wedged deep in earth, the other pointing upwards to the heavens as if to remind onlookers whence it had fallen. The *Furion* was burning, would be for hours, maybe even days, but it was no longer a threat.

'We beat you,' Richie gloated. 'You ugly alien bastards, we *beat* you.'

But Antony, kneeling alongside him on the ground, was shaking his head. He regarded his companion grimly. 'What about Travis and Linden?'

Travis dragged Linden from the wreckage of Joshua Seven just as the *Furion* smashed into the hillside, too far away for it to pose any danger to them. The damage, however, could already have been done.

Linden was unconscious.

Or worse.

No. Not worse. Travis refused to contemplate that. *Just unconscious. Not . . . please, let her just be unconscious.*

Bruised and bleeding himself, Travis managed to lift Linden, her arm around his neck, and bear her limp body to one of the few trees left standing. He laid her down, leaned her upper body against it.

Checked her pulse.

'Come on come on come on. Yes.'

Found it, and it seemed all right to him. It seemed strong, the pulse of someone who was going to live. But Travis wasn't a doctor. What if . . .? *No*. Linden was going to be fine. And when she woke up . . .

Travis kissed her, on her forehead, on her cheeks, on her lips. He stroked her hair, her hair the colour of autumn leaves. When she woke up, things would be different between them. 'You were right, Linden,' he breathed. 'What you said before. Priorities. Sometimes I think I get mine wrong. It's people who matter, people who make life worth living – and worth fighting for, worth saving. The feelings we have for each other. I almost lost sight of that for a while, but not any more. Can you hear me? From now on I'm going to be what you want me to be. I'm ready to be with you, Lin, just . . . open your eyes. Open your eyes and I'm here. I'll always be here.'

A slight frown on Linden's forehead. A twitch of her nose. She was stirring. 'Travis?' Her voice weak but clear.

'*Lin*. Thank God.' Embracing her. When he pulled back, she'd eased her eyes open.

'Trav, who . . . were you talking to?'

'Don't worry about it.' He scanned her face anxiously. 'How are you? Are you okay? Does it hurt?'

'Only when I laugh.' Which could have been why she managed just a wan smile. 'Are *you* okay?'

'I am now.'

'Did I miss anything?'

'I kissed you a couple of times.'

'When I was out of it? That's kind of pervy, Travis.'

'You weren't exactly available for me to ask permission.'

'To use your own line, I am now.'

Though they hadn't expected their next show of affection to draw applause, not even of the ironic variety. A pair of familiar figures were toiling up the hillside towards them.

366

'Hey, Naughton,' called Richie. 'And you were going to start searching for us *when*?'

'I don't know what happened,' Travis said. The four teenagers stood on the summit of Vernham Hill and gazed down at the devastation wrought by the battle. A low pall of smoke, thickly black and too sluggish to drift or dissipate, hung over the hillside where fires still burned and the smouldering wreckage of the Joshuas, the crackling hulk of the *Furion*, littered the slopes like exposed corpses. 'I mean, obviously Darion did *something*. The shields were down when we attacked. But either he couldn't keep them offline or he was discovered or something. I don't know.'

'Maybe Darion was responsible for destroying the ship,' suggested Linden.

Antony nodded. 'I think that's highly likely, Linden. In which case, we all owe him our lives.'

'You saying we've got to be grateful to one of the same bunch of stinking aliens who'd have sold us off at some intergalactic slave market, Tony?' Richie resented the idea.

'You never met Darion, Richie,' Travis pointed out in quiet reproof. 'You didn't know him. Don't start thinking like a Scytharene and making racial judgements. Darion risked his life for us – lost his life for us. No one can do more for another. However it actually ended for him – and I doubt we'll ever know – he's earned our thanks, our gratitude.'

'Thank you, Darion,' whispered Linden, clinging to Travis.

'Darion,' acknowledged Antony, and mentally added the Scytharene's name to the Harrington roll of honour.

Richie shrugged. 'Whatever. You did good, Darion. For an alien.'

'Well it's not wise to wait around here any longer,' Travis said. 'If anybody else was still alive we'd have found them by now. I wonder what happened to your Joshua operator.'

'Who, Brandon?' Richie grunted. 'Reckon he'll be halfway back to the Enclave.'

'Without an atmosuit I'm afraid it won't matter much where he is,' Antony sighed, 'but I think that's the direction we should take, certainly. And immediately, before the Culler from Otterham reappears.'

'Actually,' Linden frowned, 'I'm surprised it's not back already. Glad, but surprised.'

'Off chasing shadows,' said Travis with a grim smile.

And Antony added: 'Let's hope shadows are all it found.'

They realised otherwise as they neared the site of the Enclave and saw more smoke ahead, straggling skywards in a ragged plume this time but in other respects so similar to the dark and acrid cloud lingering over Vernham Hill that the teenagers knew it could only be the product of violence. Catastrophic violence.

'Oh God,' Linden breathed.

It was the Enclave burning. It couldn't be anything else.

Mel, Travis thought. *Jessica. No.*

'The bastards found it,' Richie muttered. He glanced at Travis: 'Satchwell?'

'How?' Travis questioned. 'Simon was under lock and key. He couldn't have . . .' *Could he?*

'Immaterial.' Antony hurried forward. 'The Scytharene could still be there. Jessica and the others need our help.'

'Tony,' Richie yelled after him, 'without a gun between us?'

As it turned out, weapons would have been superfluous. There was no enemy to shoot. The Scytharene had been there but were now gone, leaving behind their usual legacy of destruction.

The hill that had concealed the Enclave was ravaged and rent. The base's once-hidden entrance tunnel gaped open like a dead man's mouth, undertaker-black.

Travis and Antony without a pause beelined for it, Linden accompanying them dutifully.

Richie was more reluctant. 'Wait a minute. Where do you think you're going?'

'Where does it look like?' replied Travis.

'You're not going in there? There could be aliens still in there. The roof looks like it's gonna fall in any second. Place is a death trap.'

'Jessica's in here,' said Antony. 'And Mel. They might still be alive. If they are, death trap or not, they'll need us.' He glanced back at the other boy pointedly. '*Us*, Richie.'

And Richie followed.

The Enclave had been reduced to ruins, no chance of salvaging any usable equipment even if the teenagers had known how to operate it. The stockpiles of weaponry had either been blown up or plundered by the Scytharene. The lighting underground was a guttering red, like a candle burning blood. Emergency power eking out its last reserves, dimming all the time.

But bright enough still to identify the bodies.

Captain Taber lay near the entrance, pistol in his hand. Richie, thinking he'd benefit more from the firearm than its present owner, attempted to appropriate it, but the old soldier's grip couldn't be broken short of prising away one frozen finger at a time, and Richie didn't have the stomach for that.

'So Taber went down facing the enemy,' Travis noted. 'He wouldn't have wanted it any other way.'

'No Scytharene corpses,' Antony observed. 'Surely our side must have killed some of them.'

'They probably remove the bodies of their dead,' Linden said. 'I'm sure the Scytharene are big on warrior funerals.'

'Excellent,' said Richie darkly. 'Think how pleased they'll be when they see the *Furion*.'

The teenagers wasted little time making for the moncom centre, where they imagined Jessica and Mel would have been watching the Joshua assault. The girls were not there now, however. Dr Mowatt was, and a small group of scientists and techs. All dead.

'Does this mean they escaped?' Linden wanted to know. 'That's what this means, isn't it, Trav? That they're alive.'

If only he could simply say yes and by declaring so make it the truth. But Travis had tried wishing the dead alive before, at the tender age of ten. It hadn't worked then and he doubted it would now. But that didn't mean he'd abandoned hope. Hope was life. 'All this means, Lin,' he said, 'is that Jessica and Mel aren't here. Which means we have to keep searching.'

'Searching's good, Naughton,' muttered Richie as the light flickered. 'Searching fast is better.' He didn't relish the prospect of having to grope his way out of the Enclave in pitch blackness and trampling over dead bodies on the way.

They found Simon by the stairwell.

'So he did get out somehow,' Richie said. 'Simes, you—'

'Shut up, Richie.' Travis knelt beside the body. Simon was

370

lying on his side and his hands and arms were crossed over his wounds as if to stem the flow of blood that had now rusted on his clothes and on the floor. His glasses had slipped off and one lens was cracked. Travis remembered how vulnerable Simon had felt without his glasses. He picked them up, eased the boy on to his back and put them on him, gently, like a friend. 'Simon . . .'

And in death the misery, the bitterness and the hurt had melted from Simon's features and he seemed innocent where he lay and younger than his years, at peace, like he was sleeping. Travis remembered him in the kitchen at Jessica's sixteenth birthday party, lost, alone, the butt of everyone's jokes and worse. Well, he was beyond torment now. Whatever Simon had done, Travis forgave him. He only wished he'd been able to help him more.

'I'm sorry, Simon,' he whispered. 'I let you down.'

'Travis . . .' Linden's consoling hand on his shoulder.

He felt like crying. He felt like staying with Simon longer, as if by remaining with him he could keep him somehow closer to life. But to break down now would be too much like defeat, and Simon was gone. For good. Languishing by his side would not find Jessica or Mel.

Travis rose wearily to his feet. 'We'll try the accommodation level,' he said.

They wandered in the forest aimlessly, scarcely even aware of what they were doing. When darkness fell they sank to the ground. Linden suggested making a fire. Antony began an objection based on the possibility that the subsequent firelight might be seen by others, possibly of Scytharene descent, but he ran out of either words or interest or both. Neither Travis nor Richie expressed an opinion. Linden made her fire.

They'd found no trace of either Jessica or Mel in the Enclave. They'd scoured the rooms and corridors to no avail until the power blackouts had become too frequent and too extended to dare to remain in the subterranean base any longer. In the scarlet light of the dying Enclave they'd been compelled to abandon their quest.

The burden of failure was crushing, suffocating. Even Richie seemed weighed down by it. There was no warmth for any of them in the fire.

'So what do we do now?' Linden said at length and with more than an undercurrent of despair. 'What are we going to do now?'

'We go back to the Enclave,' Travis said. 'Tomorrow, when it's light. We make torches so we can see and we go back in there and we search again and we keep searching until we're sure, I mean really sure, that Mel and Jessica aren't there, wounded or unconscious or . . . something.'

'They're not, Travis,' Antony said mournfully. 'Didn't you sense that? There's no point going back to the Enclave. The girls are gone. Perhaps the Scytharene took them.'

'They wouldn't let that happen,' Travis retorted.

'How could they prevent it?' Antony sighed. 'I want Jessica and Mel with us again safe and sound as much as anyone, but we have to be realistic. One way or another, we might have lost them.' And he remembered what he'd said to Jessica before departing in Joshua Nine: '*It's better if you stay here.*' Yeah, and what did he know? Fool. Idiot. Jessica had heeded him because she trusted him – Head Boys of the Harrington School were *meant* to be trustworthy – but by leaving her in

372

the Enclave he might well have killed her or condemned her to slavery. Whatever had happened to Jessica was his fault. His heart felt like it wanted to stop beating.

'You know,' confided Richie, 'I never thought I'd say this, but I'm gonna miss Morticia.'

'What are we going to do without them?' Linden asked bleakly.

'We won't have to do without them,' Travis snapped. 'If they're not still in the Enclave, then they're somewhere else. We'll find them.'

'Actually, Trav' – and the familiar female voice from the shadows brought all four teenagers scrambling to their feet in disbelieving wonder – 'you won't have to do that, either.'

'We've found *you*.' A second voice, as welcome as the first. 'We followed the fire and the sound of voices.'

Like ghosts, Jessica and Mel emerged from the darkness of the forest into the flickering light of the fire. Their friends gawped.

'Well,' said Mel, 'anybody pleased to see us?'

And the girls weren't ghosts. They were real. Their bodies were warm and alive as the others hugged and kissed them, shouting out in jubilation at their safe return regardless of whether any alien was within earshot or not. Even Richie planted a wet one on both Jessica and Mel, and though neither girl was particularly enamoured by his attentions, they accepted them in the spirit in which they were intended and kept smiling. Mel's smile didn't falter either when Antony claimed the last and longest embrace with Jessica for himself – but she had to look away.

Later, and in hushed, gloomy tones, the two girls recounted the events surrounding the fall of the Enclave. Mel made much of Jessica's new-found marksmanship. 'On the other hand, I was just about useless,' she admitted.

'No change there, then,' quipped Richie.

'What are you talking about, Mel?' Jessica leapt to her friend's defence. 'You weren't useless at all.'

'Well, put it like this, if it hadn't been for Jess, the Scytharene would have got us and we'd never have reached the tunnel, let alone the woods. We wouldn't be here now.'

'I'm glad you are,' said Travis with feeling.

'We all are,' echoed Linden. 'Everyone together again.'

'Everyone minus one.' Mel frowned. 'We don't know what happened to Simon.'

'We do,' said Antony, and the four of them who'd fought with the Joshuas told their story in turn.

'Poor Darion,' pitied Mel when they'd finished. 'I kind of liked him. Poor Dyona when she hears.'

'At least she'll know he died for a cause they both believed in,' said Travis. 'She can be proud of that.'

'What about Simon?' Jessica ventured. 'Yes, he betrayed us, but still . . . once he was one of us. We can't just leave him lying there in the Enclave. We ought to bury him.'

'What? After he tried to bury us?' Richie wasn't impressed.

Mel's eyes flashed. 'Jessie's right. We owe Simon that for the past before the Sickness. You most of all, Richie.'

'Okay,' Travis agreed, and clearly, the differences that seemed to have arisen between Mel and Jessica appeared now to have been resolved. He was relieved. 'Looks like we'll be going back to the Enclave tomorrow after all, Antony.'

'But what then?' Linden returned to her original theme. 'What do we do then?'

She gazed around the fire. Antony cuddling Jessica while

Mel, arms hugging her drawn-up knees in the absence of a partner, divided her gaze between the blond couple and the heart of the flames. Herself with Travis holding her, which left just Richie – not that she liked to look in his direction in case they caught each other's eye and hinted to Travis what he must never know – Richie on the very rim of the fire's illumination, half in darkness, half in light. Six of them. Six against the Scytharene.

'What do we do?' Travis mused. 'Well, it's obvious the kind of military hardware we can bring to bear isn't powerful enough to trouble the Scytharene, but there has to be some way to stop them. Has to be. And we've got to learn what it is. That's what we do.'

'Yeah. I don't want to sound like a major-league party pooper, Naughton,' Richie grunted, 'but I think you're overlooking something. *How?*'

Travis was ready with an answer. 'We use the sheet Mowatt gave Jessie to begin with. We locate these other Enclaves. If they're still operational, we might find help there.'

'And if we don't?'

'Then, Richie, we'll find it elsewhere,' replied Travis determinedly, 'because we'll keep looking. We'll never stop looking, or hoping, or fighting. The Scytharene have had an easy ride so far. The Sickness. The suddenness of their invasion. At first we didn't understand the true nature of the enemy we were dealing with, but we do now. We're prepared.' Travis leaned closer to the fire and the flames lit up his face and the blaze burned in his eyes. 'Now they need to realise who *they're* dealing with. We're human beings and we're not an inferior race. We're not going to surrender. We're going to resist, to refuse to be slaves. We're going to stand against them and we're going to beat them. The Scytharene'll be sorry they ever came to Earth. We'll *make* them sorry. If we believe in ourselves and stay strong, we'll find a way, however long it takes, and when we've found it, on that day, the Scytharene will be defeated.'

To be concluded in
THE TOMORROW SEED

About the Author

Andrew Butcher was once an English teacher but now devotes his time to a ragtag group of orphaned teenagers fighting a desperate resistance against alien invaders. He lives in Dorset with an unfeasibly large comic collection.

Find out more about Andrew and other Atom authors at www.atombooks.co.uk